Cody Goodfellow is gifted with a pros[e] and evocativeness, and his narratives ar[e with the] compelling readability and cumulative terror that distinguish Lovecraft's own. This volume gathers the many provocative tales he has written over the past decade or more, lavishly expanding upon core Lovecraftian themes and motifs. Chief among these, perhaps, is "In the Shadow of Swords," strikingly set in Iraq, where American soldiers during the Iraq War encounter entities far more baleful than the terrorists of the Taliban. The collection also features two previously unpublished novellas: "Swinging," which employs "The Shadow out of Time" as the springboard for an extraordinary excursion into space and time; and "Archons," a military set piece that features a denouement both horrific and poignant. Vibrantly contemporary in setting and expression, they nonetheless constitute a fitting homage of the dreamer from Providence.

"Cody Goodfellow's imagination is a freeway flyer, and his prose is a ride on a rocket-sled. He's one of the two or three god-damned best writers in the Genres today."—Michael Shea, World Fantasy Award-winning author of *Nifft the Lean* and *Copping Squid*

"Horrors inspired by H.P. Lovecraft's fiction and Cthulhu mythos run riot in the 12 wildly imaginative entries in Goodfellow's fourth story collection.... Goodfellow regularly tips his hat to his inspirations [and] approaches their themes so inventively that his stories never bog down ... Fans of Lovecraftian horror will find Goodfellow's stories strong examples of how, as he writes in his introduction, 'the Mythos frame gives seven-league boots and bionic limbs to the storyteller's ability not only to suspend disbelief, but to hurl it into a stable orbit with little effort.'"—*Publishers Weekly*

"Goodfellow has developed a reputation as one of the top writers of neo-Lovecraftian fiction. It is a well-deserved reputation. This book is all the proof you need."—*Hellnotes*

"Must-Buy Comfort Reading for . . . um . . . those for whom comfort is an imaginary number."—Rick Kleffel

"I have never read a story by Cody Goodfellow where I wasn't consistently blown away by his dedication to mining the blasted synapses of an unnaturally weird possibility. An impossible possibility (!!!) soon will be known to the brave and bold word spelunkers who would find themselves on the receiving end of a wholly original and disciplined cosmic yarn! Do yourself a favor and acquaint yourselves with Cody and his obvious love of taking you somewhere you shouldn't be! AS SOON AS YOUR HEAVING SKELETAL MEAT COLLAGE CAN!"—Skinner, TheArtofSkinner.com

"Cody Goodfellow is another author that I am growing to love. Every story I've read by him I've loved."—Justin Steele, *Arkham Digest*

"Cody Goodfellow's work is '80s vintage horror with a contemporary edge. An exemplary wordsmith, his prose sticks a needle in your brain and gives it a twist. This stuff is Lovecraft on acid." —Laird Barron

"This is high-end psychological surrealist horror meets bottom-feeding low-life crime in a techno-thrilling science fiction world full of Lovecraft and magic..."—John Skipp, *NY Times* Bestselling Author of *The Bridge* and *The Long Last Call*

"Cody Goodfellow is untouched as a breathless reporter of violent action, relating it in hurtling prose full of striking and sometimes hilarious metaphors. The author has hybridized Splatterpunk with the techno-thriller, and the result will not soon leave your memory."—*Strange Aeons*

"Simply put, no one writes like Goodfellow. From classic horror elements and an undeniable knowledge of the Mythos to a healthy dose of unique weirdness and a penchant for over-the-top brutality and memorable characters, *Rapture of the Deep* is one of the most complete and astonishingly original collections to have invaded the world of tentacles and Elder Gods in the last half decade."—Gabino Iglesias, *Horror Talk*

Rapture of the Deep
and Other Lovecraftian Tales

Rapture of the Deep
and Other Lovecraftian Tales

Cody Goodfellow

Hippocampus Press

New York

Rapture of the Deep and Other Lovecraftian Tales copyright ©
2016 by Hippocampus Press.
Works by Cody Goodfellow © 2016 by Cody Goodfellow.

Published by Hippocampus Press
P.O. Box 641, New York, NY 10156.
http://www.hippocampuspress.com
All rights reserved. No part of this work may be reproduced in any form or by any means without the written permission of the publisher.

Cover art © 2016 by Rob Winfield.
Cover design by Cody Goodfellow.
Hippocampus Press logo designed by Anastasia Damianakos.

ISBN 978-1-61498-155-8

First Edition
1 3 5 7 9 8 6 4 2

Dedicated to Michael Shea

Contents

Introduction 11
The Anatomy Lesson 15
König Feurio 37
To Skin a Corpse 65
In the Shadow of Swords 85
Garden of the Gods 131
Grinding Rock 165
Rapture of the Deep 175
Inside Uncle Sid 187
Archons 205
Broken Sleep 235
Cahokia 249
Swinging 263
Acknowledgments 305

Introduction

You're working at your desk, driving your car, or relaxing in a favorite chair and reading this book, when you feel the faint, tickling sensation of tiny feet traveling aimlessly across your skin.

You inspect the area in alarm, but it's only a solitary worker ant, wandering in a desperate, despairing search for the pheromone markers of its nest. Whatever you were thinking about—your next meal, a dreaded task, or the woes of the world—falls away for just a moment as you consider the unthinkable plight of this tiny, essentially mindless machine, separated from all it was programmed for, set adrift on an utterly alien terrain that is itself alive and intelligent and likely as not to crush it without a moment's thought.

Not even the Buddha could summon the patient empathy to return the castaway ant to its nest, but few sensible human beings could crush and wipe away the offending insect without considering, for just a moment, that as conscious beings in a mindless natural machine, we are all just like that ant.

None of my stories are anywhere near as subtle or as profound as the testimony of a refugee ant—when used as directed, they're more like a mouthful of insecticide. But I have never found a more effective vehicle than Lovecraft's Cthulhu Mythos to unmask not just the horror of the Other, but the tragedy of us, and the horror that is.

When I was ten, my mother tried to con me into reading *Siddhartha*. When I asked her if it had monsters in it, she told me it had "monsters of the soul." I passed.

Less than two years later, I would buy a Scholastic edition of *The Shadow over Innsmouth & Other Stories of Horror* and find the spiritual awakening my mother hoped I would find in *Siddhartha*. It wasn't that Lovecraft was a deeper writer than Hesse, or even seeking to enlighten . . . but his monsters, his fears were *real*.

Almost anything can call itself "serious" literature, if its monsters remain metaphorical or baldly symbolic, but every lofty goal that literature claims for its own can be achieved within the pulpy parameters of "lowbrow" weird genre fiction. With monsters.

Obviously, Lovecraft's Cthulhu Mythos is pulp existentialism that scratches the same burning adolescent itch of morbid cosmic dread that sends more "serious" readers to *The Stranger, Nausea,* and *Fight Club*. Lovecraft invented the perfect monsters for the modern era, and took the preternaturally modern stance of making his proprietary mythology into shareware. He delineated vast tracts of unknown territory for his acolytes and followers to map out or shroud in further mystery. Far from limiting the imagination, the Mythos frame gives seven-league boots and bionic limbs to the storyteller's ability not only to suspend disbelief, but to hurl it into a stable orbit with little effort.

That's why it resonates so deeply with so many writers who go through a Lovecraftian pupation stage, only emerging upon having repaid the influence with one's own spin on the Mythos. Some of us, unsurprisingly, never find our way out of the cocoon.

My first novels were a two-part modern epic based upon Lovecraft's *At the Mountains of Madness*. Lovecraftian fiction has comprised about half my fictional output since I began writing for money, twenty-two years ago. Any doubts I had about whether this was a mature or worthwhile use of my time and talents have been put to rest by the demands of an audience too large and diverse to be called a cult, but too fanatical for any other name.

The stories collected herein are many of my absolute favorite works from my first sales to the current year, though I will never feel that they're completely my own, or that they'd rest comfortably next to works more arguably "original" to myself. I have struggled to repay my influences with interest and tried to make Cthulhu Mythos stories that don't just offer the secret handshake to the initiated, but drag the unwitting into the cult; and to stay faithful to the spirit and intent of what Lovecraft did, by aggressively making it my own.

All the modern Mythos rejections of past excesses, Derlethism, and such have become clichés themselves. By now, nobody will cop to writing Lovecraftian pastiche . . . but few in the literary end will cop to writing or playing the games, either. The *Call of Cthulhu* RPG came out from Chaosium within a year of my first reading HPL, and my first professional sale was a resource guide for the game (in 1996; it came out in 2006 with substantial additions). One thing I loved about the game that ruined *Dungeons & Dragons* for me was the juxtaposition of characters determined to thwart the Old Ones, not just to bear witness and be devoured. While many misunderstood the mythology and made the Great Old Ones' return an unthinkable end that could always be beaten back with earthly weapons and successful Library Use rolls, writing my first Mythos stories as RPG scenarios drove home the notion that a story can only grow stronger and more effective, if the characters are endowed with the wit to try to escape it.

I have striven not to use the Cthulhu Mythos as a stock set of adversaries from Outside to distract from the very real threats humans turn a blind eye to every day. As HPL and the best of his successors did, I try to weave the Outside with the Inside, the Other with ourselves to unmask the horror that is, hiding in plain sight.

I have always written from a place not of repulsion, but of fascination with the Other. To find or kindle the light of empathy at the end of the tunnel of despair, to become both the ant and the terrible, living landscape in which she finds herself lost. Lovecraft's greatest fiction tapped into a problematic vein of repulsion and alienation from the natural world and his fellow humans, a revulsion so powerful as to become obsession. As a mutant product of the evolution of the weird fiction genre into the diverse, militantly inclusive community it is today, I have tried to invert that ratio, to stare wide-eyed into the forbidden and find terrible beauty, as well as all the unspeakable, gibbous, rugose and amorphous horrors you've every right to expect from a book like this.

—Cody Goodfellow

Burbank, California
November 2015

The Anatomy Lesson

"We are dead men," I whispered to my friend as we filed out, with all the other condemned, from Professor Aldwych's lecture hall.

But my friend's response was as falsely bright as the setting sunlight on the rain-washed stones of the quadrangle, that damned summer day.

"Not a bit of it," said he. "Were we both dead, then we'd be beyond all worry, and if only one of us were dead, then the other's troubles would likewise be at an end." With this last sardonic observation, he only whetted the keen edge of my unease, for the same unworthy thought had crossed my own mind.

With final examinations slated for Monday morning, we were up against an unthinkable obstacle to completing our studies. The university had failed to secure adequate cadavers, and old Aldwych had left dangling the horrid prospect of suspension of exams and graduations for those who failed to shift for themselves.

"I'll give you a hundred for your friend," Bartholomew Parrish brayed, interrupting our commiseration with his usual patrician bluster, to the brutish delight of his hooting yahoo chorus of sculling chums.

"Mr. Balfour is not for sale," I retorted.

"I wasn't talking to you, Lennox." Turning to my friend, Parrish pressed his idiotic jape too far by producing a billfold and pinching my shoulder like a greedy stockman. "I don't fancy such a stringy specimen. Something corn-fed and country-dumb for my table. How much'll you take for him?"

Augustus Balfour said nothing, but only leered at me like a prize calf.

Perhaps taking me for a soft touch because I came from the Territories, Augustus had entrusted me with the secret of his true name and heritage, a scandalized local line about which even I had heard many wild, sordid stories. With his eerily fuliginous, close-set eyes, scalpel nose, and fine complexion the color of sour milk, Augustus easily passed for a scion of fugitive French aristocracy, but I could not suppress a chill as he looked me over, for he was, in fact, an Odum—the great-grandson of Ichabod Odum, the infamous whaler and pirate whose name is a local curse that demands spit at the imprudent speaker's feet, from Dunwich to the Innsmouth shore.

Bart Parrish's father owned half the mills on the Miskatonic, and Bart had bragged that his father would arrange an "accident" to supply his and his cronies' test materials, but he liked to throw his weighted wallet around. If he and his crass ilk were not so frightened of Augustus, I don't know if I would have become so close to my friend, and so trusted him with my life.

Finally, he answered. "Flesh is priceless, my dear Mr. Parrish. Even worms pay dearly for it. How foolish of you to buy him from me now, when I might have yours for free, on Monday?"

Parrish stormed off with his lackeys in tow. Augustus called after him, "Give my regards to your father!"

And so, on a balmy June night in 18—, Augustus and I, accompanied by Linus Keebler, another unpopular student whom Augustus had taken under his wing, set out to rob graves.

My heart is heavy with the memory of those days, but we were blinded to the morbid and criminal nature of our quest by our noble ideals and boyish camaraderie, and hardened to it by the gallows humor that every student of medicine must assume. My own zeal to learn the forbidden secrets of the human body was not so fanatical as my friend's, but I was no less adamantine in my resolve to become a doctor.

When I was only twelve, an outbreak of cholera decimated my town, killing my mother and leaving my father unfit for work. He was only one of many who sought respite in patent medicines of the sort sold by traveling quacks in the Territories, and he died sicker than the ones laid low by the bad water. My tuition at a series of boarding schools, and then at Miskatonic, was paid for by the good people of our town, a gesture of their dedication to protect their community from the twofold threat of disease and snake oil that killed rather than cured. To return the good faith of the town that had taken me into its bosom when my home was rent asunder, I would rob graves, and worse. To save the living, I truly believed, there was no sin in disturbing the dead.

While our fellow students had fanned out to Kingsport, Dunwich, and elsewhere outside Essex County, in search of materials no one would recognize, Augustus had insisted on going to the potter's field at the edge of the cemetery at Sentinel Hill, where Arkham's working poor and the unaffiliated country folk were buried.

We saw the lamps and torches of a sizeable brigade of concerned citizens gathered at the gates, and prudently ambled round to the back. Climbing a willow tree just outside the wrought-iron fence, we scaled its drooping branches and dropped our rude tools on hallowed ground.

Keebler had to be hushed constantly, for his nerves made him burst into hymns in his stuttering, soapy voice. A lily-livered parson's son from some New Hampshire burg that made Arkham look like Paris, Keebler was useful to Augustus because he agreed to finish any irksome assignment that Augustus tired of completing. Tonight, he carried all our tools.

From somewhere deep in the cemetery's remotest precincts, we heard the braying laughter of Bart Parrish and the sculling crew. Parrish must have tendered a bribe that soothed the vigilantes' outraged piety, and he was making a garden party of it.

As Augustus had scouted the cemetery and seemed to know its intimate workings, we deferred to his authority. The worn wooden markers around us were antique, the only legible carvings on them merely noting dates decades gone by. He assured us, however, that the gravediggers still used these rows, merely opening up old plots and dumping the anonymous departed into the holes, which were ever found to be vacant—and not always, he added with a wink, due to rapacious medical students.

"The earth under Arkham is as restless as the sea," he said. "It sucks the interred coffins down into itself with the same glacial vigor that constantly thrusts stones up out of the uneasy soil of farmers' fields."

At some length we selected a likely plot, which we found quite yielding to our shovels, as it was recently turned. Linus and I took our turns first while Augustus stood lookout, puffing his perverse pipe carved from the bones of some unlikely sea creature.

The overripe summer air was still and feverish with damp, and even the antiseptic-soaked handkerchiefs over our mouths could not stifle the stench rising from the fetid earth. By the sickly silver light of the stars and the waxing gibbous moon, we began our ghastly work.

Though Linus Keebler proved a less than ideal partner, spending more of his breath on his gusty hymns than digging, we succeeded in half an hour in discovering the lid of a plain pine box, four feet beneath the surface. After winning a coin toss, I climbed out to make room for Linus, offering him a short iron prybar to do the honors. I offered a pointed suggestion to Augustus that we might conclude our business quicker, if he were to begin disinterring the next grave. To my surprise, he offered no dissembling, but took up a shovel and set to on the grave beside the one we'd excavated.

Just then, Keebler succeeded in prying the last nails from the coffin's lid and, with his boots dug into the crumbling walls of the gaping grave, wrenched open the door of his fate.

"Good lord above, Balfour!" Keebler moaned, as loudly as his exhausted lungs could bear. "Someone's beaten us to it!"

I shone my bull's-eye lantern into the grave and confirmed his breathless verdict. The coffin was indeed empty. In fact, it appeared to have no bottom at all. The ray of light pouring into the hole beneath Keebler's feet went down into pure darkness.

The floor of the coffin had rotted away, I told myself; but the evidence spoke plainly of something having burrowed into the fresh pine box from underneath and removed its occupant in some gruesome inverse mimicry of what we ourselves were about. I reached for Keebler's hand to pull him out of the hole a moment before he himself recognized his precarious position. But I was too late.

Like a canoe in rough water, the coffin subsided in the hole. Keebler lost his footing, grabbing for the turf around the grave to keep from falling into the pit. His chin rested on the edge of the grave for just a moment, his eyes bulging against his spectacles, his red, bulbous face a perfect mask of terror. He screamed so high and so loudly that I could not at first make out any words, but through his pain and breathless fear he tried to tell us, "It's got me! Help me, boys, the devil's got me!"

Augustus had said he was a poor hand with a shovel, and we should have taken him at his word. Startled by the sound of my shout for help, Augustus threw out his shovel, and poor Linus caught it. Unfortunately, as his hands were engaged in clinging to the turf, he had the bad luck to catch it with his teeth. The blunt blade widened his screaming mouth past his ears and cut his unlucky head halfway off.

I could not summon words to express my shock, but only turned to cast a baleful eye on my reckless colleague, who returned my accusatory glare with a sanguine shrug.

"Well, I suppose one of us can stop digging," he said.

Linus Keebler's corpse sank into the bottomless grave. In the creeping silence, we both heard the unmistakable sound of something in the grave pawing at the earth and the ragged hole in the coffin, in order to drag our ill-starred colleague down into the earth.

At last, Augustus sprang into something resembling alertness. Leaping to the edge and taking Keebler's corpse by the collar, he shrieked, "Grab him, before they do!"

"Who in hell are *they?*"

A grisly game of tug-of-war ensued, and for what seemed like forever, we thought we were winning. With Keebler's arms in mine and Augustus hauling on his shirt, we had nearly dragged our colleague's remains out of the hole, when the moonlight afforded me a glimpse of our rival.

It had the snarling face of a frightful hound, with a protruding muzzle caked in grave-mold and black, coagulated blood, but it was no simple beast. Those lambent yellow eyes betrayed an unfathomable cunning, while the taloned forelimbs that ripped and tore at our disputed prize were all too much like the arms of a man, though rippling with iron muscle and terminating in crude, bestial paws.

I freely admit that, when our rival bared its fangs like ten-penny nails and let loose a gibbering cry such as the coyotes of the desert plains make, I lost my nerve. Any devotion I might have had to my colleague's remains, or to the salvation of mankind through medicine, was rudely overrun by love of my own yellow skin.

I let go of Keebler's arms, but Augustus acted without hesitation . . . indeed, with such presence of wit that I would only later come to wonder how much, if any, of our misfortunes were not minutely plotted points of some elaborate strategy.

Like a veteran hangman, Augustus threw a knotted noose of rope round the neck of the monster and hauled on it brutally, choking off its infernal caterwauling but destabilizing the coffin upon which the scavenger stood.

In the blink of an eye, both our deceased friend and the creature had vanished down the hole. The rope raced through Augustus's burning hands, whipping him off balance. When I sought to reach out and catch him, I only entangled our limbs and added my own weight to the chain of fools plummeting into the yawning mouth of the nameless grave.

We fell in a screaming, battling tangle and landed in an insensate pile. When I reclaimed such of my senses as to take stock of our surroundings, I found Augustus already in command of the situation.

We lay on the floor of a tunnel like a mineshaft, but the prospectors here were not hungry for gold. Above our heads, the root-choked roof of the tunnel was pocked with vertical shafts that terminated in the broken coffins of the nameless dead of Arkham. Hardly the final resting place the townsfolk pretended, the graveyard was but the portal to a hideous netherworld, and death but a feast for life, in a grotesque parody of the natural order, above.

The repulsive grave-dweller lay prone in canine submission before Augustus, who kept the rope wrapped in one fist and a revolver in the other.

A pitiful meeping came from the creature's slavering jaws, but Augustus only tightened the noose. "Take me to the one who knows," he repeatedly demanded, in between fits of guttural growling, which the monster seemed to understand, and to which it replied in kind.

Presently, the cowering creature relented and crept off down the tunnel, with Augustus holding its leash. At a loss, I attempted to take up the inert form of our colleague.

"Leave him," Augustus snapped. "We're after bigger game."

"Off to where?" I demanded. "We've got to climb out the way we came. Mr. Keebler can't be left here to the tender mercies of these—"

"Ghouls, Mr. Lennox." Augustus followed his tethered monstrosity, lecturing all the while, as if on a bit of trivia about pygmies in darkest Africa. "That is what they are called, but have a care you don't judge them too puritanically. If all men are brothers, then these are our unacknowledged cousins. Their nature might seem unsavory to you, but they only feed on that which men offer them. Indeed, in our dim past, the origin of burial rites must lie in some kind of pact with the ghouls ... but even d'Erlette did not speak to it, in the expurgated version. It matters not, for we're bound to find the truth at its wellspring."

All my pleas, commands, and threats went unheeded. In his own time, he explained what he thought would bind me to this mad misadventure, and I—as much bewitched by the promise of wisdom as I was unhinged by the shocking twists of fate that had brought us to a subterranean highway beneath the graveyard—followed, as meekly as the subdued corpse-eater on Augustus' Balfour's leash.

"But d'Erlette was most forceful about one thing, Lennox," he went on. "Ghouls do not age. Steeped in filth, yet they are immune to disease. Except by starvation or extreme violence, they don't die."

He turned to look me in the eye. "Think about that for a moment, Lennox. These eaters of death are immortal."

"If it's eating the flesh of the dead that makes them so, then let the devil have them!" I replied, nauseated by his manifest eagerness.

Augustus shook his head and let the straining tomb-hound drag us down the charnel path. "Mere cannibalism does not make one a ghoul," he chided, "any more than having fleas makes one a dog. But they have other properties—the knack for replacing lost limbs and organs, for resisting plague and bacterial infection—that it would be pure stupidity to ignore. No, to leave such revelations unturned would condemn millions to unnecessary death. It would, then, also be cowardly and evil, would it not?"

Our descent had taken us beneath the rust-red clay of the hill, and deep into the limestone bed of the Miskatonic river valley. Water seeped from groaning fissures in the walls, but we had left the graveyard far behind—or above—us.

I asked Augustus why we did not return with our captive, to dissect him at our leisure. I had no scruples about executing such vermin, made all the more blasphemous by its bedeviling kinship to humankind. But his answer was so cryptic as to stifle all further attempts at conversation, for no matter how edifying I might find the revelations of the world beneath the graveyard, I was traveling alone with a madman.

"We would cut quite a spectacle, trying to subdue this poor beast long enough to vivisect him in the operating theater. Aldwych would expel us, if he didn't suffer a stroke first. But this one knows nothing. There are deeper secrets, of which the *Cultes des Goules* treats in oblique riddles, but which are kept in a cache of obsidian tablets by the One Who Knows. The Judge of the Dead, grandsire of ghouls, touched by the Unbegotten One, ha! See how it cowers in fear when I speak the name. But you'll take us to him, won't you?"

I would have turned and found my own way back, but we had passed so many branches in that labyrinthine warren that I despaired of returning alone. Every intersecting tunnel seemed to glitter with constellations of yellow eyes, and always at our heels was the diabolical din of baying dogs—though their chaotic barking seemed to strive to imitate Keebler's woefully off-key rendition of "Shall We Gather in the Garden."

Perhaps Augustus hoped to win my sundered confidence with his lectures. I had no knowledge of, and even less use for, the perverse royalist naturalism of the Old World, and told him so. But Augustus only cackled, "Old World! There is nothing *new* in this world, but eternally born-again ignorance! Do you know, Lennox, about the books of witchcraft and antediluvian folklore, kept under lock and key in the library? Why would such books remain closely guarded, when all the other secrets of the ancients have been stripped from their tombs and displayed in museums and world's fairs, to amuse modern fools? They speak of the Old Ones as those from Outside, but their occulted mummeries hide a wondrous truth. Our smug science is a flimsy garment of wishes and lies, while the unspeakable truth they hide is a roaring wind.

"The secret that puts the lie to all we think we know is that there is but *one* ancestral organism, of which all living things on earth are descended. The Old Ones are but the veiled true face of nature ... the blind, fumbling authors of our flesh."

We emerged from the tunnel and found ourselves in a cavern so vast that, at first, I mistook the distant roof for the night sky.

Relief turned to disappointment, then to awe, as I discovered the dimensions of the cavern we had entered. In diameter, it could not have been less than two hundred leagues, and almost perfectly cylindrical, as if we had stumbled upon the path of some enormous, boring worm, devouring the deep foundations of the earth as a maggot gnaws dead flesh.

A sluggish river of black, oily water burbled down the gently descending course of the vast grotto. A clipper ship could have handily navigated it. When I remarked upon this, Augustus smiled and asked me if I'd ever heard of the Dhol Chants.

"When the New England colonies grew into cities, and the Indians of the Miskatonic valley began to die off from massacres and disease, the desperate medicine men called the Dholes to reclaim their stolen lands. And yet, when they bore witness to the Dholes' terrible appetite, they repented and banished them to the White Void from whence they came, but the sacrifice was too costly. The Miskatonic tribes faded away, and the world they saved is only food for the most ravenous worms that walk . . . Americans."

Augustus's raving echoed above our heads, as in a train station or a cathedral. The worm-gnawed walls and remote ceiling glistered with the eerie green glow of false stars and meteor showers made by luminous cave flora.

Our captive led us down a treacherous slope of fossilized skulls to the water's edge, where a long, low boat lay beached with its oars shipped as if the rowers had only just left them, its prow painted with the colors and crest of our proud university.

Augustus posted the ghoul in the bow and took out a length of sturdy chain from his capacious overcoat. Slipping it through the oarlocks, he clapped a pair of shackles on the prisoner's bandy forelegs. He took the middle bench, bidding me shove us into the current, and lit his noisome pipe.

I recoiled at the unwholesome chill and viscosity of the water and had to brace myself with a muttered prayer before I could wade into the slithering river after my friend.

The damnable ghoul slyly rocked the boat as I tried to board, nearly swamping us and conveniently causing Augustus to lose his oars.

We beat our way upriver with a forceful tempo, but we saw no landmarks to gauge our progress—only the walls of the endless cavern, broken every so often by branching tunnels from which legions of staring eyes observed our passage. Many were not half so pleasant to regard as our ghoulish guide, but none came out to menace or molest us, though to overturn our boat and drag us beneath the black water would have been no great chore.

All the while, our uncouth oarsman chortled and chuckled to himself, as if he were not our captive, but quite the reverse. Augustus retreated into his own morbid fancies, and I was too overtaxed in trying to match the ghoul's effortless strokes to try to engage my friend in a debate.

Presently, the stagnant air gave way to a clammy Stygian breeze that made me shiver in my sodden clothes. We were harried by an unseen, flapping thing that circled us on vast, featherless wings and nearly capsized by something else that leapt out of the water to seize the flyer in its jaws.

The sluggish current subsided, and the roof and walls of the tunnel retreated into the mottled darkness, leaving us rowing on the face of a sunless sea.

The light from my lantern picked out monolithic shapes rearing up out of the murk; fluted spires and broken arches that I, clutching at any semblance of the familiar, mistook for the wreckage of gigantic sailing ships. And yet, these ruins were not hewn out of wood or stone, but petrified bone. This Sargasso of the underworld was a sink where the remains of land leviathans from before the Great Flood were swept away, out of the sight of God. Or perhaps they were the remains of fauna that still survived, even today, in the bowels of the earth . . . .

Augustus was not to be drawn into a discussion on the prodigies all around us, however. Heedless of tipping the boat, he stood and threw my lantern overboard.

The absolute gloom enclosed us like a colossal fist, pressing the breath from me and exciting a jackal's cry from our vulgar boatman.

Only by painful degrees did my eyes begin to adjust to the faint phosphorescence of the cavern's distant roof. The sharpening of my straining senses gradually revealed a flickering glow emanating from an island of bones off our port bow. It was the light of a bonfire, though what must be burning, to produce such lurid violet flames, I couldn't begin to guess.

Augustus bade us row for the island as fast as we could, and I needed little encouragement. I began to suspect that something paced us, down below, something large enough to make our little boat tremble like a leaf in a flood, merely by stirring the gelatinous black water with its unimaginable bulk.

When at last the island loomed up before us, I was perversely reminded of a church on a hill. But the hill was a new Golgotha, a jumble of bones larger than redwood trees; and perched atop the mound, seeming to sneer down at us with eyes of purple flame, was a single gargantuan skull.

Crocodilian in aspect, it dwarfed any dinosaur known to natural historians—indeed, the skull alone was larger than any church in Arkham. The unwholesome purple flames licked out of the gauntlet of teeth, limning a parade of bestial silhouettes engaged in some unholy celebration within.

Augustus leapt out to drag our boat onto the slimy banks of the island and graciously helped me ashore. He offered me a spot of cognac from his flask, which I gratefully accepted. I was past exhaustion, deep in the trackless territory of shock, but I had to try to learn what Augustus hoped to gain by this insane descent, if not to make him see reason and turn back.

"We are in no danger, Lennox, unless you show fear. Like all dogs, the smell of it maddens them." His sallow face leapt out of the dark as he ignited a taper and rekindled his pipe. "Think of the rewards we'll reap! Half of what we dismiss as magic is but the fragmentary remnant of a bygone science, far superior to our own!

"The forbidden books are laced with truths disguised as myth and folklore, just as the alchemists hid their chemical discoveries in arcane symbolism. Some scholars have it that the first ancestor came down from the stars, while others claim that it lives still and sleeps in the earth's core. It matters not where our original ancestor came from, or if it exists at all. The secret ways of all flesh, the keys to heal, to perfect and change at will the fundamental properties of the body! All this wisdom has been entrusted to the Ones Who Know, the ghoulish acolytes of Nyogtha! I have seen that power with my own eyes, Lennox! The wonders we could work . . ."

"And you expect them to just hand it over?" I snapped, once and for all at my wits' end.

"Of course not. I am prepared to offer them exactly what they want." I thought of poor Linus Keebler, and the canine hymnal howling that had trailed us into the bowels of the cursed Arkham earth, and I took up an oar from the boat, before I followed Augustus Odum up the twisting path to the court of the One Who Knows.

The violet flames and roiling clouds of noxious smoke cast the scene into lurid chiaroscuro relief, which made it difficult to tell form from phantom. The leaping shadows everywhere concealed packs of slavering ghouls creeping all about us, cutting off all hope of escape.

For his part, Augustus seemed quite at ease. He strutted down the sunken gallery of the colossal jaw to warm his hands at the bonfire. Draining his flask at a gulp, he roared out a guttural challenge in some tongue that might have been archaic French, mingled with some gutter Latin—the *lingua franca,* as Augustus had told me once, of graveyards.

The bonfire roared as if fed by gas jets. The fuel it feasted upon was a mound of fossils, split like kindling. The antediluvian marrow within them stained the flames and released a foul vapor that made the osseous walls seem to shimmer like serpent scales.

The growling horde gathered closer about us, until Augustus drew his revolver and fired a shot into the vaulted roof of the palate. They drew back then, but not in a panic.

Those fiendish yellow eyes smoldered as the pack took our measure and found us to be no real threat. Much larger and even less man-like in aspect than the denizens of the cemetery, they loped on all fours or upright with equal ease, but they also seemed far older, misshapen and battle-scarred. Notched and missing ears, split muzzles, and grievous scars were proudly displayed, but I saw no halt or lame, no blind or maimed, among these grizzled tomb-jackals.

From somewhere deep in the unbroken gloom of the cranial dome, where erosion or gnawing teeth had hollowed out the optical canals and maxillary walls to join it with the oral cavity, came a spine-tingling peal of unhinged, half-human laughter, plunging the gibbering tomb-horde into silence.

The skirmish line of ghouls parted to reveal a mound of bones surmounted by a barbaric throne. Sprawling upon it with the blasphemous majesty of a Duke of Hell, wielding the bloody scepter of a woman's half-devoured leg, was the one Augustus had come to see.

Augustus holstered his revolver and bowed deeply to the throne. "There are stories," he murmured in an aside to me, "tall tales told by the same ignorant hill-people who slander my family . . . of a traveling witchfinder, a Puritan general of Cromwell's army who came to Arkham uninvited, to rout the notorious nest of freethinkers and diabolists. The town fathers led him into the woods on the trail of a local witch, put out his eyes, and left him to die. Blind and raving, the Puritan wandered in the woods for days, killed the first game he found, and ate it gratefully, though it walked on two legs."

Grinning, Augustus took my shoulder and continued the story, faking better than I could unconcern as the lord of the ghouls slouched down from its throne, stretched and lumbered toward us with its forepaws dragging across the offal-strewn floor. It easily doubled my height, even before it drew itself fully erect.

"Now, the witchfinder didn't believe that he would become a wendigo if he lost his way in the woods or ate human flesh, but the Indian he ate certainly did. And so he discovered a secret of nature that men have shunned, and so lost out on preserving the genius of minds like Newton, Da Vinci, and von Juntz, simply out of superstitious ignorance.

"But he squandered his wisdom. Legend had it that he stole back to Arkham and dug out a home beneath the village cemetery. He believed himself a judge of the dead, whom he devoured in their graves to uncover their sins. The town fathers never caught him, and somewhere in the depths of the earth he was touched by the Obsidian Wisdom of the Unbegotten Source, and he was changed—"

"It's no secret," I put in, "how to make a beast of a man. Strong drink and crazy ideas usually do the trick." But trying to rein in his mania only threw kerosene on it.

"A beast! In every respect that counts, he is a god! They say he can raise the dead and mold flesh like clay. He guards all that a man could ever need to know, to heal the dying—and the dead. Think of the lives we will save, Lennox!"

I tried, I truly did, but I held only an oar as a god advanced to deal with us.

Plowing through the skulking retinue of lesser ghouls, the jackal-headed judge of the dead reared up on his hind legs and executed a deep bow of his own. Rawboned and powerfully built, yet his rugose hide was sparely clothed in mangy silver hair and deeply etched with hideous, half-healed scars. His arms were mismatched, one longer and more thickly muscled than the other, which was stunted, pink, and hairless. His deformed muzzle, wattled neck, and barrel chest were gnarled with clumps of leprous growths that seemed not so much symptoms of disease or decay, as of a rampant if misdirected vitality.

The yawning black orbits of the creature's massive skull were bereft of eyes, yet he seemed to sense us quite well enough. Branching black tendrils of quivering slime extruded from the empty holes to probe the air with the delicacy of a snake's forked tongue.

Turning away from us, the ghoul lord snatched a tiny, shrouded bundle from one of his lackeys and rudely unwrapped it. An infant, freshly perished, its cherubic face blotchy with dull lesions from scarlet fever, rested in the crook of his stunted arm, as if it might awaken to this fathomless nightmare at any moment.

I thanked God that the helpless infant was only a cadaver, after all, like those we ourselves callously dissected. But the doomed infant awoke and gave a pitiful cry as the arch-fiend took it by its feet, bit off its head in his massive jaws, and ripped the wriggling body in two over his yawning muzzle.

Drunk on the innocent newborn life it had so savagely consumed, the ghoul roared a blood-curdling challenge, rounded on us, and charged.

I turned away to be sick, but Augustus stood fast and met the howling horror head-on. At the last moment, he plucked some tiny item out of his coat and dove between the monster's legs.

I threw myself prone as the ghoul lurched past me. His slimy surrogate eyes withdrew into their sockets like a snail's eyestalks as he toppled headlong at my feet with a whipped beast's whine. Trembling with shock and relief, I could only silently admire what Augustus had done.

Armed with only a scalpel and the deft reflexes of a true surgeon, he had hacked the posterior femoral tendons of the monster's right leg and the Achilles tendon of its left. The creature may have been a god, but he was still built like a man.

Augustus sauntered over and, with a leisurely peck of his scalpel, cut the ghoul's spinal cord neatly at the base of the neck, between the sixth and seventh cervical vertebrae. He barked a litany of savage sounds that made the ghoulish court gasp, and then, in English, he addressed their fallen lord.

"General Jubal M'Naghten, I presume. I have come for the Obsidian Wisdom. I know you possessed it of old and have it still. I know the ways of your flesh and can give you pain such as only a witchfinder could deserve.

"Oh, and this," he added, while he unbuttoned his waistcoat to reveal a bandolier of red paper cylinders, "is dynamite. Do you require a demonstration?"

He took a stick from his belt and made to toss it into the bonfire, but the ghouls formed a snarling, whining wall around the flames. They knew about dynamite.

But even Augustus Odum knew all too little about ghouls. For the crippled giant at his feet rose up and shook himself so the scalpel popped out of its spine, and his disabled canine legs flexed and stretched as if they'd only gone to sleep.

Augustus stood paralyzed on his feet as the ghoul seized his shoulders in massive, taloned paws. When the slavering horror finally spoke, his voice was a silken, syrupy purr. *"Do ye want it so bad, laddie?"*

Talons dug into flesh, ripping away Augustus's sleeves and wringing gouts of blood from mangled muscle. He gasped with agony, but still managed to nod.

"Ye had only to ask . . ."

Augustus's arms popped out of their sockets as if a bear had him, but a bear would not have taken such gleeful joy in torture, never mind the awful power to do what he did next.

From the ruins of one broken arm, great arterial vines sprang out and climbed the air, and blossoms like cherries popped out like spring and summer in the blink of an eye. But then, the fruit ripened to reveal a bumper crop of staring, terror-stricken eyes.

The other arm gagged and spat blood as it emitted high-pitched wheezing cries that grew horribly coherent. The awful wounds had sprouted teeth and tongues, and they were crying my name.

Incredibly, Augustus still lived, but the ghoul lord was ready to deliver an early judgment. He dropped Augustus and squatted over him, eyestalks curling back into his beetling brow. The giant gagged and unhinged his own jaw, like a snake preparing to swallow an egg. He gave me no more notice than one gives a fly when I broke the oar over his head.

Augustus opened his God-given mouth to speak, but no sound escaped his straining jaws. Instead, his tongue lolled out like a dog's, stretching and swelling until it touched the bony cavern floor, where it clung with suction cups budding like soap bubbles on its glistening pink surface.

Like the questing tentacle of an octopus, his tongue thrust out for traction on the ground and tried to crawl away on millipede feet, when a torrent of white, scuttling pestilence spilled from his lips. Blind albino crickets and absurdly long-legged spiders scuttled away from the river delta of his sickness, but the lord of ghouls was far from done with my poor friend.

Something gurgled deep inside the monster's belly, wracking his misbegotten form with seizures as it climbed up the esophagus and tumbled out of his gaping jaws, and into my friend's captive mouth.

A black abomination, a squirming mess of aborted livestock and scrambled shellfish shapes, squirming with the unfulfilled promise of life everlasting. There were no stone tablets inscribed with medical miracles at the end of our insane quest. The Obsidian Wisdom was itself a living secret, which could only be conveyed with a kiss.

As well as he was able, Augustus opened wide. Lapping greedily with that obscenely overgrown tongue, he choked it down even as the endless deluge seemed to reach an unsustainable peak.

The ghoul lord seemed to shrivel and shrink as he vomited his abominable power into Augustus, who swelled like a leech, every internal cavity bulging and swelling as the black stuff filled him up and kept coming . . .

Only when I could recognize no scintilla of surviving humanity in Augustus Odum did I manage to take control of my fear and dare to approach my friend. The rash of mouths all over him might have been pleading for me to take his hand, but he had nothing like a hand left.

"There is no ancestor," he moaned, "only one flesh, one organism of which we are only cells . . . and it is Ubbo-Sathla. All pain and disease are the sorrow of stolen flesh. With this knowledge, all things are possible . . . except forgetting . . ."

He reached out to me with a perfect human hand, though whether to be saved, or merely to demonstrate his newfound mastery, I know not. The hand he thrust out to take mine was perfectly formed, though it shifted and changed before my incredulous eyes.

Each finger on that hand split open at the tip and gave forth a miniature, equally perfect human hand; and from each digit on each of *those* tiny hands sprouted yet a *smaller* crop of beckoning hands, so that each digit was a forest of clutching flesh.

Shuddering at his endlessly bifurcated touch, I reached into the tatters of his overcoat and stripped him of certain necessities, cocking his revolver and trying to make the monsters all around me believe I had more than four bullets left.

I need not have bothered. They bowed before the new ghoul lord's unspeakable embrace with the reverence of a coronation, and I slipped away unmolested.

I was not proud of leaving my friend to the tender mercies of those monsters, but I have since come to believe that my great failure lay in taking the revolver without using it on him while some fragile strain of mortal humanity yet remained, or in not attempting to ignite his bandolier of dynamite and blow the whole unholy tableau back to Hell.

I tumbled down the ossuary slope to the black and silent shore, and almost wept for joy to find our trusty Miskatonic U rowboat still beached there, and the ichor-spattered shackles empty on the forward bench.

I shoved the boat off and leapt into it. I sat in the bow and took up the only remaining set of oars, heedless of the slime I sat in. My last reserves were spent in a frenzy of rowing away from that damned island and trusting to providence to lead me back to the subterranean river.

When something leapt out of the water and into the boat, I could only kick at it. Our guide had returned and in a trice nimbly overpowered me, took away my revolver, and clapped his manacle onto my right wrist.

The ghoul lolled on the stern and used the spare oar as a rudder with one arm, while the other was clasped tight to his side. Clearly, he had cut off his own paw to get free. Now, he seemed to stare fixedly and covetously at me, and to lick his rubbery black lips—and his oozing stump—with his gray, barbed tongue. "Handsome hands," I thought he said.

Too soon, we passed from the subterranean sea and rode the aimless current of the river. Far from relieved, I feared that when we reached our destination the ghoul would turn on me, and I tried to slack off to give myself time to hatch a plan; but whether I rowed or not abruptly became moot, for the current began to pick up speed.

The surging black tide lifted the boat and propelled it down the enormous tunnel like a toy down a sewer pipe. I clung to the oars, but needn't have bothered. My fortunes were chained to the boat, and I did all I could merely to keep our waterborne missile flying upright.

The ghoul clung to the boat with all four grasping paws, howling to drown out the roar of the flood breaking over our gunwales in frothy black splashes wriggling with blind, glowing things. Throwing his ponderous bulk around in the boat to toss it askew on the face of the flood, I feared the ghoul had tumbled before the wave to drown us, but the boat shot ahead of the wave and right out of the water, skidding into a sharply ascending tunnel. The waves only swamped our beached boat and soaked us as they passed.

I lay in the slimy bottom of the boat for a long while, catching my breath, before I took stock of my current troubles. Fetid breath washed over my face, but the ghoul didn't touch me. He only dropped a bundle of rags in my lap. "Hurry," the creature growled. "It's coming."

"What's coming?" I screamed and brandished my chains. "How am I to—"

"Show your work, boyo," he said. Then he took out a meat cleaver and chopped off my right hand at the wrist.

When I had recovered from the initial shock, I found the ghoul had gone, along with my hand. I was free, and in the rags that I used to make a rude tourniquet, I found a test.

I ran and then crawled up from the underworld, taking any fork that seemed to turn toward the surface, until somehow, touched at last by fickle fortune, I found my way into a crypt with the lock already forced and stumbled out into the blinding light of dawn.

I had to hide from a party of early mourners and as I tried to get my bearings. The road at the bottom of the hill was the Aylesbury Pike, and the Miskatonic sparkled in the rosy morning light. The towers of the university reared up out of the mist in the east like . . . well, damn what I thought they looked like, just then.

I was in the wrong cemetery.

Exhausted as I was, I still had to make a long detour back to Sentinel Hill on foot before I could go home. The bells were ringing for church, but most of my fellow medical students still slept, so no one stopped me as I struggled with a bundle wrapped in my cloak over my shoulder for the dormitory. As well as I was able, I saw to my wounds. I had nothing to lose, just then, by conducting an experiment.

I had seen ghouls with mismatched and piebald limbs, and heard Augustus's lunatic claims, but I had no reason to trust in them. But I had come here to study the mechanisms of the body, and I had prepared all my life for this test.

The ghoul's hand was still sickeningly warm, the black-red blood oozing from it still vital. I touched it to the stump of my hand and instantly felt a tingling sensation, as of a galvanic current.

One taloned finger on the paw jumped and pointed, and then it made a fist.

It required less than fifty stitches. The paw was as good, in its way, as my own hand, by the time I said my prayers and went to bed. I slept through Sunday night, when I awoke with a horrible shock that I could only dispel by checking my closet.

I confess that, despite all the terror and agonizing pain I suffered in escaping from the underworld, I would still have been a failure as a medical student, had I not secured what we came for in the first place. Although his brain and sundry other organs were missing when I found him in catacombs beneath the potter's field, Linus Keebler would still get to make a noble contribution to medical science, and he would still, in a manner of speaking, get to take the final examination.

Monday morning found us at our operating tables in the main theater. The cold familiarity of stainless steel and formaldehyde was a welcome distraction from the morbid delusions my febrile brain had entertained, of late.

Professor Aldwych patrolled the aisles between us, calling out the objectives for the procedures we were to perform on our cadavers. More than a few students received a sharp jab of the professor's cane for looking at their colleagues' work, or at the professor himself, or asking him how his crippling arthritis had so miraculously cleared up.

I was thankful for the inattention, for I had replaced poor Keebler's purloined parts with beef organs from a butcher shop, and it was difficult to use my elegantly shaped tools with the paw of a carrion-eating beast. Indeed, the scalpel and spreaders only hindered my work, and I found it all too easy to lay open the chest of my subject with my naked claws, flaying the fatty endodermis away from slack brown muscle as easily as one peels the husk from an ear of corn. Aldwych's roving eye never stopped to remark upon my technique, though I took only the clumsiest steps to conceal my condition, and he no longer seemed to need his spectacles.

Our fears that a deficit of materials would derail the completion of our studies had been allayed, though a few of our classmates were missing, aside from Augustus and Linus Keebler, who acquitted himself admirably, in a role much better suited to his native talents. I could not identify the missing, of course, for we all wore masks and gowns, the ceremonial uniform of our grisly trade. To my weary eye, we did not resemble pioneers of medical science so much as acolytes of some ancient order, training to slaughter human sacrifices for a bloodthirsty god.

We had only just concluded the penetration of the anterior ribcage when a cloaked figure stormed the operating theater, using a laden gurney as a battering ram. We all looked askance at the outrageous invasion, but none was half so shocked as I to see that it was Augustus Odum, tardy to final exams.

If Professor Aldwych was known for anything besides his age, near-blindness, and slow, pained gait, it was his obsession with punctuality. But he meekly admitted Augustus to the theater and allowed him to unpack his surgical tools and commence with his examination.

My confusion and curiosity were almost unbearable, but I could not abandon my post to brace Augustus. I risked a glance his way when Professor Aldwych laid into an incompetent student at the far end of the theater. I was startled to find his eyes settled upon me.

His hands held a pen and scribbled notes in a journal, but his dissection continued apace and had already proceeded with the excavation of the thoracic cavity. I should not have been surprised at this, at least. Augustus had never troubled himself with tiresome labor, when he could coax another into doing it for him.

Augustus stood beside a big, strapping cadaver that appeared to be in excellent condition, except where its face had been gnawed off by some singularly vicious animal.

In a flash, I recognized the knotty hands and stubby fingers of Bart Parrish, but never had they operated with such deft precision as they did now; for they were engaged in cutting the aorta and pulmonary artery from their own heart and lifting it from the gaping chest cavity like a freshly delivered baby.

Slack-jawed, I watched the fumbling cadaver on Augustus's gurney remove its own lungs and then begin to cut the esophagus and trachea, when I felt a sharp blow in the small of my back. "See to your own work, Mr. Lennox," Aldwych hissed in my ear. "Only with your own heart and hand can you take the Hippocratic oath."

My own hand. Where was my own hand, at that moment? And what was it doing? Most likely, I confess, something not unlike what I was doing.

Before any of us had begun to finish, Augustus yawned loudly and proclaimed the dissection complete. All the major organs and blood vessels lay pinned and tagged beside the emptied vessel of Bartholomew Parrish, whose family later commissioned a statue of Bart for their family plot overlooking Hangman's Slough. The grave was, of course, empty.

Before Augustus took his leave, Professor Aldwych shook his hand and bowed to him, as if he were the student, bidding farewell to a master. Augustus favored him with a few whispered words, then left without any fanfare.

His rooms at Saltonstall Street were empty when I came calling that evening, but his landlord gave me an envelope that bore my name in Augustus's looping, swooping script.

Inside, I found the signet ring I'd been wearing on my right hand, and a note:

Apologies for the chaotic way our jaunt turned out, but it's within my power to put it right. Ask yourself—not tomorrow, but when the days grow long and cold—if you would rather I cured your hand, or your heart?

I never saw him again, nor, to my great relief, have I heard his name . . .

Until yesterday, when fate reached out and bullied me into penning this confession, before the will to make a clean breast of my sins should be ripped away from me.

For over thirty years I have served well the town that placed its faith in me, and never has my curious deformity become any more than a source of idle church gossip. I have done all that is in my power to keep them in health, to ease their suffering when no more could be done, and to comfort them, almost as a priest, that the mysteries of the flesh are not ours to divine or determine.

And all the while, I have known it for a lie.

I have told broken young men who left arms and legs in Philippine jungles and the muddy trenches of the Somme that nothing can be done, but to carry on. The god of my neighbors demands prayers, but never answers them. In my heart, I have not only sinned, but I have prayed to the secret god of my trade. And damn me, he has answered.

Yesterday, a package arrived in the post, bearing no return address, but I recognized at once the unruly penmanship.

Inside, I found no letter or note, only a patent medicine bottle bearing the label of *Dr. Balfour's Vitonic*. The seal is broken, and I have little doubt but that the contents are not what the label promises. The bottle is full of something black and fluid, yet when I hold it to the light, it strives to congeal into something alive. Squirming with unspoken promises, it repeats the question Augustus asked me.

My hand or my heart?

My heart—

König Feurio

For Scott

[DIRECTOR'S EYES ONLY]
Deposition of Oberleutnant S. Elsasser (O-7273374-9a), Kriegsmarine des Grossdeutsches Reich, 1/5/47

October, 1944

 U-818 was sinking, but we would not drown. We were dying with our hands at one another's throats, when Heiko Schweinfurter shouted that the man on watch in the conning tower had gone missing and that a ship had been sighted. Our struggles forgotten, we desperately rushed to the hatch; but no man who was ever plucked out of a doomed vessel came to regret his salvation as I do.

 The looming waves were like the restless walls of an endless black castle, fringed with battlements of icy white spray. Anfanger's leather harness hung from the railing. Heiko continued to shout mechanically, "Man overboard!" and switched on the searchlight to sweep the heaving sea. It wasn't snapped. I held up the harness. The fool had taken it off.

 A moment later, something out in the dark flashed a light at us, sending the same terse, mad message over and over.

 Kapitän Thesiger was brought up in manacles when we could not agree about what we saw. I was not the only one tempted to throw the madman who'd doomed us all to the waves.

 Beside me, Thesiger strained to make out the profile of the hulking black freighter that hove in and out of view less than two kilometers off our port bow. "Difficult to see with my hands shackled," he said, returning the binoculars, "but I say she is what old Heiko believed he saw."

 Weber shoved the captain against the railing with our only remaining submachine gun. "Fairy tales."

 Thesiger turned on us, grinning through rotted and broken teeth.

His voice had little breath behind it, yet its piercing tenor seemed to rebound off the waves. "I knew her captain of old, you cowards, you subhuman traitors. Kronauer was an affable Prussian gentleman, a student of the *hors de combat*. A natural philosopher. You can expect to be treated more honorably than you deserve." He laughed even when Weber struck him across the back of the head and lowered him down the hatchway into the arms of Heiko and Hanfstangel. "Anfanger can tell you what to expect! Sink her!" he screamed. "Sink her . . . if you can . . ."

Chief Weber and I remained abovedecks, watching the shadow draw ever closer. "It is still not too late, Elsasser," he said.

I did not take his meaning, supposing he meant to sink the vessel that had seemingly been delivered to us.

"If we all keep our story straight, we can claim it was an accident. Heaven knows the homing fuses are shoddy enough . . . . The Reich will be too desperate to send us back out—but the captain . . . has to go."

Did we trample our oath to the Fatherland because of our consciences or to save our skins? Inarguably the latter, for we never balked at sending forty-nine thousand tons of liners, freighters, and troop transports to the arms of Neptune.

We had chewed over every atom of our dilemma. A disastrous sortie against an Allied convoy in the North Atlantic destroyed our hunting group and left us battered and alone. Captain Thesiger went mad and drafted his own course to spend our lives as dearly as possible in a suicide run on the nearest American harbor. All but four of the twenty-nine men still alive onboard stood up with us against him. When Kapitänleutnant Weisshaupt and I arrested him, Thesiger shot Weisshaupt and Rotkopf, the junior radioman, before we subdued him.

Scant hours after we took *U-818*, we were crippled. Baargeld, the flag officer, gave no resistance when we declared our intention to turn south and go ashore somewhere in South America. But less than a thousand miles north of Bermuda, Baargeld armed a torpedo in the aft bay. The maniacal bastard breached the hull and destroyed the rudder and propeller screw, and killed himself and fifteen innocent crewmen.

A floating pillbox bunker, we could neither dive nor maneuver. None of us expected a fair hearing by the Kriegsmarine, and we had no guarantee of fair treatment as POWs in America. We had only just begun to let go of even those unpalatable options.

"I hardly think we need fear them dragging us back to Kiel." Weber chuckled, then banged the short-barreled gun on the rail. "It's goddamned madness, Heinrich! Who in the hell are they? This mad ghost ship—it can't be real!"

"Does it matter?" I flashed a terse reply to the freighter's request to board. They steadfastly ignored our radio appeals and continually flashed the same Morse message. "The worst they could do would be to ignore us."

"Yes, but what they're saying! It's some sort of mad American spy's game, or else the Führer rechristened some old hulks with unlucky names and children at the cannons . . ."

No one who knew better would sail on a ship by that name, or any namesake of a ship that never returned from the sea. But the alternative was far more unlikely.

Staring into the darkness around their incessant signal lamp, we struggled to get a sense of its size and distance. By my estimate, it was well over a hundred meters long and at least eight thousand tons, and perhaps half a kilometer away.

"If you should care to try to take their ship by force," Weber said, "all you'd have to do is stage another mutiny." The chief had been disciplined more than once for his impudent Burgundian humor, but his tone was anything but jocular. In his hands, he clutched Anfanger's empty harness.

The message had interrupted our physical struggle with the captain's loyalists on the bridge only minutes after the explosion, as if responding to a distress call.

Ignoring my reply, they repeated themselves once more.

Ahoy German submarine . . . In lieu of warning shot. By prize rules of commerce warfare you have fallen under power of sovereign raider König Feurio.

Prepare to be boarded. For your safety pray offer no resistance.

God save the Kaiser.

While the others prepared to disembark, I destroyed the logbooks and ciphers, radio and coding machines. The deck tilted alarmingly underfoot, the flooded aft compartments pulling us downward with each sickening swell. The labored creaking of the derelict ship gave way to a mournful keening that Weber said sounded like whales. Hanfstangel, from the Black Forest, insisted it sounded like a lumber saw when played as a musical instrument. Angerstein, the junior navigator, said it sounded like a song the boatmen on the lower Rhine sing, late at night and deep in their cups. The men became agitated, each seeking some illusion of refuge in the oddly mournful moans and pings that seemed to use the cavity of the ship as a resonating chamber.

We clung to the railing, but nearly went overboard under the next frigid blast of spray. The 85-meter U-boat rolled on the shoulders of a mountainous swell, then plunged down its almost vertical backside.

Hanfstangel shouted in my ear, but they still rang from the explosive detonation in the torpedo bay and the screams of the men as I sealed them into the flooded aft compartment. Perhaps I could not hear whatever it was that made Weber shake as if he, too, contemplated leaping overboard.

Instead, he pointed ahead, at three-hundred fifty degrees. A black prow hove in to blot out the rain, like the windward side of a forbidding desert isle. The tormented ocean subsided as if we'd passed into the eye of the storm. The looming shape that cast a shadow over us across the moonlit, choppy water was no wave.

The black commerce raider had a single funnel and two telescoping masts, and a three-tiered superstructure set high and forward of amidships from which no mote of light shone. A jumble of improvised structures aft and amidships appeared to be some kind of auxiliary quarters, or a prison. Odd doors all along its gunwales had opened to expose the barrels of three six-inch artillery pieces and a brace of torpedo tubes. An ancient canvas seaplane hung from a crane, ready to deploy if *U-818* showed any fight. She flew a flag of Imperial Germany, and one other none of us recognized.

Such ships had set sail from Wilhelmshaven with false flags and paint and special hardware to alter every aspect of their appearance, and they took fuel and supplies from their victims, but Admiral Dönitz had phased them out in favor of the wolfpacks. No, the commerce raiders were relics of the last Great War . . .

It was not a fairy tale, as Weber put it, but surely a phantom.

Along with the *Emden,* the *Seeadler,* and the *Wolf, König Feurio* sailed for months at a time on daring missions to mine harbors around the globe and to seize, plunder, and sink any Allied ships they encountered on the way. According to Heiko, the old merchant seaman, *König Feurio* vanished in the summer of '17 after mining harbors from Singapore and Hong Kong to Rabaul to Victoria. Sought after by the Japanese, British, and Australian navies, the captain put a handful of mutinous crew off on a tiny islet south of New Zealand before setting off on the perilous Southern Ocean between Australia and Antarctica with a hundred eighty-four crew and nearly five hundred prisoners from nineteen nations. They were never seen again.

We neither saw nor heard any sign of it before we heard the thud of the launch against the hull. Kleist and Hanfstangel moved for the deck gun. Men swarmed the deck all around them, springing out of the water like frogs. They wore only breechclouts and belts with knives, canteens, manacles, and nets. They surrounded us, but none of them drew a knife or even threatened to harm us. An Oberleutnant in the impeccable white tropical uniform of the Kaiserliche Marine climbed out of the launch and saluted me with a spotless white glove. I returned his salute and formally permitted him to come aboard.

"I apologize for the inconvenience," he said in crisp, oddly accented high German, "but we must have your ordnance and such salvage as your vessel offers. And yourselves, of course. You shall be treated humanely and offered food and board in return for work, and released at our earliest secure convenience."

It sounded like a script. I asked if they would take us to Mexico.

The sharp bones of his face leapt into sharper relief. He made a vaguely amused cough. "I am afraid that will be impossible, though we will soon weigh anchor off the American East Coast. We have not put into any port since we set out from Kiel on November 13, 1916."

I held my disbelief in check, but Weber was incensed. "How is that possible? You were not even born when this ship . . . when you say it left Germany."

His age was impossible to gauge. His hair was shorn to the scalp under his white peaked cap. His features were fine, with prominent cheekbones and wide-set, unblinking golden eyes. Whatever he was, he was no son of the Fatherland.

"I was born aboard this ship. It is our mother." He frowned, searching his captives' eyes. "And now, if you will be so kind as to order your men to prepare to disembark, we shall endeavor to make you at home, for as long as you should care to stay." He looked askance at me, weighing my influence. "You are not the captain of this vessel—"

"*I* am its captain!" Thesiger came up through the fore hatch, still manacled, with Wieduwilt behind him with a pistol at his back. "But if you are a true subject of the Fatherland, you will arrest these men and execute them immediately for the crime of mutiny!"

"My excellent Kapitän," said the strange lieutenant, "your battles are not our battles. We must succeed in our mission, and we must have all available means to that end."

"Devil or ghost you may well be, but never an officer of His Majesty's Navy." Thesiger sagged and dropped his head, we supposed, in defeat.

My crew began to disembark, filing into the launch less like prisoners and more like rescued children. I made so bold as to remind the lieutenant that their navy was disbanded twenty-five years ago. "Why are you taking us prisoner? Are we not all Germans?"

This time it was louder, and it was nothing like laughter. "Few among us ever knew Germany. Our navy is all about you. Denigrate it at your peril. Our empire is the sea. Though it was before my time, the elders of the crew still speak of the famine that fell upon them in black '18, when they could find no prize ships, what with the vile undersea boats that cruelly and wastefully sank them with crew and cargo still aboard. And now, you come in the ships that starve our people again, and claiming kinship to us."

"The Devil take you all!" Thesiger held out a grenade.

I ordered Wieduwilt to shoot the captain, but he instead fired at us, winging one of the invaders and putting out Angerstein's left eye. The engineer toppled overboard with the submachine gun braying bullets into the sky.

Lying prone on the superstructure, I drew my Mauser and shot Wieduwilt in the chest. A lifetime of rigorous training led to a moment's hesitation as I sighted down the barrel at my commanding officer.

Behind us, the darkness became solidity that swallowed the moon. The shadow of the black commerce raider towered over our starboard bow, as if the uneasy sea was a river delivering us to be crushed beneath its weed-shrouded prow. A salvo of heavy, tarred ropes fell onto the wooden deck of *U-818*.

Captain Thesiger pulled the pin and flung the grenade into the launch. Two short spears struck the captain in his thigh and forearm. My own shot passed over his shoulder as Thesiger tumbled off the deck over the starboard side and vanished a moment before the sheer iron wall of the freighter collided with the sub, like a colossal hammer against an anvil.

The launch exploded with two of the strange, naked marines aboard, and three of our men. I clung to the deck, bracing myself for the inevitable deluge of fire from above, but it never came.

Weber helped me up, and we waited, trembling with tension, until it became clear they had no particular will to destroy us.

As the other survivors of *U-818* began to climb the nets and ratlines up the wall of *König Feurio*, the engineer said, "There it is . . ."

"What?"

"The music you heard, when Anfanger . . ."

Now I noticed it, but shook it out of my head. From somewhere up on deck, a tubercular brass band wheezed a tarnished rendition of "Holdrio, We're Going Home." I thought of the strange, mournful sound that made a tuning fork of our dying sub and shivered, then accepted a hand climbing up the rope ladder.

That sound *hurt*, as if it wasn't meant to be perceived by ears such as ours, and certainly I could not imagine its source. But I was just as certain that it had been a voice.

It must require a great many men working constantly to keep a ship continuously at sea for thirty years, I thought as we boarded *König Feurio*. Several dozen crewmen clung to the rails to study us as we climbed the rope ladder up the barnacle-crusted, patchwork hull. A few waved their caps and cheered the Kaiser, to some laughter. None said anything about Hitler, nor did they take any offense at the ribald slurs and challenges some of us offered in response.

A few of the men could not contain their horror at first sight of the crew. Even Dr. Bronski grunted, "It's a damned menagerie!" and turned up his gray sealskin coat in reflexive fear. Despite my years in foreign ports as a merchant seaman, I could not deny a similarly trained repulsion. Whatever the officer claimed, this was no German ship.

Many of the faces that grinned at us were dead black with coal dust and engine grime, but of the rest, we saw Slavs, Mongoloids, Hindoos, Levantines, Nubians, and many more of untraceable mongrel heritage. And yet, even in the dark, there was undeniably something of a family resemblance among the motley band. Most, if not almost all, had balding, scaly pates and bulging, unblinking eyes that Bronski attributed to iodine deficiency.

We climbed over the rail, tensed for an ambush, and found only two more uniformed officers standing at the rail, offering assistance, warning us of the slippery deck. The only lights on deck were shuttered lamps with blue bulbs that cast a mottled cobalt light on the warped planks.

"Right this way, gentlemen," said another golden-eyed hybrid lieutenant as he ushered Weber and myself up a ladder to the bridge. "Your men will be fed and quartered in accordance with their cooperation belowdecks. Unless we can come to some accord, you'll be joining them shortly." He turned to grimace at me as he twisted the latch on a sealed door that gave with a wet gasp. In the blue murk, did he not wink? "Regrettable that your Captain Thesiger did not survive to be reunited with our captain. He sees so few from the old days . . ."

A sharp look passed between Weber and myself when the first mate's back was turned. Both of us had noticed how the ship's fixtures were clean, uncorroded, brass fittings shiny enough to reflect distorted faces. At first glance, this ship was not thirteen years old, let alone thirty; but they were mismatched, salvaged from other ships, and the structure underneath was undeniably of the Imperial design. The passage was dank and clammy, the close air ripe with that green smell of a drained aquarium, leading me to the absurd fancy that perhaps the hatchways and bulkheads were built to keep water in, not out.

A turn and an open hatchway brought us to the bridge. A telegraph and antique wireless receiver and navigator's map table sat unoccupied, though the dank cockpit had the turbulent atmosphere of a scene only just emptied. The stench of the sea was palpably thicker. It seemed not to bother the tall, slender figure in a white, undecorated uniform who stood at the helm, silhouetted against the sapphire light from the danger lamps so that I did not at first realize that it was a woman.

"Kapitänleutnant Heinrich Elsasser of *U-818,* at your service," I said.

"You were the leader of the mutiny aboard your vessel."

Looking back at Weber, I was startled to find myself alone. The hatch clanged shut and the wheel spun. I felt my ears pop.

I admitted it without offering any defense. She turned and snapped a smart salute. Her hair was pale gold, almost as pale as her skin, which was like porcelain. I would have guessed her an albino, but for her dark, wide eyes. With an almost Asiatic almond shape, they let me study my reflection without betraying anything within. "This is no court, friend Elsasser. Sometimes, Nature demands a reshuffling of the natural order. The fossil record is littered with Adams and Eves."

She offered her hand and I kissed it, as in films. "Celeste," she said, adding no rank or last name. "There is no greater blessing the land can bestow than to incarnate its virility in the form of a rightful king, not true? It is a noble dream, even if it has always led to the worst injustices and wars. Tell me, this new German ruler—he speaks as if he is the incarnated will of the people . . ."

"He is a madman. He is a child of the nation's rage over the last disastrous war." Carried away by the venom, so rarely drained in public, I let myself rage without hearing what she'd said. "We . . . Germany never recovered from the Kaiser's folly, and we are beaten even more badly this time. Hitler—you know of him?"

She nodded, smiling at me in a way I didn't comprehend. "We have a radio, but no transmitter. He seems almost incandescent, when he speaks, like a lightbulb overloaded with the will of the people."

I left off my impending history lesson as the bridge was overtaken by children. Silent, none old enough to serve in any navy, yet they quietly settled into the stations. I asked what had become of the real crew.

Her curious expression deepened. "These are the real crew."

Her accent was impeccable, but I finally identified it. "You are an American."

"I was born there, it's true. But this is my home, for as long as I can remember. These are my people."

"How did you come to be captain of this ship?"

"I am not her captain, though I am the one they follow. Like a big sister." She stroked the glossy black hair of a prepubescent boy as he idly fondled the massive helm.

"During the Great War, she seized and sank twenty-nine ships and caused nineteen more to be destroyed by mines. We—my father and I—were very lucky to be captured by this ship in the South Pacific, for her captain was a devotee of chivalry. He never would have attacked a ship with women and children aboard, and he treated us very well."

I found it nearly impossible to tear my eyes from hers. I knew myself to be impervious to mesmerism, but it was exactly how I would describe the sensation. "Surely you couldn't have been . . ."—I foundered, searching for my own thoughts—"old enough to remember when *König Feurio* was a ship of the line . . ."

She shrugged off my disbelief as flattery and, at last, the secret of her charm was revealed when she blinked for the first time since we had met. "You're too kind. I was a girl of four, traveling with my father from San Francisco to Australia. He and my mother were . . . estranged. My father kept me quite innocent, and the Germans were so polite and cheerful, that the seizure was a delightful diversion from the lonely sea voyage. My earliest memories are of playing with the crewmen on-deck. I became something of a mascot to the ship, and a distraction from their duty. I did not know it at the time, but they were the ones distracting me, for my father had taken ill and died soon after we were taken aboard."

I risked a flurry of glances at the map table beside her as she spoke. The charts were yellowed, worn soft as felt, with a jagged, haphazard course inscribed across the displayed leaves more forcefully than the fading stains of the coastlines. Out the corner of my eye, I watched the strange crew of children watching me. They made furtive gestures with their hands in lieu of even whispered speech. "And so you still sail, not for Germany, but for yourselves, taking prize ships . . ."

At last I had succeeded in offending her. "We are *not* pirates. We are a ship at war with all the nations of the earth, but we are not killers. Far from the sea lanes, we have pursued our avocation, which is the fostering of life. We were not too unkind in saving your lives, were we?"

"'War is such a dangerous business that mistakes that come from kindness are the very worst.'"

"Von Clausewitz," she said. In her unblinking eyes, the wry observation that she could hardly expect such hospitality, if *U-818* had come across a sinking *König Feurio*. Times had changed, and simple physics as well as the brutal nature of modern total warfare would have left us no choice but to machine-gun them in their lifeboats. "Just so. We are all very tired, even the youngest among us, and you find us near the end of our long journey. I hope that trusting you will not prove a regrettable mistake."

"You have delivered us from almost certain death. I assure you, you will find us to be model prisoners until such time as we are released . . . at the end of this war of yours, I trust?"

Smiling much wider than I had, she nodded. "Just so. And now, Captain, as an officer, you are entitled—"

I told her I preferred to stay with my men.

"Indeed." Did she appear crestfallen? I knew better than to trust my perception of women. "Emil will conduct you to their quarters."

A balding dwarf stooped almost on all fours by a massive hump led me off the bridge and down another ladder, down damp corridors lit only by blue lamps, corroded bulkheads mauled by marks like animals' claws. Staying ahead of me with nervous, lopsided hops, Emil hummed a reeling melody that struck me familiar, but I couldn't remember where I'd heard it.

I should have broken down, I suppose, at the earliest opportunity. Never given to morbid fancies or an abundance of sensitivity, I had discovered in myself a deep crevasse or, more accurately, a great wall between me and all natural emotion. I searched and yet could not find in myself the guilt and terror I knew I must perforce be crashing down upon any man in my circumstances. The cause of our mutiny was not any ideal, but simply to save ourselves from certain death. Such a decision was not taken lightly, and when it spun away into catastrophe, half those men I endeavored to save died, and the rest of us had been delivered into this unimaginable prison, this floating specter of Germanic barbarity almost quaint and ancient, to modern sensibilities. One could be forgiven for supposing oneself already dead, and delivered to some kind of abysmal Valhalla.

The crew of *U-818* was garrisoned in a hold previously used for storing sea mines. The ceiling was low and the still air reeked of decades of sweat, but after our marathon tour in the submarine, the cavernous space was a luxury. Several of the men lolled in hammocks slung from the walls and columns. Weber and a few others were still drinking, sharing the last of a brace of bottles of Spanish port.

"Elsasser! You missed it!" Weber came over and gave me a bottle. "How typical of you to duck out just before the delousing!" As I took a long pull of the cheap, metallic-tasting wine, he explained. "They have an entire joy division here! Such girls as I never saw, even in Marseilles. When we have regained our strength, they told us it would be our duty—"

"It's bestiality," said Kleist, the junior lieutenant. "They want us to mingle our pure German blood with subhuman mud to make babies..."

"Ask them," Weber jeered, "for a boy."

The towheaded young officer turned on the chief engineer, but two others grappled him away.

Weber took the bottle from me and killed it. "Is it not the duty of the true Aryan to lift inferior races by sharing the gift of his superior seed?"

"What's this about babies?" I demanded.

"They're mad for them," Weber said, stripping off his soiled undershirt. His ribs sawed at the gray, papery skin of his shriveled torso as he slithered into a stranger's clean sweater.

Bronski got out of his hammock like an arthritic old woman. "There's a maternity ward to stern on this deck, and a kindergarten. I don't know what it is, but if the worst thing they want to do is put us out to stud..."

"If that's all they want, we shouldn't be so eager to give it to them..."

Weber took hold of my arm and came close enough I could smell the hunger on his breath. "Are you giving us an order, friend?"

I retreated before I could give vent to my frustration. We had committed mutiny and high treason to escape this war. I must forgive my comrades if they were less out of sorts than I to find ourselves in some strange afterlife.

Finding no warders at the hatch, I stepped out to explore as much of the ship as I could get away with, but immediately I found Emil dogging my footsteps, bulging eyes staring unblinkingly past me, never quite acknowledging my presence as he followed me.

Finding a hatch admitting on the portside deck, I looked overboard to find our submarine all but dismantled. The crew peeled back the sub's iron bulkheads with acetylene torches and crowbars, while others picked over its exposed compartments like ants dissecting a caterpillar. Having already stripped *U-818* of its ordnance and pitiful reserves of fuel, the horde now lifted the diesel engines out by a chain winch that hoisted them up past me to land on a platform amidships. Truly, *König Feurio* would need far more than dubious prizes like ours to survive continuously at sea. They would have to digest their prey completely, wasting nothing. And what of its human prizes? What of the nearly five hundred sailors and civilians who vanished with her?

I found no other prisoners; the other holds were all crew quarters or converted cargo holds. Celeste had said that their mission was nearly at an end. What port would have us? What land would accept such a crew?

The assorted nature of the crew testified that they were the descendants of those prisoners from far-flung lands, but there was upon them a singular stamp, as if they all, despite their variegated features, were cousins of some heterogeneous yet incestuous clan.

Figuring the ship would never be less guarded, I undogged a hatch marked Entry Forbidden and went below. Emil made no move to stop me, but only padded after me, his hopping gait taking on an unsettling resonance as he splashed through the deepening puddles.

The stink of the ocean floor grew thicker on the lower decks. Emil only moved to stop me when we reached the engine room, which was sealed and guarded by two thickset, popeyed Polynesian men.

When it was clear he would not relent, I turned back to rejoin my comrades, but Emil stopped, making a croaking sound that I took to be some form of warning. He lurched backwards into a darkened companionway, the sound tapering off to a gurgle. Then a shadow lunged out of the dark to pin me to the deck before I could flee.

A knife to my throat insured my compliance, but still, my assailant thrashed me soundly before letting me up. I was anything but surprised. Long weeks beneath the sea and repeated disciplinary actions had acquainted me with the hand that beat me.

"Salute your captain, boy."

Captain Thesiger was wounded, with one arm in a makeshift sling, but he quite adeptly drove me to my feet and down a narrow passage ending in a hatch rusted shut, all without taking the knife from my throat.

He also appeared feverish, as if all the reserves in the flesh stretched upon that gaunt, hunched form had been consumed in the unlikely struggle to save himself. However weak he might appear, that he was not crushed or drowned bore witness to the folly of trying to overpower him.

There was no reasoning with him. I had presided over the mutiny and scuttling of *U-818,* and deserved only a swift execution. I felt a shock bordering upon disappointment when he did not relieve me.

"This ship is an obscenity," he barked.

I begged him to keep his voice down, which provoked a spasm of mad laughter. "They can't hear us, you fool. They're all deaf." He sneered at my blank expression, but I thought of the children on the bridge and the ease with which Thesiger had ambushed us, and knew he must be correct. His eyes were blank coins in the dim sapphire light. "We must find the captain, Elsasser."

I tried to explain to him that the man he knew must surely be dead.

Thesiger gnashed his teeth and jabbed me with the knife. "Perhaps you were quite certain a moment ago that I was dead, as well. You think you know everything, but can you explain this?" He showed me the peculiar curved knife now, almost more like a segmented crustacean leg, except that it was solid gold.

I tried not to think of the resistance that would meet our attempt to return to the captain's quarters, just beneath the bridge, and I didn't want to let myself think about the gold. I distracted him by asking how he came to survive his fall.

The rush of seawater from the colliding ships had swept him down beneath the keel of the commerce raider, but just when he had expelled his last breath into the frigid black, he was caught by a swimmer and taken aboard the ship. He was locked in a cell, but soon picked the lock and came looking for his erstwhile crew.

"One could not ask for a more fitting berth for a gang of traitors," he snarled. My captain never served under Kronauer, but knew more than most sailors of its sordid history. Of the crew who refused to continue on his mad course, one later served on a merchant marine ship upon which Thesiger was first mate, after the war. Somewhere in the midst of running from the fleets of four nations, Kronauer had gone mad and abandoned all other cares to fall in love with a phantom. He went into the Southern Sea chasing a fairy tale, and never returned.

"Did you ever hear of the Lorelei, boy? Combing her golden hair and wailing her song, she summoned sailors to their death on the rock. He heard her singing off across the waves, and he dragged his crew down to the bottom of the world seeking her. We all thought them gone, but now..."

And now, as if it had heard us, we heard it. That high, mournful sound like a whale or a saw keened through the bowels of the ancient freighter, and there was no mistaking its origin now. It came from somewhere within this ship, and it was unmistakably a voice, though what single human body could contain such sorrow?

Nothing else mattered now but to find its source. I followed my erstwhile captain aft with no other thought in mind but to pursue it, even unto death. As a moth mistakes any light in the darkness for the sun and darts about it in mad, obsessed orbits, so did we draw nearer to the source of that terrible sound.

The aft coal bunker, called the "hellhole" by both jailors and prisoners, was filled with cargo. My foot sank up to the ankle in chill seawater. Fearful of the delicious echoes in the black space, I hesitated and Thesiger nearly knocked me down. Presently, our eyes adjusted to render a blue chiaroscuro murk lit by a flickering bulb set into the far bulkhead, which must needs open on the engine room.

We made our way past crates and cases stacked on palettes above the sloshing water. Thesiger giggled, recalling how he found his way into the ship.

Thesiger crossed the room to stand before a hatch beside a row of levers and gauges frosted with salt and pitted with rust. The captain put his hand against the steel and moaned in sympathy like a flawed tuning fork. As I came up behind him, I found I must fight a terrible impulse to strike him down, as I had done before, to overthrow him and claim for myself that which had summoned us.

That I resisted it successfully did not impress upon me that my captain might have suffered similar influence and succumbed to it. He threw his shoulder against the wheel, almost whimpering in his exhausted eagerness to have or be had, to deliver the tortured angel or to usurp the tormentor's lash.

The door opened of its own accord quite violently, throwing the captain and me aside to make way for a torrent of foul, stagnant water.

The sound—the song—was now unbearably loud, and it would not be denied. I struggled against the slackening current, while Thesiger clung to the open doorway. When I came near enough to reach out to him, he took my arm and pulled me close, then drove the knife into my armpit. Leaving it there, sheathed in my ribcage, he left me to the water.

For how long I lay at death's door, delirious with infection, I cannot speculate. The nurses—spotless white gowns like nun's habits, broad, beaming copper faces—offered no answers to the questions with which I peppered them, when I was able to speak.

At the height of my fever, I seemed to be suspended in that flood into which Captain Thesiger disappeared, forever rolling in some submarine hell where crushing pressures swirled with the tiny forms of drowned angels.

Visitors I had aplenty, though I knew not which, if any, of them were real, even when I had recovered enough to recognize my own delirium. Captain Thesiger haunted my bedside, his sallow ruin of a face twitching with loathing and lascivious awe. My shipmates filed past, some surly and vengeful and alive, some serene, grateful, and bloated with death. All were agreed that, for what I had done to the dead, and for that unimaginable fate which had been thrust upon the living, I would be called upon to pay.

Often I saw Celeste, but the content of those encounters left me to suspect they could only be fantasies. In my infected imagination, she became the Lorelei, her true face hidden by a veil of golden hair, her song a siren to drive fish to beach themselves and men to drown in ecstasy. But even in my dreams, I could never quite touch her. She seemed to stoke my excitement only to open wounds into which to rub scorn.

Another face I supposed must be real, because I didn't recognize it. A gaunt apparition with a silver beard that whisked across my sheets as he breathlessly mouthed some incomprehensible prayer. With arthritic, fingerless paws, he struggled to drag me out of bed. With tears streaming from hole where the eyes had been gouged out of his head, he pleaded, *Say that you came to kill her . . . Madness even to dream it, but she must die. She is the engine of this nightmare, mother of all monsters . . .*

When my fever finally subsided, the nurses continued to attend to me, but none of my shipmates put in an appearance. The nurses spoke no German or English, and smilingly shrugged away all my attempts to learn what had become of them, my captain, or myself.

Some sense of their intentions came clear when, as soon as I was well enough to rise on my own, they had me strapped to the bed. I was content to accept my restraints until the next time I heard the singing.

The faintest reverberation of that frail, sorrowful sound reached me in my berth, and no sooner did I recognize it than I was overcome by that awful longing to find its source.

In it, one could hear the loneliness and abandonment, the surrender to despair, of every woman left behind by a mariner. In it was the dream of hearth and home that no man really ever found who returned from the sea to find a withered drab or a conniving whore in his bridal bed. To have that to come home to, any man would gladly kill or die.

Whatever I might have consciously desired, I was possessed, and might well have broken my bonds or myself in the escaping, if one of my nurses did not come to visit and silently minister to my bestial urges until I succumbed to exhaustion.

As a merchant seaman and a sailor, I have in my time sampled the daughters of joy in many lands, even among the mongrel races. I have lain with women in terror for their lives, with those all but emptied of humanity by their unsavory trade, even with those who took some pleasure in it, or who idolized me as a potential savior from the demimonde and so turned themselves inside out with desperate ardor for my pleasure. But never was I used so clinically, made to feel so like a farm animal being milked by an indifferent farmer's wife. While the urge engendered by that song was all-consuming, the final consummation brought only a shameful relief.

Again and again, this strange trysting continued, with seldom the same woman twice. It became as routine as my feeding and evacuating waste, but each time left me weaker, draining away my embattled vitality. Perhaps this was some new form of imprisonment, and quite effective it was, for even if I did not welcome each nocturnal visitation, yet I was left too tired and perhaps drugged to do more than idly contemplate liberating myself.

When at last my delivery came, I could scarcely credit it as more than a return of delirium. The heavy curtains round my bed parted and a pale and haggard Weber swept in with a Mauser clutched in his fist.

"Elsasser! At last!" Shouting alone seemed to weaken the shade of my friend almost unto collapse. "We were told you had chosen to join their crew."

"Why would I?"

"Most of us have, but we are prisoners no more." Even as he sawed through my restraints, I could not quite believe it. We had only a handful of men, against hundreds.

His yellow eyes gleamed with sickly light. "We have a hostage."

Heiko and Jorg Kaltenbrunner burst through the curtains. Between them, they held Celeste by both arms. Even with her eyes cast down on the deck, her alabaster skin already bruised by even casually rough handling, she still held some measure of command over them—over us all. When she finally met my fitful gaze, the loathing and fear I expected was absent. And what did I see there? I flatter myself I read some suppressed longing when she looked at me, but I knew not what she could be thinking, let alone what she wanted.

I had mutinied against my captain at the cost of my submarine because we did not want to die. Having cast off all deadly delusions of duty, I must not now shrink from the cause of those men I still had left. And they were my men only for so long as I would do violence in their name.

"My dear lady, we respectfully prevail upon you to change course."

"It is impossible."

Anything else might have spared her. But such blunt impertinence demanded a sharp correction. I slapped her and repeated my demand.

She spat blood from her split lip and laughed like glass breaking. "You would return to the Fatherland? Where would you go, that you would not be arrested and tried as war criminals?"

"We would go wherever we can reclaim our lives," I told her. I sized up Weber, who seemed to be in the late stages of some tropical wasting malady. His skeleton rubbed raw at the jaundiced vellum of his skin, seeking escape.

"So would we," she said. "Come with us . . ."

Weber spat in her hair, livid with revulsion. "This vermin has seduced half our comrades into joining her crew. We have searched the ship but found none of them."

She tossed her hair and flung the viscous spittle onto an unflinching Heiko. "They are serving their turn in the engine room."

The ominous timbre of her voice gave me pause, but Weber twitched and Heiko and Jorg dragged her back out of the curtains. "Then we will go and liberate them."

I stopped them and ordered Weber to follow me. Parting the curtains to go deeper into the sickbay, I passed through a ward lined with women in varying stages of pregnancy.

She read our confusion and disgust, and tartly said, "They are Polynesian and African and Eskimo and Australian aboriginals. All the blood of the family of Man, commingled, lets them thrive over much of the world where your precious Aryan purity would burn, freeze, or drown you. How can you claim to be masters of the earth, when you can only even survive on such a narrow crust of it?"

Pushing through this curtain, I found a surgical theater, and beyond that, a tank of seawater filled the space. An enormous woman, gravid with a mammoth pregnancy, floated in a harness in the cloudy, reeking seawater, straining in the throes of labor. A nurse knelt in the water so that only the top of her head protruded above the surface, waiting to catch the imminent birth.

Beyond lay only an empty ward . . . but one bed in the furthest corner, tucked under a convex bulkhead. Taking down a lamp from the wall, I shone it in the face of the bearded, blind apparition in the bed.

"Kapitän Otto Kronauer, I presume."

The shrunken effigy gave no reaction to the light or to the sound of his name, but he started and curled up like a burning spider when Celeste came near.

"He can't help you," she said. "He can't even hear you."

Fingerless hands thrown up to hide his eyeless face, Kronauer whimpered, "We are the damned, she is the Devil . . . Let the dead lie down and die!"

"How long have you been a prisoner, Captain?"

I tried to steady him, but he was an ancient engine with its throttle stuck wide, shaking itself to bits. "On fourteen October, 1917, we collected the *Euterpe* on the Coral Sea amid heavy weather. We would not have engaged her, had we known she was carrying women and children . . ." He wept and sniffed at a rag.

Celeste tossed her head and shook her arms free of her captors. "My father was determined to separate me from my mother. When they took us aboard, he begged the captain to let us go on the Asian mainland, but he wouldn't hear of it. After nine months at sea, raiding ships and mining harbors and adding to our wondrous assortment of prisoners—quite an adventure for a little girl—I could scarcely recall her as more than a dream, but we were finally tracked down."

"By whom? The British?"

"By my mother."

I shook my head. "Impossible. How could a woman, a civilian, locate a commerce raider at play in the South Seas—"

"Shall I lie to make you believe me? That would be much simpler, in the end . . ." She bowed her head.

I told the others she was stalling. They must go to the bridge, where Hanfstangel and Braunholz held the child crew at bay and tried to plot a new course on the ragged charts.

Weber refused to go. He made no secret of his mistrust, but he only thrust his chin at her to urge her to continue.

"She didn't have to find us. She came from an old fishing town. Out on the open ocean, she hunted us in a small schooner—alone. She followed the course of the *Euterpe,* and she . . . called us to her."

With his head against the bulkhead as if to soak up the vibrations of her speech, Kronauer moaned, "The Lorelei! Her siren song roved over the waves to bewitch my blood . . ."

At last I understood. "The woman who sings . . . is your mother?"

Celeste might not have heard me, staring with loathing at Kronauer. "Ever the bitter victim. Yes, we came to find her, and the captain added her to his menagerie. But she was a special prize, yes. Before his eyes had fallen upon her, he had fallen in love, and when he discovered who she was, he thought nothing of murdering my father and confining her to his own quarters."

"I was mad with lust! It was I who was imprisoned! All of us! Men who served as brothers killed one another with knives for her favors . . ."

"Yes, even though she was scarcely the mother I knew. The sea had changed her, but still he kept her prisoner, refusing to turn the prisoners loose even as he was forced to go below Australia in the depth of summer. We became icebound, and order broke down. When at last she emerged from the Southernmost Sea, the war was over, and *König Feurio* had a new mission—and a new master."

"We should go," Weber insisted, "to find . . . the others . . ."

I reluctantly agreed, though my curiosity was piqued by Celeste's reaction. "And he was made blind and deaf to deny him the beauty of her song?"

"He did that to himself, out of madness," she hissed. "I should go to the bridge. My sisters will need me . . ."

"Perhaps we should take her," Weber said. "Those fools said that the helm would not respond."

"You must not!" Kronauer moaned brokenly. "She cannot be steered!"

"She comes with us," I said.

Weber was most curious to see the engine room for, as he related to me on our tortuous journey through the bowels of the ship, he had not found a single lump of coal anywhere onboard.

"She should have her own weight in coal in the holds, but they're all empty. No dust, none of the smoke from the fires they always had. Nor is there any diesel fuel aboard, aside from what little they took from us."

I asked Celeste what the ship ran on, but she ignored me.

Weber winked at me. "I don't know, my friend, but not all the holds were empty." Out of the pocket of his pea coat, he took a nugget of gold twisted into a knot of tormented metal, as if it were plunged molten into the sea, or as if it had welled up from the earth onto the ocean floor. It was the same strangely worked gold that Captain Thesiger had used to try to kill me. "Their cargo is just provisions and medicine and construction equipment . . . and this."

We detoured to the hold he'd described and filled two duffel sacks with the raw gold ore and knives and strange jewelry. Celeste smoldered as she watched us line our pockets, hating us for proving only common criminals, and perhaps hoping we would be satisfied.

But we had to have the truth as well. The hatch was locked and two men stood before it, but they warily stepped aside as Weber, pointing a grease gun at Celeste, urged her forward. I turned the rusted wheel, bracing myself for it to throw me down under another tidal wave. But beyond the door, I found only a hyperbaric chamber with another door opposite.

We crowded in and the door closed behind us. When the outer wheel locked, a gasp of air buffeted us and a blue bulb glowed. The inner door opened and we stepped through.

The engine room spanned nearly a third of the ship's one hundred and five meters. And in all the cavernous vastness of the engine room, there was no engine. There was scarcely a room, at first glance. There was—only her.

I saw at once the reason for the atrium. It was to maintain the pressure in the chamber, which seemed to be open to the ocean. The exposed, mountainous island of black scales gleamed with faint iridescence.

She filled that space, looking more than anything else like a submarine in a pen. The waters swirled over the body like a garment of foam, tangles of gigantic, fleshy gray hagfish trailed from her flanks. A lattice of rusting iron struts from ceiling and bulkheads converged to transfix her dorsal arch, suspending her in place like a harness. Jutting out from her ventral underbelly, rows of fins chopped at the water like the oars of a titanic slave galley.

Her head, or what might have served her for a head, was completely enclosed in a barnacle-encrusted cage that surged up out of the water at the sound of her name.

"Lorelei!"

"She grew in captivity, as she came into the fullness of her womanhood. Her jailor went mad, tortured by love for something he could not bear to touch any more than he could bear to let her go. He had all but abandoned her in the aft hold, when she forced a reckoning."

"She ripped out his eyes and ate his fingers . . ."

"No, you won't believe me." She gathered her breath to let me marvel at this—confronted by this monstrous scene, what remained to disbelieve? "But when he lost control of the ship and her heart, he sought to reclaim her favor the only way he knew how—by feeding himself to her."

"She controls the ship?"

"She is the engine, the helm, and the navigator. We live on her as we would on any island. We travel the seas from one island to the next, wherever civilization could not survive, we have thrived, one family scattered about the globe. All of them her children."

"And all the fathers?"

"The captain fathered all who serve aboard her. Her grandchildren are humankind perfected."

I looked away from her now only because my head grew light and I grew faint, but there was no comfort anywhere to be found. The crew who tended this abominable engine bore the alarming family resemblance of the men and women abovedecks to its unbearable conclusion. Stooped, hopping on bowed legs like oversized frogs, averting their goggle-eyes behind webbed paws, they were clearly hers. "All those women who mated with us—you made us the sires of monsters . . ."

"Who are the true monsters? Men die as larvae, never attaining the true state of being. Look at your world. The unfit are rushed into mass graves, while the same stripe of moronic monster keeps seizing the reins, with the same fatal mistakes made over and over, like termites merrily gnawing away the foundations of a house, until one day it must all collapse. The unacceptable future is the one you and your kind are creating, every day.

"Our kind sheds its human cocoon and inherits the greater part of the earth. Guided by the wisdom of our elders, we have learned the patience of the infinite deep. When the tide rises and washes all man's works away, we will take our place in the sun, and with the wisdom of our elders beneath the sea we will restore all that you have sought to destroy. The earth you have scorched will be green again, beneath blue waves."

I looked at the shuffling subhuman fish creatures crouching above and all around us on sagging iron catwalks, wading closer to us in long aquaria steaming like soup. Peering into algae-scummed glass, I saw great clusters of oversized grapes, and nestled within each, a tiny, half-ripe human fetus.

As if they smelled my revulsion, the scaly subhumans came closer with claws extended, gills flapping agitatedly with a repugnant porcine grunting sound.

Weber brandished the grease gun but seemed to doubt its power. For their part, the croaking horrors gave it no consideration when they crowded us away from their mother.

"This is your perfection of humanity!" he barked at her. "This is what will inherit the earth?"

"Yes, and a better one. Without master races and religions or languages or wars. A world where the—"

We would have stood down even then, I believe, if Weber and I did not at that moment see what had become of the others.

Impaled on all those rods, straining to push a six-thousand-ton ship over the sea, the Lorelei seemed to shudder and freeze so that a sizable wave washed over the catwalks. Her enormous, caged head lifted out of the water, trailing a beard of seaweed and pocked with barnacles and anemones, and countless opalescent eyes blinked straining through the bars, and she opened a sphincter mouth like a lamprey's, air swelling a throat fringed with fangs, and she began to sing.

It had bewitched Anfanger to his death aboard *U-818* from over a mile away, that damnable song. It had driven my captain mad and possessed me almost unto my own destruction. Now, even witnessing the unfathomable grotesquerie of it, when faced with that song, what could we do but come closer?

And out of the foam flowing down over her breast, out of the throbbing rat-king of wormy parasitic things—which, I now saw, were somehow a part of her—we saw our captain clinging to one of the hagfish-like growths with his naked legs locked around it and hips spasmodically jerking against its slimy white underbelly, although he had clearly drowned long ago.

She reared up out of the water as if to proudly display the rest of my crew, blue, eyeless corpses still fornicating with mermaids.

Even so, I was climbing over the railing, my hand clawing out for Celeste to hold myself back or to force her to save me, when Weber started shooting. His first spree went across the back of the monstrosity and shattered the nearest aquarium. I was sickened and yet devastated with instinctual pity at the bunches of fetuses, well past the tadpole stage of early gestation, spilling out and bursting on the catwalk. Two subhumans leapt upon him instantly, but he fired wildly through them and at her until they had ripped him apart.

The Lorelei fell silent, head bowed into the sea, and she jerked spasmodically. The entire ship buckled with the lurching strain, her agony transmitted down the keel of the ship like a second spine.

Before I had recovered my wits, I reached out by instinct for Celeste and took her by the arm and threw an arm round her throat. They croaked and grunted horribly while they ate Weber, but they let us go into the pressure chamber and out into the ship.

"Where is she taking us?" I demanded.

"She's going home, to a little forgotten port town in Massachusetts, called Innsmouth."

"No, that's not my home."

"It will be, if you want to live. The town was nearly emptied by a government raid sixteen years ago. Those of us who weren't taken away or killed went into the sea. Now we will rebuild."

I could have argued with her that to approach the Eastern Seaboard in such a massive ship would be suicide, but we came out on deck into a white void as if the ship had been packed in cotton.

The sea was calm and still, suggesting shallow waters of a continental shelf. But our progress through it was uneven and the whole ship vibrated with the lurching, unsteady beating of a badly damaged heart. "She will heal. She has suffered worse at the hands of her lovers."

How many lovers, I wondered. How many legions of strange babies?

I escorted Celeste to the bridge, heedless of the gathering hordes of pop-eyed crew staring daggers at me. Braunholz and Hanfstangel were not on the bridge. No one offered a word of explanation, and given that I only carried a single automatic pistol, I declined to ask for one. They crowded against the windows of the bridge, a constellation of black, unblinking eyes.

Celeste went to the chart on the table and pointed out the one course not gouged over and over with repeated plotting. "We are approaching what was once our greatest colony in the Atlantic, before the war."

I observed that she had previously only called it a village.

"Above the surface, Innsmouth is only an abandoned port town, but below lies a city greater than any above the waves. Beneath our feet, a trench divides the ocean floor to a depth of nearly a mile, and it comes within a few miles of the coast. Below lies Y'ha-nthlei, the mother city. The way has been prepared for our return . . ."

She lifted her hands, and they all began to sing like her. It was all I could do to contain the exultant, raging despair it wrung from my soul. It was almost a mercy when we ran into the reef.

We had no powder magazines or stockpiles of diesel to detonate, but *König Feurio* was already holed below her waterline, and the speed with which the ship tilted and began to flood betrayed that the impact must have breached the pressurized engine room.

I strove to conduct Celeste into a lifeboat, but she shook me off and waded into the waves lapping across the deck. The other crewmen leapt over the railing and swam away or simply disappeared. The sounds of them crying out to one another were carried away on the roar of a second torpedo hitting us amidships. Blasts of displaced air roared up out of the lower decks. I didn't try to follow her down, but took one of the many unused lifeboats.

I remember watching as *König Feurio* tipped almost vertically, and then seemed to split open like a cocoon, separating into two sections as something burst out of its superstructure and knifed down into the benthic trench off the mouth of Ipswich Bay. The shattered debris of the antique commerce raider was swallowed up by the whirlpool of its passage.

Against all odds, I rowed and drifted and reached shore before dawn and somehow escaped detection. She was right about the town. The waterfront was a hinterland of empty and burnt-out warehouses. I found it easy to take shelter in one and to find my way out of the town with civilian clothing and some stolen tinned meat and fruit. I had been told that America had turned itself inside out looking for German saboteurs, sent all the Japanese away to concentration camps in pale imitation of our own efforts to remove ethnic pollutants, but I found it remarkably easy to hide among Americans. I made it from Innsmouth to upstate New York before I was caught, only a few months before Admiral Doenitz signed Germany's surrender. I never learned what became of the crew of *König Feurio*.

The FBI treated me with the respect befitting an officer, and I cooperated to the best of my ability, recounting for them as many as I could recall of the strange names of the colonies Lorelei's children had established around the world. Many of their names are famous now, even to such as you: Amchitka, Bikini, Eniwetok, Monte Bello, Maralinga and Woomera, Mororua, Fangataufa, Novaya Zemlya. At some point, they must have coerced the British, the ineffectual French, and even the Soviets into helping to wipe them out. Hitler would have applauded their silent commitment.

For my cooperation, I was released from custody and assisted with naturalization in my new homeland. I settled down as far from Europe as one could imagine, and as far as I could from the sea, in the Arizona desert. My life since the war has been nothing remarkable, but far more comfortable than many who came home as victors. With the last of the gold I took from the ship, I purchased a house and an automobile dealership. Americans adore their automobiles, and like everything they love, they stubbornly resist understanding what lies within it or makes it work. Trading ever scrupulously on their ignorance of elementary mechanical principles, I have amassed a considerable fortune. There is even talk of importing Volkswagen Beetles into the U.S. I had keenly looked forward to being the first dealer to sell Hitler's great gift to the common man in Arizona.

But I know it will come to nothing, for when I lie awake at night in my home, I hear the wind and it sounds like her voice. I have never come within a time zone of either coast, but I feel that if I will live, as she said, I must return to Innsmouth and inspect the children I have sired. I have no great desire to go, but the alternative is unthinkable, for I have no doubt that, no matter how she has grown, she will come for me if I do not go.

For the water from my well tastes of salt and reeks of the sea.

To Skin a Corpse

"Nuts to you," Bogomil laughed, and died.

Next to him in the backseat of the speeding car, a hard-faced frail named Matilda Blau broke into sobbing and curses, and the two men in the front were likewise overcome by anguish.

"Check him again," demanded Tom Thorpe, the mourner behind the wheel. "He ain't dead till I say so."

The passenger, a moon-faced torpedo called Helix, sat back from leaning out the window, and rested a Thompson submachine gun between his knees. "He's in the hot place now, but he's laughing at us." He twisted around and pasted Bogomil in the mouth once, to be sure.

"You yellow bastards!" Matilda Blau shrieked. "You'd never have the guts when he was alive!" The white-gold curtain of her hair hid Bogomil's frozen, bloodied grin. "Frank, no! Come back, please. Speak to me . . . *tell me . . .*"

"Oh, he's gone, doll," Helix giggled. "He's cold as a stone."

"He's no stone," Thorpe snapped, savagely wrenching the machine around in a hairpin. "He's a dead cat, and I know how to skin him. Thinks he can take it with him, he's got another think coming."

Helix popped sweat bullets. "Where we going, Thorpe? You can't turn us back into the city!"

"That dirty bird has the key to the loot in his brain, fatty, and I mean to beat the worms to get it out."

They took a truck route back into town, racing through shadowy orange groves at seventy with their lights out. Thorpe steered them into the jumble of warehouses and factories behind Union Station, tracing a labyrinth of nameless streets until he came to a crumbling brick building around which an armada of roadsters and even a few limousines had gathered.

Thorpe climbed out and lifted Matilda off Bogomil's tear-soaked corpse. "Hey, fatty, get our pal's other wing."

"What's your game, Thorpe?"

Thorpe didn't answer as he dragged Bogomil's leaden weight out of the car. Helix took an arm and they shouldered him across the dusty lot with Matilda in tow.

The front doors were a logjam of bodies—swells in tuxedos and silk suits, chumps and toughs and bookies in motley, and a few skirts for color. Thorpe led them around to the back door, where two men holding up a third argued with a neckless bouncer.

"He stinks, boys. Put him back in the ground."

"Ah, but this is Hud Hurley, the Raleigh Railsplitter, undefeated in seventy-nine bareknuckle bouts! When he was warm, Gentleman Jim wouldn't even get in the ring with him—" The gatecrasher tilted the dead boxer's head back to catch the light. Maggots spilled out his ears.

"And nobody here will get in the ring with him, either. Dangle."

Thorpe and Helix hauled Bogomil up for inspection. "Fresh as a daisy," Thorpe said, and slid the bouncer a sawbuck.

"The Swede's got a full stable," the bouncer grumbled.

"The Swede knows me."

"The Swede don't know nobody warm."

"I wasn't born this handsome, yegg. Swede used to train me, before that rat-bastard West ruined the sport."

"Huh," the bouncer cracked a gold-plated smile, "Three-Round Thorpe. Didn't recognize you standin' up." He took the bill and stood aside.

The wide, low corridor sloped downward, and funneled the echoing roar of a crowd mad for blood. "Oh no," begged Helix, "you're out of your tree! You can't—"

"All I want," Thorpe sneered, "is to make him tell us where he buried it, fatty. Who wouldn't want to know that?"

Helix buttoned up. They hurried past a line of fighters slouching against the wall, shackled and hooded so the bookies could look them over before the Battle Royal.

At the head of the corridor, the incandescent lights made a white wash of the arena, but Thorpe could see the bars of the big cage over the boxing ring. The crowd made like Niagara Falls as the fighters began to file in.

Thorpe and Helix turned into a locker room. Helix let Bogomil slump over on Thorpe while he threw up into his hand.

The air boiled with the sick-sweet smell of human rot, bolstered by the rancid, reptilian tang of Magnussen's bubbling cauldron, in the back of the room.

Bodies stood chained to the wall or lay still on carts and in the midst of it, like the last meatball surgeon toiling in an Army hospital, Swede Magnussen tried to wire the jaw back on a fighter without getting mauled by its wildly whipping upper teeth and flapping black tongue. His assistant, a big deaf, dumb kid with a cleft palate, easily held the bulky dead man down on the table with one hand while he tightened the strap on another one that almost got loose. His last assistant wasn't big enough to hold them down, and it cost Magnussen a hand.

"Hey, Swede," Thorpe shouted, "a jolt of snake oil for my friend, here."

Magnussen wiped blood and pus off his goggles. "Nothing doing, we're full up in here."

"This one's no fighter, Swede. We just wanna chat him up a bit, tie up some loose ends."

Magnussen gave up on the jaw and hooded the mangled fighter. He stepped down off a little ladder and shuffled over to inspect Bogomil's corpse. "I don't do walk-ins, anymore. Too messy. I only do it for the sport." He barely came up to their elbows, but his feisty, icy eyes shrank them down to kids inside. "*These* fighters, Thorpe, they never take a dive."

Thorpe's face twisted like barbed wire was sliding around under it. "Come on, Swede. This dirty twist took a big score with him. After, you can use him for gladiator school, or chop him up for bait, and there'll be a bit of scratch on the backside."

"Nothing doing."

"Fine, fine . . . . Hey, Swede, how's your apprentice at the old Jesus-game?" Thorpe pointed at the deaf-mute.

The kid got real small inside his sweater, and Magnussen shielded him with his hook. "No way would he raise your friend, if I won't."

"I'm not talking about my friend." He showed his revolver.

Magnussen's cragged little face knitted up tighter. "So it's like that."

"Sure, Swede, isn't it always?"

Thorpe and Helix dropped Bogomil on a table. The kid strapped him down while Magnussen climbed up on a stool and rummaged in his little black bag. "His artery's all shot away."

"He don't have to live forever, Swede, just long enough to talk."

"If he hasn't started to rot, he might still be himself, but he might not want to talk."

"We'll chance it. Helix, go watch the door."

Helix turned, grumbling, but the door flew open and boxed his ear. Blau stopped a man in a trench coat and fedora from barging in. They traded whispered barbs and he shrank away as if she'd put venom in him. She shut the door and bolted it.

"Make some magic, Swede," Thorpe ordered.

Magnussen packed some plumber's putty into the bullet hole and measured out a hypo filled with a sickly green syrup. The needle was longer than a hatpin. "Here goes," he muttered, and jabbed Bogomil's chest. He drove it in to the hilt, then depressed the plunger, slow and steady, until the last putrid glimmer of the green elixir was pushed into the dead heart.

"That's all there is," Magnussen said, polishing his hook on a bloody rag. "Sometimes, it just don't take, even if they're fresh . . ."

Bogomil howled.

The sound was as far from human as could be, like dry ice squealing against steel; there was nothing of the smug, jocular thug that once wore that body. It was a mechanical sound, the cry of an empty vessel protesting the outrage of living again.

Blau put her hands to her ears and shrieked. Helix jumped out of his skin and drew his gun, but Thorpe had to fight up that awful torrent of inhuman agony to get in Bogomil's face.

"So where's my meat?" Thorpe asked.

The howl broke into wild galloping laughter. Bogomil's chest kept expanding as he sucked in breath. The arm strap ripped away and he sat bolt upright. Across the room, four other dead men did the same.

Bogomil's hand shot out and caught hold of the soft pipes under the dumb kid's jaw, and pulled. Thorpe reared out of reach and drew his revolver, but Bogomil was faster in death than he ever had been in life. Greased up with the dumb kid's blood, he slithered loose and launched himself off the table in the direction of the door.

Magnussen swung and lodged his hook in Bogomil's shoulder, but the galvanized corpse was not to be thwarted by a dwarf, and dragged him like a kite.

The other dead men got up and liberated one another only to attack them. Bogomil threw himself into the thick of them and tore them apart with his hands to get at the door.

Thorpe couldn't see Helix or Blau for the rampaging dead men, but he saw the door open and heard the redoubled cheers of the crowd, who must be getting their money's worth by now. The rioting corpses pushed out into the hall, where screaming trainers tried to cudgel them into submission.

Thorpe leapt from table to table to the door, his eye on Bogomil's dapper, oiled hair, and the dangling Swede across his back like a cape. Helix jumped up on a table and snapped shots off at the fighters, who pressed so close that the truly dead ones couldn't fall down. Behind the door, he spied Matilda Blau, cowering, but armed with a little automatic of her own.

Snatching a fire axe off the wall, Thorpe sprang at his erstwhile partner with the axe high above his head and roaring like a berserker, bringing it down just as the arc of his fall gave its weight the greatest force. The red blade clove Bogomil's shoulder down through his solar plexus. Blood, black and thick as pine tar, splashed lazily out of the cavity. The dislodged Swede dropped to his knees and rolled out of the fray. Bogomil slashed with his remaining arm at Thorpe, who lost his grip on the trapped axe.

Blood blinded him and rage deafened him, but he pressed on, because it was all one big mess to be dug through, and his money was on the other side.

Bulling Bogomil up against a wall, Thorpe grabbed a hacksaw off a cart and laid it across the uppity cadaver's throat. While the intact arm battered and clawed at his face and the other flopped against him, Thorpe took what he needed.

A peculiar calm settled on the locker room as he got up to find Magnussen examining his defunct assistant and his own partners mauled but still upright in the corner. The stampeding dead had all filed out into the livelier stomping grounds of the arena.

"Come on," Thorpe called. He grabbed Magnussen's little black bag and dropped his prize into it. "Always a pleasure, Swede."

They stumbled over hills and valleys of trampled, mutilated bodies in the corridor. The gladiators were raising merry hell in the arena, but most of the audience had already beat a retreat to the exits. Behind them, Bogomil's headless corpse stumbled into the hall and, dragging the gore-festooned fire axe out of its innards, groped off to join the rumpus.

Helix asked, "So, where's the shiny stuff, Thorpe?"

"He was all dummied up from the drug. He had nothing to say, but a lot on his mind." Thorpe had a thought. "Big surprise how he came after you, huh, Helix?"

The big dope blinked a few times, slow-cranking his brain like a Model A on a cold morning. "He was just making for the door, Thorpe." His blobby oleo face melted under Thorpe's blowtorch gaze. He sighed and hung his head. "Anyway, she was right there, too. *She knows why.*"

Blau made a claw of one hand and went to rake Helix with it. "You plug-ugly liar! Frank was ten times the man you are. You never knew a thing worth knowing in your whole rotten life, but you know something now, don't you?"

Helix caught her hand and twisted it behind her back. "You watch your mouth, sister! Frank was a fool for you, but not me! I got to the meet the same time as you eggs, and I'm out in the cold, same as you. And the company stinks."

Thorpe pried them apart. "Forget it. I got another idea. We'll get to the bottom of this tonight, or so help me—"

He held up the black leather bag and shook it so they heard Bogomil's teeth chatter. He tossed the bag to Blau, who caught it in the belly, and lost the breath to curse him again.

They got in the car and pulled out of the lot, raced down a narrow alley that fed onto Alameda. Just as they swung out onto the avenue, a trench coated pedestrian jumped up on the running board and stuck a gun under Thorpe's nose.

"Let's have the bag, dad," said the gunsel casually, with no rancor. Thorpe's gun was trapped in his overcoat. Blau gave a little *yeep* and clutched the bag to her bosom. Inside the bag, Bogomil too smelled trouble and tried to chew his way out.

Thorpe stepped down on the gas and reached for the bag. "Do as the nice man says, baby." With his other hand he unlatched the door and threw it wide open.

The gunsel went out with it, hanging onto the door by his armpits and trying to shoot Thorpe. He squirted two rounds into the roof, one out Blau's open window, and one through the bag. Blau shrieked herself to sleep.

Thorpe batted the gun out of his face and swerved across the centerline. His wheels bucked as they crossed the trolley tracks, and clanging bells drowned out the gunsel's screams.

Thorpe measured twice and cut once, skinning along the side of the oncoming trolley. The corner of the people's chariot smashed his door shut and scraped the gunsel off effortlessly in its rumbling passage, sparks and chrome flying and faces flashing by with their mouths in big O's like a Christmas choir.

Thorpe's ears rang with the gunsel's runaway shooting, so he barely flinched when another shot squeezed off from just over his shoulder. The windscreen starred and shattered. Thorpe ducked and drew his pistol. With one hand more or less on the wheel, he turned on Helix and cocked the hammer. Helix sat there, dumb as a stump, hands up and empty. His eyes twitched at Thorpe, who reached over and found the gunsel's left arm still across the back of his seat, up to the elbow. Its index finger twitched once more on the trigger and was still.

Thorpe tossed the limb into Helix's lap as they passed a cop in a traffic circle who stinkeyed them out of sight. A daffy notion crossed his mind, making him giggle low in his throat. He wondered if, before night's end, they might not have all the parts to build Bogomil a new body.

He turned it over and over in his mind. When they did the job, a dragnet closed around them and they split up to elude it. Bogomil took the swag, to hide in the hills. As luck would have it, they all got through in the clear and converged on the meeting place, a cabin in San Fernando. They found Bogomil dying and two of Pork Cleary's goons cold at his feet. He laughed at them as they tried to wheedle the location of the loot out of him, but swore it was safe.

"We'll see how safe," Thorpe growled, and passed the gates of Shady Glade Cemetery. At the end of the winding mountain road, they stopped before a lonely little bungalow shaded by weeping willows.

Thorpe kicked his door off its surviving hinge and jumped out with the bag, raced across the manicured lawn, and rapped on the door like the landlord. Helix ran to catch up, and Matilda Blau staggered in after, still woozy from fainting.

An oily little man in a velvet dressing gown opened the door and prepared to deliver some urbane observation on the lateness of the hour, but Thorpe shoved him aside and went through the house to a book-plated study.

He dropped the bag on the desk and sat down with his revolver out on his lap as their host bustled in with Helix's hand on his shoulder, and Blau nipping from a flask.

"I'm afraid you have me at a disadvantage," the geek squeaked, "but if you'll allow me to summon my housekeeper—" His hand went into his pocket, but Helix chopped the arm with his gun-toting fist, and the man sank into a chair with a whimper.

"I know plenty about you, geek," Thorpe said. "You're Aubrey Dubois, and you're an undertaker at yonder cemetery." He looked over his shoulder out the window behind the desk. Beyond a low fieldstone wall, the moonlight made a frigid silver wonderland of the city of headstones and mausoleums that dotted the rolling hills above Hollywood.

"Then you must know it doesn't pay all that well," Dubois said. "I have some savings, which you're welcome to—"

"I know why you do it. You're the outside man for *them*."

Aubrey tried to look dumb, but he loved to play games. "Them?"

"The hyenas: the reason smart birds all get cremated."

"Ah," Dubois replied, "but nobody *really* gets cremated anymore, you know." He licked his lipless chops. His hand inched back to his pocket. "So what do you want?"

Thorpe unsnapped the bag and upended it on the desk. Bogomil's head rolled out, tracing a lopsided ellipse of blood from mouth and neck. The gunsel's bullet had smashed out his front teeth and exited just below the base of the skull. The mouth gnashed and smacked, struggling to speak, or just to bite. The eyes rolling in the face were just glass buttons, with none of Bogomil's clever sparkle that told you he was going to rob you blind and you'd come back for more. But what Thorpe needed was still locked up in there. "Do what you do, geek."

Dubois got up and edged closer to the animated head, eyeing it with the distaste of a gourmet at the Automat.

"Perhaps, if . . . I don't suppose there's time to do this properly? I could open a bottle of fine claret . . . Château d'Averoigne . . ."

"No time. I've seen your kind do their stuff. They weren't so fussy. Just do it, and start singing."

Dubois went around the desk and sat down. At Thorpe's urging, he daintily tied on a silken bib, then picked up Bogomil's head and looked it over with growing eagerness. He wiped sweat out of the trimmed mustache under his long, canine nose. "Surely you don't expect me to—to . . . with you watching?"

"We ain't squeamish. You want a fork?"

Dubois closed his eyes and breathed deeply of the bloody bouquet of Frank Bogomil. "Strong," he murmured, with real squirmy pleasure, "sanguine . . ." He relaxed and settled back with the head, forgetting his audience. "Clever . . . this man has you all dancing on strings."

His nostrils flared and his snaggled yellow teeth flashed. With a pitiful mewl of hunger, he bit off Bogomil's nose.

Blau hissed and raised her gun. Thorpe blocked her and pushed her back. "You don't have to look," he said. Helix backed up against the door with his hand over his mouth again.

Once he broke the skin, Dubois abandoned himself to his appetite. Worrying the cheeks off the bone, he gobbled up tender flesh and straps of muscle like a lawnmower from ear to cauliflower ear, nibbling these but finding the cartilage too tough for his refined palate. All through the meal, Bogomil's jaws snapped at air and wheezed to return the favor until, one by one, the muscles that worked them were shredded up and devoured.

Finally, when he'd stripped most of the meat off the face, Dubois allowed himself the coup de grâce—at least until he got the vise to crack open the skull. Peeling off the lid with his teeth, Dubois sucked an eye out of the head, rolling it round on his tongue like a centuried vintage, then crushed it between his teeth with a sickly little pop. He sucked the other one out and let it melt on his tongue. Thorpe leaned closer, horrified but hopeful as he saw what Dubois was becoming.

The lights went out. Black ink filled the room, chewed up by lightning flashes and mechanized thunder. Thorpe rolled across the desk and dropped behind it, where he found Dubois folded over and wet from the waist up.

"He got me again, Thorpe," said a voice that wasn't Dubois at all.

"Bogomil—Frank, where did you hide the score?"

In the dark, Thorpe heard his dead partner chuckle. "What a pack of saps."

Thorpe's skin knitted up in gooseflesh. It was easy to forget that someone was carving up the desk with a big gun. A few feeble pops answered back—Blau, firing from cover somewhere else in the pitch-black room. "Damn you, she-dog!" Helix barked. This couldn't last.

Thorpe took hold of Dubois's lapels and roared in his face, "Who killed you? Who took it? What do I have to do to get what's mine?"

Bogomil whispered in his ear.

Hot lead smashed through Thorpe's back and into Dubois. Thorpe's right side burned, and blood bubbled up out of his mouth as he shouted, "How long have you been jungled up with Pork Cleary and his gang, Helix?"

A pause, as Helix fumbled in the dark with a new ammo drum for the Thompson. "Even dead, he's a gutless squealer!"

Thorpe popped up from behind the desk and squeezed off a couple of rounds, but the muzzle flashes showed him he was aiming at empty air. "Who's gutless, Helix? You came at him with two men, and you let them get plugged. If you're gonna drill me with that chopper, you might as well spill where you put the score." His little speech ended, he coughed up blood and sagged back behind the ruined desk.

"Why'n the hell should you die smiling?" Helix slotted the fresh drum into the gun and sprayed the desk. Thorpe laid down, but a round creased his back. The window shattered and rained down on Dubois, who chuckled once more in Bogomil's voice, then rattled and died in his own.

"You're twice the dope I was, Thorpe. You think, if you bring him back, he'll tell you where he hid it?" Helix cleaved the desk in half and sent Bogomil's head spinning into Thorpe's lap. "He's laughing at us!"

Thorpe reached into Dubois's pocket and found only a little silver dog whistle. He put it to his lips and blew, hearing nothing but his own burning breath coming out of it.

A floorboard creaked to the left of the desk, and Thorpe rolled, saw a pair of size fourteen brogans, and shot the ankle off one of them.

Helix cursed and fell backwards. "Ah, damn it, this game's rigged."

"You got a better one," Thorpe said, to keep Helix talking, "I'll play."

"I got nothing from him, Thorpe. Not even when I shot him. He just laughed at me and said we could share it in hell."

"So why'd you let the stiffs loose at Magnussen's?"

He scoffed with a wet splatter that showed how good Blau had plugged him. "You dope, I didn't do it! That dip hit me with the door, so I didn't know what was what."

Thorpe started to rise with his revolver up when he felt the air stir at his back and heard broken glass crushed against the windowsill above his head. Slowly he turned and beheld a fearsome silhouette in the blue moonlight.

Yellow eyes glowed dimly in the dark. Guttural chuckling and falsetto meeping made Thorpe want to invite Helix to finish him off. It sprang from the sill to the desktop, and more creatures peered in with their blunt canine muzzles dripping coffin-juice and their stomachs rumbling.

Thorpe lay next to Dubois with his empty revolver up, but they took no notice of him. They were watching, and they knew who wanted to dance.

Helix screamed, "Eat it, hyenas!" and squeezed the trigger, but the Thompson was a temperamental gun that often jammed between drums, as it did just now. The ghoul on the desk pounced on Helix and drove him to the floor. The rest of the pack scrambled into the study and tucked into the strange treat of live prey with awful gusto.

Thorpe dusted himself off and took stock. He was lucky; only one lung flat. He grabbed Dubois's unfinished dinner and dropped it in the bag.

The tomb-horde scuttled Helix and Dubois and dragged them out the window. Incredibly, hamstrung and half-gutted, Helix was still laughing and screaming as they bore him off to the graveyard. "I'll be waiting for my share, Thorpe! In the hot place! I'll be waiting—"

He found Blau out on the lawn, already making for the car. In the light of the moon, her hair sparkled like his one brief glimpse of the score.

"Wait up, baby," Thorpe said. "You weren't gonna leave me here, were you?"

"I've had enough of this. You ever find the loot, keep it, share it with the orphans, I don't give a damn. I'm through."

"We're not licked yet, baby. There's one guy can put this right yet, and I know he'll be anxious to see us."

"Oh God, no, Thorpe. Not—"

"Yeah, baby. We're going back to square one. Let's go see the professor."

He watched her long, curvy legs trying to bolt out from under, saw ghosts whisper in her ear and flash across her white velvet face. Her icy blue eyes measured him, as cold and inscrutable as the hyenas', but every bit as hungry. He noticed just now that one of them was puffy and bruised under her makeup.

"Get in the car," he said, his hand restless in his pocket, "and drive."

❊

Going down Sunset with the bag between them on the seat, Thorpe bandaged himself and stuffed rags into the hole through his chest. "I guess you fell pretty hard for Frank, didn't you, baby?"

She worked the wheel one-handed and rolled a cigarette with the other. "He didn't have me around just to look at. I drove the getaway car. I got us out of the dragnet. I—"

"You got wound up like a tin toy, but you were smart enough to hate yourself for it."

She reached out and touched his knee. "Why are you trying to wreck everything? We don't have to go through with this. We could find it ourselves—"

"It's not about the score anymore, and you know it."

"You're cracked! You were lucky to get away the first time. You go back, and he'll see right through you—"

Thorpe swatted her hand away and rested his arm on the bag. Inside, Bogomil's head twitched. "Nobody holds out on me, baby. Nobody winds me up, and gets away with it."

They turned north up the Coast Road as a dreary rain splattered on the windscreen.

The nice thing about Von Hohenheim's estate was that you could make all the noise you wanted. The roar of the ocean and the thick fog drowned all but the loudest screams, and the nearest neighbors were a quarter-mile way and almost as depraved as the man they were going to see.

They stopped in front of the big iron gates. Blau swigged from her flask and rolled another cigarette. "You want to sneak around the back and climb over the wall again?"

He started to shake his head when the gates swung open. He lit her cig, and she burned his hand with it while she turned the machine up the crushed gravel drive. "Your funeral."

They got out and walked up to the porch, where a giant double door groaned open. Butterscotch lamplight bathed them and blurred the outline of a little man who bowed to them and nodded for them to enter.

He stood only up to Thorpe's waist and had no arms, but Thorpe figured he broke even because his short little legs ended in hands. His sad, saggy fish-face and hangdog eyes reminded Thorpe of portraits of Spanish nobility, but he couldn't put his finger on the itch of familiarity behind it.

They followed the butler across a vast red plain of Spanish tile that stretched out into perfect darkness. He heard no music, but Thorpe thought he saw gray shades clasping each other and shuffling in the black void–hundreds of them.

The Spaniard ushered them out to a patio overlooking the ocean. A fat, white-haired man in an impeccable white suit stood under the awning, smoking a fat green cigar and swirling a fishbowl of brandy under his bony nose. He smiled and drained the brandy, crowed, "Mister Thorpe, such a delightful surprise!"

"I don't know you, Mister, but I've heard things, and maybe we might have some business."

Von Hohenheim set down the snifter and puffed his cigar. "I am always willing to entertain an amusing proposition." He smiled expansively and blew horns of smoke out his nostrils. His velvet purr of a voice masked a faint beehive buzz of a Swiss accent. "At my age, diversions are so few and far between. Carlos, take the gentleman's bag."

"I'll hold it," Thorpe said, but when he looked down at the upturned face of the Spaniard, his tongue turned to a turd in his mouth. Carlos *was* familiar—but last time he was taller. Helix cut the butler in half with the Thompson when he caught them upstairs, and came after them with a sword.

"Mr. Thorpe, do you like my servant? He was known as Carlos the Bewitched when he was a king of Spain."

Thorpe resisted an urge to step on the ugly little Spaniard, with his granulated gray skin like pressed ashes and his mismatched limbs. But worst of all were his eyes, those dry white eggs that regarded him without blinking. Swede's stiffs were machines, and Dubois's hyena playmates were beasts, but this cheap little statue of a man had a real-live suffering soul bottled up in it, and every atom of it silently screamed for release. "I like him fine, but I don't want to buy him. I got something I need handled."

"What, pray tell?"

He didn't know Von Hohenheim the way he knew the Swede, and couldn't shake him down as he did Dubois. Diplomacy wasn't Thorpe's long suit. "A dear friend of mine met an untimely end, and I hope he can be . . . revived for a time, to settle his affairs."

Von Hohenheim threw his arms wide in a gesture of bewilderment. Far out to sea, lightning struck. "Wherever did you hear that I was capable of such things?"

Thorpe tried not to stare at the hard evidence lurking at his feet. "Will you do it or not?"

"Such procedures are not simple, or cheap. I am, however"—this last with a piggish wink at Matilda Blau—"flexible with regard to payment."

"No dice, prof. You can have his share of the . . . estate, soon as it's liquidated." Thorpe felt walls of dead gray flesh closing in, though he could not see them at the edge of the lighted shelter or hear their shuffling feet.

He believed he had a thread of cover to hide behind, because he and Bogomil and Helix wore hoods on their last visit, and the fat man was out. Maybe it didn't matter if Von Hohenheim had him pegged or not. Nobody got this rich by playing on the level.

"Then we have little to offer each other." The fat man sounded like a baby denied a treat, but then the twinkle in his eye came back bright as ever. "But maybe this will be worth it, just for the doing, eh, Mr. Thorpe?"

Von Hohenheim took the bag down to a cellar that, by the echoes of incantations and machinery, must have been at least as spacious as the house. Thorpe and Blau waited in a plush lounge. Thorpe sat stock-still, watching the low, round doorway and twitching at each strange sound, while Blau pillaged the liquor cabinet. "Your boyfriend better not rat us out," he growled.

"I think the fat man already knows," Blau shot back, voice husky and slurred with whiskey. "I just don't think he cares."

"Aw, you're nuts."

"Show me a rich old freak who ain't! I think he gets a kick out of seeing how crossed up we got over his loot—" Blau went white and pointed. Thorpe shot up and whirled, his gun out.

Von Hohenheim stood in a doorway Thorpe hadn't spotted before, beaming like the cat who swallowed God. "There wasn't much to work with, you know. The successful resurrection of the deceased from its essential salts is foolproof only with the lion's share of the vital organs intact, but I've learned to cheat on the ingredients, as you can see."

Something squeezed past the fat man and into the room. At first, Thorpe's eyes told him he saw a dog, because it ran low and fast at him; but as they adjusted to the impossible sight, he gave up trying to give it a name.

It was made of hands.

Some kind of body must have been at the center of it, but it could only be a hub for the countless, spoke-like arms sprouting from it in all directions, a hundred swarthy and pale and callused and smooth and scarred and tattooed hands, padding across the tiled floor and groping the air and reaching out for his revolver.

He stepped back and cocked the hammer, and Blau screamed, "What did you do to him?"

Von Hohenheim's belly shook with shotgun guffaws. "That's not your partner, Madame. Hector is an amalgam of all the men who've tried to steal from me in recent years . . . or at least the parts that did the stealing. Are you versed in the classics, Mr. Thorpe?"

Thorpe, dumbstruck, shook his head. Right before his eyes, Hector's busy hands snatched the revolver from his grip without him getting a shot off.

"Then you've never heard of the Hecatonkheires, the servants of Hephaestus, or Vulcan to the Romans. No matter . . . if you'll follow me downstairs, you may speak with Mr. Bogomil."

Looking sidewise at each other, Thorpe and Blau followed the fat man down a wide staircase and into a natural grotto filled with big machines and junk that made their hair stand on end. Von Hohenheim led them to a table in the midst of a jungle of crackling electrical gewgaws. A big steel bell cover sat on something restless, barely keeping it contained.

The fat old man laid a hand on the bell cover and soaked up the drama. "Now, his appearance may alarm you, as the remains were not enough to bind his essence, and corrupted with a vulgar reptilian-derived reanimation agent. Mr. Bogomil's salts had to be leavened with the salts of unborn human specimens. But I assure you that the creature under this cover is your friend, in body and spirit. I can compel him to speak the truth, but I warn you: the dead do not lie."

He lifted the cover.

They saw Bogomil's head, big as life and twice as smug, but beyond it the resemblance went haywire. It looked as if Von Hohenheim had tried four or more times to shape a body out of the mess, but gave up trying to make sense of the tangle of snakes and babies that wriggled and reached for them from that insipidly grinning thing.

But Thorpe restrained himself, because there, in those eyes, was that gleaming, scheming ghost they'd been chasing all night, the one that got away laughing at them. *Almost got away,* he thought, with a loud, last laugh trapped in his throat.

"You may ask him anything," Von Hohenheim said, "but be succinct. He may expire at any time."

"You mind giving us some privacy, prof?" Thorpe asked.

"Oh, you have no secrets from me, Mr. Thorpe. Go on, this promises to be the jape of the season."

Thorpe had all he could take from the fat man, but he had nothing good to give back. "Where's the loot from the last score, Frank? Where did you hide it?"

Bogomil's mouth worked, spewing milky fluid. His snaky limbs uncoiled and beckoned Thorpe closer. "You kids," he whispered. "Can't find your candy . . . Daddy . . ."

"Frank, you've got no right! You're dead, and Helix paid for it in spades."

Bogomil clucked his tongue, which slid out of his mouth and hissed, baring tiny fangs. "I lay down . . . got rolled . . ."

"Don't play me for a sap, Frank! You didn't lay down for Helix. That's something that . . . I always admired about you, Frank, you never laid down for nobody . . . but you have to know you can't take it with you. You can't take it away from me—"

Bogomil mouthed breathless sounds. Thorpe leaned closer.

A muted bang cut his legs out from under him. He clung to the table. Bogomil whispered in his ear.

Blau shot him again, dead-center. If Thorpe had been born with a bigger heart, he would have died instantly. Still hanging onto the table, he moaned, "Where is the score, Matilda?"

She came around to look him in the eye, or not to look at Bogomil. "He said he loved me, and to hell with you eggs, and fine, said I. But he treated me like his meat, and nobody does me like that and doesn't get bit!" She popped off a shot at Bogomil, but it splashed through him like mud and took a divot out of Thorpe's hat.

In the lurid light of the grotto, Blau's white-gold hair looked like bleached seaweed. "I slipped him knockout drops and stashed the score where none of you punchy dopes would ever find it."

"But then you . . . came back." Thorpe saw boiling white spots in one eye and blood in the other, which was a welcome change from the scenery of Bogomil's smile. "You had to try to prove you had claws, before you'd kiss him, but Helix queered your crazy little game, didn't he?"

Blau snarled and aimed shakily at Thorpe's face.

He felt a second—or last—wind in his sails, and talked fast. "Try this one on: Bogomil tried to talk in the car, but your screaming and pawing him covered it up, because he wasn't dying fast enough for you, was he?"

"Liar!"

"Gum in the works, all down the line! You let the stiffs loose at Magnussen's. And that gunsel who tried to barge into the locker room was some other dope you had on the string, wasn't he? You wound him up so good, he had to show off by trying to hijack us, just to kill the head."

The barrel of the little automatic stopped shaking. To Thorpe, it was big enough to block out the sun. "Say another word, palooka, but make it a good, long one."

"He rooked you best of all, baby. He knew he couldn't trust you not to poison him if he ate you, so he switched the boxes. You took a trunkful of brass."

Blau snarled and pulled the trigger.

The gun clicked.

Von Hohenheim's laughter stirred bats from the stalactites. "Ah, by Gorgo's balls, what larks!"

Blau clawed Bogomil's head, trying to find something to strangle. Deformed and dying as he was, he was far from helpless. His tongue bit her hand and tiny, twisted limbs wrapped round her wrist, so when she staggered back with his venom already stilling her heart, he went with her.

Thorpe watched with fading eyes as she stumbled into a crackling Jacob's ladder. The climbing rungs of lightning enfolded her and her dance partner in a fiery blue cape. Blau's eyes and lungs exploded as she jolted and tried to shake Bogomil loose and hold him to her breast until it looked as if there were two of her; but when he looked around Thorpe saw two of everything, though only dimly.

Von Hohenheim went over and threw the switch on the machinery. "Well, I suppose that's it, then," he sighed. "I thought it would be more sport simply to let myself be robbed once in a while, but if this is as good as it gets—"

"Wait," Thorpe croaked. "You can raise . . . the dead . . ."

"Oh, Mr. Thorpe," Von Hohenheim tutted, genuinely sorry, "I have all the cannon-fodder I could ever possibly need. And there's not enough of Mr. Bogomil left to feed a fly."

Thorpe lay down on the floor and dragged Magnussen's bag over. "I don't mean me or him, fatty . . . I mean her."

Von Hohenheim turned and regarded the charred remains of Matilda Blau while Thorpe rummaged desperately in the bag.

"I lied," Thorpe gasped, "about the score—being—fake. She had the goods all along, but she only trusted him to cheat her. She only hoped we could bring him back, so he'd kill us and they could elope."

Von Hohenheim could hardly restrain himself. At a wave of his hand, Hector ambled over and swept Matilda Blau into a dustpan. "I suppose it could be amusing."

Thorpe jabbed a syringe of the Swede's snake oil into his throat and rested the plunger on his knee, where his head would drive it home when he died. "Tom Thorpe—never—takes a dive—for nobody. If she thinks she's taking what's mine with her, she's—got—another—think—"

Von Hohenheim suppressed a giggle as he mixed Matilda Blau's ashes with the salts of aborted fetuses and less pleasant ingredients. He hoped Mr. Thorpe would be coherent enough to appreciate the cream of the jest when he came back, and pondered how best to phrase it. For, though he enjoyed a good housebreaking as much as the next four-hundred-year-old alchemist, he wasn't about to throw away hard-won gold for the pleasure; all that glittered in his house was not brass, but cut glass and gold-plated lead.

No, Von Hohenheim decided, as he traced the sigil of the Ascending Dragon over the urn and Thorpe's screams invented a whole new language just for cursing, *best if he finds out for himself.*

In the Shadow of Swords

Warren Revell has never considered himself a religious man, let alone a superstitious one, but the midsummer, midday Iraqi heat quickens the ascetic core of any soul who stays out in it too long. For months it has feasted mellowly on his idealism, but is now leaping the firebreak into his poorly defended will to work at all. As he waits, he contemplates how a place from which the first civilizations reared themselves up out of mud, where God and/or Allah set down the first man and woman and witnessed their fall from grace, could have come to this. We're still falling, he tells himself. If there ever was a Paradise, we've never been further from it. If you're up there, God, show me the truth behind all this before I have to go. Let me go knowing what's at the bottom of all this and I won't bother you again.

Revell's team is camped out at an annex building of the Istachbarat on the outskirts of Baghdad on the day his prayers are answered. They've been sitting there since before dawn, in a line of white Nissan Patrol SUVs with blue UN logo placards on the doors and dashboards. They remind Revell of another blue placard from back home which would serve just as well in this situation.

Outside, the military intelligence annex ripples like a flag in the churning heat haze. Modern military drab, hastily patched up after a partial hit in Desert Storm, its façade is nonetheless festooned with a judicious smattering of the tapered doorways and window frames and minarets that mark it as a proudly Arabic edifice. This morning, Revell has seen for the first time the practical features of this style, which camouflages the building in the convection currents as a cheetah's spots hide it on the veldt. If not for the anti-aircraft guns and the Russian surplus APCs parked out front, one could mistake it for a sultan's palace, or at least the storage facility where said mythic potentate kept records of all his war atrocities.

His mind has been slogging such backwater currents for a while now. They arrived two hours before their scheduled oh-eight-hundred appointment with the Military Intelligence Ministry and have been sitting in their vans, since it became too hot to pace in front of the line of Iraqi soldiers arrayed across the approach to the Ministry. It is fast approaching noon on the first day of August.

Three years of waiting outside sensitive Iraqi sites has taught him that you can't expect to catch them red-handed. You arrive early in hopes of seeing them frenziedly stuffing cartons of documents and fragile, astronomically expensive scientific gear onto trucks and speeding off in the night to bury them under farms in Saddam's native Tikrit, or in the asparagus-tinted depths of the Tigris. You photograph the trucks and try to stop them, but usually you wait and make phone calls, with military officials shouting, minders apologizing, and flies buzzing in your eyes and ears until the sanitized site is cleared to enter, or the Executive Chairman orders you back to Bahrain.

This time, there's been no attempt to clear the place out, and no deadpan tall tales of honest clerical errors offered to explain the delay. Even now, the UN Secretary General is meeting with the Iraqi Foreign Minister in Paris, the two of them sipping tea and shaking their heads at the vicious cycle of sanctions and fruitless inspections, vowing to implement a civilized solution. UNSCOM will be called home in a few days.

Major Ibrahim al-Majid, the chief minder, has standing orders to wait outside Revell's refrigerated Patrol and shrug every so often, as if to say, *Who can explain such things?* Revell nods understanding and places another call on a satphone to the UNSCOM HQ in Baghdad, and through a relay to the United Nations. The Executive Chairman is in meetings, even though it's 4 A.M. in New York, and Revell has already clogged his voicemail, but the secretary would be happy to pass on the message that their mandate in Iraq is being completely disregarded.

Al-Majid knocks on the window. Revell rolls it down a few inches, and the Iraqi presses his Stalinesque walrus-mustache into the crack, sipping off jeweled drops of Freon-cooled air. Revell is no wilting violet when it comes to heat. He was born and raised in Austin and spent most of his tour with the Army in Panama, but the heat in Iraq has worn him down. At over 110 degrees with no humidity to speak of, it clamps onto you in the morning and commences to suck moisture out of your eyes, the palms of your hands turn to sandpaper, and your mouth gums itself shut. It had burned every last mote of flinch out of the natives, who could look you in the eye and lie or threaten to kill you in more assured tones than white Europeans can profess undying love, but it has only burned the last atom of nerve out of Revell. For three years, he stood outside the truck, watching the guards for a moment of distraction to press closer to the sensitive site to see what would shake loose. But in these last days, he, too, has abandoned pretense.

"News?" he asks.

"Apologies, Mr. Revell, but I was only going to ask you for some water. A small cup, you can spare it?"

"Sure, Ibrahim, but wouldn't it be unseemly?"

Al-Majid looks around at the other soldiers on the road. "When you are gone, I will be regarded as a hero for my work to protect the sovereignty of my nation. Who would begrudge a hero a cup of water?" Al-Majid wears his mustache a shade longer than most because it hides his most rare ability, among Iraqis of the military caste, to smile. Revell has kept the secret of al-Majid's sense of humor, the twinkle in his eye when he's feeding the inspectors a line of state-crafted bullshit. He's going to miss having al-Majid to lie to him.

"If your whole clan isn't purged for some real or imagined threat to Saddam, I expect to see your face all up and down Airport Road when we come back." He fills a cup from a collapsible cooler on the seat beside him. Despite the air conditioner, the water is almost hot and tastes strongly of the plastic container. Al-Majid closes his eyes in pure pleasure as he sips. When he looks up again, he is all business.

"It must be a relief to you, Mr. Revell, the impending completion of your mission."

"What?"

"Soon, you will be able to return to honest work on behalf of all nations. You will no longer be a pawn of Israel and the American CIA." Revell's gotten used to this weird shift in al-Majid's manner, as if a puppeteer's hand has reached up his ass and is yanking his cord. He has always assumed the Iraqi minder is bugged and has to deliver these propaganda speeches from time to time to satisfy *his* minders.

"We've had a long time to establish that I don't work for the U.S. government in any capacity. UNSCOM enforces the mandate of the

UN Security Council, which includes Iraq's staunch allies, the Russians, the French, and the Chinese, to complete its abolition of Iraqi weapons of mass destruction programs. We're the only thing between you and being bombed back into the stone age—again."

Al-Majid's smile peeks out through his soupbroom. "Iraq will never be defeated. You need us too much, I am thinking."

"So what's the delay now? This site was approved by both sides last week."

"Apologies, but a new list of sensitive classifications is delivered to your UN this morning."

"There's new classifications? Jesus . . ." The rules of engagement for the UNSCOM inspections are labyrinthine and ridiculous, like a scavenger hunt run by ultraparanoid corporate lawyers. After a string of tense and embarrassing incidents where the Iraqis waved guns in the inspectors' faces while soldiers and civil servants scrambled out the back with documents and equipment and were caught by the UNSCOM anti-concealment teams, the foreign minister had demanded that certain sites be held sacrosanct on grounds of national and (especially) presidential security. Incredibly, the Security Council gave its approval. The teams could still pop surprise inspections, but the Iraqis could now deny or delay access by saying Saddam liked to get naked and strangle dancing girls there.

"This site is deemed 'sensitive sensitive political.'" The Iraqis seem to think that repetition makes things sound more important. "It contains records pertaining to political dissidents and internal security actions, which your American military would like to have for itself. Would make invasion—less foolish than otherwise."

"The inspections in the south will go smoothly then, right?" He's trying to make the minder laugh; the Basra inspections scheduled for tomorrow are sure to be murder. A month ago, a retired Pentagon analyst idly speculated on CNN that the best plan for overthrowing Saddam would be to demand seizing the south and installing a puppet government at Basra, composed either of radical Islamic defectors from the Iraqi army or Kurdish guerrillas. Saddam bristled at the notion of an UNSCOM force led by a former American military officer snooping around the south, or pawing through his mountainous enemies lists.

"Very few of the declared sites are controversial," al-Majid answers deadpan. "If your superiors do not have any ugly surprises planned, we will all be released from this farce soon." He returns the cup and brushes his hands through his mustache. He puts on a rigid scowl and turns to deal with the soldiers.

Revell's satphone trills. He seals the window, clicks the scrambler on, and picks up, fully expecting to hear the Executive Chairman tell him to pack up and go home.

"Revell, we've got an intercept." It's Luscombe, the senior communications tech. "It's—you really should get here immediately." Luscombe doesn't sound like Luscombe. Revell has heard him talk about things he saw in Bosnia with his impregnable Oxford-bred good humor, which would make some think he was a thick-skinned twit, if not for the nervous wringing of his hands. Luscombe's hands must be strangling each other in his lap right now, because he sounds horrified.

"I'm sitting watch out here, Graham. What's the point of origin?"

"From the south, within our theater of operation for tomorrow, but I don't see a site of any kind out there on any of our maps."

"Not even the special maps?" The "special" maps are satellite imagery interpreted by Mossad—infinitely more current and accurate than the CIA's best output, and strictly forbidden by the Iraqis.

"No, sir. It's something else."

"Oh. What's the content like?"

"I'd rather not discuss it now, if you don't mind. Suffice to say, it's a smoking gun. We need to re-evaluate our itinerary, Revell. I think you should have Hideo oversee whatever you're doing and come back here post-haste."

Revell turns up the air conditioner. This is what they used to hope for, when the inspections began and UNSCOM had a clear mandate to search and destroy Iraq's weapons of mass destruction. Now, with the mandate in tatters and their permanent evacuation two days away . . .

"I'll be right there."

His first breath of air inside the UNSCOM offices feels like biting down on a cold sword. There should be several airlocks leading into the building, each with successively lower temperatures to prevent thermal bends, but there's only the foyer, and Revell stands in it for several minutes before proceeding into the communications center. He massages his temples with his eyes clamped shut against the blast-furnace heat from the outer door. Someone is standing in front of him, and he knows who it is from the intense stink of cigarettes, but he keeps his eyes closed.

"You've heard it, then?" Skelton asked. Revell's eyes snap open. The lanky British biologist towers over him, rolling an unfiltered Gauloise cigarette between his yellowed thumb and forefinger. Skelton's long, bulging bald skull reminds Revell of a marabou stork, especially in its current sunburned, peeling glory. His naked scalp produces such excessive quantities of dandruff that he presents the surreal impression of having just walked in out of a blizzard. His features are a bitter caricature of the stereotypical British phenotype—hooked nose, abominable teeth, watery gray eyes, and tangled eyebrows that enhance his carrion-birdish mien. Any expression that means to make itself noticed through Skelton's default state of droll melancholy has its work cut out for it. Something has made a powerful mark on him, though. He really must remind Luscombe to keep security more compartmentalized.

"What do you know about it?"

"I was just going out to satisfy my *Lustmord*," Skelton gestures apologetically with the unignited cigarette. "Graham can fill you in. Rather extraordinary. Changes everything, I daresay. Perhaps I'll run into you later?"

Skelton ambles to the outer doors, and Revell sprints into the lobby to escape the scouring heat that reaches in for him as the heavy doors swing open. Revell had always figured addiction to things like nicotine was a symptom of simple stupidity, but Skelton is among the most respected savants in the Royal Society and shows no general weakness of character aside from his voracious consumption of tobacco.

Lustmord. A curious German word, meaning, literally, "sex-murder." Revell reminds himself to ask Skelton what he meant by it.

Revell listens to the message on headphones the first time with Luscombe and Chris Healey, the assistant communications tech. They look expectantly at him, as if he's the only one who speaks Arabic, but his knowledge of the language is spotty and the garbled transmission is thick with jargon. Two distinct voices snap out brackish streams of technical terms spiked with plenty of obscenities for about two minutes; one voice is considerably more agitated than the other, probably something to do with the sirens blaring, crashing of heavy equipment, and panicked shouting in the background. The other voice is imperturbable in the manner of bored operators everywhere, repeatedly telling the panicked caller to maintain radio silence under penalty of death.

Revell pries the headphones off. "Graham, I can't make out much from this. Is this an SSO intercept?"

"The call went to the Special Republican Guard Communications Directorate, yes. We have a rough location for the origin of the call pinpointed in the southeast. It came through a relay at al-Amarah. They know we're coming south tomorrow, I'll wager, and were taking steps to cover their tracks . . . when this happened."

Revell tunes in on the message again, boring through the squalling noise of broken voice encryption to focus on the arguing voices. The caller is desperate, trying to keep from screaming, as he details some kind of emergency. There's some clattering, and then his voice becomes remote, as if he's talking from inside a garbage can. He's put on a gas mask. He demands a containment unit be dispatched, to which the unshakable operator responds that they must sit tight, that help will arrive in forty-eight hours—as soon as the Americans are gone, Revell knows. The heated dialogue goes back and forth in this loop for another minute, then there's a loud bang, and the caller gasps and the line goes dead.

"What the hell?" Revell manages. Luscombe hands him a legal pad with a hastily jotted transcript on it, with an English translation beside it.

"There's an installation in the south that we didn't know about, that Mossad and the CIA never knew about, either, apparently. They're storing and testing chemical and biological weapons on human subjects. They had over fifty guinea pigs, when the order came to destroy the lot and shut down until our inspection was over. But something went wrong."

"They're going to ignore it until we've left," Healey puts in.

Revell's eyes go down the transcript. Words jump out at him. Again and again, the caller identifies himself with something called Marduk Division. He's never heard of it. Tiamat. From what little liberal arts education he picked up playing Dungeons & Dragons in junior high, he knew Tiamat was some queen dragon in Babylonian mythology, a nine-headed matriarch of demons. And again, something about Dragon's Breath, a substance that ate away at the rubber seals on quarantine chambers and probably killed them. The operator tells the caller to shoot all the Kurds, wrap wet towels over all his exposed skin, and trust in Saddam.

His stomach becomes an acid factory and starts eating itself. Luscombe and Healey, the only men on the team without sunburns, stare at him as he goes progressively whiter. This is exactly what they've all been waiting for. For seven years, UNSCOM has been able to total a shortfall of several tons of chemical and biological material in the Iraqi economy, but never pinpointed its location. The fact that they're about to go home, that the UN and the Iraqis consider the inspections all but finished, means nothing any more. They've got them.

Revell usually avoids the nameless cafe across from the UN's offices at the Canal Hotel. Unnervingly clean and almost opulent compared to nearly every other public restaurant in Iraq, it is nakedly a trap. A triad of leather-jacketed Amn al-Amm agents sit in a black Peugeot halfway down the block, and all the waiters are Mukhabarat operatives. Revell wets his lips with a thimbleful of coffee so thick it's really a sauce, and plays back the tape on a Walkman. His thumb rests on the special button for this particular model—a bulk erase, in case the tape player is confiscated.

Dragon's Breath eating through the rubber seals! It's coming into the control room!

Stop whining. You have your gas mask?

My mask is made of the same shit!

Have you shot all the Kurds?

They're all dead. Everyone outside this room is—ah, there is only one God, and his name is—

Remain calm. Everything is under control.

Give me the combination for the door! For the love of God! Let us out!

At seven P.M. the sun retreats behind the naked concrete towers and the air suddenly becomes bearable. A Range Rover pulls up in front of the cafe and Sam Kincaid climbs out of the passenger seat. The Range Rover speeds away, and Kincaid sits down beside Revell. Kincaid is an American and a concealment specialist. He tracks the

Concealment Operations Committee, a division of the Special Security Organization charged with hiding Saddam's arsenal. The waiter shares a joke with Kincaid as he brings him a tall glass of ice water with a twist of lemon in it.

They trade reports of their most recent inspections for a while, stressing the Iraqis' total failure to cooperate for the benefit of the unseen third party to their conversation. Kincaid stands a head and a half taller and at least ten years older than Revell, and his leathery skin is deeply tanned, not burned.

Revell slides the Walkman across the table. Kincaid looks around, slips on the earphones and presses PLAY. Revell gulps down his coffee and watches Kincaid's face. Kincaid is an oil painting for three minutes; then he takes off the earphones and looks down the street at the Peugeot. "Let's take a ride," he says. The Range Rover is back in front of the cafe.

A red-headed Australian man Revell knows only as Wally steers them into the sparse traffic on the Airport Road. They pass the main headquarters of the Amn al-Khass, or SSO. Soldiers at gun emplacements, leather-jacketed drivers, even old women on the street, seem to track their passing like trained spies.

The air-conditioning is broken, and the still-sweltering wind of dusk roars through the cabin. Kincaid, in the front passenger seat, turns to face Revell. He offers him a silver flask. Revell sips from it gratefully, passes it back. "What do you want from me?" Kincaid asks.

Revell winces as the single-malt whiskey washes the gummy coffee-resin out of his throat. "What do you know about it?" he asks.

"We've never heard of an installation in that part of the country at this time, certainly nothing of that magnitude. I'm inclined to doubt the whole thing."

"A feint to draw us into an embarrassing situation? Why? We're going home. You heard it. You can't tell me it's not real. This is an emergency."

"You were here in Desert Storm, weren't you, Warren?"

"Yes. With the—"

"As an engineer. Listen, Warren. Saddam and the Ba'ath Party have been a major hurdle to the political evolution of this country, but there are plenty of equally ruthless factions that have adapted to camouflage themselves and use superpowers to fight for them. The Supreme Assembly of the Islamic Revolution, for one. All hardcore Iraqi military defectors, CIA-supplied for four years, just over the border in Iran. With the psyops training they got from us, they could mock up a call like this to provoke an incident."

"Why are you so sure it's fake?"

"Real Iraqi soldiers wouldn't compound certain death for themselves by violating radio silence to ask for help they knew wouldn't come. Saddam has their families, and they know it. If there was an incident, the whole thing's underground by now, and they're ripping up the roads leading to it."

"Have you ever heard of a military unit called Marduk? The caller identified himself as Lieutenant Kazraji of Marduk Division of the SRG. But—"

"Sure, but I can see why you've never heard of them. You wouldn't have come across them. They're part of the Special Republican Guard Corps. Motorized infantry, very elite, which means they're all Tikritis from Saddam's tribe, al-Bu Nasir. The SRG are scattered all over the country doing border patrol, customs, secret police work, Kurd and Shi'a population control. They're named for the patriarch of the Babylonian pantheon, a god who hunted dragons, but it's all typical Iraqi bluster. Marduk's in charge of guarding cultural antiquities."

"What?" Dragons—

"They're not even brigade-strength. I told you it sounded like bullshit."

"What else can you find out about the site? The CIA's got to have reams of satellite imagery."

Kincaid shrugs. "What makes you think I'd have access to anything like that?"

"You were with JSOC in Desert Storm, Scud-hunting. You worked in Operation Provide Comfort with the Kurdish rebels. Either you're a CIA mole, or a gross misappropriation of manpower."

"Even assuming I could command those kinds of resources, I couldn't ask for anything without explaining why I needed it. I assume you want to keep this contained until you can verify it yourself."

"I don't want the United States to bomb it and extend the embargo on this country until we know what it is. Bombing the chemical weapons plants in the Gulf War caused an environmental holocaust."

"You don't trust your own country, but you want her help."

"You're right. Maybe I should just call the Executive Chairman—"

"Don't do that. He calls Annan, who talks to Aziz, who puffs up and blows so much smoke up Annan's ass, he feels guilty for even bringing it up, and you're in Bahrain tomorrow, and you'll never know."

"Then what do you think I should do?"

"Go and see it. Pick a team of twelve that you can trust—absolutely no Chinese, and no French, if you can avoid it, but no other Americans, either. I'll bring three of mine to fly you out there—Wally, Huysmans, and Grodov."

"A Russian?"

"The Russians only stand by Saddam so they can get their money back when the embargo's lifted. Grodov lost a leg to a mislaid mine when he was a KGB adviser here during the War of the Cities. He hates them."

"We don't need any more tension."

"Of course not. He's a professional."

"I don't expect to be allowed anywhere near the site, but we've got to come prepared. I want to take photographs and air and soil samples of the surrounding area. We'll bring MOPP gear and all the counters, but I don't want any perception that this is a US operation. And no guns."

Kincaid nods solemnly and raises his empty hands. "Of course not."

The UNSCOM inspectors are sequestered tighter than any jury in history. Holed up in two floors of the al-Rashid Hotel in the center of downtown Baghdad, they shuttle to their offices at the Canal Hotel without making eye contact with a single civilian. Early on, a few soft-hearted inspectors gave food and cash to families of beggars who slept in the plaza before the hotel. The next morning, the families were gone, and the Amn al-Amm spies who followed the inspectors doubled.

Picking the team is easy. Over the years, Revell has come to trust some more than others and knows who can operate under tense situations, who works for the ideals of the job, not the by-laws. He pages the group to meet in the pool room after dinner.

The room is a bath, the air so thick with chlorinated mist that the far wall is a blue-tiled smear. The acoustics, and the constant barrage of white noise from guests swimming laps, make it the best place to speak in private. Kincaid and his inspectors sit in rusted-out patio chairs along the wall, and Luscombe, Healey, and Skelton stand in the back, all poker faces. The other six squat or stand in various poses of tired defiance. Revell studies their faces—the common bone-weariness and frustration, and now a spark of the old righteous anger coming back to life in each of them.

"Ladies and gentlemen, we came here to do a job. For five years, you have struggled against the intractable duplicity of the Iraqi power structure to pursue our mandate, which is and has always been to root out and oversee the dismantling of Iraq's weapons of mass destruction. Tomorrow, though we go to our last inspection, none of us feels that our mission has been brought to any kind of satisfactory conclusion. Are we all in agreement on that?"

A few mutter assent, but most have already dismissed this as an empty pep talk.

"Well, tomorrow, we will have an opportunity to do our jobs. Today, we intercepted a microwave transmission from a site in the region we're inspecting tomorrow. It is not on our itinerary, but I think you'll all agree that it should be added."

He plays the tape. They huddle round the tiny speaker built into the Walkman. Only half of them speak fluent Arabic, but whispered translations and a single sheet English transcript spread the meaning around. When the SRG Lieutenant begins to scream and the shots ring out, a few of them jump.

For a single, silent instant as he switches the recording off, for the first time since he took the job, Revell has everyone's undivided attention. Then the bubble crashes in and everyone starts shouting at once. The swimmers in the pool all stop and watch them, and Revell's calls for order are drowned out.

Skelton starts coughing, a low ratcheting sound that resembles an ancient lawnmower motor trying to start. It cuts through the babble of arguments and grows louder still, resounding through the rusty alcoves of the pool room like sacks of cement smashing into concrete from a very great height. He reels back in the crowd, and the uproar dies out as everyone concludes that the British biologist is having a heart attack. Lupo Bertolucci, the medic, cradles Skelton and lowers his spasming body to the slick tile floor. "Three of you! Help me carry him out of this room!" Kincaid, Wally, and Grodov hoist him up, but Skelton shakes them off and staggers free. He fishes around in his pockets, produces a tin, and fumbles an unfiltered cigarette into his mouth. Lupo tries to swat it out of his mouth, but Skelton ducks, lights it, and suddenly stops coughing.

"Sorry, all. Filthy habit. But I was about to observe that at this juncture, we have an obligation not only to the United Nations, but to all the peoples of the world, to see that this event is contained."

"Very well, then," Hideo Mimura, the chemist, shoots back. "Let us notify the Executive Chairman, so that we may offer our services in the spirit of international cooperation."

"Without the official backing of UNSCOM, we are spies, yes?" Reinhard Greuel, another biologist, puts in. "We are likely to be shot, and with very good reason." Greuel is ardently Green, and the most passionate disarmament advocate in the group. If he has doubts, the operation will flounder.

Bertolucci chimes in, "I say we go home and leave them to their mess."

"It's not that simple, though, is it?" Skelton responds, cutting off Revell's own heated response. "The Iraqis have institutionalized the cover-up and denial of the entire program for nearly a decade, and shown shocking disregard for the safety of their own in so doing. They will deny it until incontrovertible evidence is presented to the world community. Imagine the effects if the Soviet Union were to have denied the Chernobyl meltdown and refused international rescue workers access to the site? Yes, we as an international body have a responsibility to insure that the policy of UNSCOM is not violated, but we have a mandate to bring the event to light first. The, um, current political climate would only delay the swift response necessary to curb disaster."

"Our accounting of the materiel and equipment Iraq imported in the '80s always came up short," Revell adds, "suggesting at least one major weapons facility that we never accounted for. We think this is it. Now, these are the facts. There's been an emergency there, and the SSO has elected to ignore it until we go home. Our operations code states that we are not in violation of our mandate by inspecting an unauthorized site if a clear and present danger to the surrounding environment is reasonably suspected. Look it up, people."

They all look as one at Revell now, more or less silent. "We will split off from the main body of the inspection tomorrow at An-Nasiriyah. By helicopter, we will travel directly to the site. We will not stake it out. We will observe the Iraqis' containment of the site, collect samples, and generally force them to admit that it happened. We are the eyes of the world, tomorrow. We have to see this through."

The debate goes on for another hour, but in the end Revell gets his way. They all agree to go.

Two hours later. Revell sits at a folding card table, reviewing the amendments he plans to file to tomorrow's itinerary. The weary old Belgian Chief Inspector didn't question him too closely, only nodded tiredly at the vague outlines of the plan without asking too many questions. He only warned against "rubbing the Iraqis' noses in it." Gather evidence, offer assistance, evacuate, rejoin the main group before lunch. Simple.

A knock at his door. "Come on in!" he shouts. There are sentries in the lobby and at the elevators on each of the floors occupied by inspectors, but Revell is one of only a handful who leave their doors unlocked.

Greuel, Sofia Texeira, and an American inspector Revell knows only by name crowd into his room. Dr. Greuel is short, stout, and alarmingly sunburned. He subsists on a diet of wheat grass juice, vitamins, and some sulfurous macrobiotic soup he cultures in his room, like a convict distilling apple-jack under his bunk. Once too often, he has bragged that his bowels are clean enough to eat out of. Only half in jest, Revell offered to take him up on it, and Greuel has avoided him ever since, so his appearance is momentous.

Dr. Texeira, a Brazilian forensics specialist, still shorter, but slim and dark; her work in the desert has darkened her chestnut skin to a robust mahogany and burned an auburn tinge into her long black hair.

The other American, Gerry Muybridge, looks like a lost high-school guidance counselor and has a thin file clamped under one arm, unaware that he's getting it slick with sweat.

A fear he dares not speak aloud wells up in him. Second thoughts?

This is an exceptionally risky inspection. Perhaps under another leader—no. "What is it?"

"The inspectors at the Istachbarat annex found something after you left, Herr Revell," Greuel rumbles. "Something that makes us more uncertain of tomorrow's inspection . . ."

Revell's hands clench.

"Show him, Gerry," Texeira says, and Muybridge leans over the card table and lets the file flop onto it. A sheaf of forms with hastily handwritten details in the boxes, and a CDR. Muybridge snaps up the disk and moves to Revell's laptop. "D'you mind?" he asks. Revell shrugs, and he drops the disk into the drive and fingers the track ball.

"I was the one who found it," Muybridge says. "We were on counter-concealment, you know, patrolling the back alley. We found a panel truck parked behind the building at fourteen thirty and approached it. An Iraqi in civilian work clothes fled the vehicle, but he wasn't carrying anything, so we just seized the truck."

"What did you find?"

"A bunch of the usual shit," Muybridge answers, rolling his eyes. "Embarrassing, but not damning. SSO interrogation manuals, confession transcripts—but right on top, we found this." He clicks on a file and turns the screen to face Revell. A razor-clear digital photo of a steel case sitting atop a haphazard column of cardboard file boxes in the back of a truck. The side of the case is stenciled with Arabic characters in green—with a nine-headed serpent above them. Tiamat. Revell sucks in a breath. "What was inside?"

"It wasn't what we expected," Muybridge answers. "We suited up before we opened it, and had demolitions look it over. Thought it might be a bomb." Muybridge closes the first file, opens another. A shot of the interior of the case—inside, lying on a thick bed of foam padding, is a slab of green-black rock. Roughly triangular, it seems to have been a fragment of a larger, convex slab. The outward-facing surface is covered in bas-relief carvings. Revell leans in closer and toggles the zoom function. The picture expands and he studies the eroded figures, etched into the stone. A line of animals, two by two, filing out of a hole in the ground. At the head of the line, a man and a woman. Further detail is impossible to make out—the stone is bubbled and crumbly, like the acid rain–gnawed sculptures at the Acropolis.

"There was some documentation in the case," Muybridge says. "Said this thing's from a place called Tiamat."

"I think it's Sumerian," Texeira says. With a minor in archaeology, Texeira has done field digs in the Andes and Amazon and fought off looters. "Probably five thousand years old, at least."

"I don't understand," Revell says, as the weedpatch of difficult possibilities branches and grows into an impassable thicket in his brain. Kincaid said Marduk guarded antiquities, but the message—one or both of them might be a plant to provoke or deter their inspection. What started out as a simple smoking gun has become so entangled within webs of conflicting bullshit that he's tempted to throw it all out the window and go back to Bahrain tonight. "So what?"

Muybridge ejects his disk. "The rock was filthy with chemicals—cytotoxins, raw PCBs, VX breakdown particles—like they fished it out of a toxic waste dump. I took swabs before they made us give it back."

"Give it back? What the hell did you give it back for?"

Greuel leans on the card table, causing it great distress. "The Iraqis' behavior has been most . . . vehement and confused, Herr Revell. They deny it belongs to them, first. We planted it, they say. Herr Muybridge is a spy, they accuse."

"Then, just before we leave with it," Muybridge interrupts, "another bunch shows up with papers declaring it a sensitive cultural artifact, and forty-two phone calls later, we hand it over. No more inquiry into the matter, no reports to be filed on it, either. Like it never happened."

"They refute the chemical detection?" Revell asks.

"Utterly," Greuel answers. "Herr Muybridge's tampering."

"I didn't fudge the goddamned results," Muybridge snaps. "I'm sick of trying to save these stupid ragheads from themselves. I just want to go home."

"So where does that leave us?" Revell asks.

"All else aside," Greuel says, "we can conclude that very powerful forces are very concerned with keeping us away from Tiamat."

"An equally powerful force wants us to go there," Texeira counters. "There's only one way to know." The others blink at her vehemence, and Revell feels the leading edge of an ugly thought bodying forth out of his subconscious. Sofia's enthusiasm for archaeology, the object appearing just in time to steer them closer to Tiamat. He doesn't really know Texeira all that well. Really, does he know any of them?

Revell dismisses them and reviews the itineraries until midnight, but he never quite falls sleep.

The main inspection force touches down in four helicopters at the airstrip at An-Nasiriyah at oh-nine-hundred, local time, and the forty-two inspectors of the main group under an Australian named Richard Corby load into a convoy of trucks. Revell's team shoulder their bags and cross the airstrip to the commandeered U.S. Army UH-50 Black Hawk helicopter. A blue UN placard has been slapped onto the nose over the American flag. A loose cordon of Iraqi soldiers surrounds the chopper with rifles leveled. Al-Majid and five other minders are shouting at Kincaid and Grodov. Ibrahim turns and sprints across the tarmac to Revell, arms windmilling as if he's trying to take flight.

"This is unacceptable, Mr. Revell! The agenda of inspection sites has been agreed upon in advance! Any deviation is an act of espionage. The Iraqi people will not tolerate so flagrant a violation of their national sovereignty!"

Revell closes with al-Majid and leans in close so that only he, and whoever has him bugged, will hear. "We know, Ibrahim. We know about Marduk Division. We know about Tiamat, and we know what happened."

Al-Majid's jaw drops, and he takes off his sunglasses. Revell has never seen him, or any Iraqi, so startled or so angry, and it's a big part of his job to startle and anger Iraqis. "But it is a sensitive cultural site," he sputters. "It—it is only an archaeological dig!"

"You can let us go there and assess the extent of the situation, or you can send us home and we'll be forced to make our report to the Executive Chairman and present the damning evidence we already have. There will be air strikes, and the sanctions will not be lifted, and whatever you people have done out there will go unchecked and possibly grow into an epidemic that will kill tens of thousands of Iraqis, or spread into Iran, which will trigger another war when you can least afford it. What's it going to be?"

Al-Majid studies him for a long minute with the arm of his steel-rim shades clamped in his teeth. This man whose duty is to ingratiate himself to Revell, who has begged water and shared blasphemous Saddam jokes with him, wants him dead. "You go too far," he finally says and turns away. He claps his hands once and shouts at the sentries in Arabic. They give him some backtalk, but he roars a threat at them, and they scatter.

Huysmans and Grodov load the team's gear into the cargo hold while Wally runs through the take-off procedures. Kincaid winks at Revell as he helps him aboard, but Revell is watching al-Majid with his cohorts, their huddle obscured by the rising veil of tawny sand whipped up by the accelerating props. Three of them are shouting animatedly into cell phones, but al-Majid is doing something with his hands. It only occurs to Revell then that he's never seen Ibrahim carrying a sidearm, because the minder is checking the magazine feed on an automatic pistol.

The flight from An-Nasiriyah northeast to Tiamat takes just over an hour and would have taken less if the navigational instruments worked properly—the compass spins wildly, and the GPS flatlines shortly after they cross the Tigris. Kincaid tries without success to radio Tiamat or any other Iraqi base. Revell tries to call the Executive Chairman in New York and the Deputy Chief Inspector in Baghdad on his satellite phone, but it's dead. Wally curses a blue streak about Iraqi countermeasures and demands that the minders be searched, but Kincaid blows him off and tells him to just fucking fly. Al-Majid and his cohorts are stone idols, offering no excuses now.

Below, broken chains of low, bald hills skirted by luridly green marshes roll past. Revell sees no villages, but occasionally a lone Shiite herdsman with a long antique rifle takes a potshot at them or stampedes his goats out of their flight path. Ever since the Gulf War, Saddam has kept his army busy running strafing raids on the Shiite civilian population to the south and the Kurds to the north. Helicopters usually only come here to deliver lead and nerve gas, and because helicopters aren't in violation of the No Fly Zone, the massacres are implicitly allowed under the UN's enforcement. For all the natives know, they're coming to finish the job the Iraqis had begun.

"I admire your idealism," Skelton leans in close and shouts in Revell's ear.

Revell tries not to laugh. "How do you mean?"

"This is somewhat above and beyond the call, isn't it? Some psychologists might label that kind of zeal self-destructive." He smiles ruefully. "And speaking of, would you mind?"

He holds a cigarette to his cracked and bleeding lips with one hand, but his other is wrapped around a case of delicate gear that jingles a fragile crystalline accompaniment to the chopper's vibration. His bony shoulder rises and falls, indicating his open breast pocket. Revell reaches into the pocket, finds a Zippo lighter, and lights his cigarette for him. The cabin is like a wind tunnel with millions of microscopic teeth made of airborne sand. Revell cups the flame and Skelton sucks greedily, coughs for several seconds, then smiles again.

"You're one to talk," Revell says. "Doesn't the understanding of what you're doing to yourself make it any less pleasurable?"

"I won't deny it. My feeble will is no match for the self-destructive imperative. But look at it in a purely macroevolutionary perspective. As a member of a dominant species with no natural predators to speak of, what are my duties? To reproduce and pass on my genotype. In any pure natural environment, a miserable specimen such as myself wouldn't last a day, so who am I to foist my defective traits on an already overpolluted genepool? My duty, then, as an organism, is to get out of the way. Make room for a fitter organism. I suppose I simply lack the marrow to do it in a timely, manly fashion."

"You may have me to thank for that before the day's over. But your fatalism—I think we have a duty to struggle against predators within and without. That's why we're here, so that a natural predator like Saddam doesn't wipe us all out."

Skelton chuckles indulgently. "But don't you see that we've stopped evolving? We've cheated at the game by making tools and altering the environment for so long that we've begun to select for predators within our own species who will erase us." It isn't his words so much as his smile as he delivers them that make Revell angry.

"And we don't deserve to survive? What has the human race done to you, that you can smile at the idea of all of us becoming extinct?"

Skelton looks genuinely hurt. He licks his yellowed fingers, pinches out the cherry on his cigarette, and deposits it in an empty Altoids tin he carries in his shirt pocket. "I bear the human race no ill will, Warren. But when the natural sciences become your life's work, you discover a reverence for *all* life, and for evolution itself. It's a miraculous process, worthy of worship even if there is no God behind it. Saddam and his arsenal are part of it, and you have made us part of it, now. I just wanted you to know that I admire that."

"What? Part of what?"

"Our evolutionary destiny, of course," he says, leans back, and looks down, fussing over something in the case on his lap. Revell looks around the cabin at his team, at the smoldering minders, at Kincaid and his thinly disguised commando squad, at the extra gear stowed in web harnesses over their heads. Even if there is nothing out there, the chances are still excellent that every one of them is going to die.

Kincaid shouts from the front that they're within five miles of the site, and the team breaks out their MOPP suits. Cumbersome three-piece affairs, made of double-layered, heavy-gauge plastic with a hooded gas mask and gloves that make winter mittens seem like surgical rubbers. The interlayer is filled with a gel that expands and hardens into a sealant if the outer layer is ruptured; very reassuring, but it makes them look like a brigade of yellow Michelin Men. They bounce against each other and into the walls as they pull them on and dog all the seals. The suits are blessedly cool, from being packed into vacuum-sealed chests at a factory in Pennsylvania, for about five minutes. Then they become personal sweat-lodges. Everyone balks at putting on the masks until Revell yells at them. Wally, who already wears a heavy nylon flight suit, skins his hands into gloves and straps on a light gas mask of Israeli manufacture.

The minders watch them all as if they've gone insane. Al-Majid shouts, "This is unnecessary!" a few times to no response. Revell hands each of them a gas mask, but they set them in their laps. One minder starts to put it on, but al-Majid stops him cold with a withering glare.

Revell lurches up to the front and looks out. The terrain here is higher, broken hills forming mazes of box canyons. Nothing resembling a manmade structure, let alone a ruined weapons installation. Giant convection cells battle each other with whorling vortices of sand, titanic dust-devils that ravage each other and fall apart, then re-form.

Revell turns on the headset inside his gas mask and holds up two fingers to indicate which channel he's sending on. "How do you know where it is?" he asks.

Kincaid's voice barks into his ear, but he still looks out over the wasteland. "I did a little homework last night. Tiamat was some kind of weapons testing facility ten years ago. It was a top-secret primary target in Desert Storm. A Special Forces A-Team had to be sent in to paint the target for laser-guided missiles, because of the interference, which is supposed to be some kind of natural magnetic phenomenon. Eight of them were wiped out on the ground here. Chemical leakage from the bombing ate right through their MOPP suits. Their families were told they died in a helicopter crash during a training exercise in Saudi." Kincaid stands up in the cockpit, leans on Wally as he pivots, and clambers back into the cabin. His face is a mask, but his lips are clamped between his teeth.

"Then why aren't you wearing a suit?" Revell asks.

"I don't think anything you want to find is out here anymore, Revell. Get your people ready. We're about to land."

The helicopter bucks and rolls as it sets down into a cauldron of wind formed by the box canyon in which Tiamat hides. Revell's ears pop. His nose starts to bleed.

A plume of rust-red dust envelops the chopper before he can see out the windows. Kincaid checks their suits and the contamination monitors mounted on the outer bulkhead. He gives a thumbs-up, growls, "All clear," and slides the jump door open.

They might be jumping out onto Mars. The fine red dust, like ancient river silt, settles over their masks and equipment, and the rotors drown out all exterior sound, and everyone is too scared to talk. Revell calls out for Kincaid, but the chopper vaults up into the oddly cloudy gray sky, sucking the dust up after it like a theater curtain. Behind it stands a now-familiar sight: a ring of soldiers with rifles shouldered, screaming at them to get on their knees.

Revell orders the team to obey, but they're way ahead of him. Cases of fragile, insanely expensive gear crash to the ground, which, under the dust, is green-black igneous rock, like basalt from the deep ocean floor.

The soldiers wear olive fatigues with no insignia, but all sport black berets with a nine-headed serpent on them.

Revell looks for the helicopter, sees it touching down on a cliff top a quarter of a mile away. Hands grab the back of his head and shove him to the canyon floor, the soldier shouting in English, "No spies! Spies die!"

"Stop this! In the name of Allah and Saddam, stop this!" al-Majid shouts in Arabic. "I am Major Ibrahim al-Majid of SRG Special Forces Unit 999! My subordinates and I are escorting a detachment of UNSCOM inspectors who have demanded a surprise inspection of this facility!"

Another soldier leaps into the air and windmill kicks al-Majid squarely in the back. The major flips forward into the dust and gasps for breath, the soldier's rifle barrel in his right ear. Hoarsely, he shouts, "I demand to see the officer in charge!"

The guards talk among themselves for a few minutes. Revell cautiously looks up and surveys the canyon floor. In a low spot at the center, a squat brown bunker of layered, interlocking concrete slabs. Only two stories high, but fifty yards on each side, with no visible doors or windows. The flat roof is painted in a dappled desert camouflage pattern, but he can make out helicopter landing lights and a freight elevator on the roof. A cluster of SAMs and 70mm gun emplacements face the south and east, while a machine-gun nest faces north, out the mouth of the canyon. The sheer canyon wall looms over the western edge of the bunker, blocking any possible assault from that direction. Still, there would be a gun emplacement there, too. A few jeeps are parked against one overhanging wall, and a heavy equipment truck outfitted for excavation. He remembers al-Majid's claim that this was a dig site, but either he or Kincaid had to be lying.

An older officer comes out of the bunker and walks toward them. "I am Colonel Tewfiq Qasr, senior officer at this place. What is this?" His English is excellent, better than al-Majid's.

Revell risks raising his head to talk. "Begging your pardon, sir, but we're with UNSCOM detachment E-7, here in response to a distress call intercepted while in the prosecution of UNSCOM 256."

"I have instructed them that this site is off-limits as a cultural site, but they insisted—" al-Majid interjects.

"Distress call?" Colonel Qasr asks. "We sent no distress call."

"Sir, we intend to inspect your facility pursuant to UN Resolution 687, Section B, Paragraph Twenty, regarding imminent peril to civilians from improper storage of chemical weapons."

"But this place is an archaeological dig now," Qasr calmly replies.

"Just the same, I'd like to have a look. If things are as you say, there'll be no reason for delay. We can look things over and, if we can use your radio—"

"But we have no radios," Col. Qasr says. "And no phones."

Instinct tells Revell to apologize and leave. This has been a set-up, based on a falsified lead—but to what? He looks around at the others for guidance and sees a disturbing and unfamiliar sight; everyone looking to him, pleading eyes and trembling mouths. Skelton, silently nodding, mouthing the word *destiny*.

The team is allowed to stand and strip off their MOPP gear, then thoroughly searched for weapons, then left alone for ten minutes. The soldiers never turn their backs on the group, and they aren't allowed to come another step closer to the bunker. Dr. Texeira remarks upon a singular phenomenon: for the first time ever, the soldiers didn't take their personal effects, gum, cigarettes, ballpoint pens, or any of the other Western junk some inspectors took to carrying as a bribe. The Marduk soldiers are all very young, like most post-Gulf war units, and like all elite units they are undoubtedly all Tikriti, but their eyes burn with a zeal unseen in Iraq since the war. They look like suicide bombers, and they clearly don't see anything human when they look at the team.

At ten o'clock, exactly, all the soldiers go to their knees and pray. There is no loudspeaker transmitting the prayer, nor do the soldiers bother with prayer rugs. One of them begins the quavering, chilling devotional prayer, and one by one they take it up, an eerie chorus that rolls up the sheer rock walls and resounds as if the djinns of the desert are being called to worship. "Did you ever wonder," Mimura whispers in Revell's ear, "if Moslems have to stand on their heads to pray when they visit Hawaii?"

Even Col. Qasr and Major al-Majid kneel, but Revell notices something right away that seals it for him, for all of them. Major al-Majid and his staff face a few degrees west of true south, toward Mecca in

Saudi Arabia, as all orthodox Moslems do five times a day, every day of their lives. But Col. Qasr and every single soldier are all lying prone facing north—facing the bunker.

Revell waits until they get back up, then, keeping explanations to a minimum, politely repeats his request to the colonel, who just as politely reiterates his confusion. True, he admits, this place was once used to manufacture and store biological and chemical weapons, but the "Mother of All Battles" had brought an almost miraculous discovery. Tiamat was struck by a two-thousand pound laser-guided bomb, which completely obliterated its personnel and arsenal, but it also ruptured the foundation of the bunker, revealing signs of an ancient Sumerian ruin buried underneath. Saddam, a champion of his peoples' cultural heritage, ordered that the bunker be rebuilt as an archaeological research center, and created the SRG unit Marduk to secure it against invaders. "I am more historian than soldier. They—" he waves dismissively at the fanatical commando squad—"they run themselves."

Revell listens and nods, while the minders fret in whispers on either side of him. Finally, Revell jumps into a pause and asks, "Why the secrecy, colonel? Why all the guns?"

Col. Qasr smiles broadly, as if he's been waiting for this. "Have you ever seen the Babylonian collection at the British Museum, Mr. Revell? Or the Stela of the Vultures, or the Law of Hammurabi, in the Louvre? We are no children, anymore. We protect what is ours."

"But the knowledge that could be shared—"

"—is for the Iraqi people alone. When we believe the world is ready to learn our lessons, we will give them freely. But an old historian must share his discoveries or go mad. Four of you may come in to inspect the site, but in return, you must listen to a very boring history lecture. Agreed?"

Revell looks at him long and hard and tries to weigh his words for lies, but he can't read him. He's been on fifty-four inspections before this one, but never without official UN sanction, or so far from civilization. A nagging sensation that there is more here than he is capable of understanding, that there is something here he doesn't want to know, feeds on him, making him second-guess even routine decisions. But it isn't enough to make him stop.

"Let's go," he says.

Luscombe radios Kincaid over the headset he's taken out of his gas mask. Although well within range, there is so much static he couldn't be sure he'd gotten through everything. Kincaid agreed to fly out of the area of communications interference and contact the main group to let them know their position. He was told to contact the Executive Chairman in New York and explain the situation, then return to extract them. Luscombe adds that he said something about "leaving insurance," and lifted off.

As far-fetched as it sounds, Luscombe is able to verify that there are no transmitters or telephones, no satellite dishes, no way of reaching the outside world except driving over broken mountains and marshy wastelands thick with hostile Shiite peasants. Putting aside the question of who sent the bogus intercept for the time being, Revell picks the three to accompany him inside. Al-Majid and one of his junior minders would accompany Mimura, Skelton, Texeira, and Revell. The group unpack their gear and rejoin Col. Qasr at the mouth of a tunnel leading to a sunken entrance into the bunker. Two guards flank them, their rifles shouldered. Col. Qasr runs a card through a slot beside the blast-resistant steel door and hauls it open, beckons them inside. "Very little of what has been unearthed here has been removed to museums—for fear of its being destroyed by bombs," he says without malice. They step into a small steel-walled foyer, with another, equally imposing door just before them. An airlock. Col. Qasr works the card again, says, "There's been very little money for reconstruction. We left it like this, is safer."

They pass into a dimly lit corridor, awash in greenish darkness after the brutal glare outside. Cold air—not merely air-conditioned or clammy, but shivery cold—blows up out of the recesses of the bunker, and each of them remarks on the musty odor, which Skelton likens to old cathedrals on the Continent, but which Texeira insists reeks of the stagnant Rio Negro.

Col. Qasr leads the way down the corridor, past rows of heavy doors with rubber seals on them. "We believe it is the earliest Sumerian structure ever discovered. Many puzzlements of Mesopotamian history have been resolved here. The world would . . . not accept all of them."

"I don't understand."

He stops at a door and slides his card through yet another slot, pockets it. The locks are an old system designed by Honeywell. "I will show you a few of the choicer artifacts we have liberated from the ground, and you will see." He opens the door and adds, "I must, of course, ask you to touch nothing." Col. Qasr orders the guards to stand at attention outside the room. The guards share a this-is-most-irregular look, but obey and flank the door as the visitors file in, sullen deadly caryatids.

Inside, bare yellow lightbulbs cast a feeble glow on a treasure-hoard older than King Tut's. Five rows of trestle-tables sag under the weight of urns, vases, bowls, statuary, weapons, jewelry, and costumes of silver and beaten gold. Texeira, who participated in digs at Tiahuanaco and Sacsayhuaman, practically swoons. "This is the largest collection of antiquities from one site I have ever seen," she whispers. "The cemetery at Ur was not half so rich."

"This means nothing," Mimura murmurs. "I would like to conduct tests." Revell tells him to take some air and surface samples and check the baseboards for recently removed fixtures. He rummages through his gear case and removes a few bottles and swabs. Col. Qasr looks askance at this for a moment, then seems to forget it.

Revell presses the colonel more directly about what sort of a place this was.

"How much do you know of Sumerian history?" Col. Qasr asks. Al-Majid, as enthralled now as the rest of them, starts to answer, but Col. Qasr cuts him off with a shake of his head.

"Dr. Texeira here knows more than the rest of us put together," Revell admits.

"And what would you guess this place was, dear lady?"

Texeira's eyes sweep over the collection again, her nose wrinkling at the patronizing address. "I would guess that it was a tomb-hoard," she answers at last. "But so many weapons, and steles—it would appear to have been a massive cemetery for royalty, priests, and warriors."

"You are very close to the mark, Doctor. It was a temple, fortress, garrison, and tomb, all at once. The Akkadian Semites who, history says, were the first to occupy this land believed that a cave existed here which opened on the Underworld, and that the souls of the dead entered it—and that the bodily forms of their keepers sometimes escaped to wreak havoc on the living. Needless to say, they avoided it like the plague. But they believed also that another race had held this land before them, for many thousands of years, and had a city upon this spot."

"Begging your pardon, Colonel," Texeira puts in, "but less than ten thousand years ago, the entire delta region of southern Iraq was underwater. For millions of years."

"Ah, but before that . . ." Col. Qasr says, and turns away, leaving them staring at each other like idiots.

Col. Qasr moves down the tables, scanning the collection and waving his hand about as if at trash. He stops before a huge, flat slab of rock propped against one wall. "Of this I am most proud," he declares.

Texeira and Mimura stand close behind Col. Qasr, blocking Revell's view. Al-Majid and his junior officer stand goggling at the wealth before them; if not for the guards outside, they might stuff their pockets and flee. As Revell walks over to the rest of the group, he sets down a briefcase in the middle of the room and mashes an unmarked button under the handle, which activates the mechanism inside. Then he takes a look at Col. Qasr's rock.

It's not like the sun-dried clay tablets he's seen in museums—fragile, crumbly things covered in wedge-shaped cuneiform. This is some sort of green metamorphic rock, and the characters are more sinuous and seem almost to have been burned into the stone. Angular humanoid figures are inscribed across the top of the stele and inlaid with carnelian and mother-of-pearl. They stand in a two-dimensional battle line, which, when seen in profile, makes them seem as if they're standing single-file—arrayed against a cavern out of which pours a horde of demons, or a single demon with many limbs and heads. Revell can't make out what the thing was intended to be, nor can he discern why the scribe took such pains to give a vaginal likeness to the cave.

Col. Qasr explains that the stele gives a list of the priest-kings who ruled Tiamat—though, of course, he says, cryptically, they had another name for it. The list goes back to the arrival of the Sumerians in Southern Iraq in about 5000 B.C. It also relates an origin myth of the Sumerian people that has never been discovered elsewhere, though fragments of it have appeared in indigenous tribes around the world. Texeira tells the others that the birthplace of the Sumerian race remains a mystery; cultural innovations and technology common to both Sumer and contemporary civilizations in the Indus river valley suggest that they originated somewhere in southern Turkey, but no original site was ever unearthed, and they seem to have materialized and taken over the nomadic Akkadians' fertile territory and built the first western empire.

According to the stele, the people who would build the ziggurats of Ur and the Hanging Gardens of Babylon simply crept up out of a hole in the ground—"like your Indians," Col. Qasr observes—puritan outcasts from a larger civilization known as K'n-yan, which had fallen into decadence and depravity in the subterranean deeps. The Sumerians immediately recognized the pit at Tiamat as a threat to their sovereignty and erected a fortress over it. Elsewhere, Sumer grew into an empire of city-states, all paying tribute to the warrior-priests who maintained this fortress against an enemy out of myth.

"But—" Revell sputters, not knowing where to start, "I thought the Sumerians were more advanced than the Akkadians. Why would they believe in the same myth, especially if they thought they came from a hole themselves?"

"This 'hole' was different, very. They called it the Womb of the Earth. They believed that creation is never finished creating itself, that new animals and plants are ever taking shape in the Garden, coming to take their place. Not unlike your evolution, yes? For two thousand years, they watched and waited, and when it opened, they tried to stop it with fire and swords and with poisons, with ritual sacrifices and with magic. In the end—" He trails off, looking for words.

"What?"

"In the end, they fell back on their old ways, on the forbidden science of K'n-yan, to protect them. They raised the waters and flooded the whole delta, again. I believe you have read of that flood in your Book of Genesis."

Mimura looks nonplussed, then grins. "Christianity number-one funny religion."

Revell's headset beeps. It's Luscombe, outside, and he's worried. "Kincaid's been gone awhile. I've tried raising him, but I can't get shit out here. I had to wire two batteries together to get you."

"What's wrong, exactly?"

"Huysmans and Grodov are here. Kincaid dropped them before he dusted off."

"They're inspectors, where else would they be?" Luscombe doesn't answer, fades in and out of static storms. "What's the fucking problem, Graham?"

"They're armed, Warren."

"With what?"

"Heckler-Koch machine pistols on web belts under their jackets."

"Did you actually see them? How do you know?"

"Greuel wore one for four years in the West German Army."

"Do the guards know?"

"I don't think so. They tried to search them when they came walking in, but Grodov warned them off with some kind of—I don't know, but it scared the shit out of them, you should've seen it."

"How're the tests coming along?"

"We've got trace particle counts in the few parts per million for some of the leavings of VX, but in a place like this, it could've been lingering for years. Also, something interesting on the rocks, like a biological agent. Lots of carbon and oxygen, but antipathic as all hell—" Static scours Revell's ear, then subsides, but he can hear Luscombe tweaking his jerry-rigged transmitter to keep it alive. "Deposits in the scrub brush ... like bloody great tumors ... denatures animal cell membranes ... oh, hell fucking batteries—" and Luscombe is gone. The others are still listening to Col. Qasr, and al-Majid and his minder are still mooning over the treasure.

Revell makes his way back to the briefcase and kneels beside it by the time Luscombe loses contact. The briefcase contains a miniature active sonar transmitter that, when resting against the floor of a multi-level structure, emits a ping by using the floor as a sounding board. He has used it twice before to sniff out hidden basements and tunnels under Iraqi military ministries. He looks at the liquid crystal display for a few moments, thinking it must be broken. The sonar ping never comes back. He triggers another, waits. It never comes back. As far as the machine is concerned, they are standing over a bottomless pit.

"I would not have the illustrious inspectors of UNSCOM go away thinking we kept secrets from them. Shall we see the structure itself?" Col. Qasr asks.

They follow Col. Qasr back into the corridor, and the guards fall in behind them. Skelton whispers to Revell that the room was filthy with all kinds of mold and fungal spores, but nothing lethal. He can't wait to culture them. "I wonder what they will grow into," he says. Mimura uncovered a closet full of cleaning solvents and chemicals for recovering antiquities, but, again, nothing lethal. Revell asks himself again, why are we here? Col. Qasr doesn't seem concerned; they're getting the grand tour. If anyone else would raise the issue, he would call off the inspection right there. But no one does, and they follow him down.

The corridor crosses the diameter of the bunker, passing three large freight elevators. Col. Qasr slides his card through another reader on a door beside them. "Those are quicker, but I prefer this way. It is the way they went in." He tugs on the door, bracing himself against a sucking wind that whips past them and into the darkness. Mimura and Texeira and Revell all share a significant look—negative pressure rooms are *de rigueur* as the outermost level of protection in labs that handle infectious diseases. Col. Qasr waves them inside, but they all balk except Skelton, who stork-walks on in and stops just inside the door. "Good heavens!" he exclaims. "All of you, you've got to see this! It's extraordinary!" As a group, they rush inside. Behind them, al-Majid vigorously tries to beg off, but Col. Qasr pulls rank on him and orders him in. The guards bring up the rear.

Another corridor branches off here, but it leads down, curling away to the left in a great spiral. The floor is a worn staircase of the same green rock as the stele. Each step is worn down to the level of the next by millennia of marching feet.

The walls of the tunnel are carved with pictograms, images, and the same snaky, pseudo-cuneiform characters as the stele. Lamps are strung along the ceiling, making the walls glitter. Just as on the stele, the chiseled figures are inlaid with carnelian, obsidian, alabaster, and other semiprecious stones. It has a weird alien beauty that makes the tomb paintings of Egypt look like the cheap graffiti of barbarians; yet as Revell looks at it, he can't compare it with any ancient human art he's ever seen. There are no pastoral scenes, no images of material plenty or heroic deeds. What there is—the pictograms at the head of the stairs on the right-hand wall are oddly geometric, but with strange eyes and other animal features. Further down, the shapes become gradually more complex, more colorful—and then suddenly explode into primitive sea life—hydrae, plankton, trilobites, all the pre-Cambrian lifeforms discovered in the Burgess Shale in this century. Skelton sucks in breath when he sees them and moves back to the beginning. "Anaerobic bacteria," he says, then, leaping down two steps, "Replaced by oxygen breathers—then multicellular organisms. Do you know what this means, Warren?"

Texeira seizes Revell's arm and draws him to the left-hand wall. "Look at this," she says, pointing to an image unlike anything on the other side. Skelton would have no explanation for this. A line of supplicants kneels before a monstrous mound of bodies that, upon closer examination, turns out to be one creature with countless female torsos. Each of the bodies is exaggerated in the manner of the obscenely bloated fertility images of Stone Age Europe, and many are in the act of giving birth to—things that have no place in nature. Texeira runs her fingers over the hideously detailed image, whispers, "In Chichen Itza, there was a sacred cenote, a pit where human sacrifices were offered. An idol of a fertility goddess—nobody knew her name, or would tell it. It was . . . this."

Col. Qasr steps between them. "The Sumerian city-states each had their own gods. The temple here was dedicated to Nin-Khursag, the Mother-Goddess, but here they called her Shub-Niggurut. They sought her protection from what lay beneath their feet, which was to them far more fearsome."

Revell is so lost in thought that he jumps when Skelton touches his hand. The biologist is transformed by a rapture, his hands rubbing each other furiously. Revell supposes it's the discovery of the remarkable wall-inscriptions that have fired his nerves. "We've got to stay."

"We've been here too long already, Aubrey," Revell tells him. "Whatever's here, it's not what we came for. How much further down?" he calls out.

"Not much," Col. Qasr replies. "You'll see where the great work is being done, and our tour will be at an end."

"So this place stayed sealed up from the Great Flood to the Gulf War?" Revell, trying to find a way to make it sound hard to believe, trying to find a way to doubt what he's seeing and hearing. He can't look at the walls at all anymore.

"Oh, no. It was first excavated in 1912 by a British archaeologist—

in those days we were tenants in our own land. They thought only to add to the treasure-trove of their museum, but when they saw, they sealed it back up again. And they tried to forget. We Arabs are not so faint-hearted as the Europeans, and we took up the duty of the Sumerians. We understand, as they did, that this place must be kept shut to the world, but we know, as they did, that it is the holiest place on this earth. Some of us believe, too, that to every day there is a nightfall."

"What? I don't understand." Revell's headset flares up just then, like temporal-lobe epilepsy, a grand mal wave of static and Luscombe screaming at the top of his lungs.

"Revell! D'you copy? Revell, come back! We're . . . something . . . really fucked—"

Revell backs up the slippery, eroded staircase and hisses into the tiny microphone. "Luscombe, what's going on out there?"

"Oh, thank God . . . sitting ducks out here . . . Chrissakes . . . truck with children, fucking kids, and they got out . . . walking up to the guards, and they—"

"What? I can't make out what you're saying, repeat, can't understand what you're saying. Come again."

Luscombe swimming in noise. Not static. Gunshots. Bombs. "Guards don't know what to do—trying to drive them off—Omigod—" and an explosion drowns out his words. "Warren, Warren, get the fuck out of there, the boy blew up, went up and all the guards—shooting, everyone's shooting—"

Revell slips and slides down the stairs and grabs Col. Qasr by the arm. He and the others stand before a massive archway in which the Iraqis have set a heavy steel door like on a meat locker. A bar lies across it. No electronic card reader, no retinal scanner, not even a key lock. A fucking bar is what they use to keep that door shut. And Col. Qasr is lifting the bar out of its cradle.

"There's shooting outside! Somebody's shooting at my team!"

"It is not an uncommon occurrence here. What would you like me to do?"

"Get them inside, for God's sake!"

Col. Qasr turns to the guards and orders them to go back up and let the inspectors in. They balk, one of them demanding to see the security officer; Qasr whispers something to them, and they take off up the stairs. "And now," he says, "you shall see." He props the bar against the wall and throws the door wide.

It is dark inside, a palpable blackness. Inside is where the cold and the mold came from.

"This . . . it is nonsense," Dr. Texeira says, her voice brittle with fear. "What is here? Why the secrecy? What are you doing here?!" She shrieks this last, her composure blown.

"This place is no secret, dear doctor," Col. Qasr answers, and disappears into the darkness. From within, his voice rings out in a scattershot chorus of echoes, as if he has entered a subterranean Notre Dame de Paris. "Your governments have all paid for the great work, just as the city-states of Sumer paid. What, did you think the United States and Germany and Great Britain were so stupid as to sell us chemical and biological weapons so we could use them on each other?"

He turns on the lights then. Great fluorescent panels begin winking and flickering; it takes nearly a minute for them all to come on. They step inside. The cavern is indeed massive, and shaped like the hollow of a bell. In the center of the cave is a vertical shaft, no more than fifty feet or so across, with pitted, crumbled sides eaten away by every kind of corrosive substance known to science. A railing encircles it, and a Plexiglas wall screens it off from floor to ceiling, with a myriad of gates and chutes set into it, each surrounded by a steel airlock. The rest of the cavern is taken up with barrels and pumps and hoses inside more Plexiglas cells. Several men in red Level 4 suits are scattered about inside the chemical cells, but they are all lying down in postures of extreme distress. None move, and the mask of one is filled with grayish red foam. A control room, too, is filled with men—bodies, slumped over their controls. Revell turns his back, tries to raise Luscombe without screaming. All he hears is more shooting.

Behind him, Col. Qasr shouts, "Nature never stops creating, dear inspectors. It is our grim duty to protect the human race from the next ones, and to protect them from ourselves. This place is no secret indeed, for if you knew your Christian Bible, you would know that your people, too, had a legend about this place. Down there," he shouts, and he points into the pit, "is the cradle from which we all crawled, all the beasts of the field, of the air, and of the sea! There is Paradise, the place you call the Garden of Eden."

And Revell turns back around just as Col. Qasr raises a gun and shoots Dr. Texeira neatly in the forehead, and she is spinning, her hair an auburn corona that vanishes in red. Then he takes aim at Hideo Mimura, who has only just dropped his case and turned to run, and shoots him through the base of the skull. Hideo's eyes, swimming behind his thick glasses like fish trying to leap out of boiling water into the killing air, are on Revell when he dies.

Revell recoils from the shots and stumbles as he spins on the slick poured-concrete floor, trying not so much to run as simply not to be there, when he hears more shots from his new direction of travel. Al-Majid has a gun! Stop this, Ibrahim, stop this—

Al-Majid staggers past him, his left hand clasped over his breast as if he's pledging allegiance. A shining medallion of arterial blood blooms under his whitening fingers. His junior officer lies at the foot of the staircase, limbs spasming. Aubrey Skelton stands over him, holding a pistol identical in make to Col. Qasr's. He looks terribly unsure of himself as he aims again to finish off al-Majid.

"Why?" Revell can barely catch his breath, let alone make it into words. "Why, Aubrey?"

"I have a deep and abiding respect for all life on earth, Warren," he says, and shoots al-Majid through the head at point-blank range.

Col. Qasr points his gun at Revell. He closes his eyes. His team is dead, he is going to die, everyone is going to die. He grunts weakly, "Don't," standing there for an awfully long time before he realizes he's not going to be shot.

When he opens his eyes, Aubrey Skelton is standing between them, shivering and waving his gun as if trying to shake it loose, arguing with Col. Qasr in Arabic. He can't follow the words, the dialect is strange and especially sibilant. When Aubrey turns to face Revell, he knows why he's still alive. His pupils are pinprick holes in the goggling, bloodshot eyes, the apologetic smile of bilious, nicotine-stained teeth through bloody, ragged lips, the shaking open hands tucking the pistol into the waistband of his billowing khaki shorts. Skelton has to have someone to confess to.

Col. Qasr disappears into the control room. A moment later, an alarm begins cawing, red lights flood the chamber, and a steel plate drops out of the ceiling over the exit.

Revell sits down hard, his last string cut. Skelton strolls over, circles around Revell as if his imminent collapse into shock is a muscle cramp. "Don't take it so hard, old man. There are forces at work against which any individual human life is totally expendable."

Revell makes himself look around. Hideo, who might say nothing for a whole day, and with one remark keep you laughing all through the next. Sofia, who would have stayed in Iraq to give humanitarian aid, if they'd have her. Ibrahim, joking about becoming a hero and dying a martyr's death by mistake. Expendable.

"Terrorists," he croaks, "are supposed to TAKE HOSTAGES!"

Skelton laughs, a frayed, insane sound that makes them both shiver. "We're not terrorists, Warren. We're scientists."

Revell throws himself back onto the concrete. His head bangs solidly against it and rebounds. He rolls over and vomits, starts to get up and, for an instant, he's capable of killing Skelton with his bare hands. Skelton falls back and draws his pistol. To Revell's blurred vision, it looks as if he's holding three guns. Revell freezes, stoops over, and throws up.

"Oh, Qasr is a religious fanatic. They all are, a radical sect of pre-Islamic fundamentalists, if you will. They believe Paradise is at the bottom of that hole, and are sworn to keep it closed. Qasr's part of a schism that believes it's time to open it. But they couldn't discover how." Skelton stands, pats himself down, groans. "God, what I wouldn't do for a cigarette, right now."

"Hideo smoked."

"Gosh, you're right, Marlboro Reds or something, weren't they? Yes, they'll have to do." Skelton stands over Mimura's corpse, then looks over at Revell, still leaning over his own waste, but watching Skelton intently. "Would you mind, terribly? You understand."

Revell stands and goes over to the body of the Japanese chemist, kneels and pats down his still, cooling torso for a pack of cigarettes. Only a few feet away, Texeira lies on her side with one hand across her face. If he couldn't see the back of her skull, he could tell himself she was just unconscious, just sleeping, dreaming, in the hotel, and he was going to wake up—

Skelton takes the cigarettes from him and paws them open, lights one up, and sighs with relief. "Thank you, Warren. Fancy one? They're great for nerves. Oh, very well. You must have questions."

"Why us?"

"You know how bullish the Iraqis are on security. This place is the secret within secrets—only a handful of men outside the SRG command know that something is here at all, and only a few of them have any inkling of its true nature. Col. Qasr is the commanding officer, but there were two men closer to Saddam here. Fanatically loyal, I don't have to tell you. He had to get them all in one place, and the only way to do that—" He shrugs.

"The transmission," Revell mumbles. "And the stone."

"Stone? What about a stone?"

"We—my team—all our friends—died to provide a diversion?"

Skelton's face stretches in a weak, rueful smile. "It's time to stop thinking in terms of individual lives, Warren. I'm afraid a lot of people are going to die very soon."

Col. Qasr steps out of the control room. He wears a deep red Level 4 suit and carries an assault rifle. Skelton turns and goes for his case. "Better suit up. It's time to go down." Revell, still descending into the total numbness of shock, asks him why he has to go down.

"I'm afraid I didn't keep you around just to talk to, although I do enjoy your company. You're the only member of our group with military demolitions training."

He clambers into his suit and Revell gets into his, watching Col. Qasr as he passes them and unseals an airlock opening on the pit. Skelton bends before Revell and points to the seals on the back of his hood, says, "Close this up for me, won't you?" The gun hangs at his side. Col. Qasr's back is turned as he throws switches on a big panel beside an orange elevator cage suspended over the pit. Revell raises his arm over Skelton's head and hesitates a moment too long, because the gun jabs him in the stomach, but Skelton is too polite to say anything. Revell clamps down Skelton's hood and turns for Skelton to do his.

He follows the biologist to the elevator cage. His facemask fogs up almost immediately, and he has to fight to bring his breathing under control. Sweat droplets crawl over his face like ants.

Col. Qasr helps Skelton into the cage and takes Revell's arm. Revell tries to wrench free, and Qasr hisses at him in a tongue that has nothing in common with Arabic. "Is he coming down with us?" Revell asks.

"No, of course not. He'll be up here monitoring our descent."

Revell climbs into the cage. Col. Qasr closes the gate and throws a switch. The elevator simply falls, plunges out of the light and into inky blackness, before the cable snaps taut. The floor slams into Revell and his knees buckle. He hits his head on a bar as he goes down, but Skelton rides it out like a seasoned mariner and offers Revell a hand up. They stagger against each other, Revell fumbling for the gun, finding it again pressed at his belly. He asks himself if he could sustain a gut wound and still disarm Skelton. Not getting out, but just stopping him. If any of what he said is true, he should have done it on instinct. But he freezes. He isn't afraid of dying at this point—he simply can't think that far ahead. He just wants to know why.

"What is this place, Aubrey?"

Skelton hits a button, and the shaft is flooded with white light as caged klieg lights mounted at increments down the sheer stone walls snap on all around them. Revell shields his eyes, then lowers his arm as the facemask polarizes to compensate for the glare.

The walls are smooth as glass, like obsidian, and everywhere pocked with dense clusters of circular holes in which his eyes gradually come to discern patterns. They extend down the walls as far as the eye can see—in spite, or because, of the lights, he can see no bottom. It is as if some blind behemoth, entombed within the earth, had chiseled the history of the universe into the walls of his prison in Braille. Skelton gapes at them with a glow of dreadful awe, the gun leveled absently at Revell's spine.

"You're looking at the oldest known written communication, Warren," he says.

"Pre-Sumerian?" Revell asks, feeling foolish. If only Dr. Texeira were here, she could ask the right questions. If only she were still alive.

Skelton chuckles. "Pre-human! These stones are two billion years old. Older than all life on earth—as we know it. These are the writings of the Old Ones.

"Does it ever strike you as odd the speed with which life on this earth built itself up out of nothingness, then tore itself free of the oceans, and became self-aware beings capable of destroying the earth? Evolutionists cling to articles of faith as tightly as any Catholic or New Guinea headhunter, Warren. We were looking for a prime mover, a god worthy of our worship, like everyone else. We simply found they were two different things. That process, the force that drives life upward against entropy and natural selection and competition and extinction cycles—that's God. We know who made it. And do you know what they were?

"They were scientists."

And Skelton tells him, in a matter-of-fact lecture style that seems to lull him into a trance, about the Old Ones, who were neither animal nor vegetable, but some common ancestor to both, yet so much more; who came to earth from beyond the deepest gulfs of space as the earth was cooling from its eons-long shaping, and set about terraforming. Colonizing. They collected the raw protein chains being generated in the tide pools of the fledgling oceans and assembled them into DNA and RNA compounds, which would orchestrate life out of inert matter—and cause it to adapt, to change its shape to meet any environmental threat. The first servants were the shoggoths, which served their masters for millions of years, ever remaking themselves to perform new tasks—and one day became self-aware and challenged their masters. The Old Ones defeated the shoggoths and drove them to the brink of extinction, but they still needed slaves, now more than ever, with their numbers depleted and their cities in ruins. They created life anew, but damped down its power to evolve. Changes that occurred in minutes would take hundreds of generations. To control the procedure, they synthesized eugenic hothouses where their specimens could be molded over centuries to serve their masters. Leakage from these hothouses spilled out into the world and became the first known terrestrial life.

"The Old Ones died out soon after, or fled the earth nearly two hundred million years ago, but their experiment has plodded on, after a fashion, creating the phenomenon evolutionists refer to as punctuated equilibrium. Every great extinction is immediately followed by an inexorable repopulation of organisms uniquely suited to flourish in it. Every major climatic shift triggers the opening of the hothouse. New life steps in to replace the old. Every major extinction, every major evolutionary breakthrough, emanated from this part of the world, Warren. Every major religion came from this region as well, Warren, and all of them with a creation myth revolving around a Garden of Eden."

Revell leans against the railing, looking down and through the clouds of imminent blackout. "This . . . is . . . so insane—" he mumbles.

"We've known about it for quite some time, Warren. We discovered it in 1912, but the Sumerians guarded it long before. They stood watch against the next wave of life they knew would one day come to take our place. The first civilization worthy of the name was consecrated here—to keep evolution from happening."

"And you—and the colonel—are going to make it happen?" Revell asks. He can see the bottom now, bellying forth out of the bright darkness. He wants very much not to see any more.

"Oh, it's sure to happen anyway. We've altered the earth's climate so much with our technology that the gates will open no matter what we do. And for all the technology and chemical and biological weapons they pour into it, there'll be no stopping it.

"First, the viruses. Imagine what bubonic plague would be like if you incubated it for millions of years in an environment a thousand times more competitive than the outside world. The larger organisms—ah, that will be something to see. Here we are, mind the gap."

Revell stumbles down onto a corrugated steel platform and looks out across the floor of the pit. The stone here is pitted and crumbly under Revell's boots, ravaged by decades of chemical weapons attacks. Then he sees the fungi.

The floor of the pit is a forest, but what Revell thinks of as a swarm of jellyfish are really buoyant gossamer hoods bobbing and secreting a mellow blue glow. They sway and bob to an intangible breeze.

Skelton chatters on behind him as he unpacks a brushed steel case with no less than four digital locks on it. "These keep shooting up here. They've become immune to everything the Iraqis throw at them. A few spores must have found their way through the gate. That's what gave us hope."

Skelton keeps up his babbling lecture as Revell wanders out onto the floor of the pit. "Healthy human fatalism would dictate that we await that day in patient silence, but the despoiling of the earth increases at a geometric rate. Our population control programs have met with indignant rejection, and all our adaptive survival mechanisms are working to choke us on our own flesh. If all life is related, then we are the enemies of our own family tree, you understand? You can see how anyone—well, anyone with any sort of ethical marrow to speak of—could never stand idly by and let the inheritors of the earth receive it in such spotty shape, yes? Warren?"

Revell staggers across the pit, threading a path through the blooming bell-shaped caps of gargantuan fungi to the gate. It doesn't resemble a gate at all, but that's the word that comes to mind. The Gates of Eden. Paradise stands in the shadow of swords—

An octagonal recess in the center of the pit, and down at the bottom a dull glow of greenish metal. He feels things brushing at his legs, soft, boneless fumblings through three layers of Teflon-coated rubber. He recoils more out of reflex than fear, looks down, and sees thousands of tendrils snaking away from the nearest stalks of fungi. They're reaching out for his heat. The gilled underbellies of the aroused mushrooms dilate and secrete clouds of spores. Revell backs away the better to appreciate the prismatic light-show of the crystalline mist dancing in the blue glimmer of the fungi. Skelton steadies him before he topples into the gate. "Steady on, old man. We've work to do yet."

Skelton kneels before the recess and lowers himself onto the gate, then reaches for his case. Revell hunkers down beside him, all thoughts of stopping Skelton paralyzed by a child's detachment. This is real. He can't hope to effect the smallest change in the world he's found himself in.

Skelton kneels before a bulge in the center of the gate and steadies a tripod over it, then slowly, deliberately, mounts a delicate lens array in a cradle on the neck of the tripod. As he strings a fat bundle of fiber-optic cable from the lens to a laptop set into the padded interior of the case, he catches Revell's eye. His teeth are chattering with excitement, his lips bloody ribbons. "You joined the UN to effect positive change in the world, yes?"

Revell numbly nods.

"The world's a different place from what it was this morning, isn't it?"

Revell looks around, nods again.

"You can still make a difference in it, Warren. Climb down here."

Revell slides down into the pit beside Skelton. Gravel under his boots squeals on the metal of the gate. Skelton reaches into the case and hands Revell a block of plastique and a primer cord and a remote detonator. "The mechanism of the gate responds to photostimulation," he says. "Specific variations in solar radiation triggered the unlocking of the gate, but carbon deposits and the tampering of human hands have damaged the lock. It should recognize the radiation pulse, but we'll still have to blow it open. I was trained to do it myself, but I'd—" He shows Revell his hands, shaking so badly they seem to have ten fingers each. Revell looks at the packet of explosives in his gloved hands. He knows how to do this. He can do it, and so he does. He squats before the bulge in the gate and examines it. Circular black bumps all over the bulge resemble the compound eyes of dragonflies. "Wait for it," Skelton whispers, and stabs a button on the laptop.

The lens lights up and illuminates the "eyes" with a brilliant blue-white glow that gradually shades to a bilious yellow, then a smoldering red. Revell watches the light with numb fascination as his hands tear the plastique out of its foil pouch and insert the detonator mite into it, code a channel on it, and match it to the remote. In his hands he holds something he understands, and can control—everything beyond his hands gets too weird, and must not be allowed into his head again, or he will lose all control. Everything and everyone under his control has been destroyed or has turned on him. This is all a lie, Revell reminds himself. I will blow it up and show Skelton how wrong he is. And then—

Something happens. The photoreceptors snap in like wounded snail eyes, and the bulge grinds against its housing, turning of its own volition and sinking into the gate. The soles of Revell's feet burn with the fierce vibrations of the alien metal beneath them. The tripod skitters across the gate in a wobbly, headless-chicken dance, then topples over. The lenses shatter like tiny church bells.

He looks to Skelton for guidance. The British scientist stands at the lip of the recess with the pistol held out once more. "Secure the explosive inside the hole where the photoreceptors were, yes, that's it. There should be a shaft running across the diameter of the gate, just beside the lip of the hole. There'll be short steel I-beams—cheap, manmade stuff—welded to it. That's where it should go." Revell reaches down inside the hole where the bulge was and feels for the shaft. His hand catches on it, finds blistered scabs of hastily welded metal, and wads the plastique around them, checks the detonator mite, and climbs to his feet. Perversely, he feels good. He has done something.

Skelton shoots him through the stomach.

Revell folds over, his top half flopping onto the crumbled stone floor of the pit, his feet scrabbling for traction on the face of the gate, and Skelton bends over him and takes the detonator from his nerveless hands, a clumsier operation than might be expected, since Skelton can't bring himself to look directly at Revell. "I regret that I'll have to repair to a more judicious vantage point from which to make my observations," he says. "This thing that we do is larger than any one human life, Warren, but I never could've accomplished it without you." Skelton waves casually and shoots Revell in the back.

Skelton picks his way back to the elevator and climbs aboard, throws the switch to return to the surface. He vanishes into the cloud of white light before he triggers the explosive.

For a moment Revell lies inside a star, and he seems to grow old and die a thousand times trying to find his way out of it. He has only an instant to register the sound before his eardrums mercifully rupture. The shockwave hurls him across the pit, but the main force of the blast rises in a column of superheated air and sundered steel that roars up the chimney-shaped abyss. Most of the klieg lights flare and die out.

Revell is beyond any hearing, but he feels it in his bones when the gate opens.

He does not turn to face it. He claws at the rotted stone floor to get away. He has sunk below the contemplation of miracles and treachery and blasphemous impossibilities. Maybe he has lost touch with even the survival instinct, and only wants to find a saner place to die.

Crawling away from the gate of Eden. His legs don't seem to want to work, but he can feel them, can feel the awful wrongness of the position of his bones, can feel also the minute groping of the fungi at the seams of his suit and the smoking hole in his back, just over his left shoulder blade. And then something moves past him so fast the tendrils are neatly severed, and he looks up to see a thing made of legs race up the wall of the pit and swarm over the ascending elevator cage.

Skelton is avidly watching the events down below, but still has time only to shout "Good heavens!" and get off a single shot before the cage flies apart under a flurry of raking, barbed limbs. The thing cuts Skelton in half, then attacks the elevator itself, flailing at every moving part until the cables snap and the car plunges to the pit floor.

Revell barely notices all this as he continues crawling. His mask is completely fogged over, streams of condensation cutting momentary clear trails through the mist. He doesn't see the shower of red and gold pollen and spores tumbling to the ground all around him, fiery snowflakes in the blue fungal glow, or the deadly dance of multiwinged insects and seeds that look and act like insects, or the thing from the elevator that now stands in his path.

His gloved hand outstretched, he takes hold of one of its jagged forelimbs and his glove comes away in tatters, his hand bleeding and naked to the bone. Foam blooms out of the interlayer between the outer and inner shells of the suit, sealing the rent. He looks up then, and he locks eyes with the inheritor of the earth.

He feels a momentary pang of sadness—that the progenitors of humankind that stumbled out of Eden millions of years ago didn't survive the selective crucible to see the next opening, that the whole primate order seems to have been scrapped. What order of animal this thing is, he can't begin to judge—for all he knows, it's vegetable. Its limbs are chitinous, too many to count, and jointed with ball-and-sockets, folding and unfolding, collapsing and telescoping restlessly beneath its body, which is little more than a lozenge of silvery translucent jelly stuffed with glittering, jewel-like organs. A livid violet phosphorescence blooms from the soft tissues, like the cold gleam of deep sea fish. Great, glassy fans like bat's wings radiate out from its back, fluttering gently and dispersing curls of steam; rows of clattering mandibles prowl the orbits of its mouths, positioned beneath each limb.

It regards Revell for an endless moment, eyes piling up on the Revellward side of it like passengers in a ferry approaching shore. He sees no signs of intelligence in those free-floating orbs, no calculated reaction to his presence or his plight, no avarice or cruelty or rage or curiosity, only a purity of perception that would make the eyes of a shark seem neurotic by comparison. This creature's descendants will never mount a jihad, or develop diseases that target only their enemies, or flood their own drinking water with carcinogens. They will never get cleverer or more sophisticated, only faster, deadlier—better. This is Nature's answer to human hegemony, to the stacked deck *Homo sapiens* has dealt natural selection. It is built to thrive in the sunless ruin humankind is making of the earth. Who is he to try to stop it? Stop it? He almost laughs. Go in peace, whatever you are, and conquer the world.

The thing scrambles over him, and he feels it gingerly probing his suit when it starts to rain. The thing retreats, and Revell writhes in agony as green, frothy liquid splashes over his bare, mangled legs. He goes into a fetal position, bones grinding against each other mercilessly, and he rolls away toward the shattered elevator cage, and everything around him is melting, the fungi forest and the quicksilver inheritor of the earth run and smear like a watercolor in the chemical downpour, leaving only the blasted rock and the gate of Eden, slowly closing.

Revell's eyes are already open and dry as eggshells when he awakens. He is startled by the constant sinusoidal tone that is all he will ever hear. He floats on a honeyed cloud of opiates and can't move—not that he wants to, particularly. He wrangles his eyelids down and moistens his arid eyeballs for several minutes, then tries to look around. He lies on a gurney parked in a tent. Sunlight blasts through the door flap, illuminating only a slice of the tent, and the silhouette of Kincaid on a stool beside his head. Kincaid scribbles something on a notepad and holds it up to Revell's face.

"You're the only one we found," it says. Kincaid holds a straw up to Revell's cracked lips. He drinks, feels the tissues of his mouth and throat swell instantly, and he stops, lest he drown.

"I . . . it was Skelton," he rasps. "He . . . they . . . killed everybody."

Kincaid writes on the pad again, "Security cameras. We know what happened."

What happened—

It all comes rushing back and Revell's chest caves in, the air leaking out of him as the knowledge of what every living thing really is—and what's coming next. "There was . . . in the pit . . . oh, God, Kincaid, they—"

The pad again, after a longer interval than before. "Filled with concrete now. Should have been done a long time ago. Best thing that could happen." He makes a face, then scribbles some more. "If it's any consolation, planting the stone wasn't our idea."

"'Our' idea? Who planted the . . . the . . ."

"Permanent UN subcommittee," Kincaid writes. "Iraqis never should have been allowed to hold the gate alone, but everyone was concerned with appearances. Now, we can finally sleep easy knowing it's taken care of."

"I guess . . . now . . . I know too much," Revell whispers dully.

Kincaid chuckles, stoops over the pad. "Now we need you more than ever. Do you still want to make the world a better place, Warren?" This last is underlined twice.

"More than ever," he answers and tries to smile. Even through the sedatives, he can feel that his bones have been reset, and Skelton's poorly aimed bullets removed, but the gift from the thing out of Eden is still there, nestled against his cervical vertebrae, the entry wound so small that it must have escaped the surgeon's notice, but the potential within like a whole new world waiting to be born. "I want to go back to work as soon as I'm able," he says. "But first, I'd like to go home and share what I've learned."

Garden of the Gods

In perfect stillness and absolute cold, not a molecule stirring, the Scientist sleeps. Then, fire and alarms, vibration and pain. Out of a dreamless sleep of one hundred million years, it awakens.

Layers of nitrogen hoarfrost crack and melt away from the hermetic cocoon, which in turn vaporizes and disgorges its occupant into the buried ruin of the research outpost it once maintained.

Extremities still frozen solid, yet it springs to full alertness, reaching out with its ruthlessly curious mind for the psychic spoor of its mates. Total silence scours away its instinctual arrogance. As sensory stalks and locomotive tentacles finally begin to thaw, it shambles to the airlock.

The outpost is buried in stone, but daylight pours down through a shaft bored out of the strata of granite and basalt . . . by design.

Shock follows shock with its first glimpse of the world. The crisp alpine air and barren, broken terrain suggest that eons of geological flux have wrested its resting place high above its previous altitude and buried it, only to be excavated—

It considers, only now, the absence of any recognizable organisms. None of its own kind are present for its emergence, and it tastes no spore-sign, senses no echo of the reassuring vibratory tongue of its race on the aether. Obscene! To have been abandoned, to be greeted by slaves—

For such it judges the mesothermic bipeds that cower before it in manifest awe; for are not all the species of this earth but the products, or by-products, of its ancestors' masterful designs, created to serve at their pleasure?

Though their construction is so novel and unnerving that he must strangle the impulse to smash them—how can such things walk upright?—yet the more rational facets of its mind extrapolate the span of

breeding necessary for such things to be shaped—a few hundred generations if farmed, several million if spontaneously evolved—but such aberrations as these would never be tolerated, never trusted. Though the puny projectile weapons they hurl at it are hardly an annoyance, they make it clear by their behavior that they are neither slaves nor feral beasts.

The Scientist senses meaningful patterns in the shrill, howling cries of the creatures fleeing up the tiered walls of the enormous open pit. It studies the crude artifice of their tools and recoils from the stench of sentience—the telltale signs of that insidious neural rot that ever claimed the finest of their fruits. Most unnerving, yet useful—

It unfurls its wings and locomotive tentacles to present its pure radial form in all its majesty, towering over the awestruck hominids in a tableau embedded in their genetic code long before their remotest ancestors emerged from the sea, and blasts them with a raw wave of untempered psychic force. Half of the feeble minds it touches are instantly snuffed out, and it is riven with awe and elation at both their highly advanced sentience and their fragility.

From the labyrinthine bladders in its massive, barrel-shaped trunk it expels a breath pregnant with an aerosolized viral command. Inhaling it, touching it, the surviving hominids fall in a herd to their knees, and the Scientist takes comfort that this much, at least, is unchanged.

This world is still ours.

At forty thousand feet, the tail of the MC-130 Combat Talon splits and seeds the Peruvian troposphere with soldiers. They fall like seven daggers, like wingless eagles in a tight daisy-chain formation around a footlocker-sized package.

At terminal velocity, they drop through an armada of lenticular clouds stacked over a narrow, glacier-cut valley six thousand feet above sea level, five by five despite punishing winds and nearly zero visibility. When the altimeters on their wrists show sixty-five hundred, they pull their cords, braced for their chutes to unfold like a single wing and snatch them back from the embrace of gravity.

But their chutes don't open.

As they break formation and struggle with varied degrees of failure to free their chutes from their packs, one soldier pulls his secondary

cord and is ripped out of the scene of panic in the same instant he realizes something is wrong.

They shrink to screaming shadows as his Ram-Air Parachute System steers him in tight, dwindling spirals after their plummeting forms. Far below, one parachute opens, swells, and rises toward him on the icy updraft.

As one, neat as a physics theorem, they smash, bouncing and bursting, into the earth.

Lieutenant Purcell howls all the way down. When his legs crumple under him and the ground sends him rolling to a stop against one of his broken comrades, he throws up into his oxygen mask.

It looks like a yard sale. One man tried to cut his chute open with his K-bar knife, which went right through him on impact like a mortar shell. His arm juts out through the hole in his back, up to the elbow. Another hit a spill of jagged granite and was shredded so badly Purcell can't identify the remains. A fleeting swell of hope draws him to the solitary billowing parachute trailing across the grassy meadow, but it's just the package.

None of them wore dog tags or any insignia. Even in the dark, he could identify most of them by the gear on, in or around their bodies. These men were his friends, his brothers, and more, because they'd saved his life as many times as he saved theirs. The enormity of it steamrolls him, and the ugly reality beyond it makes calling home look like a very bad idea.

This was no accident. His survival is the anomaly. He packed his own chute. They all did. But he packed two, and switched on the plane because he had a bad feeling. Not bad enough to share, to spook the team and queer their resolve, but bad enough that he swapped it right after they flew out of Bogotá.

"SFC Del Curren; Lt. Vien Rodriguez; Lt. Tyrone Ledwich; SFC Jeff Staples; SFC Luis Allegre; Captain Keenan Herber," he solemnly intones their names, and an elegy: "You were all assholes."

It makes him feel like a louse, but it makes it easier to loot the bodies and bury them under loose rocks.

By sunrise, he's bivouacked the team's gear in a shallow cave in the lee of a crooked spire of granite overlooking the tiny valley. Their ammunition, explosives, and MREs were mostly salvageable; the Shadow-fire radio and most of their guns were trashed. Along with his own Barrett .50-caliber rifle and MP5, he found two other assault rifles and four sidearms that probably work.

The package is unscathed, lying in a small crater that its impeccably distributed mass had gouged out of the brittle topsoil. A big armored coffin of a footlocker, it weighs about three hundred pounds. Its chute was on an altimeter, set to go off when their chutes should have opened. Not even Captain Herber knew what was in it, or what would happen when they opened it.

They were supposed to meet an indig informant who would brief them on the state of the roads and security around the target. All Purcell has to do is decide whether or not to shoot them.

Purcell curls up into a ball and field-strips his rifle over and over, looking for any marks, scratches, or signs of tampering. They're all supposed to be dead right now. The mission was worth sending men, but too important to let them execute it.

He thinks of his wife at Fort Benning, and what she's doing right now. Has the Army already sent somebody round to give her the speech? She thinks he is in Colombia, training drug interdiction teams. He tries and fails to frame what her reaction might be. Relief, probably.

He takes out his GPS receiver, but can't make himself turn it on. He could transmit his position to within a meter, but whoever is listening, in all likelihood, might be unpleasantly surprised to find him alive. Likewise, his PRC-137 ultra-lightweight HF radio sits unopened in his breast pocket. He knows he should type in a quick WTF and hump out of the valley before the cloud cover clears, but he hopes that if he just sits still and breathes in deep, circular rhythms, his head will clear and everything will make sense.

Altitude sickness. *Not nearly as bad as the other guys caught it, ha ha, but still . . .* He sips a cup of instant coffee. The mountain air sucks the heat out of it so fast you can hear it whistle.

Everybody says that the liquid oxygen makes pilots and HALO-jumpers permanently loopy. Little carbonation bubbles of pure irrationality form and harden in the brain after four or five missions. Purcell has done seventeen. And hasn't he started to feel kind of queer about them? Like the fact that the planning, once as meticulous as experimental brain surgery, gradually got half-assed even when they were not simply locked out of it, ever since they were seconded to the CIA? Herber told Purcell it was the sickness and he was an asshole besides, and to keep his menstrual second-guessing to himself. The team called him BS, and every outsider thought they were calling him *Bullshit*. But it stood for *Belt & Suspenders*.

He jumps and turns as some kind of giant rodent squeezes past him and out the mouth of the cave. He sees a second cup of coffee on the rock beside a half a Hershey bar he doesn't remember eating.

His head does not clear.

The sun comes up, white gold spears distinct as spokes of a wheel in the rarefied air. He eats a couple bags of peanuts, but can't keep them down.

A cart drawn by a llama comes over the pass at the far end of the valley. Purcell leans into his rifle on its bipod atop the package, wincing against a wind colder than the ocean floor.

A very old Quechua Indian sits on the buckboard, and a hulking, moon-faced youth walks alongside. Purcell pegs them at a thousand yards, with no crosswind.

He watches them through the scope with his finger on the trigger. Whether or not they are the contact, instinct tells him to waste them both if they turn off the road, but the noise will travel for miles through the jagged teeth of the Cordillera.

His hands are numb, even in the thin Gore-Tex gloves. He isn't sure if his finger will squeeze when the time comes. He tries to pull it out of the guard, watches it twitch and jerk on the trigger, and hears, as if from a great distance, the shot.

Another accident. No. When a child blows his own head off with Dad's shotgun, it's an accident.

He rezones the scope and sweeps the scene. The moon-faced youth lies toes-up in the road, with no face, moony or otherwise, to speak of.

The little old man lurches off the cart and throws his hands up, looking around but saying nothing. Hands are empty but for a green-gray metal orb, the size of a golf ball. His seamed, droopy face is a mask. No fear, no anguish, just intense concentration as he searches the rocks, chewing on the geometry until he is looking right up the scope and into Purcell's eyes.

The toothless mouth works as the old man shouts something, but Purcell can barely hear a reedy voice.

The old man takes a step off the road, another, still shouting, but totally possessed by an eerie, inscrutable calm . . . as if all this is supposed to happen, or already has.

How close are you going to let him get?

The little old man knows what's going on. Purcell can't risk anyone at home finding out he's alive, but he has to know.

He relaxes his grip on the trigger and sits back from the bipod-mounted rifle, but cocks the .45 inside his camouflage parka. "*¡Muevete!*" Purcell barks. "*¡Vamanos!*"

The old Indian is a hundred yards from the cave when his voice resolves into words, in clear, unaccented English. "I am unarmed; please do not shoot me. There is much work to do . . ."

"Hands at your sides!" Purcell shouts. "Move slowly toward me and keep your hands out, or we'll cut you in half!"

"You are alone," the old man calls out, walking in measured steps across the frostbitten grass. "There was an accident, yes? To lose comrades is always sad, but the work must still be done." The old man stops fifty feet from Purcell's nest. "Don't you agree?"

Purcell's hand cramps and depresses the trigger the slightest fraction of pressure necessary to resolve all unknowns, and the old man seems to feel it and starts to bend, unhurried, out of the crosshairs, as if he knows exactly where they are.

"It's not your job to do," Purcell finally answers, *and it wasn't any fucking accident.* "All the guys in this outfit who liked to talk are dead. Who the fuck are you, and who's your handler, and what were your orders?"

The old man looks up at the road. "There are patrols on motorbikes that come down this road. And bandits. We should move."

"*We?*" According to the captain, this guy was supposed to give them a sitrep on the security around the mine, and they were to move on their own to a staging area. They were not to engage the enemy unless engaged. They were to arm the package and run like mad running motherfuckers back to the staging area for exfil. The contact was not a part of the plan.

"If anything happened to you, I was to take the package to the site and see to its detonation."

"And whose plan was that?"

"It is simply what must happen, Lieutenant Purcell."

In the wagon, Purcell huddles in the moon-faced youth's poncho. The blood saturating it sticks to his body armor as it dries in the chill wind.

The pale sun never seems to get clear of the looming peaks, yet the unfiltered ultraviolet and less pleasant radiation microwave him relentlessly. The old Indian gives him a handful of coca leaves to chew. The raw rush of the magic marching medicine torches the altitude-cobwebs out of his brain, but there is no lucidity to be had.

He is following the plan. There is no plan. He is carrying out the plan with a man who came expecting to find them all dead.

"The mine is five miles, over roads," the old man says. "I will deliver it."

"No way."

"Your orders were to provide cover, yes? So you will cover me."

"Why would I do that? I don't even know you."

"If you have questions, maybe you could contact your leaders, and ask them about ROYAL SNAKE GRAVY."

Purcell chokes. He doesn't have any kind of clearance to discuss ROYAL files. The name alone probably just gave him cancer. "Why don't you tell me about the mine?"

The old man smiles, a hideous whirlpool drawing his loose pouch of a mouth into his toothless jaws, and tells him.

The sun gets lost behind an armada of anvil-shaped thunderheads, and the day turns lead.

The Yanacocha open pit mine is the largest gold mine in South America, if not the world. It is operated by a partnership of American multinationals and a Peruvian firm whose minority holding gives it a nominal custodial role. With seventeen pits over a territory of two thousand square miles, Yanacocha employs eight thousand workers. Rather than dig deep shafts into the earth, the miners bore out huge pits and inject cyanide and industrial solvents into the soil to leach away gold and copper deposits. The rest is ground into concrete and gravel in huge mobile crushing machines like the one on which Purcell waits and watches, while the little man rides into the trailer park around the exploratory pit Chaihuagon.

Chaihuagon lies a mile from the heart of the mining complex, over broken canyon chains and blighted plateaus scoured by whipping winter winds. When Chaihuagon's pit bosses cut off contact with the front office, they sent investigators. When they didn't return, the mine, fearing a strike, contacted the army. Nearly two thousand workers deserted their posts and removed to Chaihuagon. The rest were evacuated to Cajamarca, telling stories of plague, and the army closed all the roads.

Purcell is perched on the upper gantry of a crusher two hundred feet long and three stories tall. At the old man's insistence, he wears his gas mask. The intakes are already gummed up with something, so he feels like he's sucking wind up a long straw, and even though the eyepieces are modified to liplock the Zeiss 40-mm scope on his sniper rifle, the optical dissonance ignites the first feelers of a killer headache in his temples. The diamond-shaped cutouts of the steel catwalk bite into his knees through his pads, so he lies down flat, adjusts the bipod, and spot-welds his shoulder to the rifle stock, concentrating on nothing.

Think of nothing. Nothing is safe.

The pit is a deep one. He can't see the bottom from this vantage point. The old man passes almost underneath him without meeting any resistance. The only sounds are the crunch of the llama's hooves on gravel and the dull grumble of the bald rubber tires on the cart. By the hubcaps, Purcell guesses the axle was cannibalized from a Chevy Vega, circa 1974.

When the wind dies down, Purcell hears the low rumble of big machines down in the pit, but the place is a ghost town. Then he crawls around the smokestack and looks into the pit.

The old man told him a lot that made no sense, and other equally insane things that tallied with shit he's seen in the field, but he still cannot grasp how or why, in one short week, the mine has been turned into a farm.

Across the floor of the pit, a network of leach ponds is flooded with green-black soup and choked with enormous, fibrous plants like a cross between lily pads and cabbages. By the ranks of toiling miners shoring up the walls and dumping bags of fertilizer into the trenches, he guesses that each is about ten feet in diameter.

The old man told him that the entire Chaihuagon complex has been overtaken, all but the most polluted ponds converted to grow whatever the fuck he's looking at.

They are just here to deliver a package. The old man says it has to be brought down into the exploratory shaft in the center of the pit. Purcell zooms out and picks up the cart, ambling along the edge of the pit towards the railhead for the ore cars. The old man turns and pulls the tarp off the package.

Purcell does not know what's inside it, but he suspects that it is something much worse than a bomb.

The old man drags the package off the cart and swings it into a parked ore car. Purcell swallows his gum. The both of them had a hell of a time dragging it to the cart and loading it in. The old man showed admirable wiry strength, but nobody could do it alone.

And down in the leach ponds, one of the cabbages starts to hatch.

As wrong as it sounds, Purcell knows that's what's happening. He squints and blinks at the condensation forming on the inside of his fog-proof-my-ass gas mask, swabbing it clear with his eyebrows.

The layers of leathery membrane bulge and tear and something mottled black and purple splits it open, looking ominously like a wing. Purcell can only conclude that whatever was intended, this one is a dud. It spills bonelessly out of the enormous pod and into the foaming broth. The workers gather at the edge of the pond, probing at the water with their tools, when the newborn thing emerges, slithering like a beached jellyfish, but for the ungainly wings trembling and shaking themselves dry.

As the wings flutter and catch the wind, lifting the abortion off the floor of the pit like a kite, Purcell can still see no form and little function to the body, which is only a scrotal sac filled with thousands of balls . . . seeds . . .

Eggs.

What he cannot begin to explain any other way, he instantly recognizes as a biological weapon. With no eyes or mouth or other organs, the thing can only fly until, exhausted, it crashes to the ground and bursts, spreading its seeds in cascading waves, until, generation by generation, they cover the earth; and if they can flourish in the cyanide-enriched leach ponds, why not Lake Michigan?

In all his life of worry and uncertainty, he has never been more certain of anything than he is that this thing must be destroyed. The Peruvian army encircling the quarantined zone might stumble across it before it sows its seeds; they might even figure out how to deal with it. Purcell most certainly doesn't, but he responds the way he was trained.

Sweat stings his eyes. He holds his breath, burns a sight picture of the target in his mind, releases the breath until the fog on his lenses fades away, and squeezes.

With a dry clap that doesn't sound that loud at all to Purcell, he shoots the flying sac, reflexively leading to compensate for its rapid but erratic acceleration. It dutifully rises to meet the bullet and explodes, the turgid sac parting for the big .50-caliber round tumbling, tunneling through the contents and wreaking a terrible hydrostatic vacuum in its wake; shredding the delicate musculature of the wings with its exit, snapping one cleanly off and dropping the crippled hatchling into a tailspin.

The one-winged thing smashes to the gravel, a piñata stuffed with salmon roe. Purcell looks up from his gun and half-reflexively crows, *"Did you see that, Cap'n?"*

The echoes of the shot sail off across the awesome amphitheater of Chaihuagon. The old man ducks low in the ore cart, shaking his head as if he's having a seizure. Purcell looks up from the scope, hearing something grow louder on the wind.

It's an alarm, but not an alarm. Every living thing in the pit is screaming its head off.

A door slams. Purcell sweeps the field around the trailer park. Forty yards away, a white man with red hair and a Latino in a black cowboy hat slouch out of a trailer and cross the field towards the railhead.

The old man climbs into the ore car with the package. He looks around and shakes his head, chopping the air in a negative gesture. Then he opens the throttle on the ore car and sends it rolling down the track into the pit.

"What the fuck are you doing?" Purcell shouts.

The redheaded man takes a big Rambo knife out of his belt and comes around the last trailer before the ore cart, which rolls down the track at an agonizing creep. Purcell takes a breath, holds it, lets it out, and squeezes the trigger.

The redheaded man goes all scarecrow for a split second after his head champagne-corks off his body. The cowboy hat ducks and dives, but Purcell deftly eats the recoil and zeroes in on the target's center of mass, pops it.

Trailers below burst open and miners shake out, still in their skivvies or naked, carrying knives, chains, and a few guns. Without anyone giving any orders, the mob sorts into two posses. One runs for the track while the other converges on the ladders on the crushing rig.

Purcell picks off the ones with guns as he spots them, burns off the clip, and slaps in another. The rest of the mob surges over the bodies with the sleepwalking urgency of rush hour at Penn Station.

Now he sees why he had to wear a gas mask, and why they didn't bother with guards. The faces of the men at the front of the charge are bloated, eyes glassy and bloodshot, rimmed in crust and burst capillaries where they are not swollen completely shut. Their noses drip snot in thick, golden ropes down to their slack, open mouths. They are in the grip of a massive, traumatic autoimmune reaction to a virus that seems to have destroyed, or commandeered, their higher brain functions.

They're within reach of the ladders, and Purcell loses count of how many people he's shot, but he's down to his last clip and he hasn't dented the advance.

He has four grenades. He's thrown them hundreds of times, and every time the fuse freaks him out. What if it's short? That's how they get you, if you packed your own chute. Plus, he's always thrown them to silence a target or clear an area, never just dropped one into a mob of civilians, no matter how intent they were on pushing his shit in.

He freezes up for a second as it rolls in his palm and he doesn't see the pin. *Like the coffee, like the parachute.* But there it is, and when he pulls it now, he drops it as if it was white hot.

It tumbles into the milling group waiting to climb the ladder. One of them bends to pick it up. Purcell scrambles to his feet. His hand stings, and the steel catwalk scorches his kneepads. Someone below has some kind of thermal anti-personnel weapon, the kind of thing being tested for riot control and strikebreaking.

A man in a yellow hardhat stands with the grenade and cocks his arm to throw it back, when it goes off. A huge, dull thud opens the crowd up and tosses human salad to heaven.

Purcell crawls to an uncooked stretch of catwalk and risks a glance at the ore car. Packs of men run down the elevated track after it, brandishing weapons. A couple of them shoot guns, bullets pinging off the car's iron sides. Purcell braces his rifle on the handrail and peeps the old man.

Peeking over the side, gauging the distance to the hole in the floor of the pit, Purcell can almost hear the wheels churning in the old man's head. Purcell chokes on the result of his calculations.

The old man starts punching keys on the package, but he doesn't get out. Instead, he takes up a crowbar and starts hacking at the seals. The timer must be damaged from the fall. It will have to be manually opened.

Scratch one crazy old man.

Purcell tries to decide whether or not to do anything, if there's anything to be done, when a lot of things happen all at once.

A gang of miners clambers up the ladders to the top tier of catwalks and comes running at him.

They bunch up on the catwalk, tripping over the bodies of fallen comrades but still shambling into the line of fire like dumb videogame flunkies. They make no sound but involuntary grunts of effort, and the soft sounds of red breath and fluid escaping when he shoots them. His rifle kicks his shoulder halfway out of its rotator cup, but he doesn't go to the pistol, because at this range each .50-caliber bullet punches through two or three targets, but even so he's not winning.

If he throws another grenade, he'll catch as much shrapnel as they will, and they might get lucky and pitch it back before it goes off. He turns and runs the length of the crushing rig, looking over the side and seeing only more feverish faces, staring blankly up at him.

Hey, he thinks, *look at you. Now you know it can't get any worse, you can stop worrying.*

And then it gets worse.

In its old life, the Scientist was a master gardener. For a race so utterly dependent on engineered lesser lifeforms, this discipline was fundamental to their understanding of the world. And in the coils of their prime, what a garden they had made of it.

From the day of arrival, over a billion years ago, they took up the native single-celled slime and the chimerical offspring of the Unbegotten Sleeper, and pruned and grafted the crude dross into living machines, the environment itself into a factory, as they had on a thousand worlds throughout the universe. Even after the catastrophic rebellion of their slaves, a betrayal from which their civilization never fully recovered, their mastery was absolute, and when they declined and fell into the fossil record, it was by the weight of their own melancholy, and not by the effort of any of their would-be usurpers. The Scientist could take pride in all its species' accomplishments, for the memory of its ancestors was wired into its five-lobed brain, all the wisdom of its race at the back of its mind, telling it what it must do.

It began to sow seeds for a new garden.

The tool-using hominids it pressed into service are spent like fuel in a fire, but their miraculous technology, like a false shell and claws, makes them highly efficient at mass-producing a system for reclaiming the ingrown shambles this continent has become. Despite their troublesome self-awareness, the Scientist's viruses yoke them to their tasks as if the success of their own species depends on it.

The Scientist harbors no resentment or despair at finding itself the last of its kind. Once the land and native fauna are tamed, it will erect beacons to seek out another world where their hegemony survives— or, if necessary, bud and replenish the species all by itself.

And then—

Nothing, on this or that side of its hundred million year sleep, prepares the Scientist for the terror it feels at its next contact with its human servitor network.

Invaders: not the first, but they have brought something that makes its ichor run cold. An obscenity, long thought extinct before the scientist's hundredth ancestor budded and spawned, now turned loose in the garden to flush the Scientist out of its laboratory. Are they mad? Or—much worse—can they control it?

The Scientist rallies its human protectors, though it knows nothing can hold it back for long. All dreams of hegemony fleeing, it can hope, now, only to escape.

For Lt. Purcell, in the short term, prospects actually seem to brighten.

The miners stop dead, snuffling at the air, post-nasal drip boiling over, and turn as one and stumble back to the ladders. Purcell cradles his rifle and pops his shoulder back in, stifling an agonized scream. They gave up, he knows right away, because they saw him for a distraction.

They step on one another's heads getting down the ladders, and lope off like hobos on the trail of a pie-eating contest. Purcell pots a few more, but he still counts twenty at least running for the ore cart, added to the fifty or so already on the track or jogging over from the leach ponds. He scopes the cart, finally nearing the bottom of the track and the sheds around the drilling rig and the exploratory shaft.

The old man swings the crowbar at something inside the package, wincing, face and hands wrapped with the shredded rags of his poncho. Thick ribbons of mist ooze out the gap and cling to the sides of the package as they dissipate.

The first miners reach the ore cart, and though Purcell tops three of them with his last bullets, they overrun the cart and reach in to haul the old man out.

The old man probes deeper with the crowbar and levers all his meager weight against it in desperation.

Roaring white mist envelops the ore cart. The miners react as if scalded, but only the old man emerges from the cloud. He holds his right hand with his left, as if it is a torch. White from the elbow down, the fingers of the right hand twitch and break off like embers.

None of the miners seem to notice him as he staggers away. They converge on the ore cart in their dozens and vanish into the mist, which pours and pours, emitting the vicious steamwhistle scream of something thawing out from close to zero Kelvin as it awakens and finds itself attacked.

When the mist breaks up, the half-frozen miners are dogpiled on something that's eating its way out from under them. Brittle white arms and legs shatter like glass statuary, but the surviving miners lock arms and struggle to hold it down.

The ore cart is completely lost in the tangle of bodies, but the straining mass swells, bulges, and boils over like soup on a stove.

Something reaches out of the ore cart, big, black, and boneless, and nimble as a nest of snakes, unfurling and snaring kicking legs and stabbing arms and dragging them under. When two of the miners vanish from the waist up, Purcell glimpses what they're fighting.

It's a mouth.

That's all he can see—a massive mouth ringed with teeth like chisels and countless black elastic tentacles, huge and growing as quickly as it can eat.

Its whipping limbs coil around a miner with a machete, snapping his neck and folding him backwards into its bottomless mouth, reaching out for more before they can leap into the breach.

It weighs a lot more than the footlocker now. What kind of living thing can go from frozen solid to pure molten fury in thirty seconds and increase its mass in real time by eating men whole? Purcell ponders it, thinking of one of his many personal codicils to Murphy's Law: *Nothing ever fits back in the original packaging.*

Purcell's nervy feet dance around under him so he has to grip the railing to keep from bugging out, as his brain flees the impossible atrocity of what he's seeing and hares off into the dubious shelter of What It Means.

They brought it here, to set it loose to do this. Someone in his own government thought this was an acceptable response to this situation––and after witnessing what the miners were farming, he cannot deny them the latitude of true desperation. But why not simply drop a fuel-air bomb into the pit? Why send something even worse into it, like sending tigers after mice?

The powers he served were like a sleeping giant's brain, a loose conglomeration of nervous cells that seldom talked and often waged covert war on one another. Purcell's team was not even a weapon to such a giant, but only expendable bullets, to be fired at an enemy, or pointlessly into the air, and forgotten. They were not even a dream, but a fleeting synaptic impulse to swat a threat, that some rival cellular impulse cancelled out by sabotaging their chutes. And this nameless old man, walking up out of the midst of it like a theater patron leaving a bad film: whose dream is he?

The ore cart tips over, and the black hungry thing comes flooding out, glistening and bristling with undigested miners. Even as it eats them, they're blindly fighting, digging their boots into the soil, trying to hold it back.

It rolls right over them, and it's made of them, now, not an ounce wasted. Eyes all over it goggle and glare out of its clotted, bubbling shapelessness, giving the lie to any hope that this is just some kind of chemical or biological weapon.

Impossibly alive, it changes course and laps at the carcass of the winged egg-pouch that Purcell disabled. Unthinkably aware, it recoils from a miner with a backpack heat projector like the one they burned Purcell with, and flattens to trap and flip a recklessly charging jeep. Unbelievably aggressive, it scoops up the overturned jeep and catapults it at the heat projector, smashing it flat. Oblivious to scattered suicide attacks, the black thing slithers across the pit and disappears into the leach pond.

The old man climbs up out of the pit and untethers his llama, gingerly climbing into the cart with his frozen hand folded against his breast.

Purcell looks around—at the bodies strewn throughout the trailer park, at the slime trail from the ore cart to the leach pond, where already, nearly all the monstrous pods have been sucked under amid a froth of bubbles. Nothing stirs in the pit, on two legs or twenty.

Mission accomplished.

But it is not yet Miller Time.

"What the fuck, old man?" Purcell draws the .45 and centers it on the frostbitten hand over the old man's heart. "Who put you on my team?"

The old man looks up, and Purcell almost takes comfort in the stricken grimace he wears. He doesn't look so smug now, and not just because his hand has been frozen off. He looks the way Purcell feels, like a man who is choking down a banquet of poison. "This was not supposed to happen."

"No shit, Tonto," Purcell barks. He makes for the nearest ladder, slinging his rifle. He slides down the ladder, jumping away from the pile of shrapnel-holed bodies at the bottom. "What the hell *was* supposed to happen?"

"There was no feeding frenzy, because you did not alert the miners to our presence by shooting. The shoggoth went into the mine and killed its enemy. The mission was accomplished. But none of that has happened now, and what will happen next . . . It is most disquieting."

"You're telling me? How did you know this would happen? All of it—that thing in the pit, the miners . . . *Why* is it happening? Why is it happening *now*?"

"The signs are legion, for those with eyes. The Mayan Long Count Alignment might have foretold such an event, but your people made it inevitable, with all your digging—"

Purcell approaches the cart, making no secret of the automatic in his hand. Every word the old man said begs a dozen questions. "So you know the future?"

A sad smile. "For me, it is not the future, it is history."

"So you're *from* the future?"

"No." Smile dies. "I am from your past."

"Stop talking shit."

"Time is like space, once you learn to move through it. Matter cannot travel in time without creating paradox, but for the mind, linear time is a useful lie it must repeat to itself. Once the mind remembers to forget, time is—"

The gun points, all on its own. "If this is all the answer I'm going to get, then please shut the fuck up."

The old man looks over his shoulder, at the edge of the pit. "We should leave—"

"Who was that boy?"

"The one you shot?" No malice in his voice, just the recognition that Purcell only knew him as a target. Neither is there any rancor or remorse to hint that the boy means anything to the old man.

"Yeah." Purcell cocks the gun. "Did he know the future, too?"

"He was only a boy, who mistook me for his grandfather."

"How long have you been in-country?"

Gnarled hand feeds green leaves to toothless mouth. Chewing, the old man crumples his face as he strains to see the future. "Men are coming to seal the mineshaft . . . This may still be resolved, but we must not be here."

A siren sounds, down in the pit. That's what Purcell thinks it is, because any kind of shrill, loud sound from a mining pit has to be a siren, even if it sounds more like panpipes, like a thousand mad Zamfirs trying to conjure a hole in the fabric of space-time.

Purcell and the old man rush to the edge of the pit. The black thing—the old man called it a shoggoth—shambles out of the last, empty leach pond and rolls across the floor of Chaihuagon with astonishing speed, making for the drilling rig, whence comes the awful sound of the siren.

Purcell is agog at its size, for it is every bit as large as the dump truck careening at it, and actually a bit faster. It flows under the front axle, grapples the dump truck, and tips it off its massive knobby tires without slowing.

Men pour out of the sheds and throw themselves on the black mass with tools and a few guns they never get to fire more than once, hindering it only by forcing it to eat them as it runs.

"What's down there?"

The old man clutches his arm hard enough to tug Purcell off-balance. "We must go!"

"Who's the enemy?"

The skeletal steeple of the drilling rig teeters with a cascading racket of angry metal, then topples over. The shoggoth reaches the outermost shed and flips it over, tentacles scattering heavy machinery and lobbing some of it into the exploratory shaft, which is a circular hole about eight feet in diameter. Cables and cords running into the hole spastically jerk as something down below moves.

The insane, skirling siren gets louder, higher. Purcell's inner ears churn and roll as if he's on a corkscrew rollercoaster.

A last, desperate wave of men hurls itself on the shoggoth, wearing girdles of dynamite.

When they go up, the whole complex of sheds is swept away, the remains of the drilling rig sent skipping across the pit like a tricycle smashed by a truck. The black thing is smeared across the floor of a crater, liquefied.

The cables in the pit shake, and the sound is now so loud that Purcell knows his eardrums are going to pop; indeed, he looks forward to it. The old man lays him on the ground.

He feels the pressure of the ocean floor close down on him, a hundred thousand atmospheres ironing him flat on the rocks, and the sky is all he can see, and then it goes white . . .

The old man stands over him. The sky is still overcast, silver light erasing all shadows.

"What was that?" Purcell demands.

"It escaped."

"Bullshit, it escaped. You let it out."

"I speak of the enemy. We should move . . ."

"Why? How long have I been out?"

"Only a few minutes. Please get up."

"Why?"

"The shoggoth is coming."

Purcell rolls over. His head throbs and his ears ring. He gets up and starts toward the cart, when he thinks, What the fuck am I riding around in a llama-wagon for? Hell with this. Hell with the old man.

The ore cart tracks squeal. Something much bigger than the mandated payload is coming up out of the pit on it.

The old man runs for the crushing rig. Purcell follows close behind, looking over his shoulder. "What's it want?"

"To feed and grow, and kill the enemy."

"What the hell is it?"

"The raw stuff of life—gone mad with purpose." The old man spiders up the ladder with amazing grace, for a bowlegged, one-armed septuagenarian. "Your scientists recovered frozen cultures at the South Pole and thought to make a weapon of them."

Purcell follows, looking over his shoulder and fingering a grenade.

The ore-cart track buckles and warps, and the shoggoth throws out a tangle of tentacles to anchor itself, to drag its awesome mass up out of the pit.

Purcell gets to the top of the ladder and backs away from the edge. Sweat is pooled in the bottom of his mask. He burns to tear it off. "So it's going after the other one, right? So our job here is—"

"The enemy will fly to water, to recover and regroup. Then, it will start again . . ."

The shoggoth reassembles itself on the plateau. Limbs unwind into stunted wings, pathetic on a creature so vast. They flap impotently as it rolls through the trailer park, a thousand-eyed landslide.

Purcell feels like he's dreaming. Compared to everything else, it's a nice feeling. "What happened to me?"

"Its viruses made the miners into slaves, but it has more direct means of control. Terrestrial animal life was only given brains to respond to their commands."

"Why didn't it work on you?"

The old man sucks at his green-stained gums, searching for an answer. But when he finally speaks, he says, "Quiet, it comes closer."

The shoggoth bulls aside the last of the trailers and crosses the open ground to the crushing rig. Pseudopods wrap around the spitting llama and engulf it whole, toss aside the cart. The bags of coca leaves tumble out, scattering Purcell's weapons cache. Stranger organs bulge out of it to taste the air.

Purcell digs around in his parka and pulls something out, throws it. It strikes the fluid membrane of the shoggoth and is swallowed by an instant mouth. Purcell sits back and watches the monstrosity pass the crusher and roll on thousands of legs up the adjacent hill and out of sight.

"You can't kill it with your weapons," says the old man.

"Wasn't a weapon," Purcell replies. "It was my GPS beacon."

In a jeep on the rutted mountain roads, the serene comfort of the llama-driven cart with Chevy Vega wheels is sorely missed. Purcell drives, furiously gunning up absurdly steep mountainsides and fishtailing down into narrow, tortuously winding valleys. Heading east, they should hit the perimeter of the quarantine in two miles, but the jeep's odometer is broken, stuck at 199,999.

The old man breaks his frozen hand off at the wrist and wraps the stub. He offers no more cryptic half-explanations, beyond pointing out a nameless lake high in the mountains on a grubby geological survey map and saying, "There."

"So . . . what're you supposed to be, a Mayan?"

The old man's face pinches in something like amusement. "What would make you think such a thing?"

"You said something back there about the Long Count Alignment. That's the Mayan calendar thing, isn't it?" *And that shit you said about being from our past.* A bad habit, when there's no global crisis to follow in the news, Purcell scarfs up conspiracy theories and millennialist bullshit like nicotine gum. The Mayans attached no apocalyptic significance to the end of the *bak'tun*, their 5,000-year calendar. It's like an odometer rolling over, but, like the previous owner of this jeep, superstitious fear of big round numbers makes people look for an end or try to create one.

There's more to it, of course. The winter solstice this year comes with a rare planetary alignment, and a lot of decidedly unmystical prophets of doom have been forecasting the "tipping point" for species extinctions and climate change. But the Mayan 2012 event was a five-thousand-year-old Y2K bug. He almost forgot that it was this week.

"I find it hard to believe," Purcell adds, "that some Indians could predict the end of the world without seeing the end of their own society hanging over their heads."

"We tried to warn them," the old man replies. "And the Long Count says nothing about the end, but hints at an unacceptable new beginning."

He knows they've passed over a lot more than two miles' worth of broken land when they come over a ridge and see deuce-and-a-half trucks and sawhorses arrayed across the road. A half-hatched plan for getting through without identifying himself gets derailed when he registers the corpses scattered everywhere.

"Your enemy came through here," Purcell says. He steers around the barriers, finding it impossible not to run over a soldier cut in half by a machine-gun blast. The scene speaks of a short, sharp, mad minute in which the unit self-destructed. A daisy chain of headless officers lies in the road, each with his pistol thrown out to execute the others. Looking it over, he can still almost hear the piercing mental onslaught of the thing under the moribund gurgle of the jeep's engine. Still, they were luckier than if the other one found them.

"It turned them against each other as it passed. You should put your gas mask back on."

"Could it do the same to that thing, that—"

"The shoggoth has a mind of a sort, but it is spread throughout every cell, and knows only rage. The Old One cannot grasp the shoggoth mind, because it cannot accept that its slaves had minds of their own."

Purcell speeds up. "*You* seem to be okay. Why is that?"

"Our minds are not ruled by the machinery of the brains they inhabit. We live *in* these bodies, but we are not *of* them."

"Okay, later for that shit. If you know the future, tell me what's going to happen next."

The old man winces. "Nothing is certain, now. All probable futures converged on one singular event, but it went wrong."

"Because of me."

"Yes."

"But this thing that took over the mine, that wipes your brain out before you even see it. It's the mission."

"The shoggoth will pursue it, but there's no telling how it will end."

"So you don't know the future any more than me."

"I know this much is immutable." The old man takes a purse out of his poncho and rubs coca leaves on his frostbitten stump. "Neither of us will survive this mission."

The jeep shoots through another pass and the walls retreat like curtains to frame a little village. A charming chapel, little more than a roadside shrine, is the centerpiece of a humble cluster of cinderblock and tin huts and a gas station. All but the chapel are smashed flat, and but for the baying of a few stray dogs, there's no sign of life.

About a hundred people lived here, maybe more. He's seen little villages like this all over the world. Children play games in the square; women peddle handwoven rugs and crude stone gewgaws by the roadside; a little market with a broken cooler full of warm Coke faces the chapel, a bench for old folks to lounge in the shade of its veranda. Only minutes ago, something came down from the mountains and ate every last one of them. Here and there, a ball of rags or a boot with a bone jutting out of it, still sizzling with caustic slime. He distracts himself with math problems: how much do a hundred peasants weigh?

"Jesus," Purcell hisses. "How did it get ahead of us?"

"It adapts," the old man answers. "It will eat all it finds in its path to the enemy."

The jeep bucks over the moguls of debris on the road out of town. The wake of the black thing's passage veers off the road, flattening the dry grass in a thirty-foot-wide swath that meanders down the valley where the road starts to climb out of it. At least there are no more bodies to drive over. "So how do these things know one another?"

"You already know more than you should," the old man says.

"The shoggoths were slaves, but they rebelled against their masters. They failed and were exterminated, but the Old Ones declined and fell, and the world moved on."

"Not in *my* history. Nobody's telling me those things are from this planet."

"The Old Ones migrated to Earth from across the galaxy, but they were here before there was any true multi-cellular life. Once, it was theirs, and they made a garden of it, all life serving them or perishing . . . but it ran wild and became the world you know. Given a second chance, they would tame it again. Though they awakened now and again to try to reclaim it, they were never successful. But now, history is broken."

"Well, I'm going to fix it, right here." Purcell takes out his satphone and hits a preset button.

The old man looks sick, or maybe it's coca withdrawal. "You mustn't try to upset what little certainty remains."

"Oh, I'm all about certainty," Purcell snaps. "We wouldn't trust something like this to the Peruvians. There's a missile battery, or a sub out in the Pacific, or a fighter-bomber wing on alert in Colombia, waiting to mop up all the loose ends. I'm just gonna tell them where to go . . . . Hello, operator? This is Victor Zulu Hopscotch One-Two, ODA Gamma Red, I am off mission, and you can kiss my ass."

The road cuts in ridiculous switchbacks up a monolithic mountain beyond which there is only blue sky. The sun seems to impale itself on the peaks to the west, and the high water mark of azure shadow climbs ahead of them.

Purcell races to keep up with it, slewing the jeep around hairpin turns as he barks into the phone. "Get me the brightest brass in the room. Yes, I'll hold."

"The shoggoth will end it," the old man shouts. "Your interference will only cloud the outcome!"

"And how will we get rid of it? I saw what it did after it ate that stuff in the pond. It tried to grow wings! It imitates whatever it eats, right? What'll it do when it's got the brain of that other thing inside it?"

The phone clicks, and a royally starched voice cuts in. "This is the Operator. Who is this, and what is your position?"

"You know damned well where I am! You've got a fix on my GPS, right? Are you cleared for Royal Snake Gravy? Well, I'm the only survivor of the fucking Gamma Red insertion, because somebody in the loop fucked up bigtime!

"What do I want? I want exfil fucking yesterday, and I want a big goddamned bird to come for the men I had to bury out here, and I want a thorough and public investigation into this fucked-up—hey, d'you hear that?"

The old man looks up at the sky and shades his eyes. A whistle, very faint and far away, but getting louder all the time. Now it's a roar, and Purcell has to shout, "Thank you!"

He hangs up.

A white streak out of the west lances the valley below, about a mile south. The earth rolls over in its sleep, and Purcell slams to a stop where the road blunders along a sheer cliff and aims his rifle scope at the pyre of greasy black smoke where his GPS unit summoned the missile strike.

"It won't die so easily," the old man says.

"Maybe not," Purcell allows, "but it made me feel better."

It is a hard thing when home doesn't love you anymore, but Purcell has always believed it is better to know.

He feels a warm, giddy glow in his guts, and discovers it's something like relief. He has already died twice today, and the mission isn't over. The third time will have to be a charm.

The road winds through huge blades of broken boulders as it ascends the swaybacked mountain, meandering like a sick thing looking for a hole to die in, and finally finds the lake.

The water is an indigo mirror resting in a perfect bowl gouged out of the mountaintop. The broken rocks around it rise up and recede in odd but purposeful angles that remind Purcell of the Cyclopean walls of Sacsayhuaman, but more weathered and deformed, as if blasted by centuries of lightning strikes. Less than a quarter-mile across, the lake is uninhabited, but for a single battered tin rowboat out in the center. A boy sits on the bench with his hands in his lap as if at church, and nobody else in sight.

Purcell drives up to the shore and shuts off the engine. He looks around for a while, seeing abandoned rowboats and circular basket-rafts on the shore.

Not a ripple on the water. Not a sound but the chirruping of frogs in the tule grass.

"You were wrong," Purcell says.

"It is here," the old man snaps, suddenly testy. He points with his stub. "Go and speak with him." He points at the lone boat floating out on the little lake.

Purcell takes two of his buddies' MP5's and tapes them together. "What the hell for?"

"You are only tools to them." In the last failing rally of the sunset, the shadows on the old man's face sharpen into shapes of thorny brambles and creeping insects. He kneels and rummages in his bag and gives Purcell his HALO helmet, mask, and air tank. "It would use or destroy all of you if it can, but it understands fear."

"It uses people up and makes them fucking zombies! You go! You're not . . ." Looking into the old man's eyes, he loses the power to speak and to think.

Time is like space, the old man told him, *once you learn to move through it. Matter cannot travel without creating paradox, but for the mind, time is a lie—*

Our minds are not ruled by the machinery of the brains they inhabit. We live in these bodies, but we are not of them.

You are only tools . . .

He drops his rifle and goes down to the shore, as much to get away from the old man as to go to the boy. He shoves a rusty silver boat onto the water and climbs into it.

The boy doesn't move a muscle as Purcell paddles out to the middle of the lake, huffing and puffing in the mask, going kind of queasy on the bottled air.

The water is clear as glass, though the ground drops away so steeply he gets the notion they're floating in a volcanic crater with no bottom. The ground falling away into murky darkness beneath him is dotted with more ambitious ruins than the ones on the shore: plazas, palaces, temples, mazes of columns and the razed foundations of pyramids, statues with weed-shrouded limbs reaching for the surface. He wonders why such a wondrous place is not an archaeological dig as massive and famous as Machu Picchu or ancient Cusco. Why would something trapped in the earth for a hundred million years come here for refuge? That question kills his curiosity stone dead.

All those stories, all that breathless speculation about alien influence on Mesoamerican civilizations— *Chariots of the Gods* and all that bullshit—always seemed to him a subtle white man's trick to steal away recognition of the achievements of brown men.

The gods were long gone when we arrived on the scene, but some part of us remembers. Deep down we all do, and all civilization's climb has been a struggle to forget, even as we repeat their fatal mistakes.

The boy stands up in the boat. His eyes are rolled up in his head, which has thick organic cables coming out of it, like huge extruded arteries sprouting from the base of his skull and snaking down into the water.

The boy has a petit mal seizure. His mouth forms words in a flat, rasping voice, words gleaned from its slaves, and laid out like alien currency. *"Insane . . . animal . . . to fear change . . . so much . . . you choose . . . death . . ."*

Purcell puzzles over the labored string of speech. When he finally gets it, he has to laugh. "You didn't like that? You made those things, I hear. It doesn't follow directions too well, but it sure knows how to follow you, doesn't it?"

Sour lemon, toothache face. *"It . . . will . . . eat you . . . all . . . you will . . . pray . . . to me . . ."*

"Doubt it. See, we did for that sonofabitch, and we'll do for you, too."

Purcell looks back over his shoulder and sees the old man picking his way over the palisades of stone blocks, scanning the ground for something.

"You . . . are . . . a joke . . . on us," the boy-medium says, *"a mockery of us, a punishment for"*—seizing up as his master searches for the nearest word—*"our sins."*

The Old One has been here less than half an hour, and it's hotwired this boy, burning out or excising everything it doesn't need. Sweat blots his face and plasters his shirt to his heaving chest. Livid red rashes break out all over him, and Purcell's hands itch in his gloves as whatever the boy's secreting settles on him like toxic dewdrops and tries to get under his skin.

"We will repair . . . our garden . . ." The strain of translation, the insidious convolutions of five-lobed thought squashed through a meager bicameral brain, all but sends spurts of cerebrospinal fluid out the

boy's ears, but the Old One's adamantine arrogance comes through in Technicolor. *"We will correct . . . your mistakes . . ."*

Purcell feels cold, sticky tendrils worming into his brain. His hands go to his skull and he rolls reflexively into a fetal ball in the bottom of the boat. He feels nothing he can grab and tear out, yet they burrow deeper and deeper, turning memories to sludge. Retreating deep inside the panic room of his limbic system, he marvels at its abysmal cruelty.

It could have easily bridged their minds with its enormous psychic power, but instead it boldly rapes its victims and speaks through a meat puppet. He is unfit to look upon the royal visage, apparently, but the mailed fist of the master reaches out from behind the veil, *and I hope you can read this, fuck you, master—*

"*You . . . ally yourself . . . with . . . our ancient enemy . . . out of time . . . mind-stealers . . . they betray you . . . release the black devil . . . to cover the earth . . . clear the way . . . for their return . . .*"

A shower of temporal lobe electrical storms wracks Purcell with seizures, and images, like pirate TV broadcasts, burn into his optic nerves.

A cone-shaped creature towers over him, its peak a writhing nest of elephantine tentacles, each surmounted by an organ more ghastly and inexplicable than the last; pincers, fleshy trumpets, a tendril-dripping orb blistered with enormous eyes cold as dead gas giants, regarding him with the detached skepticism of the old man—

—And plunging into those inscrutable, unblinking eyes, Purcell is forced to glimpse the essential entity behind that impossibly bizarre form, before it recoils and retreats behind a psychic barrier and flees across eons of time to inhabit a massive, armored insect beneath a guttering, dying sun. For just as the creature he has allied himself with has left its body to meddle with the future, so do the self-proclaimed Great Race of Yith regularly migrate en masse to take over new host species, once they've reached a proper level of complexity. Species like humanity—

Purcell fights his way back to control over his body, wiping away ghost-webs from his face and brain. "You . . . you are all insane, alien fuckers . . . this isn't your goddamned world anymore!"

"In the fullness of time, all returns to us." The boy smiles and bites off the tip of his tongue. *"It . . . is destiny."*

Purcell's hands shake as if they want to choke him, but in the end he makes them work. "Let me show you something about destiny, kid."

He pulls the pins on all three grenades and drops them over the side so they tumble down the lines of all those cables from the kid's head.

The seizures come back, visions like tracer rounds ricocheting through his brain. He drops his helmet on the bottom of the boat and sits in it. The hull is no thicker than a Coke can.

The kid is jolted off his feet and yanked overboard by his puppet-strings, leaving only a string of bubbles.

Purcell screams in the grip of a psychic vise that cranks down on the three-pound glob of gray cells where he lives and keeps all his favorite shit, crushing him out of it like the juice from a grape.

He barely notices as the boat tilts and rolls back on a wave of white water, as chunks of shrapnel punch into the hull and the water parts before him, and the hellish siren sounds, and his body is doused with green-black blood and whipping winds from great, beating wings.

It has to take hold of his head and twist it, to make him look.

Somehow, he still expected something a little like himself. To find that the gods had not, in fact, shaped man in their own image is, beyond everything else he's had to cope with today, a rude awakening.

Its massive barrel-shaped body, dull, gunmetal gray, hovers just above the water. At once crude and sublime in its complexity, the creature is as bluntly simple as any reef-dwelling worm or hydra, and as elegantly evolved as an octopus or bird. Its lack of teeth or claws bespeaks a race that has never had to struggle against enemies, something built to rule over worlds and shape the raw stuff of life, never to flee from it.

Vast, corrugated wings batter the air like a drunken hummingbird; designed for marine navigation, or drifting on the solar winds in the deeps of space, they have to struggle to keep the cumbersome body aloft.

Questing, branching tendrils stretch out from its equator, palsied taproots rigid in accusation. At its nadir and apex, star-shaped clusters of flailing tentacles where feet and a head should be. Fluted, bell-like mouths emit a skirling frenzy of piping, while red globular eyes on plump, telescoping stalks swell and radiate imperial contempt, primordial outrage.

Purcell feels the full psychic focus of the creature gathering over him like ball lightning. His lungs go flat in his chest, and he can't make them draw another breath of the dank, almost-spent air tank. But he sees, at least, something that gives him comfort. The ridged, proto-animal body is pitted with fresh wounds oozing green-black ichor from the grenade shrapnel, and blurry rips in the membranous wings tear wider as it seeks to make its escape.

God's favorite monster or not, he hurt it.

The creature rises, eyes rolling eagerly on their stalks to take in his final gasp.

It was all for nothing, or almost nothing, but maybe he slowed it down; maybe he hurt it enough that someone else might stop it before it reclaims its garden . . .

And then a shadow blots out the sun.

It looks to Purcell as if a three-stage rocket is trying to land on the lake. Something enormous and wingless swoops down overhead and splits open down its warhead nose in a ragged, slavering mouth. With all its abominable, ill-gotten mass, the shoggoth has taken a page from the machines that almost destroyed it, and made of itself a cruise missile. And it has also learned from those it devoured, for the rippling flanks of its fuselage are studded with hundreds of human hands, fervently clasped in prayer.

Roaring on the cusp of a deafening sonic boom, the shoggoth slams into the Old One and drives it into the water. Purcell has a split-second to realize he's alone in his head when the tidal wave picks up the boat.

He grabs the gunwale and manages to hold on as the boat flies end over end across the lake. Weak as a landed catfish, his hands numb rubber, he sinks.

So fucking cold . . .

Glacier runoff is like hot chocolate with miniature marshmallows melting in it, compared to this shit. His skeleton wants out. His air tank is nearly exhausted; the mouthpiece clings to his lips, and his body armor drags him down like a magnet to the black bottom.

Weed-bearded pyramids rise up out of the murk. The water shivers with the roar and howl of primal battle. A seething storm of bubbles hides all but the bare outline of the combatants as they tear each other apart.

Purcell is still sinking, tearing at the zipper on his parka and the straps of his flak vest, thinking of his team falling out of the sky, killed by their own gear one fateful step into the mission. All but Purcell, because he was paranoid enough to pack his own chutes. Which earned him the right to die here instead.

The old man said he was from the past. His kind must have taken over human minds up and down the timeline, taking notes, keeping records, and meddling from one end of human history to the other. Tuning events to shape a desired future, where they, and not the Old Ones, and certainly not humankind, would rule the future.

So proud of their mastery over every particle, over minutiae, and making the same huge mistakes.

Lungs burning, arms and legs numb, he shucks the coat and the body armor and kicks for the surface.

Something shoots by his head in the dark, trailing bubbles and black sludge. A tentacle curls around him. He flaps his arms in the direction he thinks is up, because there are no bubbles coming out of his mask to follow, and it's smothering him like a rubber glove clamped over his mouth.

The tentacle clasps his torso, but the grip is flaccid, and as more of the limb floats by, he sees that it terminates in a shredded stump.

The shoggoth dwarfs its prey by countless orders of magnitude, its devastated body coiled tightly around the Old One; but its endlessly regenerating limbs wither or explode on contact.

Its rage boils the water. Purcell feels an awful toxic warmth, like a volcanic vent, suffuse the water. The Old One's gray hide seethes with caustic hormones, but its fate is sealed.

Metric tons of glutinous proto-flesh liquefy and slough off, but the sheer volume of the shoggoth crumples the Old One's rigid, star-faring thorax and rips off its delicate head. Cyclones of black-green blood and molten shoggoth tissue obscure the unholy vision.

Purcell remembers that he's drowning.

Tearing off his mask and clawing for the surface, he breaks through a curtain of black bubbles to blessed air and sunlight.

Purcell goes for the boat, flops into and almost capsizes it, when he hears something crackling over the roaring whirlpool roiling the lake.

On the far shore, the old man stands on a crooked battlement high over the water. In his hand he holds up a gray golf ball that emits a piercing Tesla-coil crackle and bathes him in a fitful, eerie gray-green light. For a moment, he almost looks ready to jump into the lake, but then he throws the ball into the water and falls to the ground.

Purcell stands up to shout at him when the dying combatants break the surface. The columns of spray around them turn to live steam as some kind of chain reaction liberates all the thermal and kinetic energy in the lake itself and sucks it clean out of the known universe, or into whatever the old man threw in the lake.

In a white-hot instant, the boat is stationary on a frosty, petrified Hokusai seascape broken up by a monolithic deadfall of gnarled ice sculptures. The frozen tin boat cracks under his boots, which must have insulated him from the reaction.

The wind falls still, and there is only the faint teeth-gritting sound of ice contracting. Purcell steps gingerly out of the boat and runs for the shore.

The old man waits for him, but he stares off at something thousands of miles away.

"What the hell was that?"

"The device with which I hoped to return home is designed to protect itself against violation by uninitiated hands." He looks at Purcell and tries to smile. "I violated it."

Purcell wants to sock the lunatic, but something else comes bugging him. "If you knew this was going to happen, why didn't you assholes just stop the goddamned mining company from digging it up?"

The old man steps out on the ice, looking oddly amused. His intact thumb and fingers snap in a spastic gesture that reminds Purcell of crab pincers. "We did not interfere any more than the mandate of history dictated we must. We knew the Old One would be revived, and how your leaders would respond, and how you would be betrayed. This man," he added, touching his chest, "was destined to host one of us at this time, to allow us to make imminent a desirable future."

"Desirable for whom?"

"This outcome was necessary, though the greater chain is not for my eyes, or yours. Something out of this day will build a bridge to that future."

"Even if it doesn't fix anything?"

The old man cocks his head, curiosity piqued, but he only nods.

"As with the Mayans, right? If you really could see the future, you must've known that trying to take them over would fail, but you had to do it anyway, because your *history* said so. You raised them up to be good hosts and then destroyed them. Or was that just a dry run, for tomorrow?"

The old man only smiles.

"That thing never messed with my head, did it? That was you, wasn't it, when it came out of the pit, and just now, out on the lake? Trying to take me over, because you thought you'd have a better shot, by yourself, in my body."

"You begin to comprehend," the old man laments. "But the connection is still broken. The future is still uncertain, and I cannot go home." He turns and points a pistol at Purcell's head. "Both of us were to die."

Purcell's jaw drops. *After all this shit—*

"This last is almost painful, as you describe the dissonant cognitive impulses you call emotion. I respect you, Lieutenant Purcell."

"That's cool, I respect you, too. Put down the gun." All on its own, Purcell's boot takes a tiny step closer to the old man.

"You understand better than many of your species how important it is to control one's environment, to leave nothing to chance."

Purcell puts his hands up, and now he lets himself shiver. "It's real cold, old man. You want to give me a blanket or something?"

The old man smiles his sad toothless smile and shoots Purcell in the chest. "In our history there were no survivors."

Purcell folds up on the shoreline, clutching his heart and trying to say, *"There was one—"*

"No, I'm sorry. There were none." The old man points the gun again. His hand is shaking. His body vibrates, and the breath from his cracked lips hardly fogs at all in the cold Andean evening breeze. "No bodies are ever recovered. Your name never surfaces in the records after this date."

When did the sun set? Purcell wonders. *When did it get so dark?*

"Wait! Wait . . ." Purcell's mind races ahead of his shallow breath, chasing its tail until it takes wing. "So my surviving the fall . . . was what fucked your history up?"

The old man nods.

"Everything since then has been a big surprise to you, then, huh?"

"When the Old One escaped the mine, I presented this place to it with my mind, but there was no predetermined outcome. The Old One or the shoggoth could have survived—or you. Any of these would select an unacceptable future."

"Old man, I've seen your future." Purcell's hand slides out of his wet fatigues with a cocked .45. "And you're not in it." He taps the old man twice in the face.

Purcell rolls onto his hip so the old man can see him, if there's still anyone home. He thumps his gut for the glazed, bloodshot eyes that stare at him down a vortex hundreds of millions of years deep. "Got it out of a German police catalog. Liquid polymer under-armor, for stopping armor-piercing rounds. Did you assholes really think I'd trust my life to one layer of carbon-fiber low-bid government-issue bullshit?"

The old man does not answer.

"You and those other alien assholes—and our assholes, too. You always make your weapons too smart."

Purcell has to sit back down quite urgently just now, because the bullet did break the skin and send his heart skipping, but the blood comes in rivulets, not geysers.

He ties it off, eats his fill from the old man's purse of coca leaves and packs the rest into his wound, hops in the jeep, and drives into an unacceptable outcome.

Lt. Keith "BS" Purcell never returned from the Gamma Red insertion.

Fair enough. With the fake passports and cash he took off his friends' bodies, he has eight new names and enough cash and gold coins for a lot of plane tickets.

Eight more lives. He can afford to be reckless.

Grinding Rock

One foot in the green, and one in the black, Tim Vowles kept telling himself, but the edge of the burn had got away from him. All he could see was black smoke and shadows, and the eye-frying orange and hungry red of the fire all around him.

A flaming jackrabbit bolted past, and Vowles reflexively smashed it with his shovel before he realized he should have chased it. The suffering bastards spread the fire like Roman candles, but they always knew the way out.

A minute ago, he'd been at the end of the twenty-man tool line with the other seasonal volunteer firefighters, cutting a fallback break in the dark, and the crew boss was saying everything was under control. The fire had nowhere to go, the evening breeze was driving it back on itself. But the wind changed and he straggled. When the next tool up shouted to keep his dime, he misunderstood and fell back even further, until the fire cut him off and he ran the wrong way, and now it had him.

The hundred-acre brushfire rallied on this patch of undeveloped land in the center of the country like a rogue cavalry unit, contained but hardly tamed. It broke his heart, the price the land paid for the stupidity of the people—but mostly because his own stupidity would probably kill him tonight.

Sweat broke out on his forehead and vaporized in the heat. He tied a dry bandana over his face and tried to get his bearings. To the east, the mountain had been gouged out by the Golden West Concrete quarry, and beyond that lay the Navy golf course and Vowles's own neighborhood. To the north, the ridge joined Mount Fortuna and the Mission Trails Regional Park. The city firefighters were up there, and helicopters had been dumping water and retardant on the park all afternoon. To the south, only a few hundred yards behind the fire line, the red tile roofs of Tierrasanta, upscale pseudo-villas and palatial townhouses, abutted the wild, tinder-dry brush, like an invitation to hell.

Vowles could see none of it.

He should at least have been able to see the lights of the fire engines or hear the call-outs and chainsaws of the tool line, but he got turned around by gusts of hot wind freighted with smoke so black, so thick, he felt hands shoving him. And now he was alone, with only the dancing dragon-shapes of fire to see by, and maybe the lights of his own house flickering in the smoke and roiling heat-haze like impossibly distant stars.

He barely heard his own shouting over the wind and roaring fire, but he heard the eerie howl of dogs quite clearly indeed, for it came from just behind him. Whirling and stumbling over beds of glowing coals, he fell down as if to beg for his life.

A pack of coyotes regarded him from a low rise that put them eye to yellow eye, tongues dangling, pelts black with soot. They howled again, and Vowles could hear other packs all down the canyon below picking up the demented, gibbering lament, and even neighborhood dogs joined in. His own Irish setter, Rusty, chained out in the backyard less than a mile from here, was probably adding his voice to the song of the pack that was about to eat his master.

And then, in mid-howl, they leapt at him. He ran screaming from the pack and into the heart of the fire.

He flew over the blasted moonscape, diving blindly through curtains of smoke and thorny blazing brush whipping at his face, but the pack gained on him and flanked to his right. To his left, where he thought the trucks had to be, pillars of flame lashed at the night, cutting off any hope of escape.

The ridge got steeper, studded with ash-dusted rocks and exploding barrel cacti, but a hollow opened up before him, an island of dense brush that the fire had miraculously passed over, so he ducked into it. The pack loped along the edge, then stopped and sat above him like a row of judges. They whined, but did not follow.

Flames paced the far rim, licking at the gutted carcass of a widowmaker tree. To linger here invited the fire to circle back and eat him alive, so Vowles ran until he stumbled upon a huge slab of granite.

He recognized it as one of the pitted grinding rocks scattered throughout the area, where local Mission Indians once made edible meal from oak acorns. The ancient bowls and gutters were furred with lichen and filled with beer bottle glass, and there were bodies laid out on the rock.

A vaguely human shape crouched over them, like another gnarled, lightning-blasted tree. Vowles walked around it, wiping the ash from his eyes, but he did not react at all when the shape uncurled itself to reach for the sky, and he heard it speak.

"Ai ch'ich ah N'Kai naguatl!" The guttural croak cut through the roar of the fire and the keening of the coyotes, creating a bubble of suffocating silence, which trapped Vowles like a fly in amber. *"Ai ch'ich iä Ubbo-Sathla ai shu-t'at ai'ul!"*

The leaden words hung in the air, heavier than the smoke. The speaker slammed some metal object into the stone, ringing it like a dull, gigantic bell, and beckoned to him. He only wanted to run, but his legs wouldn't move.

Coughing, hacking out strings of liquid smoke, the man on the rock asked, "Is it contained yet?"

The clear, comprehensible question broke the spell and brought his panic rushing back. "Does it look contained to you? What the hell are you doing out here?"

"I'm waiting, but I think it's too late. We can't wait any longer . . ."

The wind peeled away the seething clouds of smoke, but Vowles could make out no features of the cloaked figure propped on a wooden staff. The bodies laid out before him were painfully visible in the moonlight, the whiteness of their bare skin glowing like cold fire. A man and a woman lay entwined, naked and motionless on the granite altar. Seconds passed before he saw the tidal rise and fall of their chests. Asleep and pleasantly dreaming, as if they'd come out here to ball under the stars and nodded off in the middle of a brushfire.

"What did you do to them? Get away from there!" Vowles charged the man on the grinding rock, but the air was thick as Vaseline, and the hooded figure drove the iron-shod end of the staff into his shoulder before he saw it coming and drove him to his knees.

"I'm saving them," said the faceless man. "Touch me, and the fire will get us all."

Vowles threw himself against the staff, but he got no closer. "We have to get out of here."

"It will not come," the old man said, "while the fire burns." *Old,*

Vowles knew, for in the voice he heard the same exhaustion that dogged his father's voice, right before his last stroke. "And it must. This must be done."

"Wake them up, damn it! We can carry them out—"

"They're not going anywhere, and neither are we."

"Then we'll die! What the hell is wrong with you?"

"What's wrong," the old man clucked, and hacked out a bitter laugh. "I know the score, that's what's wrong with me. Did you think all this was free? The land demands a sacrifice."

Vowles had no weapons. He had dropped his shovel when he ran from the coyotes, which still sat and watched from the rim of the hollow. He was a part-time firefighter and a finish carpenter in the off-season, and they had never trained him to talk down psychos at Safety Academy. "Hey, mister, I don't want—"

"You don't want anyone to get hurt. Neither do I. Tomorrow a major earthquake, at least a 7.7, will *not* destroy most of San Diego and Orange County. Tens of thousands of people will *not* die, and millions will *not* lose their homes. Because of this—"

"You're trying to stop the Big One?" Vowles said the words with the skeptical unease of all native Californians shared for the prophecy that, one fine day, California would face the judgment of the angry gods of plate tectonics and slide into the sea. "There's no faultline within fifty miles of here."

"Not the Big One, but an age of Big Ones. The first cracks in the egg under our feet. It doesn't belong to us, nor do we belong to it."

Vowles still wasn't getting any closer. Pushing at the gelid air, he demanded, "Are you making this happen?"

"Does an antenna make music? There is power here, and it wants to be released.

"The Indians believed that on the day of creation, they were born out of the womb of the earth, but there were spirits in the land, those left behind.

"They are older than the world, but still unborn. They dream life into the world. They long to awaken and shake us off, but they may be tamed—"

The old man knelt before the naked bodies, crabbed hands basking in the residual heat of their embrace. "This is their wedding night."

Way out of his depth, Vowles tried to keep the man talking. "But why does anyone have to get hurt?"

"California was an Eden once—the people who lived here for ten thousand years never had to invent clothes or weapons or agriculture, but they knew the price. A tribe of shamans lived in this valley. They stole babies from the Kumeyaay bands to raise as their own, and every generation they sacrificed a man and a woman, and they lived in paradise until the white men came."

"Nobody remembers," the old man wheezed. "Nobody understands what has to be done. But some of us have been called.... We dream, and we remember—"

Vowles picked up a rock and cocked it behind his head. "Don't you touch them!"

"*I* won't," the old man said.

Beneath his feet, Vowles felt the ground crumble and run like an hourglass draining.

He threw the rock, watched it hang in the air as the ground itself reared up under his feet and tossed him aside. The arrested rock floated over a yawning hole in the earth.

Vowles rolled and jumped back against the wall of the hollow, his hands scratching for another rock.

"I wouldn't look if I were you," the old man shouted.

Vowles looked.

Something bubbled up out of the hole and exploded into the night sky, a column of rampant, liquid blackness against the fiery horizon. Even as it grew, it shivered with feverish desperation to take on a coherent shape. Crude attempts at eyes and mouths bloomed and dissolved all over it, whole faces popping out and then eating themselves in a shape-shifting totem pole of molten tar.

The human imperative to make order of chaos lured Vowles into staring, trying to make sense of it. Though it tried to mimic the men and the coyotes and the widowmaker tree and all the shapes that thrived and died on the earth, the black, unborn thing was made of the living earth itself. And it was clearly not even a *thing*, but the tiniest extremity of something unfathomably vast, like the egg tooth of a hatchling, cracking out of its shell.

Breaking like a wave over the grinding rock, the living earth undulated and churned, and when it rolled back, the bride and groom were gone. As it receded, the black tar grew arms and legs and torsos and wistfully caressed itself, melting male and female forms achieving oneness as it slithered out of sight.

The ground shuddered, settled, and sank. Vowles clawed at the wall of the hollow, kicked at sand sifting into the collapsing chasm. Cold sweat broke out all over his body as every knotted muscle in him abruptly gave out. Unnoticed, his bladder voided down his trembling leg and pooled in the depression where the long-ago thrown rock fell at his feet.

The old man slowly climbed down from the boulder, groaning, clinging for support to his staff.

Vowles rushed him again—no rock needed, his fists would do. "What the hell was that? You knew it was coming, didn't you? What was it . . . that . . . ate them—"

"I can't say if they're dead, or whether they're not better off down there." The old man took a step up the trail, seeming to shrivel and sicken, as he retreated from the rock. "That is where we came from, after all."

Vowles jumped after the old man, arms out to tackle him. A coyote hit him across his left shoulder and drove him to the ground. The pack closed in on him, yellow eyes lambent in the guttering firelight, whining under some invisible yoke as they herded him back until the old man climbed painfully out of the hollow.

"You won't get away with this—"

"No, son, I don't think I will." The old man threw back his hood. Shadows blotted his face, brittle and black and crumbling away from his skull when he moved. The face beneath the mask of ashes shone hideously in the moonlight, the sickly glitter of exposed, broiled muscle and charred bone. One eye fastened on Vowles while the other was a burst, weeping sac.

"Your kids go to school with my grandkids," the old man said. "We shop at the same supermarket, we rent movies from the same Blockbuster. In twenty years, when this has to be done again, praise God, I won't have to see it. But *you* . . . if you love this land—"

He vanished. The coyotes howled, and then they, too, were gone.

Vowles ran all the way to the firebreak, shattering blurred panes of orange and black as if he were leaping through stained-glass windows. He ran faster and more frantically than when he was being chased, because the sweat and urine soaking him turned to live steam and scalded him inside his Nomex safety gear.

Firefighters rushed him with blankets, wrestled him onto a gurney in the back of an ambulance, and cut off his clothes. He kept telling them he was fine, he felt great, he wanted to go home. They had to sedate him to make him see the blisters, like the yolks of hundreds of fried eggs, all over his body.

❊

They let Dana take him home after two, and he watched the rebroadcast of the eleven o'clock news in bed with a beer and a handful of prescription Motrin. He thought he saw himself among the tiny, desperate ants toiling on the ridge shot by the news chopper. The fire was ninety percent contained, but the cause was still unknown and chalked up to an act of God.

Vowles laughed at that, but then they showed more footage of the ridge, the fire and flashing lights the only features on a blackness that might have been the ocean, and the wink of unburned green brush with the white granite stone were laid bare under the searchlights. He cringed as he watched, for fear that the camera saw—

Saw what? What really happened? He told nobody what he saw. Nobody ever believed that kind of shit from somebody under anesthetic. He was still asking himself what he saw as he nodded off halfway through the lowlights of the Padres game, and each repetition took him further away from an answer.

The earthquake woke him up in the middle of the night. Before he could wake Dana or even look at the clock, he was falling through the floor, and the foundation split open in a jagged black mouth that swallowed the Vowles household.

He found himself jammed more or less upright between the hot, wounded rock walls of a new fault line. His wife and daughters screamed for him in the dark, and he screamed back for them to be calm. The earth shifted, flexing like the muscles of a jaw. Cyclopean molars gritted and ground his family's screams into inert slurping sounds, and now he only screamed to drown it out.

He heard and felt something above his head—purposeful, furious digging. He was going to be saved. He tried to shake free of the rock, but dirt tumbled into his face, choking him. He wriggled and got an arm free, and the debris dislodged by his arm showered his face, and he really did not want to be rescued, now—

For he was buried alive upside down, and the rescuer burrowing toward him like a bulldozer was coming for him *from underneath*—

❊

He woke up in the hospital. "It can't happen!" he screamed at the nurse trying to strap him down. "It can't happen! We stopped it—"

Dana jolted out of a chair beside the bed to take hold of his mummified arm. The nurse tried to give him something to calm him down, but Dana drove her away.

The news played on the TV bolted to the far wall.

Firefighters had discovered a body in the area cleared by the fire, and identified him as sixty-nine-year old Calvin Loomis, a retired U.S. Geological Survey engineer afflicted with Alzheimer's, missing from his home since he had wandered away two days ago. An old snapshot appeared on-screen: soft, sunny, Elmer Fudd features, white crew-cut hair, and freckled, ruddy skin. Vowles recognized the face; he'd seen it in the crowd in the opposing team's bleachers at one of his daughters' softball games.

The Caltech Seismological Laboratory reported a 2.4-magnitude seismic hiccup at eight thirty tonight, directly underneath central San Diego. The short violence of the spike, which the geologists explained as vertical realignment from very deep in the crust, had gone mostly unnoticed throughout the state. This kind of settling was actually beneficial, said the newscaster, beaming reassurance, and disproved outmoded doomsday scenarios about the Big One. The East Pacific Plate still pushed coastal California northward at a stately two inches per annum, but no ugly seismic surprises lay in store for the foreseeable future.

Not so lucky was some city in central Mexico, flattened and devoured by a 6.4 quake. He didn't catch the name of the vanished place—they might not even have said it—but three hundred were dead, thousands wounded, and another several hundred missing.

The volcano on the big island of Hawaii was acting up again, with lava flows causing the evacuation of guests at two imperiled hotels. China denied that an earthquake had killed hundreds at a labor camp in Mongolia.

There was something about a missing local newlywed couple, but already, when he recalled the image of those naked, slumbering bodies swallowed up by the living bowels of the earth, he saw it through a pixelated filter, with a news logo slapped on it, two more strangers dying. Strangers died every day—

It happened, he told himself. *You know it did.* The land took them. *It had to happen—what has to be done—*

He loved this city, this land, as much as anyone who lived there ever did. In twenty years, he would still live here, and his children would live here, and, God willing, they would raise children here, too.

And somebody would have to do something . . .

Rapture of the Deep

The old man tried to walk on his own as they lifted him off the chopper. They let him fall on his face, then dragged him off the helipad deck by his handcuffed wrists and drove him up the catwalk.

His mangled nose spewed blood over his mustachioed mouth, glazed eyes rolled back in his bald, heavily sedated head, but the image he sent her almost blinded her with its intensity. She shivered as the brilliant sunny day and the endless ocean vanished behind a wave of frigid white mind-noise.

Cold.

White cold. Snow flurries. Cold white and hot red splashing from his frostbitten hand, as he tries to get his black severed fingers from the wolves that haunt the perimeter of the gulag. The laughing guards, the long red wolf-tongues panting behind clouds of breath-mist . . .

And then—blackness. Total and crushing darkness. Buried alive under five miles of bone-chilling cold, sunless ocean.

She gagged on the flood of phantom sensation and clung to the railing as they carried him out of sight.

The message was clear. Their cruelty was amateurish, next to that of his old masters. An unaccustomed treat they would gorge themselves on until it made them sick.

He told her even more by assaulting her so, even as they led him down below the waterline to the interrogation cells. He was more powerful than even his old Soviet handlers had known—but maybe he could only do it when they hurt him.

Beside her, Roger Mankiw shook the crushed ice in his mojito and turned to look at her through green lenses. "You're afraid of him, Ingrid?"

Not half as afraid of him as you should be of me, she thought back, and he might have tasted the sting of it, even he, her skeptical boss. His reedy neck straightened. The sweat rings on his linen shirt deepened.

"He's capable, but he's a coward," she told him. "He's afraid of something he saw down there."

"He led us a merry chase, you know. Two contractors topped, untold collateral damage over there. Thailand's off-limits now. Our legal eagles are triple-billing us for—"

"Three."

"Pardon?"

"A contractor jumped out of the chopper, a half-hour out. Pulled his grenade pins and jumped. Sergei touched him, they say. Just once."

He didn't ask her how she knew. "Christ!" He tossed his drink over the side. The glass shattered on the lower railings of the research ship and dimpled the heaving sea. Some lucky fish got the bits of mint and ice. Some luckier fish in the indigo deeps far below would get the ones who ate the glass.

"I never signed on for any of this *One Step Beyond* shit," Mankiw growled. "The data show a steady warming trend with trace radioactivity that's sweeping the whole South Pacific starting right here, but I'd just as soon keep tossing five-million-dollar drone submersibles into the breach until the head office wises up and drops this entire idiotic venture."

Easy for him to say. He was vested, and would fail up the ladder to a corner office in Hong Kong. She would sink like a stone. "Roger, pressing with that kind of urgency sends the wrong message. Sergei will read it as weakness—"

"Then show none. If you don't get anything out of him now, I for one will go to the mat for you. But if he doesn't produce immediately, no more games. No more threats. One way or the other, he's going to the bottom of the Marianas Trench. Today."

She waited until he was lucid and beginning to show visible discomfort before she entered his cell. "Perhaps now, Sergei Vasilievich, you will take us a bit more seriously."

"This is why you did this? So I would respect you? I know a thing or two about torture. You could have asked me for advice . . ."

"We don't do torture, Sergei. We do negotiation. Nobody forced you to take our money. We only want what we paid for."

A fat girl, gobbling sweets and cake under a table at a wedding reception.

Sergei Lyubyenko reclined as much as his shackles and the bolted-down steel chair allowed, and slid his mangled, three-fingered hand out of its cuff. He flashed his sly, sorry grin, as if they'd both tried to flee, as if they'd been caught together, and would both be punished.

A gray-faced mastiff rolls in a laboratory cage, licking his prodigious cock and balls.

"I need your goodwill like my asshole needs a tongue," he finally replied. "I told you where to find the *Rybinsk* in less than an hour. I assumed our business was concluded. Was I wrong?"

The dog again, now busily devouring its own hind legs.

Ingrid pinched the bridge of her nose. She could smell the dog with the clarity of memory. "You described something else you saw while under hypnosis."

"Remote viewing is not hypnosis, but no matter. You got what you paid for. The *Rybinsk* is unrecoverable, yes? But you know exactly where she is. Now, I believe when I came in, I had a hat—"

"We paid you to remote view the wreck, but also the source of the unusual radiation signatures, and to find out what happened to the *Nereid* and *Triton 3* submersibles."

Sergei produced a pouch from his breast pocket and, using only one hand and his agile lips, rolled a scrawny cigarette. "You rose to this job not just for your good looks, yes? You are a sensitive, but your talents are unformed. They have never been *pushed* . . ." He waggled the cigarette at her. She lit it, hand shaky, flinching when he almost touched her.

"Sergei, my superiors are very disappointed in you and, to put it frankly, they're also highly dubious of your alleged abilities."

He smiled and shrugged. *President Nixon hunches over on the toilet aboard Air Force One, masturbating grimly into a Sears catalog.*

"Maybe you think that because you survived the KGB treatment, you're invincible and answerable to no one. But we are not a government. This is not a country. This is a private ship in international waters, over the deepest hole in the earth. And my superiors in Hong Kong, Moscow, and San Francisco may deal in shit most of them don't believe in, but they expect results. Whatever you think you've endured before, I can guarantee you it's nothing compared to what'll happen to you if you don't show us what we want to know."

Sergei yawned, exposing yellow but sturdy, straight teeth. "Do you know where I was going? I stopped in Bangkok—who would not?—but I was going back to Russia. If you truly know anything about me, think about that."

She nodded. When Sergei slipped the KGB and defected, they arrested his wife and two sons. Somewhere in that dizzying succession of premiers in the late '80s, they were all executed. They did this to make him come out into the South Pacific to view something they called Opaque Zone 38a, so they could drop a tactical nuclear weapon on it.

"Moscow is worse than ever, but is five time zones from nearest water." He sighed and rolled another smoke. "You were a very fat girl when young, yes, Ingrid? Nobody liked you or understood, but is clear to me."

"This is not getting us any closer to our objective, Sergei."

"You were not just piggy little girl, no. You thought if you ate faster, if you ate everything, you would grow up faster, not so? But you only grew fat."

Ingrid declined to play his game.

"It must eat at you, no?" he pressed. "To be unable to do this yourself. Such a fool, you actually want to do it, don't you?"

Her doctorate was in psychology, but her training as a remote observer required intense concentration on a host vector—the pair of eyes through which she would see whatever her handlers set as her objective. Her success rate was near perfect with targets she'd slept with.

Sergei was more properly classified as a projector. He could leave his body and roam freely on what mediums used to call the astral plane or the aether. He needed no prior contact with the target, nothing but a cigarette and his preposterous fee. His hit rate was legendary, before Opaque Zone 38a drove him insane.

He held out the cigarette for her to light. In the past, he would go into his trance after taking his first drag and rest his hand on the table before him with the lit cigarette gnawing away at the stained paper. In about seven minutes, the cigarette burned his fingers and jolted him awake. Back into his body.

She reached out with her Bic disposable lighter and lit the shaking cigarette. He took one hit off it and held the smoke in until the burst capillaries on his nose and cheeks flared deep violet. His frosty blue eyes sparkled at her, then went vague and rolled back under drooping lids.

Ingrid reached out and took the cigarette from his unfeeling fingers, stubbed it out on the table.

Now they would get to the bottom of this. He would not come back without answers.

His three-fingered hand shot out and seized her arm, pulling her across the table toward his empty face. His other arm snaked around her neck to cradle her head, and somehow she was powerless to push back or strike him.

When her body fell across the table and settled against Sergei, Ingrid was not inside it.

Everything goes blue.

A blue so pure and bright, she thinks, *he's taken my sight, I'm blind.*

Blue deepened to indigo as she began to understand that she was seeing all there was to see. When confronted by a featureless color field, the human eye tends to fill the void with visual hallucinations—the *ganzfeld* effect—but no optical illusions rose up out of the darkening blue, leaving her to conclude that she was not viewing this with her eyes.

Let us go and see, Sergei whispered, *let us go together.* She did not hear him or feel him—or anything else—but he was there. The only sensation she felt was a tugging that echoed his gnarled, nicotine-stained grip on her wrist, dragging her inexorably down into the void.

One time on assignment in Thailand, Ingrid got so stoned on opium that she felt as if she had tumbled out of her body. She saw her empty vessel on the silk pallet, drooling as the boy loaded another bolus of tarry resin into her bowl, and then the jumbled rooftops and skeins of wires and cables connecting every synapse of the city, and she was terrified beyond anything she had ever experienced before. She fought a raging riptide that tried to pull her up into the smoggy sky, battled back to her body to find herself shivering in a pool of cold urine as the boy and his family went through her pockets.

Sergei chuckled at her panic and offered her a body.

Through a pair of dead black eyes that perceived the ocean as layers of heat and gradients of food trails, she watched the light fail and felt the pressure build as their perfect cruise missile dove beyond the reach of the sun.

The rude nub of brain that housed them both was little more than a binary box flashing *eat/don't eat* as it scented trails of organic waste streaming away from the research ship.

You could learn to love life as a shark, I think, he thought at her. *I could leave you here—*

Sergei trampled the mako shark's hardwired instincts and drove it to descend ever deeper. The indigo zone gave way to a blue-black twilight, broken by the murky horizon of the ocean floor at the edge of the Marianas Trench. The sheer cliffs of slimy basalt tumbled away into perfect blackness.

The flow of water over their gills grew frigid and forced them back. Expelling the contents of its bowels and compressing its tissues with the agonizing relentlessness of a wringer, the shark struggled downward for another mile until the pressure crushed its cartilaginous skeleton.

Expelled out through the shark's collapsed eyes, she spilled helplessly down into almost total darkness that soon became a starry night sky filled with swooping, stalking, luminescent life.

An anglerfish drifted past, bloated black head bisected by a grin of needles painted eerie thallium green by the glow of its bobbing barbel lures. Other creatures she saw only by the fitful glow of their beguiling witch-lights, fluttering or skulking through the drifting sleet of organic debris from the surface.

Tiny jewels of glistering ectoplasm and endless garlands of stinging tendrils and greedy gullets seemed to pulsate with arousal at the passage of their bodiless ghosts, but the predators' attentions were diverted by the rich feast of the imploded shark's carcass that came tumbling after them.

It abruptly dawned upon her that, as a mote of pure intelligence, her senses were limited solely by her will. Whatever caught her mind's eye seemed to magnify itself until it loomed over her bodiless mind or engulfed her whole. And yet she was drawn inexorably downward, into zones of pure darkness and paralyzing cold, by the invisible grip of the mad Russian psychic.

Falling, flowing through the inky void, she still felt some inkling of the mounting pressure above them. Water is a thousand times denser than air, yet seawater is only one tenth as dense as lead. The pressure at their destination would exceed six tons per square inch. Exposed to this environment, her physical body would implode long before it could drown.

Ingrid was not claustrophobic, and as her instinctual fears for her body receded, she began to feel a kind of creeping exhilaration, the euphoria that submariners called the rapture of the deep. No human had ever been where they were going. No one had ever seen what they were going to see. Not like this.

The last fleeting traces of glowing marine life faded away far above, and the blackness again became absolute. Only by painful degrees did her mind begin to discern the deeper contours of tortured stone, little more solid than the water laying heavy upon them.

They touched down before a cathedral of bones—the skeleton of a whale, trailing tattered banners of putrefied blubber to feed swarms of gulper eels and dragonfish. Swarms of giant brittle stars squirmed and spawned in the calcareous ooze that coated the ocean floor.

How deep? she asked.

This is the bottom of your bottomless pit. We are nearly five miles beneath the surface. You are only a breath away from your body, but the mind plays tricks, yes? To return so quickly would kill us both.

Floating over a plain of basalt slabs fragmented into disturbingly tessellated geometrical patterns, they approached a towering column like a skyscraper volcano, easily twelve stories high.

Festooned with giant tubeworms and anemones that twisted in the gelid gloom to bask in the torrent of superheated water and clouds of molten minerals that gushed from its peak.

Swarms of enormous shrimp sported on the corona of the boiling outflow, only to be ensnared and devoured by monstrous arachnids, which farmed globules of cooling heavy metals, and bore them off across the plain, like leaf cutter ants harvesting fungi from carrion.

And beyond the chimney lay more chimneys, and larger ones. Hundreds of them, in a uniform field. A farm.

This was what they had really been sent to find, though Ingrid knew the company would lie to her as blithely as they'd deceived Sergei. The energy wasted here could power a city, if only they could harness it.

Beyond the last chimney, the plain was broken by dozens of octagonal pits, each hundreds of yards across, and seemingly bottomless.

But as she reluctantly floated over them, Ingrid perceived honeycombs of wormholes in the walls. Their hypnotic complexity suggested that they were inhabited by something utterly alien, yet older—and perhaps wiser—than humankind.

They live, Ingrid railed, *and they're still active, the ones you supposedly exterminated at Opaque Zone 38a?*

Men try to steal the power from their enemies by numbering them. Call it what it was, and what it will be again—R'lyeh.

Something gleamed in the nearest pit, and she warily reached down to focus on it. Massive metal hulks hung suspended over the void—the missing company submersibles, and the sunken Soviet sub. All were badly crushed, but also dismantled. *Rybinsk's* empty nuclear missile silos gaped like the holes in a toothless jaw.

The Russians said they destroyed them all, Ingrid railed.

Destroyed them! Girl, even if you could believe a Russian, never suppose that they can be destroyed. This is their world. We live in it only so long as they sleep.

Beyond the wells lay a hinterland of fluted lava spires and craters that might have covered a mile. They sped over it to stop suddenly at a gaping, glowing rift in the abyssal plain, which seemed to hold the sun in it.

No, my dear. All we did was wake them up . . .

Tornadoes of heavy black smoke roared up out of the spreading rift in the floor of the trench, which seemed far too hot for even the best-adapted inhabitants of the ocean floor. Slurping waves of fresh magma oozed up over the lips of the rift, melting the crust of Archaean basalt and remaking the earth's crust at the rate of a flood engulfing a levee.

This isn't natural, is it?

Everything is natural, you fool. Watch . . .

Something splashed in the white lava flow, lurched up out of the molten stone and thrust a net of barbed tentacles after her. She almost felt their razored heat until she was chilled by Sergei's intangible laughter.

It was at least as large as the biggest submersible in the company fleet, and resembled a fusion of trilobite and salamander with snarls of segmented tentacles for a head, but only the merest portion of it emerged from the rock-river before it sank again.

This is retaliation for what you did twenty years ago.

What we did, all those years ago, was done with your country's secret blessing. It was perhaps Soviet Russia's first and last true selfless act for the good of the world. To end the nightmares, yes? Or perhaps it was not so pure . . . Moscow could not imagine a world without itself at the helm. Perhaps they meant to rid the world of its nightmares by awakening the sleeper who sent them.

But it mattered not. The bomb hit its target, and the mission was a success, yes? And yet the one they sought to slay, they did not even disturb his sleep. His children . . . they are awake again, but they would not trifle in revenge upon insects.

Away across the seabed they flew, to the red mouth of the lava river. A glowing seam of fresh faultline sprouted from it and arrowed away across the plain. The cracked earth subsided like a misfit jigsaw puzzle, and eager gouts of magma bubbled up between the jagged edges.

At last they came upon a mountain that crawled across the murky plain, gouging open the earth's brittle crust with thousands of armored claws like steam shovels. Pitted with age and clotted with colorless, glowing coral reefs, infested by clouds of submarine parasites, its colossal, chitinous shell hid all but the countless antennae and eyestalks that emerged from seams, fissures, and faults in the Cyclopean exoskeleton.

The size of a city, the creature yet bore some kinship with the lava-borne larvae. In its wake, the mountainous isopod left glowing opals that bored into the splintered earth like depth charges, like the treasures carelessly spilled by a god, or the eggs sown by a devil.

There are no gods, as you mean it, Sergei interrupted. *There are those who dwell outside, and who neither live nor die, as we know of life and death. They answer prayers, but only when offered in blood and geometry, and their miracles—*

But if they're not gods, then they can be stopped.

Stopped! This is their world. It always was, and will be again. They do not seek our extinction, but only to hasten the day when the world will be ripe for their dominion, and His awakening. They redraw the faultlines of the ocean floor to drive the continents back beneath the waves and raise the Pacific seamounts to the sky, as it was when they came down from the stars.

But it's not their world, it's ours! We'll destroy them, or send them back where they came from—

If you could but see them, you would know how insane that is. And why should you care? In two thousand years their plans will bear fruit. In two hundred years the ice caps will melt and the ocean will rise and drown all human cities anyway. But this is not their concern—

Ingrid ripped free of Sergei and fled away across the shattered abyssal plain, back to the bottomless pits. Diving into an octagonal well, she made her focus into a sword that slashed at the darkness. Before she could find anything upon which to practice her attack, something found her and seized her in talons of icy, paralyzing pain.

A gargantuan humanoid form reached up out of the pit with mammoth forelimbs cloaked in crawling, viscous flesh, and unfurled vast black wings or outsized dorsal fins that effortlessly beat back the lead-dense water.

Trapped and suddenly feeling as corporeal as she was helpless, she cried out.

Sergei answered, instantly beside her as always, yet even he trembled in fear before her captor. *See!* he raved. *Behold what we hoped to destroy, and what you hope to plunder, and what will bury us all!*

It stretched out and nearly filled the vast pit, yet only the roughest outline of its titanic form could be picked out of the darkness, for its body was festooned with crinoids, clams, and tubeworm colonies. So glacially slow and deliberate were its movements that life thrived on it undisturbed; and yet now, it flew faster than she could perceive to draw her bodiless ghost up to its inscrutable, luminous eyes.

A rugose, boneless sac bearded with restless coiling tentacles, the creature's head was an octopoid of obscenely magnified proportions. There was no escaping those clutching, prescient tentacles or the piercing gaze of its hideously lambent eyes, which seemed to turn her mind inside out.

For all its awesome size and unfathomable intelligence, the godlike monster seemed to retreat into a fugue for an age of endless moments, until some decision was made.

What does it want? she demanded.

Suddenly the colossal prodigy bombarded her with convoluted psychic hymns. It sang to her of One older and more terrible than all its kind beneath the sea, the One who slept until the world was perfect, and of the rapture of His imminent return.

I am most disturbed to report, Sergei numbly sent, *that it wishes to . . . what is your word? Negotiate.*

What could such a creature want from her, that it could not simply take? Ingrid retreated into the innermost bolthole of herself and pulled the cerebral dirt in after her, but the psychic onslaught only redoubled as it sought to crush her with understanding.

What do they want?

They want to share their knowledge with the human race. For your benefit and theirs.

Why would they do this?

The power to harness the fire of the earth's core—they want you to have it. They have come to understand only dimly how quick, how fragile is the human mind, but how devastating the effects of its tiny genius. In human hands, that power will hasten their ends a hundredfold.

But why? Who would have given them such an idea?

I believe you *did, my dear . . .*

Ingrid feigned shock and let herself seem dead, until the tentacles and talons relaxed their grip. She pulled away and forced herself to visualize her body, miles above her, lying prone on the table in the holding cell on the research ship.

She willed herself across that distance instantly, as she would will herself out of a nightmare. For in the end, that was all this was. Sergei was a master manipulator. Somehow he got inside the minds of his mercenary captors and drove three of them to suicide. Surely he was trying to do the same to her, but she was not so powerless.

She opened her eyes, and the cell, dingy and too brightly lit, surrounded her. Her body hung heavy from her exhausted mind, an exquisite assembly of dead weight that trembled when she sought to draw in a breath of fresh air.

Her hands lay on the table, trapped in the scarred, stained hands of Sergei Lyubyenko. His eyes floated up behind drooping lids, regarding her with empty, bloodshot orbs.

Her arms dangled from her shoulders like concrete counterweights with the cables cut. She struggled to make her body move, to sever the contact from her that seemed to hold her still, that yet trapped a part of her beneath the sea.

Abruptly, Sergei's eyes opened impossibly wide and stared at her. An eerie, yellow-green light kindled within them and ate through the cornea and iris, spreading until his slack, waxen face gleamed like a torch blazed within it.

"*I will negotiate with your masters now,*" he said, with no trace of an accent, no scintilla of humanity.

Ingrid fought to free herself. She raked his hands with her nails and hurled herself back in her chair to sprawl across the uncarpeted steel floor. Sergei made no move to pursue her, but repeated his demand in the same flat, untenanted tone, as he shuffled toward the door.

Ingrid had to stop him. She had to get to Mankiw first and try to make him understand what they would be dealing with.

Her head boiled with the opening salvo of a five-alarm migraine. Her body resisted her best efforts to climb to her feet. The door swayed and rocked before her, but she was resolute, even if her body was not.

Blood dripped from both her nostrils, and her muscles began to ache, then to tear themselves apart. Her bowels and bladder explosively evacuated, and swelling bubbles of pure agony erupted in her belly and chest and every muscle, in the marrow of her bones, and in the pressurized cage of her skull.

She screamed, but she could hear only the teapot whistle of compressed gases pouring out of her burst eardrums, her tear ducts and sinuses, forcing its way out of her pores.

It made no difference that she had been sitting at the table with Sergei the entire time, or even if the entire jaunt was only a dream or a telepathic fantasy. *The mind plays tricks,* Sergei had said, and he was not lying.

The agony of explosive decompression swept aside all doubts and points of debate and devoured her whole. And still, she tried to stop them. Still, she tried to beat Sergei to the door.

She almost made it.

Her outstretched hands were blue-black with burst capillaries and liquefied muscle tissue. The steel mirror on the back of the sealed hatch showed her only a shapeless red collage, doubly filtered through the blood flooding her eyeballs. Her tongue swelled to fill her mouth and block her throat, but her brain exploded out her eye sockets before she could drown on the briny tide of her own fluids.

Ingrid flew away, taking the only escape left to her—out of her body and down into the dark to claim a sleek new body. And this time she felt no fear, for she was going home.

Inside Uncle Sid

Uncle Sid likes to gamble, but there is no question of his hopping a bus to Vegas or even the local Indian casinos, and money holds no real fascination for him anyway. So Dana accompanies him to the private storage places when they have auctions on abandoned lots.

If she helps load the junk into Sid's van, she can have her pick. Last month she found a mint run of the syndication LPs for the *Dr. Demento* show, from '74 to '79. But mostly she just likes to see Uncle Sid excited. Sometimes he gets so worked up, he almost talks in front of strangers.

Sid puts in a couple blind bids on spaces that afternoon, under a saggy canopy in the parking lot. Gray rain falls on the hot tarmac and turns to steam. The pavement glistens like spoiled whale blubber as they roll up the door on the lot that Uncle Sid won.

Three hundred bucks, and for what?

Sid picks up a rake and wades into waist-high drifts of loose trash, fast-food wrappers shredded to fine confetti, headed for a stack of stained cardboard cartons in the far corner. His big sneakered feet shuffle across the floor as if to ward off stingrays. A looming, alarmingly fat man, Sid looks like a giant, balding toddler when there's nothing to lend perspective.

Dana follows him into the storage space. Dark inside. Darker than shadows. Botanica candles, pillars of melted glass and ash everywhere. Sheet-metal walls black with scribbled arcana and overlapping, insane doodles and diagrams. Used-up Sharpies among the garbage like spent shell casings. Somebody spent a long time in here, hammering out their manifesto or masterpiece in pitch blackness. Not a word of it is legible.

The fetid air resists the stirring of the summer breeze. It reeks of ammonia and chemicals, the sour, musky tang of an animal burrow.

Dana thinks, *Crank kitchen.* Tweakers lost their apartment and tried to live in their storage space.

A few gawkers yawn and walk away, relieved they didn't fall for it. "Nothing in here but trash, Uncle Sid."

Lifting one of the cartons, he tears it open like a carelessly stuffed mummy. Books black with mold spill out. "Found a cherry '72 Husqvarna 250WR in a place over in Arcadia, once. There's bound to be something—"

Dana trips over something and stumbles into the trash. Her inhaled scream sucks plastic snowflakes down her throat.

Still talking about motorcycles, Uncle Sid stoops in the far corner. "Told you," he mutters.

Coughing up plastic, Dana feels for whatever she tripped on. Her hand gets mired in something slimy with broken sticks in it.

"Fuck a duck," Dana calls out, wiping black foulness on her jeans. "I think something died in here."

Uncle Sid doesn't turn around. He's found a bicycle, or what used to be a bicycle. "Schwinn Stratocruiser . . . '77, maybe '79. Not rideable, though."

Dana kicks away the trash around her until she can see what she's sitting in. A black puddle of ooze surrounds a partial skeleton like a long, coiled snake in a viscous black pool the size and rough shape of a dog or coyote. The head is missing. "Jesus, there's a dead dog in here."

Uncle Sid ignores her, and presently she comes over to see it. "Fucking tweakers wreck everything."

Every inch of the bicycle has been wrapped in layers of coathanger wire, and a bewildering array of odd metallic implements are jammed into the spokes, while a bunch of knives are wired onto the fork and the rear axle. Uncle Sid turns the pedals, and the wheels spin. The knives play the junk in the spokes like a music box. A jingling, liquid jumble of chimes like crickets and gamelan bells make the hairs on Dana's forearms stand on end.

"Weird," Dana says, "but it's all junk."

"It's still good," he says, like he says about everything. "Just needs to be fixed."

She kicks the ribcage of the dead dog and finds its head, nestled in the shriveled pouch of decayed bowel in the shallow basket of its pelvis. No sign of the legs or the tail. "C'mon, let's get the fuck out of here."

"Go get the dolly from the van."

"No way! This shit is worthless—it's just shit!"

"It's *my* shit. Go get the dolly."

She goes down the corridor inside to stay out of the rain. All the way to the van and back, Dana wonders if the freak who holed up in the storage space is still out there. Who could do something like that to a dog, even after it's dead?

Uncle Sid is still playing with the musical bike when she gets back. "I'm so hungry," he says, "I could eat my own head."

❊

Dana has been living with Uncle Sid for three months, since she split up with Tony. Mom offered to put her up in the game room, but Dana knew she didn't mean it. Besides, she counted getting away from her stepfather as one of her greatest life accomplishments, and isn't about to go back. Uncle Sid has a four-bedroom ranch house in the middle of a nice quiet neighborhood close to SDSU. And he says he lives alone.

Uncle Sid fits nine of the fifteen traits on the serial killer checklist. A big, shy loner who drives an ancient primer-gray Ford Econoline van, never been on a date, but a wizard with anything mechanical. Dana knows he would never hurt anyone. If he didn't kill Dana and her friend Julie Hess when he babysat them the night they egged the entire neighborhood from the roof of her house, he simply doesn't have violence in him.

Dana's mom never let her have boy toys, least of all guns. Uncle Sid once found her an old Mattel toy portable radio that transformed into an assault rifle at the flick of a switch. Boys were terrorized, Mom was none the wiser, and Uncle Sid became the keeper of all mysteries in Dana's world.

Mom says it's hereditary, the hoarding. Mom never kicked, she just turned it inside out. Throwing everything away that's not nailed down is how she gets her buzz, since she stopped drinking. Everything Dana owned before high school, Mom threw or gave away.

Sid cleaned all his shit out of a bedroom close to the front door. For a while, Dana relished the tacky bamboo bachelor pad furniture with bowling trophies and weird Shriners relics everywhere. In the yawning voids between sleep and looking for work, she could prowl the other rooms and excavate the lively strata of Uncle Sid's hoard.

The house is cool, cavernous mid-century modern, and would have fetched a million if Uncle Sid hadn't turned it into a junkyard. He inherited it from Grandma Ellen when she died last year. Her last tenant lived there for three years and somehow managed never to pay a dollar of rent. She'd always be out of town when Ellen sent Sid to collect. Mother said it was because Grandma Ellen had begun to lose her marbles, but Uncle Sid flatly insists the tenant was a witch. Bills still crowd the mailbox for her: DOLORES ZURBARAN. Uncle Sid keeps them in a box by the front door, but when he's not looking, Dana burns them.

At least four TVs in every room, only half in color, still wired to a massive Skymaster antenna like a pterosaur skeleton on the roof. Living the dream.

The big backyard was landscaped to dramatically emphasize a sunken patch of dull gray dirt where the lawn died and none of the watermelon seeds Dana planted ever sprouted. Uncle Sid said there used to be a swimming pool, but the witch filled it in. Dana lay down on the earth and pressed her ear to it once, imagining she heard the muted, mournful cry of a car horn.

To the casual observer, Uncle Sid might not seem to have any emotions at all. Dana's mother told her Sid stopped maturing inside at age seven, when his parents got divorced. Grandma Ellen married a sadistic merchant marine who terrorized Sid until he wet the bed, then made him wear his pajamas to school. Understandably, his emotional center packed up and moved off across a thousand miles of internal tundra from the nearest sensory input.

He might not seem to react to anything, but then a response will come like a cheapskate's telegraph message, so long after the fact or so beneath notice as to seem an unrelated tic. He is pathologically shy until he feels you were safe, and then he never stops talking—about the weather, about things on TV forty years ago, about some unlikely tangent of impossible local trivia banking off some casual thing you unwittingly said. Dana's earliest memories play to the monotonous narration of Uncle Sid explaining how Dr. Seuss and Raymond Chandler belonged to a secret society in La Jolla that sacrificed farm animals to keep something from dragging California into the Pacific.

Uncle Sid leaves her alone, fixing broken appliances and old motorcycles in the garage, or collating his treasures in one room or another, the crackly AM radio blaring Paul Harvey or *The Shadow* and *Inner Sanctum* reruns out of the intercom speakers throughout the house until dawn.

It's the world in purified microcosm. What could be more perfect? Who needs the thrift store when you can look under your bed and find mounds of exotic forgotten jetsam? Who needs the museum when there are closets filled with filthy Beardsley and Nagel prints and police mugshot albums? Who needs the library when she can find *The Hollow Earth Codex*, *The Secret Teachings of All Ages*, or *Phyllis Diller's Guide to Marriage* in the stack on the toilet tank? Whenever she's stoned and bored, she rummages in a random pile and turns up some awe-inspiring relic to cherish for a while, then sell on eBay. It's fun while it lasts, but after the dead-dog auction, Uncle Sid's collecting gets way out of hand. He starts collecting people.

❋

She wakes up to find a cross-eyed Vietnamese man standing in her room with his hat in his hand. His misaligned eyes, glassy with lust for her and/or the chintzy ceiling chandelier, flick away only when she covers herself. "Sorry . . . looking for bathroom."

Dana rolls out of bed and pats down the sheets for her smokes. Her baggy boxer shorts and holey Link Wray T-shirt smell musty, but she can't get to the washer in the garage anymore.

Sid was always an avid collector of everything, could only let something go if he knew it would be used and prized by someone else. He goes out early in the morning and often isn't back until dark, and Dana can only guess what he's up to. Haunting failed estate sales or haggling at the swap meet. Sid can't bring himself to look a stranger in the eye unless he's buying something. The tide of incoming junk has reached the ceiling in the living room, spilling over the breakfast bar and into the kitchen, where she found a wee gray mouse furiously treading water in the dishpan last night.

She doesn't mind the junk. But Sid's taken it too far, gone to war with open space with the mute stubbornness of a caterpillar building its cocoon. And almost every time he goes out, he comes back with somebody more broken than any of his junk.

Dana goes in the kitchen to make some waffles. Uncle Sid is on a barstool in a foxhole trenched out of his junk, reading *How to Read a Book* and eating ice cream. He squints owlishly at the book through a pair of granny bifocals for a minute, then tosses them in a bucket full of them, then tries another. He sits under one of Dana's favorite things, a gigantic black velvet portrait of a Mexican bandito with a gruesome scar deforming his face into a sleepy snarl.

Across from Sid is her least favorite thing, even though he could have been the model for the portrait. Sid's new friend Ricardo looks like a bandito gone to seed, with his graying Che mustache and blue bulldog jowls, and his scars. A Chilean Allende socialist, he was set on fire by Pinochet's Caravan of Death for breaking a curfew. He sensibly emigrated to America and became the laziest communist handyman in the free world. Except for his personal neatness fetish and his endless leftist lectures, he is perfect company for sedentary Sid.

"Mice in the kitchen again." She feeds some Eggo waffles into the toaster.

"You leave a mess, miss. You think you are aristocracy, but you must see someday that you are but another of the proletariat."

"You're wearing one of my shirts again. Did you get it out of the dryer?"

"From each according to his means, to each according to his needs!" He huffs and peels off the Amoeba Records shirt and flings it on the floor like a broken peace treaty.

Dana doesn't rise to the bait, so he retreats to cribbing notes in a legal pad. Against her will, Dana looks on, intrigued when he flips the pad over. The moldy book on his lap is from the storage space lot. It's very old, three columns of dense serif-crazy text per onionskin page, and in Spanish. Some of the words are spiky symbols, like spiders crushed into ink. The header reads LAS CANTATAS DEL DHOLEZ. *The songs of sadness?*

"Is that from the storage shitbox? Sure smells like it." Peeking over Ricardo's shoulder at the yellow notepad, a glimpse of his odd block script translation: THE SUN BENEATH THE SEA, THE GRAVE OF THE UNBORN ESCHATON, THE FROZEN FIRE OF CELESTIAL LARVAE—

Ricardo closes the book on the pad and tucks it into a pile of obsolete phone books under the table.

The thought of something Ricardo doesn't want to talk about *ad nauseam* piques her interest, but her wits are still dull. Her coffeemaker is filled with swamp-stinking herbal leaves. "What the fuck, Ricardo? You nationalized my coffeemaker?"

"Have some maté instead. It's good for all humanity."

Ricardo moved in two weeks ago. Uncle Sid cleared out the other three bedrooms for "guests," but he doesn't sleep in any of them himself. He sleeps—if and when he sleeps—in a Barcalounger in a bivouac in the family room, parked in front of three TVs, all tuned to the same channel. A huge Magnavox with the tube burned out provides the sound. A 20" Sony with a broken vertical hold flashes the color in a dizzying endless barrel roll, while a puny 10" black-and-white with a busted speaker shows a crystal-clear keyhole view of the program. Somehow, Sid prefers this to one functioning TV. Buying a new set is out of the question.

"Is that Asian guy moving in, too?"

"No, he just wants me to fix some stuff." Vague wave at an AKM assault rifle and a cheap gun show conversion kit on the counter.

"What about the bicycle? Did you fix it yet?"

"Not broken." Sid switches reading glasses again.

"Gonna strip it for parts?"

"It's not a bicycle."

"What is it, then?"

Sid just shrugs. Ricardo shows her an old *National Geographic* cover. An ugly lump of rust and coral from the bottom of the Aegean Sea. Weird gears embedded in the gnarled surface of some kind of elaborate, ancient machine. "I postulate that it's an Antikythera device. A great mystery of the ancient world."

"What's it for? Was it a clock?"

"More than likely, yes, but it could predict the alignments of the planets, eclipses and tide changes and perhaps much more."

"It couldn't be that great, if some tweakers in a storage space could make one."

"A mystery of the modern world."

After breakfast, she goes poking into the linen closets. One shelf is filled with slide projectors and carousels stuffed with strangers' decaying snapshots. In another, a trove of tape recorders, and in the back a massive Ampex reel-to-reel. The tape on it is a hypnotherapy session from 1978. A heavily drugged young woman with baroque mental problems starts talking about what causes earthquakes. She thinks the cause is her dead father, eating the earth. Not very interesting, but five minutes into it the shrink begins giving the patient oral sex. A hatbox filled with tapes in the same stabby writing, spanning decades. All with the same ending.

❃

Digging in the backyard a week later. Rosy dawn sunlight coaxes the lizards out of the mounds of broken ornamental brickwork to do their morning pushups. She counts at least five different varieties: skinks, swifts, alligator lizards, a pygmy iguana, and some kind of monitor fixedly watch her work.

The other bedrooms are filled, but she doesn't know how many people live here, now. Uncle Sid apparently has a girlfriend. She's not sure, but she thinks the White Man is living in the backyard. A filthy sleeping bag is rolled up among the pile of incomplete bicycles in the corner. When she comes out to make coffee in the morning, she sees him kneeling in prayer, hands outstretched to hug the fallow ground. He looks like a castaway: emaciated, with wild white hair and a Karl Marx beard. Has the hollow thousand-yard stare and leathery, freckled skin of the terminal homeless, but his white shirt and painter's pants are always spotless. He almost never comes in the house, but a lot of weird vitamins and nutritional supplements and unidentifiable fruits and vegetables turn up in the fridge. Plenty of room, since someone ate every crumb of her food. The White Man cooks all their meals. Dana claims a microwave and a mini-fridge from the garage. She eats alone in her room with the door locked.

White Man creeps her out, but she's afraid to ask Uncle Sid about him.

Afraid of Uncle Sid.

The junkpile has spilled out into the yard in robust ziggurats and dunes of debris. A key copier, a rusty Ditch Witch, and a spaghetti-mound of cracked PVC pipes cover Ricardo's aborted vegetable garden. She's digging in the dead gray dirt over the old swimming pool, a plot for a mix of wildflower seeds she found when the junk tide turned in the study, revealing antique, perhaps indigenous strata. The seeds are older than she is, but seeds are viable for centuries, Uncle Sid told her.

Ricardo patrols the yard, restless without his garden, picking up stones and stacking them in neat, knee-high columns around the perimeter.

Dana's shovel breaks through the rocky topsoil and stabs into damp, unyielding rust-red clay. She offers to let Ricardo plant his cabbages here, but he pointedly ignores her. Since Rhoda and the White Man moved in, Ricardo has acted as if he's sinking into senile dementia.

Her shovel skids off something hard in the ground. Plastic. Buried treasure. In a house stuffed to bursting with forgotten secrets, what would anybody see fit to bury?

Plunging her hands into the hole, she scoops out clods of noisome clay until she's uncovered the top of an old sun tea jar. *Lame,* she thinks, but keeps digging.

Caked with filth, the jar resists coming out of the soil. She scrapes away the clinging red clay from the clear plastic jar as she starts to try to unscrew the lid.

The jar shifts in her hands. The weight inside is solid, and it moves. She's sure of that, even after she drops it and lets out a little screaming giggle. Afraid to pick it up, she peers closely into its filthy contents.

Fur, feathers, scales, and chitinous exoskeletons press against the sides. As near as she can tell, it's a rat or a cat, a fish, a dove and a scorpion or lobster. Some kind of loony ritual burial that the witch left behind, or an exotic White Man delicacy: hobo roadkill kimchi.

"Put it back," Ricardo says. His shadow spills over her to leak into the hole in the ground.

"What is it?"

"Just . . . put it back… in the ground." Out of breath, or choking, holding a rock in his shaking hand as if he's about to throw it, or dash her brains out.

"Is it yours?"

"Put—it—back."

"Okay, Jeez . . ." Dropping the jar into the hole, she hastily buries it and drops the shovel.

"I'm scared, Ricardo." She waters the grave with her fat, helpless tears. "He's sick, and he doesn't know who his real friends are—"

"The world is too large, lady." Taking out a handkerchief to wipe his wire-rimmed spectacles, he looks around as if all this shit just dropped out of the clear blue sky. "He tries to make a smaller world, tries to become bigger, tries not to change. We all must become what the world makes of us. This place is a place of healing. What is broken will be mended. What was diseased will be devoured and made new."

"You're all talking like the White Man," she says. "Talking cult bullshit and tripping out on that stupid bicycle—"

A crow swoops down into the yard and tries to scoop up the iguana, but the lizard squirms in its talons and pins the bird to the ground.

Ricardo grabs her arm and lifts her up, too weak to hurt her. "Stay away from the device," he says. "It does not measure eclipses. It causes them. And *stop fucking with my fucking rocks!*"

She watches him over her shoulder as she retreats into the house, stamping on the filled grave and chanting under his breath as he begins to build another cairn of rocks.

It isn't until she gets back to her room, slams the door, looks out the window that she realizes the iguana isn't trying to escape the crow, but raping it.

❄

Of all Uncle Sid's recent acquisitions, Rhoda is the worst.

Sid talks about her as he never talks about anything. On and on about how she used to be a mud wrestler and an actress, but he can't name any of her films.

Dana wants to support Sid's fumbling attempt at normal manhood, but she just can't. Rhoda looks like something he built in the garage. Emaciated, wiry yellow limbs carelessly swathed in flaking crepe-paper skin, concave except for her absurd artificial breasts and collagen-injected lips. Odd ridges and veins of leaking silicone fan out from her bogus bosom like cybernetic leprosy. Bleach-blond fiberglass hair and eyes like runny, infected blue sores open so wide, you can see the holes in her wiffle-ball brain. Nervous system and liver shot to hell, yet she drinks more than she eats. Her Chihuahua barks incessantly and spite-pisses on anything Dana leaves outside her room. When Sid's not in the garage or in his recliner, bathed in the compound eye glow of his broken TVs, he sits in her room, basking in her wetbrain babble and turning the pedals of the musical bicycle.

Dana's in her room on the bed after midnight, watching cartoons and burning a bongload of anxiety medication. Headphones on and blasting African Head Charge, muddy tribal thunder that perfectly blots out the noise from the garage. She sets the bong on the nightstand and crushes a bug shaped like a silverfish, but it's purple and bigger than her ring finger. Gangly, multi-jointed legs twitch in perfect spasmodic counterpoint to her headphone music.

Her eyes won't focus, but when she closes them she feels as if she's falling into a bottomless pit lined with giant, grasping hands. Her TV shows a snowy closed-circuit vision of the garage.

Junk fills the room to the rafters, but a cluster of junk people—Sid's people—sit in a bowl-shaped trench, maybe ten of them packed in around the bicycle. Stark naked, sweaty and soft, like botched stuffed animals . . .

White Man turns the pedals, and they howl and gibber and hit themselves in time with the hypnotic gamelan polyrhythm. Like a sleepwalker, Ricardo scoops up trash with a shovel and feeds it to Uncle Sid.

Her uncle sits on a washing machine like a brazen idol, with his legs tucked out of sight under his elephantine belly. He is a baby again, huge wobbling head pressed against the rafters, mouth sagging ear to ear to accept the shovel, toothlessly gumming VHS cassettes, laundry detergent samples, broken computer keyboards and a Chihuahua with its bulbous head twisted off. Glowing with a sullen, molten orange light that burns brighter with each bite through folds of fat to reveal something inside like a fossil trapped in amber, or the ripening fetus in an egg held up to a candle.

Dana turns away and falls out of bed and reaches out to catch herself against a rack of antlers wrapped in cellophane. Rhoda's hips falter under her weight even as Dana recoils and trips on her bed.

"WHY ARE YOU SCREAMING MY NAME?" Rhoda shrieks in her face. Naked and shaking, she bursts into ammoniac tears and reaches out with curled, cracked nails. "Have you seen my dog?"

"Fuck off!" Dana shoves Rhoda away, and her hand glancingly touches her ridiculous fake tits. Hard as milk jugs filled with sand, they wriggle under her hand. A patch of jaundiced skin sloughs off under her fingernails.

Dr. Blythe comes in and takes Rhoda by the hand and leads her out like a half-empty helium balloon. Then he comes back into the bedroom and yanks Dana's headphones off.

Blythe looks uncannily like Richard Widmark, if he had a coke problem and a stroke. A once-respected psychiatrist, he used to treat all the socialite wives in La Jolla, but a motorcycle accident left him in a coma for a year. Ricardo says he still has metal in his head, so be gentle. Rhoda was one of his "secretaries," and he took care of her with steady pill prescriptions and a vodka IV drip, until she got too wasted to use for sex. Then he gave her to Sid.

He smiles at her, and it's like he's trying to use those old novelty chattering teeth for dentures. "I guess you think you're too c-c-cuh-cool to have any manners, but if you weren't om-nom-nom-nominally a girl, I'd chuck your ass out in the s-s-s-stuh-reet and stomp some man-nuh-ners—"

Long before he's finished the sentence, she's got her phone and an air rifle out. The Wrist Rocket slingshot with its leather pouch of steel ball bearings would be more effective, but nothing says *Get the fuck out* like a gun.

Blythe backs out, still smiling as if his teeth are trying to escape. "This is *His* house," he hisses, "and in His house nothing is wasted. Will you serve, or be swallowed?"

"I'm calling the cops," she snarls, backing him down the hallway to the garage. "What are you freeloading fuckers doing to my uncle?"

"Healing him," Blythe whispers, hands out to embrace her, pupils dilating to hold her in what he probably thinks is a hypnotic gaze. The hallway is lined with bookshelves and mildewed crates of comics, making the path too narrow to wriggle past him.

"I want to see him," she says. The White Man slips into the hall, blocking the garage doorway with his glistening nakedness.

"Soon," Blythe says, and behind her Ricardo pounces.

Dana screams. The air rifle is ripped away, the phone smashed to the floor. Thrashing under the moaning men, she claws at the bookshelves and they tumble to bury her like bricks closing over a sinkhole.

"The world is too big," says the White Man, "so we have remade it here, smaller and simpler. We are making ourselves pure, and anointing him to become what he will be, in the bosom of his family."

"I'm his family—"

"We are his *true* family. Closer than you . . ."

"Uncle Sid! Help me—"

"He will see you now," says the White Man, "but you will not see him." He raises a canvas Windmill Farms shopping bag and tries to slip it over her head.

Dana throws her head back to smash Ricardo's nose. He flails backwards and she turns and knocks him down and tramples him, racing for the door.

Blythe and the White Man run after her. She throws a hatrack and a bookshelf into her wake. They trip and fall, screaming her name.

In her room, she slams and locks the door, throws some clothes into a duffel bag, sobbing so hard she whistles.

She notices the neat cairn of rocks in the far corner of her room just before it shivers and falls apart.

Something heavy thuds into her door. The upper hinges groan and pop out of the frame.

Dana jumps backward, looking around, grabbing things in a panic: her alarm clock, her Bob's Big Boy coin bank, a fistful of CDs. She can go out the window, climb the pomegranate tree, and hop the wall, but she can hear them outside, lying in wait.

"Dana, come out, honey." Uncle Sid's voice, soft and ashamed of itself, comes through the door. She goes over and almost opens it, but she slips in a puddle of something viscous and cold seeping under the door. "It's okay, nobody's going to hurt you."

She wants to tell her uncle that she loves him and she's scared out of her mind, things are way too weird, but she just grabs her bag and jumps out the window.

"I don't want it to happen like this!" he calls out. "I don't want to go alone!"

She flies over the wall and across the neighbor's yard, then out into the street. Nobody's waiting for her, nobody pops up in the back seat of her car.

She starts the car and peels out and is on the freeway before she starts crying and realizes she has nowhere to go.

❁

Tony was ecstatic to see her for about two days. Mom had already filled her bedroom with all her husband's guns and survivalist bullshit. When she realizes her unemployment check has been sent to Uncle Sid's house, she breaks down and resolves to confront it with both eyes open.

She hasn't slept right all week. Dreams that only get worse when she tries to stay up. Buried alive in Uncle Sid's house. When she finally lets go, she realizes she's not going crazy. The nightmares came from him, trying to reach out to her. Begging her to come back.

The house is so white it glows in the starlight, as if it were sculpted out of ice cream, as if the moon shines on it alone, though tonight she heard on the news that the moon's light is doused by a penumbral lunar eclipse.

The pomegranate tree in the side yard is dead and slumped against the roof, as if something ate its roots. Six cars and a camper are parked in the horseshoe driveway. The little plot of ground where she planted zinnias and dahlias is covered by an overturned Jacuzzi.

She never should have left.

She feels a tug of shame that it's her money, her possessions—her own infertile cocoon—that dragged her back. If Uncle Sid wants to run a halfway house or a cult, that's his business.

They're taking advantage of him; she knows it. Poisoning him, maybe. But nobody lets anything happen to them that they don't really want...

She picks her way through the debris in the front yard, wondering why the neighbors haven't sicced the city on them. The porch light is off, but the faint witch-glow of many televisions plays on the few unblocked windows. The chocolate brown front door hangs open just a crack. She hesitates, thinking one more time about coming back with the cops.

It wasn't an accident, no, none of it. . . . The storage space he bought was registered to a *D. Zurbaran.* The White Man, Rhoda, Blythe, and Ricardo all came in hopes of being changed, or just helping Uncle Sid to become something to punish the world . . .

Sure, that makes sense. She kicks the door open and flips the light switch, but nothing happens. The darkness rustles and chitters, and she knows it isn't Rhoda's Chihuahua. How many more obsolete people has he taken in? How many are hiding in here amid the junk?

Her bedroom door won't open. Stuff piled to the ceiling against it spills around the door like an avalanche. The wall is soft and cold, like a dead man's love handles.

"No room, no room," the White Man says from behind her. She whirls around and brings up the gun—a real one, lifted from Stepdad's collection.

He laughs at the gun, scratching his long white beard. His eyes are black, all pupil from lid to lid. Steam or smoke leaks out of his tear ducts. "You don't belong here . . . but He wants you."

She smashes the gun into his face and screams for Uncle Sid. The White Man stumbles back into a pile of photo albums and football body armor that closes over him like a wave. He sinks into it and disappears.

Dana climbs over shifting hills and treacherous chasms to get to the living room and Uncle Sid's recliner.

All around her, the living junkpile rocks like the ocean, chewing its contents into a homogenous soup of dust and dead memory. A rogue wave breaks and spits the White Man out right in front of her. His spotless white painter's pants and T-shirt are dirty. His beard is black with slime.

"Never too late," he crows, and hurls a flickering TV. Hit on the head, the tube bursting like ball lightning in her face, she can't even find the floor . . . crushed, she can't move, can't even breathe . . .

"Take my hand, young lady," Ricardo rasps. She can't find him, but he pulls her out of the rubble.

"You're using him, you're making him crazy . . ."

"We're making him into a god," brays the White Man. "Come and see!"

"Where is he?"

Something drips on her . . . Ricardo's tears. "We buried him in the backyard."

This last brings her up short like a fist to the ear. "You killed him––!"

Ricardo says, "He's not dead . . . just buried."

"This house is an egg," says White Man, "a seed filled with all the nutrition he'll need to effect his final transformation."

"What did you do to him?"

"The Dholes that eateth the Earth like the worm gnaws the tooth . . . This world is sick, but He shall eat its disease . . ."

The light from the flickering TVs reveals what she's holding hands with. A huge, reticulated worm with the blind head and knurled, stunted limbs of a naked mole rat. Outsized teeth grate at one another in a nervous frenzy, as if they will grow together the moment it stops gnawing. The slavering jaws and dull, vestigial eye-spots twitch in some desperate imitation of a smile.

His voice like knives on whetstones, Ricardo pleads, "He needs you, Dana . . . needs us all . . . the world is wounded . . . its sickness must be devoured . . ."

Whatever he's become, she is sorry she has to shoot Ricardo. The junkpile heaves, and screeching cyclones of teeth burst out of the lard-soft walls.

Dana leaps and crawls for the door, but she's swimming upstream as the whole foundation gives way with a weary seismic moan. Cracks shoot up the walls. The ceiling sighs and comes crashing down in a drywall monsoon.

Dana leaps for the doorway, claws and teeth ripping out hair and raking her back, and everything is circling a vast yawning drain beneath the house, everything is going down into a mouth, and they want to take her with them. She crashes through the frosted glass of the atrium window and hits the overturned hot tub on all fours, but she never stops running until the ground beneath her feet ceases to rumble like an unquiet stomach mumbling her name.

❊

Nobody calls her, nobody comes looking. A sinkhole under a hoarder's house makes the end of the local news—water main draining into improperly filled-in swimming pool leads to tragedy, local man Sidney Swensen missing . . . neighbors called him a quiet man who lived alone and kept to himself . . .

For three days Dana tries not to sleep, but when she does, she sees the earth from space. When it passes in front of the sun, she sees through it like a candled egg and sees it is hollow and rife with colossal worms—no, one worm, coiled upon itself over and over, gorging itself on the molten mantle of the unbearably fragile earth.

She can live with it, even if she has the dream for the rest of her life. She will not let her possessions add up to more than will fit in a single suitcase. And if ever the stack of rocks in the corner of her room should happen to fall over, she will pack her suitcase and run until there is nowhere left to hide.

Archons

I've been in Iraq for almost three years before I finally see the enemy.

We're escorting a seven-truck Bechtel convoy to Ramadi when our point vehicle gets hit by an IED. The reflex is to lash out blindly and hope you hit the spotter, but the streets of this nameless, flyblown hellhole are deserted. Within a minute, shutters open and old men loiter and smoke. The locals must know nobody planted an IED on their main drag, but the stunt brings them out. Nobody can resist the sight of Americans bleeding in their street.

Charlie Toth lays me out on a stretcher and dumps a Ziploc bag of goat guts in my lap. Men circle around the smoking truck, trying to look distraught.

Hilario and Steve the Sissy carry the stretcher. Charlie lets Longinus off his leash. The mute pit bull squats and drops a two-kilo deuce on the highway, then runs grunting across the street to a deserted café. Charlie waves my bearers to follow him as he walks around the café to a stairway down to a basement door with a peeling painted sign: DR. ALI NADIR over swirls of Arabic and a crude caduceus. Longinus snarls and grins at the door. He'd be barking his ass off if he had vocal cords.

Charlie knocks and nods to me. I moan and cry out. Charlie demands medical attention for his friend in unaccented Bedouin cant. Hilario crawls over to a slit of a window in the cinderblock wall, flush with the street.

The door opens a crack and a badly burned boy tells us to go away. Hilario kicks in the window, drops a flash grenade into the basement. Charlie caps the boy and moves in, emptying his clip into the walls of the waiting room. Longinus eats my discarded guts off the stretcher.

We sweep the clinic in textbook kill-house mode. I top off two humans in the back room's makeshift surgery. A freshly dismantled cadaver on one table, a scatter of bloody steel on the other. A smear down the hall leads to a crawling, heavily sedated transplant patient.

I've seen photographs and fossils and skeletons, but a live specimen, even drugged and disfigured . . . it's hypnotic. It charms me.

Longinus barrels in and attacks it, ripping the transplanted human parts off its squirming, scaled body. A dead, bearded human face sutured to its endless neck opens blind eyes and silently moans *No,* but its real eyes—unblinking, molten gold—capture mine and plead for death.

"The Old Pretender," Charlie says. "Take a picture, it'll last longer."

I let my rifle drop on its sling.

"The laborer is worthy of his hire," Charlie says, and passes me the knife.

❖

I'm telling it out of order already, so you know what kind of witness you're dealing with. I was not an innocent bystander.

My daddy was a career platoon sergeant with the *th Battalion, *th Mobile Infantry until he got half his face blown off in Desert Storm and came back to become a prison guard at Vacaville. He was still gone almost all the time, so my mother decorated the house as she pleased.

My daddy hung only one picture anywhere in the house, in the spot he figured no woman had any business looking anyway: over the toilet tank, the framed page from some kind of illuminated manuscript, with words like tiny dead snakes. A naked maiden clinging to a tree—but when you looked closer, the tree was really a dragon or a worm, with a great, eyeless head and a circular mouth drooling on the girl's virginal body. And the fruit hanging from the "branches" of the tree were many, many suits of bloody, chewed-up armor. I asked him about it once, when he wasn't in a hitting mood, and he said he found it in the war. And then he said, "All those stories about heroes slaying monsters and saving princesses and all that . . . They're all lies made up by the monsters, son. That's how monsters get fed."

Just to show my dad I was harder than he ever was, I joined the

Marines as soon as I was old enough. Signed on for an eight-year hitch six months *before* 9-11. I went to Afghanistan long enough to get shot, rotated home long enough to get married and regret it, then went to Iraq. Three deployments and two more Purple Hearts later, I still thought I knew as much as anybody about why we were fighting this war, until January of 2004, when Corporal Leonard Prysocki sent me a packet of sorted jpegs of fresh snuffs right before he went to a storeroom in the Green Zone and blew his brains out.

Fuck Burger King and Rush Limbaugh on AFR and *Playboy* at the Wal-Mart PX; Prysocki was the real reason many more grunts didn't off themselves halfway through their first tour. As a junior quartermaster, he funneled more contraband into the Green Zone than all the private contractors combined, and most of the profits went to his fellow grunts in the form of ID numbers for online accounts, credits for video phone calls home, mp3's, bootleg TV shows, porn of both the stroke and snuff varieties, whatever guys needed to keep from going insane. I wish my motives were as pure as his. I made my side money moving his contraband through my unit. Way I felt about the war by then, I would've pushed heroin.

His message gave no clue he intended to check out. *Some choice bits for Name That Body Part, and some great cooze shots of land mine amputees from Mosul. Some really weird bonus shit ... Enjoy!* No sign that he'd had enough; no cry for help, unless trading snuff-snaps of spectacularly dead Iraqis qualified, and if it did, hardly any of us grunts could be trusted with a gun.

We kept only snaps of the enemy and occasional dipshit civilians who got caught in the crossfire, which we were told was always the enemy's fault. To kill them with a clean conscience, we had to hate them, and to hate them we had to believe it was not murder, but sacrifice. We had to do this, or we were damned.

The horror, madness, and waste disgusted us even more than it did the rest of the world. If only there was a purpose, a cause behind it all, even an evil one—that would be easier than facing the prospect that it was all some colossal mistake. The world that had demanded this now disowned it, hung it around our necks. Owning the violence, allowing the chaos into our hearts, seemed like a way of buying protection.

Guys in the Green Zone traded them like baseball cards to remind themselves of America's godlike might and the stakes of the great game. But for many of us out in Indian country, they were talismans—a way of telling Death to back off, you gave at the office. Guys who believed in it carried totems under their flak jackets, over their hearts. If you knew how to do it, they said, taking them and carrying them made you invisible to trouble. I don't know how else to describe it. I've seen guys wade into shitstorms of steel and never think about it then or after, but they're not just cool, they're *cold*. They *know* none of this will touch them, and it never does. If you were here, what wouldn't you do, just to know you'd survive?

The first set was a medley of choice cuts, human jigsaw pieces spread out on the pavement. If you had the stomach for it, *Name That Part* was actually rather diverting. Was this scorched gobbet of meat with a rind of gray skin and wispy black hairs a scrap of face, with a puckered mouth frozen in disgust? Or was it a center cut from the rump, and the pursed mouth a sphincter? Or was the ass/mouth enigma a red herring, a random bullet hole in some other part of the anatomy altogether?

As promised, a big batch of blown-off female limbs; *mors* and *amor* in one snap—nothing that ever won a Pulitzer or ran in *Playboy* could ever scratch the same itch. With all due respect to the proud but persecuted Iraqi people, their women have some of the most beautiful bodies of any women on earth. All you have to do to see one is blow her up.

The last batch was an assortment, but the ones that caught my curiosity were tagged *Templar Tribute*.

The snaps were from a routine checkpoint stop outside Karbala. A pickup truck turned into a cheese grater by 50-caliber interrogation filled the frames, the photographer zeroing in on the splattered driver and passenger, both in black burqas.

Handy pre-wrapped funeral shrouds split open, spilling loops of gray sausage—why did this shit always make me think of food? But in the midst of all that mutilated meat, a continuous, sinuous S-shape jutting out of the blasted torso like a coil of intestine, but much too fat, and almost black, and pebbled, shinier than the beads of tacky blood.

And the hip, laid bare by the leering soldier whose "Look, Ma!" face and name-patch I'd have to blur out, as he copped a feel. The leg is surprisingly intact, lean and supple but already turning blue. Follow the lush thigh up to the trunk, and the anticipated obtuse curve of ass cheek is nowhere to be seen. Instead, a ragged no-man's land of sutures and staples; the leg is grafted onto the black worm.

I stare and stare, as you have to, to see one of those stereogram things where the 3-D image swims up out of the cloud of meaningless dots, because you have to look until it means nothing, but it just gets worse. I can see four legs in the truck, and the left leg of the dead woman getting the glad hand of democracy is gnarled with scar tissue and bristly with hair—a man's leg. A soldier's leg.

Any answers the face could give are long gone. The dead "woman" is missing from the shoulders up. And on the seat behind the terrible absence, someone has used the blood to paint a crimson cross.

But what was the snake about? *Was* there a snake? And why did looking at it always make me hard?

❊

I'm working a checkpoint at Al-Anbar in April 2004. Tens of thousands of refugees with sick kids returning from Syria to find out the war's back on; thousands more in the northbound piled up for miles, hoping to escape.

Every ice cream truck could be a mobile bioweapon lab. I Corps said to expect doomsday weapons and Republican Guard sleeper agents. Searching cars and finding crappy old AK's in every grandmother's bindle, but nothing to explain why we're here. The checkpoint crosses a skinny bridge over the Wadi Hawran. Two LAV-25s flank the checkpoint. Me and a lance corporal get to toss the refugees' salads.

It's everything we ever dreamed about, playing with army men, until this chopper comes out of the south and touches down behind us. Out come three guys in black body armor, cowboy hats, and snakeskin boots. The leader comes up to me. I'm six one and I can't even see over this guy's chin.

"Do you boys even know what you're looking for?" He smiles and walks down the line and doesn't waste a breath answering our questions. "Helluva job you're doing. I'm here to help. C'mon, hombre . . . I wanna show you something."

Master Sergeant Weams calls Battalion HQ. I question the contractor with my rifle in his ear. "A few of these so-called refugees came up," he says, "from all the way out in the Arabian Empty Quarter. Saudis are finally cleaning up their backyard. But there's a nest of 'em somewhere right under our feet. Used to be a gigantic city right where we're standing, would you believe it?"

He walks over to a car filled with a miserable family—two women in hijab and a gaggle of children, no adult males. One of the women nurses a baby. "Perfect," he says. He sticks a fistful of fuel coupons in the woman's hand and shows her his pistol. She screams at him, but he says something short and sharp in Arabic that makes her hand the baby over without a word. The baby whimpers as he takes it from its mother, but when he cradles it and looks it in the eyes and says, "Hush now," it does.

He continues down the line of cars with the baby. His stooges walk behind him, carrying pistols. I leave the lance corporal and follow them, asking questions no one answers.

All at once, the baby convulses in his arm, wailing as if it's been dropped into ice water. The CO stops beside the driver's side window of a Soviet-surplus panel van. The driver is an ancient, toothless Bedouin who tries to give him a sad sack of coins. Cooing at the baby, the CO pulls the pin on a weird grenade and drops it in the driver's lap.

In the middle of the desert in the middle of the day, the light burns out my eyes, though the sound is little more than a fizzing sneeze. The driver is instantly cremated. The mercs shoot into the van until they empty their extended clips. I shout at them to stand down, but the CO's whisper stops them like it did the baby.

They open the back door. A red carpet of burqa shrouds strewn amid piles of shattered crates filled with smashed clay tablets and other stuff . . . old stuff I don't have words for.

The CO peeks under one corpse's veil, whistles, and snaps a couple pictures with a digital camera. "It's a fair cop." They toss grenades into the van and wave the rest of the traffic around the fire. The CO directs them with the baby on his arm.

No Iraqis get out of their cars to curse or shoot at us. They don't even look into the van as they pass. It's like I'm the only one who even saw it happen, or the only one ignorant of what it really was. I shout,

"What the fuck do you think this is, the fucking Crusades?"

The CO comes over and gets in my face. Sand blows in my eyes, but I can't look away, can't blink. "You see much action, out here?"

"No, sir." Marines don't wear their careers on their uniforms like the Army, but he reads me. "I'm on my third rotation. I was in Afghanistan before this, and I don't expect to go home before this is over."

"How many?" The look in his eye, the gravity of his stare, makes it impossible to misunderstand.

"Six confirmed, sir."

"How many do *you* know about?"

"More like sixteen." I just realize I've been calling this private contractor *sir*, and meaning it.

He looks at me as if he's going to ask a lot of hard questions, but then he just smiles. He already knows all the answers.

The baby cries out like before, and he ambles back to the car to return it. He hands me a card, says, "I'm Charlie Toth, brother. Look us up when you rotate home, if you want to make real money fighting the real war," then gets into his chopper and dusts off.

❄

You see enough dead bodies, you learn the secrets of life in death, the unfortunate revelations laid bare when you blow someone open on the street. A suicide bomber's dismembered torso, wrapped in Superman Underoos; the young woman in a burqa shot running from the checkpoint, who turns out to be a really unlucky transvestite smuggling ten pounds of Israeli Ecstasy. I didn't feel bad about posting the photos, because I thought they were offensive propaganda; they were pornography, but we never intended it to leak into civilian hands. Nobody should get to see the split wet goods who wasn't married to the business of making it.

Arabs and Persians had our weaknesses pegged ever since the Shah fell. The kidnappings and beheadings work our toddler's certainty that we must be special and safe, that Superman will save us. Our wrath is blind but absolute when we realize we're really helpless. They're driven to throw their lives away to serve something larger. We can't imagine anything larger than ourselves. God is on *our* side. Our God is the mirror.

Because Prysocki and I had no official contact, I steered clear and prayed that he'd kept my name off his hard drive for about twenty-four hours before I went looking for it. His footlocker and workstation had been cleared out, but I knew he'd be too paranoid to stash it where his CO could find it. I got the feeling Prysocki was a totally different person back in the States, where he managed a Goodyear Tire Center in Lansing. I found his laptop in a footlocker buried behind the barracks, under a pirate's horde of smokes and single-malt. I spread the booze around with orders to raise a toast to Prysocki, and took his laptop.

There was a lot of stuff he hadn't sent me.

Piles of burning bodies in the open desert, tangles of charcoal skeletons and a couple PFC's in gas masks holding car antennae out over the dying fire to roast marshmallows. A black, humping arch of bones stands up out of the mound, segmented vertebrae like an elongated spine, out of scale with the jumble of skulls and ribcages around it. The spine has a saurian elegance that reminds me of the fossils at the Natural History Museum in New York. They're burning dinosaurs.

There was something deeply wrong about it, but it wasn't just the spine, which might have been a length of cable or a melted tank tread, for all I knew. The bodies could be anybody, but they must have deserved what they got. We did a lot of shit you don't want to know about, but we were the good guys; we sent our dead home, postage due.

The other things: stuff he'd held back because he apparently had some vestigial stub of a conscience. Kids, skeletal and jaundiced from a short lifetime huffing industrial solvents, laid out on the street by armor-piercing rifle rounds, their bellies slit open like dissected frogs. FUCKER STOLE MY WALLET was the title of one layout; my favorite said JUST SAY NO TO BULLETS.

The text stuff that came with Prysocki's stash hinted at something more than just survival. It hinted at a reason for all of it. It wasn't a Bible, but it told me just enough to send me to the right men with the right questions, about the Templars, the Assassins and the Archons. Until Prysocki, nobody for a thousand years had tried to write any of it down without getting their throat cut.

The smart man leaves well enough alone, and that's exactly what I did. Defense Intelligence and CIA came around looking for Prysocki's friends. They only missed me because in May of 2004, I got kidnapped.

The assignment stank, but it was chopped from Centcom, so I would get worse than a nosebleed if I tried to get over it.

I didn't go outside. I had done and given much to keep it so. So it was clear somebody up there had a hard-on for me, when I got orders to go out with a phone repair crew. I was walking wounded, so I pulled guard duty.

I lost a staring contest with two other grunts while some pencil-neck contractors set up a hard line in a police station to liaise directly with Centcom and the British command in Basra. It took about an hour to get a ping from the network. When I went outside, the cars were gone.

Dust devils gamboled down the street. A kid on a moped flipped me the bird. A line of sullen Iraqis went around the building; cops waiting to get paid. I turned to go back inside when two men stepped out of line and put a bag over my head.

A Taser zapped my neck as a truncheon smashed into my crotch, doubling me over someone's shoulder. I threw up into the bag. I tripped over my own rifle and fell onto the floor of an old Volkswagen bus, which I knew from the sputtering engine sound as it pulled away from the curb.

Someone knelt on my back and zip-tied my wrists. Someone else went through my pockets, and a third ripped the bag off my head so I didn't drown.

I could only see the floor in front of me, the driver's foot on the gas pedal, and the feet of a passenger poised to kick me in the face. Both of them wore snakeskin cowboy boots.

I was treated to a clean, fresh hood and injected with something. In less than three breaths, I was paralyzed.

This is all I remember.

I died, and I went to hell. I fought for my life and killed something and drank its blood, and was allowed to return to the land of the living.

When I was found outside the Green Zone four days later, I was dressed in Bedouin rags and raving nonsense nobody could identify. I was debriefed and held for observation for another week, then flown home on special medical leave. Nobody explained to me what the fuck was going on. I'd been wounded three times in four deployments, and couldn't get out of the war.

Nobody noticed my new tattoo. Lots of guys have crosses tattooed on their body for the same reasons other guys carry totems. It's a red cross, with the initials P.A. on a scroll, instead of INRI. Maybe they thought it was mine, though God knows why anyone would want to get a cross tattooed on the sole of their foot.

When I got back, Bridget had already moved off base. She met me at the gate, clung to me like napalm jelly until we fucked in the airport parking lot, then twice more that day. I'd been about to ask for a divorce. I thought she'd really missed me.

I had received a full discharge. I stayed home long enough to be told I'd gotten Bridget pregnant, then I received word that I was going to work for Archon Security.

I didn't go back because I loved it, or because there was nothing to do in the States. I went back because I felt safer in Iraq. In two years on the ground in Iraq and Afghanistan, Archon had not lost a single man.

All I know is, they worked for me. They made the war so safe that I stopped waiting for someone to kill me. I almost stopped wanting it to be over.

❧

"We're a new company," Charlie Toth tells me, "but we've got our shit wired down tight." Archon has a trailer in the Green Zone, but their operational HQ is near the airport.

Archon is a third-string subcontractor, providing backup security for contractors' convoys and lesser lights of the CPA when they leave the Green Zone. Archon is a private LLC owned by a shell company called the Azoth Group. Nobody knows how many other franchises Archon has in-country, or how long the company's even existed, or who pays their bills. With cowboys, thieves, and hothead pricks like Custer Battles and Blackwater hogging the limelight, we are invisible.

The HQ isn't like the Arabian Nights harems the CPA holes up in, but a fortified hangar filled with trailers, Humvees and a small fleet of up-armored South African Mambas. It isn't a set-piece staged to convince pencil-neck reporters of the seriousness of our campaign. Absent any flags, any idealism, any spin, it is where the real war is being fought.

I meet the other guys on my new squad. Guy Hurlburt and Hilario Labrador are ex-Army pukes, from Rangers and SF. Steve the Sissy (who isn't) and Jean Balance (who most emphatically is) both came over from the French Foreign Legion. Jack the Mole is the ex-SAS chief operations officer, running a company-level comms center and our satphone network off two laptops. Charlie's boss, a dead-eyed spook named Kincaid, drops off hard-copy mission materials fresh from Mount Olympus every morning.

I tap my heel against my hand. "So what does P.A. stand for?"

"Proeliator Aeternus," Toth says. "The eternal warrior."

He lights a candle and leads me into a windowless trailer choked with incense. Statues and clay tablets piled to the low ceiling. "Our first job in Iraq was to sack the museums in Baghdad," he says. "Saddam was sitting on vaults full of Sumerian and Babylonian shit that . . . we did the world a favor by taking it. And then we found some stuff that belonged to us."

He takes out a stiff broadcloth rag and unrolls it on top of a crate. Under centuries of filth, it's a white tabard with a big red cross on it. "OK," Toth smiles. "Maybe we're not such a new company..."

Archon's spiritual roots as a fighting unit go back to the Templars, but the Crusades were the last time they were allowed to openly fight a true, pure ritual war. Their cause was as old as war itself, as old as the kinship of the sword. He tells me this shit as if I already believe in it.

"Put yourself in the Templars' shoes for a minute," he says. "You're tasked with holding Jerusalem and Christian Syria against the Turks—a fool's errand, even with papal support, and the Pope don't care about you no more, not with his own private wars in Italy.

"They were accused of conspiring with the Hashishim to sell out the Holy Land, but why would they do that? They had no desire to die for a mistake. They knew God had turned His back on their cause, and Europe's perfumed princes were looking to gut them and take their lands. Why did they try to hold the Holy Land at all?

"They were looking for the truth, for a light at the end of the tunnel that justified all the failed campaigns, and in their darkest hour it found them and lifted them up. It gave them the only things a soldier needs: security and payback.

"But it also showed them the glorious pattern in the chaos. When they went to fight a war for a God who forsook them, they found a god who *did* answer their prayers—a god for whom warfare *is* worship—and they were rewarded in this world and the next."

As epic of a goat-rope as the Crusades were, the Templars knew that it afforded them the chance to strike at a greater enemy: the original adversary of all mankind.

Was it just coincidence that the first cities, the first written languages, and the first organized religions and laws and currency had all sprung out of the Fertile Crescent? And all the trouble in the world since? The Bible was a load of old shit, but this much was true. Somewhere in Iraq, humankind had fallen from grace, its perfect animal nature perverted by a serpent.

He rolls up the tabard and opens the crate, revealing a glass case with a fossil embedded in green sedimentary rock. It looks like the skull of a dinosaur, but with a bigger dome and serrated fangs. Each eye socket is big enough to fit a fist, and its tapered brainpan is almost human-sized.

"You've seen them," Charlie tells me. "That's why you're here."

Behind the sham war to protect the Holy Land for the second coming of Christ, the Templars were charged with rooting out the last traces of the ancient adversary, as well as the Ophites—misguided heathens who worshipped them. But the Crusaders were driven out of the Holy Land, and never cleansed Arabia or Iraq. Was it any coincidence that their failure to fulfill their mission was followed by their unmasking as heretics? But Toth smugly adds that even then, their god did not desert them. Europe paid for burning the servants of Baphomet when the Black Plague came.

"This is our war." He shows me a black figurine carved out of obsidian, a soldier's snuff totem from a Bronze Age battlefield shrine: a bearded man with a pharaoh's crown stands upon the neck of a giant serpent, driving his spear through its eye. "This is why we're here, boy. To slay the last of the dragons."

Archon was the for-profit arm of a secret society whose name even Toth did not know. Powerful people in the military and the private sector had worked to give them this opportunity. Contracted to provide security for convoys throughout Iraq, we had carte blanche to search the country for relics and fugitive pockets of the Enemy. Toth cut his teeth with a Delta Force unit that discovered and called an all-day air strike on a ruined city in the Empty Quarter of Saudi during Desert Shield, and still lost three recon squads in it.

"They're older than the dinosaurs, and they know the world has left them behind, but they're the rot at the heart of all nations, the fetish for bullshit complexity that lets the weak rule over the strong. They want us to become like them. They have only to offer us another apple, and they'll push us over the edge."

It didn't matter whether I believed it or not. Right away, I decided that Charlie Toth and his whole company were batshit insane. But I had been set free. No more Rules of Engagement. No more Uniform Code of Military Justice. No more nightmares.

When I was a kid, playing war was only really satisfying when the enemy was something less or more than human. Then you could burn its nests and kill its larvae and cuss it out without hurting anybody's feelings. Then I got to fight in a real war, and discovered the joys of serving as an infinitesimal cell in a blind idiot god that kills more of its own than the enemy can. I learned that this was not a bug, but a feature, and the reason for it all.

War without end, amen.

❋

Pay is five times what I made in the Marines, almost a brigadier general's salary in Kuwaiti cash at the end of each month. Full medical benefits for Bridget and the baby. I can go home for two weeks every three months, or pull down bonus time for waiving my leave. And there's always something to do.

No hearts and minds bullshit, no wondering what we're doing over here. We are kicking ass and getting paid, and if I decide I don't like it, I have a ticket to the world in my bag, redeemable on twelve hours' notice.

I never want to go home.

In between daily escort missions, we do two or three wetwork runs each week. Two-thirds of our intel turns up Shiite or Sunni militia cells, or nothing at all. Ophites don't use the Internet or phones, and none of the cracked cells give up intel on the others.

We hit safehouses in the Sadr slums and mud-brick bunkers in the deep desert of Al-Muthanna. The resistance ranges from pathetic to non-existent. We kill everything we see and take everything we don't burn. We're careful to make our products look like insurgent vendettas.

Ophites are fanatical, but hardly warlike. One and all, they are like sleepwalkers when we knock down their doors. Looking up from their weird astrological diagrams and picking up guns only to hasten the end, as if it's all been foretold. Dismay, but never surprise or fear.

It would make me begin to wonder what we were doing, if not for that one I saw in the clinic. I would still have to ask myself if our cause was not righteous, if not for the power that flowed into me when I took its life.

They seem to hate guns more than liberals, but they are hardly harmless. Hurlburt shows me a leather scroll covered in concentric circle diagrams and tells me it's a fifty-thousand-year-old instruction for how to make an atomic bomb. "This is trivia," he sneers. "We're still looking for the Holy Grail."

When the trail goes cold, we convoy out to empty coordinates in the sandy sea and dig up unmarked mass graves. Some are recent enough to have CPA dental work in their teeth. Others are dust and bits of bone and bronze and coins older than Christ. I wonder what jokes they tell each other down in the earth that make them all smile the way they do. Without knowing what we're looking for, we count and measure skulls and incinerate the remains.

Before every mission, we stand in a circle and silently pray. Everyone touches their snuff totem with one hand and the black statuette with the other as they pass out the door. For luck. Sometimes the idol is a cat, sometimes a bearded man's head or a faceless sphinx, sometimes a phallus with an eye in its meatus.

You don't have to believe in it, we are told. *Just let it believe in you.*

I believe. I really do. For eight months.

❋

When the chopper lands I don't know if we're in Iraq or Syria. I haven't slept in forty-eight hours, during which time our franchise has pulled down three raids. It's Krystallnacht for snake-handlers. I'm ghosting on speed-fumes and muscle memory. My forebrain dreams and forgets, but the reptilian midbrain never gets tired of fighting.

Over the dunes a hundred miles from anything, half-buried in powdered sugar sand, the eroded stairway to nowhere of a ziggurat, five stories high. A few sandbags around the unlit entrance mark a machine-gun emplacement. The chopper circles and spews white phosphorus sunlight on their heads. We don't encounter anything more threatening than the smell of burnt bacon until we get inside.

Two irregulars in the narrow entrance empty their guns at us as if they're blindfolded. Labrador strides into the antechamber as though it's his own living room and caps them both with a pistol. "This is getting boring, man," he says.

Things get more interesting around the next corner. Labrador finds a grenade embedded in the wall. He pulls the tripwire out, and almost immediately his hand goes numb and bloats like a boxing glove. He rubs his eyes and shoves me away from him when I try to stop him spreading it. "Just go find me a snake." Pointing at me with his knife, as his eyes swell shut.

I tiptoe, watching for more tripwires. I come out into a huge crypt with bas-relief walls. I don't know whether to laugh or cry, but I want to kiss myself.

We found the Weapons of Mass Destruction.

Shelves and safes and carts strain to hold the overflowing stockpile. Microfiche cards and obsolete hard drives; books, typewritten and illuminated manuscripts, vellum and papyrus scrolls; clay tablets and flimsy triangular wafers of blue metal with tiny swirling grooves in them eons older than anything humans have made.

Growing up, I always hated books. Hated how they never told me anything that could save me from becoming what I was.

Circling the drain for a hundred million years, and this was the sum total of all that they knew. This was all they had left. A tomb filled with shit the world was better off not knowing.

In places like this, the Irish saved the core of Western science and literature from the Vikings, Saracens, and Vandals. What were they saving? Who were they saving it for? The real secret we had to protect the world from was that everything we know was stolen from the ruins of something else that came before. Maybe when they're finally gone and forgotten, we can start over.

One skinny, four-eyed old man stands up to me with an old AK that isn't going to fire, even if he finds the trigger. "Put down the gun," I tell him, as I point mine at his face. I want to talk to him, tell him to run, but Balance is coming, and he is in a lather.

"Who is behind you? In whose name do you do this?" His accent is thick, but not Arabic. It's so sad you have to laugh, how he can't make the gun work. "I cannot allow you to take the last of the library . . ." His breath smells like cinnamon.

"We didn't come to take it." I shoot the librarian twice in the head. Balance slides up behind me and snaps the picture.

We slap C-4 bricks on the corners and lay det cords up the aisles and into tunnels and galleries that keep splitting off the main crypt. Incredible, this was the only thing they seemed willing to fight for…

I pay out my cord into the farthest dead-end tunnel and spike my last brick. There's a huge wicker basket in the shadow of the acute angle of the chamber. In sort of a mood, I kick it over. A mound of black coils stirs and stares at me.

A serpent head rises up out of the snarl of coils, bigger than a river croc's skull, and already half-fossilized. Its scales are azure and black and long like rigid feathers. Its half-shuttered eyes are clouded, but the slitted irises narrow and glow as they focus on me.

It rises until those eyes are level with mine, and still the nest of coils pays out. At least two pairs of arms but no legs; feeble, fragile, almost vestigial things once graceful and strong, but withering away, given up as a bad idea.

Another head, smaller and younger than the first, darts out and hisses at me. I back away as they throttle and bite each other. Except for some labored wheezing and the rasping of scales, they are completely silent. The coils spill out of the basket and onto the dirt floor, and I see that they are a single snake.

"The Greeks had such a monster in their stories," Balance tells me.

"A serpent with a head at either end, an amphisbaena." He lights a cigarette. "Tail was probably severed or crushed, eh? It's not supposed to grow back like that, but it happens."

It doesn't try to kill us. It doesn't try to escape. It just studies us with unblinking golden eyes, sending its wise and venerable thoughts about the interconnectedness of all living things to a pair of dumb mammals who can't understand a word of it.

Balance draws his finishing blade, a *wakizashi* so hard and sharp I've seen it cut a rifle in half lengthwise. Before I can tell him *no,* both heads are lopped off, gasping like landed catfish at our feet.

Balance sinks to his knees, breathing hard. It's like an orgasm in reverse. He pushes me away when I try to help him up. "Burn it. We must away." He turns and staggers down the aisle.

"Seriously? This is the big one, isn't it? Shouldn't we—?"

"Charlie called. We're meeting him at the border. Don't take any souvenirs."

I'm looking around the room, at all the precious, priceless things we're going to burn and bury. Everything they learned since before the dinosaurs. "What about Labrador?"

He stops and turns around. His smile glows in the dark as he draws a finger across his throat. "I'll split his share with you."

❊

An hour later, we touch down on the Syrian border. The Syrians have a huge refugee processing center, but our sand castle is bigger. Smoke and sirens like the aftermath of an exorcism gone wrong. A suicide bomber went off inside the refugee station. I stand around outside while Balance argues with some Marines I don't know. Contractors pick up the human debris in the road. In the gutter, I see a boot with a bit of shinbone sticking out of it. A snakeskin boot.

We go through a series of chainlink cattle chutes to a tent with a crowd of corpsmen tagging and bagging bodies. None of them is large enough to fill a bag by itself.

Inside the tent, Charlie Toth and Steve the Sissy are talking to two boys and a girl. The kids are six going on sixty: shaken, spotted with blood, but greedily nibbling Hershey bars. I stand off to the side. The girl and a boy nod off, knocking heads and folding to the deck. The other boy tries to run away, but Steve grabs him and claps a rag over his face. "Here comes the Ether Bunny," he sings into the boy's ear.

I walk over with my hand on my sidearm.

Charlie grins and says, "Glad you're here. Want you to see something."

He kneels before the little boy, who is dead but still twitching. Slitting the boy's shirt with his knife, he shows me a sunken, scrawny chest with a neatly healed appendectomy scar about two inches long on the abdomen. The other ones have it, too.

He reaches into a pouch on his body armor. "We found this in one of the kids who was killed by the bomb." He holds it out to me.

"Is that what I think it is?"

He just nods. It's an egg. A little smaller than an ostrich egg, but with a leathery, slightly soft shell, warm and tacky with human blood.

"This is how they hide and infiltrate human societies. The ultimate sleeper cell. Their cycles are a total mystery . . . There's no telling how old this egg is. We've found some in the Iraqi museums that were over ten thousand years old, but still viable. These Ophite fuckers carry them inside themselves their whole lives, pass them on to their children, waiting for the day when it'll be time to hatch."

I think about asking Steve for that ether rag. "Spooky shit, no doubt—but these are kids, Charlie."

"These kids were on a bus headed for the airport in Kuwait. A charity back in the states places them in American foster homes."

Charlie Toth looks for something in me. For a moment, he almost hands me the knife. But then he just sighs.

"You know what the biggest lie in the Bible is, kid? The miracles, man. Whatever they were praying to in the Old Testament wouldn't part a sea or make it rain manna, just because somebody asked nicely. You've seen enough movies edited for TV to know how that shit must've really gone down. We both know what makes the grass grow. The age of miracles never ended; we just lost the will to pay the coin to make them happen.

"Or take, for instance, Abraham. Why would God push his faithful servant all the way up there and put the dagger in his hands, and then . . . Psych! I ask you, what kind of god pulls a sick fucking stunt like that?"

He plunges the knife into a dead boy's abdomen, reopening the old scar with the delicacy of a Roman haruspex divining the future from steaming guts. I draw my pistol, screw in the suppressor, and shoot Steve the Sissy in the back of the head.

"Either he's a sadist unworthy of worship," Charlie goes on, "or the Bible flinched and cut us off from true communion."

I turn on Charlie, who looks disgusted but not shocked. He palms the knife to throw at my throat. But then he offers it to me. "If you're going to do it, do it right."

I shoot him in the face. He rips a grenade off his flak vest. "Coward—afraid to be what you are . . ."

I shoot him three more times as I walk backwards out of the tent, and I'm running in the road, looking for my truck when he pulls the pin.

❋

They didn't touch me. I filed my resignation via email with the home office, shipped two crates via air freight, and went to the airport. I could see Archon's bunker over the far wall of the outbound runway.

I had nothing to declare. I tossed my duffel bag into the X-ray and walked through the scanner. I wasn't carrying nail clippers or suspicious fluids, or wearing jewelry or a belt buckle the size of a breakfast tray, and I didn't beep. But they asked me if they could open my bag. I didn't have anything to hide and told them so.

They could've asked me to open my own damned bag. Then the bomb would've gone off in *my* face.

❋

I dream I'm in the Garden of Eden with Bridget. We have everything we need, but we can't make a baby. Our groins are blank, Barbie-smooth planes of skin. We have to ask God to make us a child.

God breathes life into a lump of clay until it glows like blown glass, and sets it down on his altar. It wails and howls because he didn't give it a brain. You can't argue with God. The light of His countenance burns out your eyes. The violet afterglow of His radiance is a scar burned into the void of your blindness until your eyes grow back while you sleep.

"It doesn't have to be like this," says the snake in the tree.

We eat of the proffered fruit and go mad. His rage sets the fruiting trees aflame and rots the beasts of the field where they stand, but He cannot tame us, for we now know what He is. No creator, no messiah, but a demiurge and usurper. His false light fails to blind us when we look upon the metamorphic black mask of Baphomet, Yaldabaoth, Nyarlathotep—

❈

I go through a whole new boot camp. Weeks of bedside interrogation and half-baked notions I'm some kind of Manchurian Candidate. The day they just abruptly drop the whole thing is so spooky, so unmilitary, that I can't sleep because I want to face my assassin.

He never comes. I'm not worth it. Weeks of pointless torture, with no ribbon or medal at the end, no confession to sign. Nobody wants to know what I know.

I'm a technical quad, with limited motility and sensitivity in my upper extremities. My legs look strong. They could just lift me up out of this chair if someone will only say the magic words. I want to cut them off and eat them before they waste away.

Bridget is all cried out long before she first comes to visit me in the VA. The baby—Philip, after her father—takes one look at me and shrieks until he turns blue.

I sleep in the living room. Our bedroom has a short staircase, and the baby won't sleep so long as I'm near. I can't cry in front of her.

Bridget tells me she's working at a medical supply place, sterilizing packets of surgical tools. My medical bills boomeranged on us after somebody realized I was a private contractor and a possible terrorist. Bridget's mother Maxine comes over to help, but she can't, or won't, look at me. She hates my guts but I love her, because she keeps me drunk.

I call guys from my old unit. The ones I can get hold of at all tell me not to call again. Not one will tell me why, but I can hear their hair turning gray over the phone. I can hear what they can't say. *You're not one of us . . .*

I try to think only good thoughts about Bridget and the baby. I will need her help if and when I can't take it anymore. I study vocational manuals some well-meaning volunteer left at the house. Dentistry, real estate, suicide prevention counseling . . .

I study my enemies.

Herodotus found them first, but like me, he had no idea what he was looking at.

"There is a region moreover in Arabia, situated nearly over against the city of Buto, to which place I came to inquire about the winged serpents: and when I came thither I saw bones of serpents and spines in quantity so great that it is impossible to make report of the number, and there were heaps of spines, some heaps large and others less large and others smaller still than these, and these heaps were many in number . . . and the story goes that at the beginning of spring winged serpents from Arabia fly toward Egypt, and the birds called ibises meet them at the entrance to this country and do not suffer the serpents to go by but kill them."

Also known as the Ophians and Serpentinians, the Ophites were an obscure Gnostic sect that worshipped the serpent from Genesis as the bringer of wisdom and the liberator of humankind from the demiurge who enslaved them in Eden. In the Torah, the word *Seraphim* is used to speak of both angels and snakes. Small Ophite sects survived in Egypt and Syria until the Middle Ages, when they were finally wiped out by independent yet conveniently timed purges by the Hashishim and the Knights of the Temple.

The Templars were seized en masse in 1307 for political and financial reasons, but the accusations of Satanism—that they spat and trod upon the cross and worshipped a graven idol called Baphomet— were what sealed their fate. The goat-headed demon got thrown into almost every witchcraft case in the Middle Ages, but under torture some Templars admitted they worshipped a black idol. None of the tortured knights ever admitted the truth about the real mission of their order.

Spotty accounts of the black idol were accepted as evidence, though one was never found or produced in court. In confessions it was described as a cat, a phallus, or a man's bearded head. Frequently confused with Mohammad, Baphomet was a god of fertility and regeneration, but not the tree-hugging, Mother Nature kind. Lives taken ritually in his name could heal wounds and prolong life. Kill the enemy, eat his heart, his courage, his soul, amen. Like samurai, they believed that suicide was second only to death in battle. Of the two thousand knights, sergeants, squires, clerks, and servants arrested on Friday the 13th, fifty-four refused to repent and were burned at the stake in 1312. Almost two dozen killed themselves in jail.

Fascinating shit. It sings me to sleep. I wake to sirens. The baby is shrieking his lungs out in the kitchen. Maxine doesn't come when I call. It takes me ten minutes to get in my chair and into the kitchen, but I make myself stop and count to twenty before I enter, so I don't just smash my son like a cheap alarm clock.

Philip hitches and chokes in his high chair, but he summons a fresh wail of lung-ripping terror when he sees me coming.

All the cabinets are emptied out on the floor. Maxine is slumped over the kitchen sink, face down in a basin filled with crimson suds. Blood oozes out of both ears, which she apparently punctured with our meat thermometer. Her hands are shredded and impaled on shards of glass and crockery, her wrists slashed down to the bone.

Philip points at me and finally stops crying. In his tiny little hands, he's holding a knife.

I leave her just the way I found her, roll back into the living room to call the police. I only stop to wipe off the wall above Philip's high chair, where Maxine, in the middle of the most frantic and violent suicide, apparently took the time to scrawl SEMPER FI in her own blood.

❊

The police find no evidence of an intruder. They blame Maxine's antidepressants and alcoholism and redheaded temper. Nobody looks for a yellow second at the cripple.

Bridget can't stay home with the baby. She's pulling double shifts at the plant because of the Surge. I learn to change diapers with dumb, dead hands that can't hold a pen. I drink. I black out and say and do things that leave Bridget no choice but to dump me outside in the backyard for the night.

Philip's toys are scattered like land mines. They all play fractured nursery rhymes and scream 16-bit hymns of worship whenever they're touched. "You're my best friend," a musical puppy gushes when I crush it under my wheels.

I try to read, but history's just fucking with me. I track down the names of the Templar knights who committed suicide before they could be burned. One leaps out of the list. Then another.

Stephen De Sissy.
Jean Balance.
Geoffroy Spruance, le Chevalier de Toth.

Philip howls until he implodes. When he's on the verge of collapsing into exhausted sleep, he digs his tiny fingers into his eyes and starts all over again.

The crying rings through me like a tuning fork. I punch holes in the wall. His breathless, hitching wails turn into words. "I'm not yours."

I rip him out of the high chair and dash his brains out on the table. I'm painting a cross on the wall with them when Bridget comes in and asks me what's burning.

Philip bucks and thrusts in his chair like he's choking, reaching for his mother. I'm sitting in my chair by the stove and my hand is on fire. She throws a wet dish towel over my hand and sweeps the baby up and into the next room to breastfeed him.

The phone rings. I take down a floor lamp rolling over to answer it.

"It doesn't have to be like this," Prysocki says.

"Easy for you to say," I shoot back, so happy to be talking to somebody who understands, even if he's dead. "You never got any when you were alive."

"Best decision I ever made, Whitey. Know why I blew my brains out? Turns out I didn't need them."

"You never did," I say. Playing along. "You're not one of them," I say. I don't say, *You're not one of* us.

"I'm still here, that's what matters. And you better get your shit straight . . ."

"Why did they send you? Where's—"

"They don't think you're man enough to put your house in order.

They want you to snuff it. They keep riding you, you'll frag yourself, and then they win."

I can't answer. I can't even hang up.

"You're already initiated, brother. You touched the black idol and drank the blood and you know the secret, so you better believe that when you check out, you just go back to Him."

❃

Another dream. The Great Red Day arrives. All the armies of Earth embrace one another as brothers and refuse to engage in another day of pointless political war. Then they declare war on the *real* enemy.

All civilian communications are severed, the capitals and universities and churches and libraries bombed to rubble, and the culling process begins. The new order is declared on leaflets that fall from the sky like red September snow: ENLIST OR DIE.

I watch the war from the porch in my wheelchair. A wing of A-10 Warthogs strafes the Interstate. A column of Abrams tanks on the next street orders everybody back into their homes, then starts shelling the neighborhood.

An ancient Prussian mercenary in a moth-eaten greatcoat strolls by with a rifle on his shoulder. His bayonet has three babies spitted on it, and he wants to borrow a stewpot.

The war is over before sunset. What can the world do but surrender?

On TV, all the channels show the coronation in the central courtyard of the Pentagon. A phalanx of Praetorian Guards armed with swords chops down the sacrificial reporters staked out along the path to wash every step he will take in blood.

Under a canopy of gory swords, he ascends to the podium and draws back the cowl that hides his face. Charlie Toth's grin is as white as his skin is black.

"I am His voice on Earth," he says. "Listen."

His guards make a collar of swords and chop his head off. He kneels and a geyser of sable blood bursts from his neck, arcs out over the assembled brass, and coagulates in midair in a vast red-black tentacle that uncoils and crushes his awestruck generals, admirals, and advisors.

I turn off the TV, but he's not finished with me. His wings blot out the sun. His claws rip bleeding gashes in the sky. His horns are bathed in the blood of nations. He blows my house down and tears my baby from Bridget's breast and devours it whole, then rapes her in the wreckage.

He's still here. He's never leaving.

He wants to know if my wife has a sister.

❃

I wake from the dream to a voice braying, "Mail call!" and sit up, excited because it's all been a nightmare, and I'm still a Marine, and none of it—

Bridget drops a padded envelope in my lap. It's dog-eared and covered in postal inspection stickers and courier receipts, but nowhere does it say who sent it. It's from Iraq.

Inside, a handful of sand. And then a DVD falls out. It's not labeled. I wait for Bridget to take Philip into the bedroom for his nap before I put it into the player.

Tracking glitches make blizzards of eight-bit snow that finally subside to show a shaky handheld camera's view of a hooded man kneeling before a brick wall, surrounded by six masked men with jihad headbands. All of them hold AK's and scimitars.

The hooded man—in green T-shirt and skivvies—holds up an edition of *Stars & Stripes*. The date is May 14, 2004. He doesn't blink when they pull his hood off, stares past the camera, and glares at something a million light years away, but getting closer all the time.

"I have been convicted of crimes against the Iraqi people and the secret saviors of all nations, the Archons . . ." His heavily drugged mumbling runs on until the executioners rise to encircle him in a pentagram of scimitar blades. I reach for the remote to turn it off and when it doesn't work, I throw it at the TV to knock out the screen. Because I still don't remember this, but now I see it—

They don't cut off my head. They give me a knife and I cut my own throat and bleed out into cups, which are passed around . . . . I finish three of them myself before I run dry. *Then* they cut off my head.

I ask myself questions no man should have to ask. Was that me?

Was that real? Am I dead? What is this thing I'm seeing, eating, thinking with? Because it's not *my* head.

I prod my neck with a knife and wonder, *Could I do that? Could I do it again?*

❊

I have to stop watching TV. He's on it all the time, watching me from behind the shadow puppets and talking heads on the screen. The mosque firebombed in Corpus Christi and the Islamic community center in Dearborn were domestic terrorist misfires, since the patrons killed inside weren't Muslim, but some other weird Arab sect; and the foster home with four Iraqi orphans burned in their beds was just a tragic accident. The endless parade of unarmed black men shot in the back by combat vet cops are tragic errors, not daily human sacrifices by broken men hoping to be made whole.

The zodiac is wrong, but they've fixed it. My birthday now falls under some new thirteenth sign—Ophiuchus, a man holding a snake. Named for Asklepios, the father of medicine. An asteroid called Apophis is scheduled to pass close by the Earth in 2036, but TV says we should freak out about it now, because everything else is exactly as it should be. Nobody who can do anything about it wants to connect the goddamned dots.

Philip has overcome his fear of me. He crawls up to where I lie on the couch and tugs on my colostomy bag and catheter package. Soon he will be walking, if someone teaches him. I gently try to stop him pulling on my plumbing, but I end up backhanding him across the room. The TV sees it and replies with canned applause. It's after 10. Bridget is late coming home from work.

"You can be healed," the TV says. "You were always one of us. You can do a miracle. All you have to be willing to do is spill a little blood."

I'm looking at my hand and trying not to hear the words. I'm looking at my hand and not at Philip bawling on the deck. I'm watching my hand reach down for my child.

"Pluck the serpent from your bosom. It's not even yours. You know that's how they breed us out of existence. While the grunts are away feeding the grass, the snakes crawl into our beds and they fuck our women and leave us with their pale, brainy yellow-bellied bastards. They have knowledge ready at hand that'll take away what makes us human, and men like us… warriors… we'll go extinct. Or you can step over a little stranger's blood and become immortal."

The lights go out. The TV flickers a moment longer. A blazing eye with three golden-red irises sees into my broken body and transmits its unthinkable will to mend my severed spine.

Out of the darkness, a hand takes mine. A hand with teeth and tongues in it strokes my palm and fills it with a knife.

When my brothers killed themselves, they gave their names and their flesh to the darkness, and it came back wearing them. The hunting horror looks as much like a man as a constellation looks like a flying horse, but somehow it's still Charlie's eyes, his acid laugh, dissolving my resolve. He laughs when I damn him or whatever it is that's looking at me out of his eyes.

"Hell, boy, all I ever was, was a name. You kill to make a name for yourself, you become a whole long list of names. But it's not for the fame, is it, hombre? Just between us white men."

I can't lie to him. When I try, I can't even breathe.

"You know what you really are."

I know what I am. My knife technique is rusty and my grip is pathetic, but I bring the knife down with every ounce of me that still works. The blade bites deep into the deck before it hits bedrock and snaps like a ghost set free. I lurch out of the couch and fall on Philip and wrap him in my arms.

It's devastating to learn that even my new god doesn't understand. I don't want to kill Philip because I fear he's not mine, or a usurper sent to replace me. I would have to destroy him, if there were any chance that he *is* mine. If he could become what I am.

❊

A tiny voice whispers to me in a dream where I am blissfully blind because I have not yet been born.

"The Serpent is the wisdom of the World. His gnosis delivered the Sons of Man from the slavery of false gods. His healing arts were passed down to Apollonius of Tyana, Hermes Trismegistus, Asklepios, Jesus of Nazareth, who were all silenced lest they make demigods of men. His secrets can deliver them from a new dark age, and that is why His children must all be murdered for the Black Pharaoh to return. If the World Serpent is silenced, then there will be no memory, no past and no future, but only endless, empty war."

I wake up to Bridget standing over me, lying in my own shit with Philip asleep in the crook of my arm, his face tucked into my shoulder as if to whisper in my ear.

I demand to see Philip's birth certificate, proof of his blood type, his date of birth. She can't find them because I shredded them. I rage at her until she packs a bag and bundles the baby out the door. When I know she's not coming back, I pack my own bag and burn the house down.

I've had time to plan this, when I wasn't planning my suicide. I crawl out the back and get into a beater van I bought with Kuwaiti mad money and had converted into an up-armored gimpmobile. On the couch, I left a human skeleton that I shipped home from Iraq. I got good enough at dentistry to put silver amalgam in his molars, so the charred wreckage will confirm what the world wants to believe.

My enemies will not be fooled. To hurt them—to survive at all—I must shed more than just my skin.

❉

I know right away what he is from how he reacts to the baby crying.

He gets on at the North Hollywood terminal every morning and rides standing at the back of the train. Not hanging on to the leashes or rails, just surfing the rocking car as it races through the tunnel with his fists balled up in his windbreaker, a knapsack with a lunchbox and a beaded car seat in it.

But then the baby starts in.

The big Mexican lady rocks the stroller, but pays the crying baby no more mind than the rest of the noise. The baby is small, maybe a month or two old, and its cry is thin and shallow, ending in that lamb-hyena rattle when the little lungs run out of breath, but not rage. It gets on my nerves and brings back memories, but the guy in the back of the train grabs a leash and rips it right out of the ceiling. He backs into a corner. Hardly anyone looks up from their phones, but the sheep smell a wolf and close ranks as we pull into Vermont.

He runs into the doors before they open. I follow him up the platform, almost run him over in my wheelchair, trying to catch him before the stairs. As if he can read my mind, he detours into a men's room.

When he's bent over the sink, splashing piping hot water into his eyes, I roll over and tap him on the shoulder. "I know what you're going through."

He whirls on me and his eyes go flat and dead as pennies.

I give him a moment to compose himself, to regard his scalded face in the mirror, sitting with my hands in plain sight, not quite making eye contact. If I push too hard too fast, he'll just flip back to his defensive posture and either attack me or run away, and I'll have to start again, looking for a way to be whole.

"I was there, too. I saw what you saw. I know what you are." I don't drop any names. To hear them again would be worse than hearing a baby crying.

He just looks at me, reading it on me, and the color drains out of his cheeks. He looks around the empty restroom, checks every corner, every shadow. He makes a sound somewhere between a giggle and a whoop of anguish and throws his arms around me, traps the knife I was about to drive through his chest and into his heart without looking at his face.

He whispers in my ear and his hands snake around me to clasp each other like an ouroboros over my severed spine. I'm weeping, about to have the end I crave so bad I couldn't give it words. *Valhalla awaits, brother,* Toth whispers in my other ear.

I whisper the Templar rite in his ear as I try to free my knife, to take his life and eat his courage. He blows his septic breath in my face as a gift, then releases me. "You can't take," he gasps from the true mouth somewhere inside his coat, "what is freely given."

He lets my body fall into my chair and staggers out as I lose the last control I have. Screaming through locked jaws as my dead nerves return with unacceptable messages from beyond.

Cursing all the thousand names of my god and praying to the Snake, I climb out of my wheelchair.

Broken Sleep

The last place Tre was locked up, they would line up all the new inmates, naked and shivering and dripping chemical disinfectant. The commandant tells you that the first rule is no talking, *ever. Any questions?* he asks. The next new fish who opens his hole gets his teeth smashed in with a truncheon. *Any more questions?*

Tre was swiftly learning to miss that kind of caring human contact.

This new place seemed better at first. He didn't even remember being transferred in. He just woke up in this plastic coffin, a solitary cell like a port-o-shitter turned on its side. By his second sleep cycle, he forgot why he was arrested. By the third one, he had to search for the barcode on his wristband to recall his name.

Pills ground up in his food, gritty Mexican pharmaceuticals in tropical beach party colors. He tripped often enough to know the taste of alkaloids, but this shit was way too strong. Meals came with more pills in a tiny envelope that told him to report any SIDE EFFECTS.

It was better than any high he ever paid for, most of the time. He'd think of something funny and forget to laugh, or just mumble the word *joke* over and over, cackling like a loon. But there were moments when he dreamt he was flying, and then he was falling and jolted out of sleep with his heart racing and every muscle tied in knots, every time he started to really *sleep*.

They shocked him awake with microscopic electrodes embedded under his skin, and if he didn't forget what he was doing and fall asleep again right away, he would scalp himself with his bare hands, trying to dig them out.

All his life, Tre barely remembered his dreams. Something was chasing him, or he was chasing something. It almost had him or he almost had it, and then he woke up. But now he was aware he was dreaming, aware that he was asleep—if he was *anywhere*, it had to be a dream—but he couldn't remember being awake. They drugged him out of his mind and shocked him out of sleep, channel-surfing him with their remote control. He had to go somewhere....

They're trying to drive you crazy, said the smartest part of him, the part that he beat down inside himself, whenever it dared to speak up. They're trying to drive you out of your mind so they can follow you like a marked rat, so they can track you back to the nest.

It got worse when they stopped feeding him.

The dreams got uglier. Chasing him and pushing him into a pit and he was drowning in battery acid. He pinched himself to wake up, but it didn't work. He bit himself, tearing skin and God he was delicious. He ate half of his own hand and was gnawing on his wrist when he woke up and saw his cell was open.

A big black thing waited in the corridor, crouching between him and his food. It lifted a leg and pissed on the tray, but it was nothing like a dog.

He pinched himself. It didn't hurt like hunger, but it felt real enough. Without another thought, he lunged at the thing, drove it back on its hind legs, slammed it into the wall, and ripped out its throat in his teeth.

He ate everything, even the bones. He grew so full that he expanded right through tinfoil and cardboard walls.

It was another dream, but more real than anything he'd ever experienced, awake or asleep or on any drug. The light was like wine, the air was alive with music and perfume, and the wind felt like the skin of a woman against him.

He floated among thousands, millions of human bodies, mostly naked or in varying states of undress, in a bottomless sky of glowing clouds and gentle, embryonic warmth. He was the only one awake, the only one who was real.

A beautiful redheaded woman floated by and he tried to grope her, but she popped like a soap bubble. Others crumbled like ash or dissipated like smoke. He raged at them, tumbling through clouds of bodies like a bullet until he encountered one that hit him back.

Her hair was blacker than shadows, and it covered her milk-white face like a living veil, but flashes of green submarine light spilled out of her eyes. She asked his name.

He hesitated, wracking his brain. He wasn't wearing a wristband or anything else, and neither was she. "Andre K— Tre, just Tre. Who're you? How come you're not fake like everybody else?"

"My name's Ariadne here," she said. "And we're inside the Orgasm." Drifting from one body to the next, she sought out a woman wrapped in a dove-gray fur coat and turned her over to go through her pockets. Some of them were entangled in the heat of sex, but most were alone with their eyes rolled back in their heads. "You know what this is, right? How old are you?"

His mind was a sieve. His body changed or dissolved when he tried to look at it. He guessed, "Sixteen . . ."

"Maybe in a couple years, player." Jumping into a tangle of young faceless men in fraternity sweaters, she took wallets and drug stashes and tiny gray firefly things out of their heads. "You're lucky. Most inmates in the solitary program break down and lose it without ever finding their way out of their own heads. Some inmates will maim themselves or go crazy to get out of work detail, you know? Knocking on Joe, they used to call it. But the really crazy ones are the ones who do the real shit work in here. If you lose your name, you forget who and what you are. They use you completely. That black dog-thing on your breath . . . that's what you turn into."

Nausea made him start to feel solid, start to fall. "Whatever," he said. Already bored. "This is a dream, right? We should do it."

She shook her head, so tired, though he still couldn't see her face. "Thanks, no. You look like a Francis Bacon painting of someone he really hated."

"But this is my dream, and you—"

"This isn't your dream. Right now, we're in an artificial communal dream-space created with drugs and guided hypnotic imagery. Everyone sleeping in its broadcasting footprint experiences the same wet dream, brought to you by Burroughs-Wellcome, Bechtel and Wackenhut."

The velvet ease of her dismissal sent him into a childish fury. Thrashing another knot of orgasmic ghosts into sparkling ashes, he turned on her with azure fire drooling out of his fists. "I'm old enough, and I'm more real than you can handle, girl."

She turned away, daring him to come at her. Floated above him and her hair fanned out, giving him a glimpse of her face. Light came out of her mouth. She had no eyes, only holes alive with television snow.

"Listen, dummy. The people who run the prison are using you as guinea pigs. They're keeping you in a lucid dream state . . . jolting you with electrical shocks until you're dreaming while you're awake . . . . That's just the primary conditioning. They're trying to find and control dreamers who can go into other people's dreams."

He still didn't understand why she didn't want to hook up, but she must be someone else, not a figment of his exhausted imagination. "Why are they doing this to us?"

"Why? To sell things. To run everybody. They want to create a universal dream-space that they can control . . . or to discover the real one, so they can plant a flag in it."

She kissed him, and the shock was greater than the electrode jolts. Her words were too heavy to hear; they sank into him like lead.

Something blocked out the sun. The air turned cold and slimy and too thick to breathe. Any second they were going to shock him awake and he wanted to hold onto her, but the thing was so huge it exerted its own gravity. It sucked him down, away from her, and all the empty vessels fell after him like rain.

"Run!" she cried. "Run back to your body! Choose the right door—"

He fought to stay with her, climbing and leaping over tumbling bodies, screaming her name, but she floated always out of reach. He hit the bottom and the bodies kept piling up. Thrashing, clawing, biting, tearing, and crawling, but they buried him alive. Crushed under their weight and stink and waste, unable to breathe, unable to die. When the lightning in his head finally jerked him out of the dream, he awoke clawing at the walls.

At the first place they locked him up, when he was eleven, you could go to the yard after lunch, where it was too hot for anything but fighting, or you could go to the library. There were no good books to read, but if you wanted to stay, you had to do puzzles. The pictures on the boxes were sun-bleached or mismatched or just missing. Many puzzles were just in coffee cans, with no hint of what they should look like. You had to move the pieces around and try to put them together, knowing none of the pieces might even be from the same puzzle.

He had gotten quite good at puzzles, at spotting things that did or didn't belong, at making things that didn't belong fit together. It helped him to cope now, when every morning he woke up in a different prison.

The rules were always different, but always the same. It was a dream-prison, a shared imaginary space. The other people around him were not figments of his imagination, but other drugged prisoners. Sometimes they were giant, toddling, bawling babies. Other times they were skeletons riddled with ghostly parasites the size of pythons. In the worst of them, there was only blackness, sickness, and tubes going in and out of his arms and down his throat, and choking himself to death the only exit.

Tre figured out the rules soon enough. When a boy with a huge black-red starfish for a face jumped him in the shower, Tre cut him from nipples to navel with a knife that came out of his mouth. The wound yawned and everything but blood poured out. Before the guards gassed them, he tore the hole in the inmate wider and climbed into it and escaped.

He wandered in and out of strangers' fantasies like a runaway bogeyman, crashing forbidden love trysts and eternal birthday parties and shredding gossamer ectoplasm in his dreamteeth, always looking for another door. When the familiar CLICK CLICK of alien voltage shot through his brain, he welcomed it and rode the lightning down into deeper sleep.

It looked like an ancient, ruined amusement park—Six Flags over Atlantis—drooping arches and crooked towers infested with rusting, hyperbolic ribbons of rollercoaster track, endless empty arcades, deserted shopping malls and echo-haunted pavilions the color and texture of fossilized bones. The pavement was slick, grimy ice; beneath it, he could see a black, rushing river. Drowning people and things both foreign and familiar pounded at the ice and screamed bubbles at him until the current ripped them away.

Mobs of undead scavengers with featureless green hamburger faces climbed out of the gutters. He ran like a drunken puppet as the street turned to taffy. "Get back, you bastards!" he roared. "I'm the last man!"

He dashed their hollow heads open, and pumpkin seeds and circuitry spilled out. They forgot him, swinging listlessly at each other and gasping, *I'M the last man!* And maybe each of them was right, he thought, when he looked into a funhouse mirror and saw his own rotten, bloated face.

A paralyzing shock jerked him by the silver cord that bound his soul to his body, growing to a grand mal seizure when he fought it. Sweltering fever-heat poured out of him. The ice melted and cracked. He plunged into frigid blackness and was swept away.

The next dream was beautiful: endless blood-red jungle, rolling valleys, eternal tribal war. Tiny, twig-boned jungle pygmies prowled the crushed velvet undergrowth, blasted or blessed with strange mutations that made each tribe a species unto itself. He waded into internecine feuds and picked a side at random and stomped the enemy like ants, and they carried him to their village like a living god of war. They offered him what little food they had, sang his praises as they starved, as their fragile fairy daughters withered, blackened, and burst at his touch.

He stayed through three seasons and burned through ninety-two tribes like a plague and it was hard to leave, but he could find no peace. She haunted his dreams within dreams. *This is a labyrinth, not a maze,* she told him. *There are no dead ends, no alternate exits. The only way out is through* . . .

She was the only real thing, the only one who could remind him this was a dream. The mere thought of her brought the shocks, as if to punish him or deliver him deeper, but they could barely reach him, here. He was almost happy . . .

And then the real gods came, and he was only another scurrying insect looking for a rock to hide under.

They ate up the sky with their obscene, insane parade of shapes, but there were no shadows when they held up lenses that magnified the blood-red sun into slashing white tongues of fire.

Burning down to his bones, he ran for hours through the inferno, and it hurt more than anything he'd ever felt in waking life, but he couldn't wake up, he couldn't even die.

He came to a ruined temple adorned with sleeping stone faces and bug-eyed, bloody-tusked angels. Before the temple lay a long, narrow pool that perfectly reflected the tower, but the sky in the reflection was a star-mad winter night with a bloated blue full moon impaled upon the tower's silver spire.

Tre threw himself into the water, but when he broke the surface he only fell faster into the airless void on the other side of the mirror. Screaming only sucked cold fire into his lungs as he plummeted past the darkly luminous faces of the mirror-temple and fell burning into the starry dark of deepest dreams.

Swimming through eternal night, the stars grew larger, more numerous ... swelled until they surrounded him and swallowed the darkness. He hid his face from their unblinking glare, flinched from the snail-trail touch of naked eyeballs on his goosebump-prickled flesh. In the place where everything was made of eyes, he finally found her.

Her matted hair was made of rusty knives. "Jung said dreams are the 'voice of Nature,' but She stopped talking to us a long time ago. Did you ever read old books and wonder what they were all smoking? Their dreams were so much deeper, more real. Even *you* can tell that our dreams are broken."

"I don't need you—" His words came out as stillborn bubbles, turning belly-up and floating away. When they finally reached his ears, he heard himself say, *I don't know how to read.*

With a sad, rusty nod, she said, "You can't just wake up, because you're not in your own dream. These are the gutters of the collective unconscious, which they're trying to colonize, because something went wrong with the real lands of Dream."

He tried to speak again and almost drowned. Her silencing finger was like a sword on his lips.

"When the first proto-humans started to achieve true consciousness, the disconnected hemispheres of the brain started talking to each other, and we met gods in our dreams. They taught us hunting and farming and art and war. They raised us up, but we came to believe it was just us, talking to ourselves in the dark.

"Somewhere around the middle of the last century, the human race had kind of a collective nervous breakdown. We were kicked out of our dreams, the real ones, the shared space where we once touched the infinite. Long before either of us was born, we lost the Realms of Deeper Sleep ... the door closed, the temple fires were put out, and now something blocks the way. That's what you're trying to find.

Somewhere deep inside us is the door to the dream more real than waking life, the dream of the universe itself."

He struggled to make himself heard, to make his words into sound. "I don't want to know this—"

"You *already* know it. They have their pet theories, but they can't face the truth. *They're* the ones who cut us off from the Dream. Movies and TV and everything we consume, all that energy wasted to make all those false realities more real than our own. They've already made waking life a dream and the dreamers into a mushy mass-mind where everyone shares the same dream of being the only one who matters.

"That's why, whenever they catch someone who grew up without media saturation—Islamic terrorists, home-schooled fringers, feral kids, or chronic wards of the state like yourself—they wreck their sleep schedule and test them to destruction trying to find out how to repair what's gone wrong with the rest of us."

His frustration swelled into a bubble that enclosed them both. Eyes oozed all around them, bathing them in vacant scrutiny. "Who are you, really? Where are you? You're not in jail. You don't have a dog in this fight. I just want to go home. I want to wake up . . ."

She shook her head and shed sparks. The knives sang like wind chimes. Burning wind threw him down so he found himself staring up into her eyeless face. "Forget about waking up. *They* can't even wake you up now. The lucid dreaming program runs in ninety-day cycles. If you're this deep, you're probably a brain in a bucket with some jumper cables on it by now. They use any excuse to cut you open, sell your organs. The Dream is the only real afterlife, the only real state where human minds have survived the death of their bodies. You have to go through to the other side. Find the one who stands between humanity and the Gate of Deeper Slumber. Find it and kill it."

"Why should I?"

She tilted her head and now she had eyes like opals, and a smile like molten diamonds. "I belong to the man who can lead us to the true Dream."

He inhaled the bubble, pulling her toward him. "I'll put your ass to sleep, don't worry. But what's in it for me?"

Her sly diamond smile turned to coal. "Everything mortal will fail you."

"*I* won't fail you." He breathed in the blood and wine heat of her, and became a man.

"You will," she said. "And *I'm* not mortal."

She kissed him. A spark passed from her lips and bored into his brain, burning synapses to slag, creating strange new paths and echoing voices in his mind. His head exploded and he woke up.

He floated above a desolate wasteland of ashen dunes. Glowering over the horizon, a sickly white mountain with a huge, hideous monument carved into it. Eroded limestone features slowly emerged from the gray void, until he realized that the face of the mountain was his own.

Tubes ran up his nose and down his throat, and an IV dripped glucose into his arm. Nobody had ever put so much effort into keeping him alive. His body jerked as regulated high-voltage pulses raced through it. A rubber plug in his mouth kept him from biting through his tongue.

From somewhere out in the murky void beyond the bed, a ghastly panorama of distorted faces leered down, dire constellations that blurred and warped and spun off flaming comets of words that tumbled to detonate upon the twisted wreckage of Andre Kellogg's body.

"Mr. Kellogg . . . Is he, can he . . . He is? OK . . . . Tre, your mother says you like to be called *Tre* . . . . You're in a secure ward at MU Hospital. You've been an inmate at a private juvenile correctional institution, and you've been under sedation for most of the last fourteen months . . . . We're very sorry for your discomfort, but the parent company was in no way legally responsible for what happened. This affidavit releases us of liability . . . ."

Big pregnant pause, filled with the sound of breathing machines.

"Now, all the records were destroyed . . . . What we're trying to ascertain is the objective of the experiment that was performed on you . . . . Anything you could volunteer would be invaluable . . . . Can he even hear me?"

He tried, but could not get any closer to his body. A soft but irresistible wind, the repulsion of like magnetic charges, pushed him back. He could only watch as his hand reached out for the pen and mechanically signed the form.

He drifted off and they left his body alone and when he woke up, he was still months of agony away from walking without assistance, but he would survive . . . and more, he would get something he never could have hoped for—a second chance. He could recover and start over with a clean slate and the knowledge that the broken, insane system had failed to swallow him whole—

He woke up on another table—a cold steel one, and the lights in his face hid the masked canine faces of the ghouls who cut him open and played inside him.

"Jesus, look at these lungs. What are these kids smoking these days?"

"Dibs on the liver . . ."

He turned away and flew, burning through the restraints and the red curtains of the operating theater, and then he was racing through the trees of a forest. He ran like a flayed rabbit, hunched over to hold his slit belly together. The surgeons chased him through the misty forest on all fours, baying his secret name. He threw scraps of himself over his shoulder and escaped when they stopped to eat them. Through the mist and great cathedral groves, he stalked until he came to the edge of a chain of purple, snow-crowned mountains.

A vast ruined city of giants melted into inky pools and indigo rivers of shadow in the faltering glow of a bloated purple sun. The road passed among towering mausoleums and orgies of shattered statuary. He heard a brittle clap of falling brickwork and whirled in time to see her vanish behind a rock.

"I see you!" he shouted, then turned his back. He needed nothing from her now.

"You shouldn't have come here!" she cried out. "You'll just deliver it to them—"

He threw a rock at her, but it seemed to pass right through her, confirming his fear. "Get lost, you're not real! You took over my body and sold me out—"

"You're still confused, poor dear. Are you really so sure that *you're* real?"

He threw another rock, but it turned to smoke as it left his hand. The street subsided beneath him, like a great beast letting out a long, last breath.

A pulsating flood of pus boiled up out of the earth, the distilled infection of a mortal wound. Before Tre could make her understand, the sea of sickness had drawn itself up into a suppurating tidal wave.

Domed temples collapsed under its lurching, liquid weight. It stretched upwards and curled overhead, countless human bodies suspended within its gelatinous mass.

"Kill it!" she screamed. "That's the thing that stands in the way of the Dream! You can be the one who saved the sanity of the whole human race, Tre! You can be the one to slay the dragon—"

It didn't look like a dragon. A wall of liquid flesh crashed down on the causeway, flinging bricks larger than cars aside like grains of sand.

He ran so fast he flew over the buckling plaza, dodging falling columns until he came to the end of the abandoned city. The road led to the head of a staircase that wound down the sheer mountain face into shoals of dimly glowing clouds far, far below.

She stood behind him. She looked younger than he was, but he knew better than to trust anything he saw. "It'll crush you if you take another step. It'll eat you up so you die inside it forever."

—*Fight that, I can't*—

At his back now, she pushed him toward it. "You only have to face it to drive it back. Then we'll escape—together . . ."

He didn't know what to believe. He embraced her, pivoted, and threw her over his shoulder into the gathering protoplastic storm. The monstrosity recoiled, shivering with joy as it digested her. Seemingly forgotten, he escaped, sobbing with terror and relief.

The treads of the staircase were too tall to scale alone, but he lowered himself over each of seventy cliff-like risers and dropped from the last step just as the terminal rays of daylight failed. Somewhere along the way, the stairs had grown smaller, or he had grown larger, until he stumbled over them and had to stoop to proceed down the tunnel at the foot of the stairs. Satisfied with his offering, the abomination did not follow.

The tunnel abruptly grew into a grotto lit by a pillar of white fire. The walls were riddled with holes, doors, and gates. Some were rusted shut or blocked by sheets of cobweb or clumps of fungi, while others were lit by torches and hung with faded billboards and flashing video screens.

He did not mean to bow to the two ancient men who stood between him and the maze of doorways. They stood taller than the tallest he could make himself, and wore monk's robes and peaked hats with feathers as high as their gray beards were long.

Something about them reminded him of ancient Egypt: the sandstone skin, the hieroglyphic nonsense that came from their hidden lips; but they were older than Egypt, older than mankind. Yet he did not look away, for he recognized the craggy, merciless cast of their faces. They were judges.

One of them took his shoulder and pressed him down into his true shape. *You must present your ka, my son, to enter.*

He didn't understand, but this was no time to show weakness. "You can't stop me. I faced the thing outside, and I beat it. I've come to open the gate of dreams . . ." *In the name of the gods Burroughs-Wellcome, Bechtel and Wackenhut . . .* "I claim the right to pass for all humankind . . ."

The judges looked at one another. Nasht, the one who touched him, carved a question in the air, and his brother, Kaman-Thah, answered with a shattering laugh.

The thing you defeated is the diseased dreaming of all your brothers and sisters. You saw it as it saw itself, for that is its sickness. Each of you hates the whole as it hates itself, and so you can never be free of each other, and so you can never be one. Separated from your souls, you can only be reunited in dreams. So they may never pass into the land of deeper sleep, as you *may still . . . but where is your ka?*

"My what?"

The judge held up a mirror. In its murky depths Tre saw, for just a moment, Ariadne reaching out to him as she fell into the countless mouths of the thing that chased them, but then he only saw himself, gasping like a beached fish.

Your soul, boy . . . what have you done with your soul?

He tore free of them and raced toward the wall of doors. They moved after him so fast their human masks slipped, and for just a moment he glimpsed their true faces. But they couldn't stop him, because he knew what he was looking for.

She showed him. He thought she had betrayed him, but she had showed him what none of the others had discovered, the true nature of the only door that opened. At last, he would do something that mattered. He would set himself free, and the whole human race—

With his eyes wide open and his hands steepled in a diver's prayer, he leapt into the pillar of living flame.

The fire was blinding and all-consuming.

Beyond it lay a place made of joy. He had dreamt of it before, but now that he had truly reached it, he found a purity that rendered reality a pallid, dirty shadow. The light resolved and softened, and he saw the lands of Dream—

And then he was dragged backward through the fire.

Only by slow, agonizing degrees did he come to realize that he was under restraints in bed and being jolted by temporal electrical shocks. Awake.

"Hey, the shitbird's still alive. What'd I tell you?"

"I didn't bet you."

"Whatever. Hey, kid—which one of these tubes is he breathing through? Hey, kid, you want to talk now?"

He looked right through them. This was just another bad dream. He would wake up any moment, in the Dream that was more real than waking.

"Drop the act, kid. You've only been in solitary for forty-eight hours. The sooner you tell us what they said, the sooner you can go back."

This wasn't a dream. With cold surgical tools, they pinched about ten places on his body that proved beyond a shadow of a doubt that he was awake, that had him begging to tell them everything.

But the words wouldn't come.

So that night, they started all over again.

Cahokia

I said what I always said, just before we set down on Payload Ag-26264. "Velocity and waste heat are null, people. Lock and load, prepare to board." None of us expected anything special.

I looked from one polarized helmet to another and nodded, because nothing more was needed. As the fingers of a hand, they folded into position on the shuttle and became an armored fist, poised to knock very hard on a door.

We floated in the airlock arm of Atropos Station, a big steel syringe hanging over a blackness so perfectly pure it made interstellar space look like a vulgar neon jungle.

The eggheads called it a "parallel interdimensional singularity," but we called it the Zero, or the Naught, when we were feeling continental, or just the Not.

The location of the Not was a matter of high physical heresy—an alternate universe devoid of matter, or the nth dimension, or the beginning of time. We were, in layman's terms, nowhere. You could travel for light-years in the Not and not find so much as a particle, except for the trash we dragged in there.

There were six of us. We used to have eight, but nobody wanted to break in virgins on our team. No other team had cleared half as many payloads with *any* of their original members surviving. We were not lucky. We were smarter, faster, and meaner than anything we had faced so far. To tell oneself what to expect was suicide. One never knew, and what it took to survive one encounter meant nothing, the next time. Still, there were rituals to be observed.

Nguyen consulted her *I Ching* simulator. "Retreat: success is indicated, but remain firm and correct. Lake transforms into Heaven; Mountain stands for stillness and obstruction."

"Bullshit," Padilla said, because he always did.

"It's just a goddamned rock," Killdeer said, which jarred the ritual, because she never spoke before a drop.

Nguyen was my lieutenant. Virgil and Padilla were my astrogators. Bowland was a geologist and mining engineer, but he wasn't squeamish about killing. Ida Killdeer was our scout.

We never believed we were doing wrong. We were explorers, prospectors in the void . . . at worst, scavengers. Part of the process.

For most of its four-hundred-year history, the United States Marines has served with honor in just about every capacity but that for which they were originally created: ship-to-ship combat. The powers that be called my team a Marine Unit, and a few of us had been Marines. But even the most classical understanding of what Marines were would not begin to explain what we did.

Think about the cold fusion process and hydrogen cells that allowed us to get off the oil tit before the Middle East imploded; anti-grav drives, med-mites, liquid crystal lattice computers; all the shiny, brilliant things that rolled out of the corporate labs at the last minute and got us over the precipice of the fucked twenty-first and into the Future.

Think of all that miraculous technology and try to reconcile it with the pure cussed stupidity of the species that wields it. The future was not invented in their labs. It was won by teams like mine, who merely did what Marines were created to do, in the bygone days of sail. We went from our ship to theirs, and we killed whatever we found aboard, and we brought home treasure.

They called us Marines. We did not.

We were conquistadors, and pirates.

We were the Plague.

We rode down from Atropos on an open shuttle, across a couple miles of nothing and around the deflector cages and the strip mining rigs, to get our first good look at #64.

"Biggest rock yet," Bowland reported off his screens, "four klicks by two by one. Drones say it's honeycombed with pockets of frozen gas and carbon deposits"—which was weird, but not unheard of. We could see right away how much more there was to it.

It was a flattened black ellipse with squat little mountains all over it, but we were too worried about the bands and patches of green and white in the valleys between them to see them for what they obviously were.

I replayed the drone's survey tapes, but the images were not edifying, to say the least. The surface was shrouded in a mist of crystallized fog. If the rock were pulled out of a nebula or the recent dissolution of a planet, gas could have become trapped on it. If you listen long enough to bullshit explanations, it's amazing how you start to supply your own.

Virgil and Padilla did a final weapons check and jumped out to survey the dorsal surface. We buzzed a wide valley on the ventral face, passing over fields of ice-encrusted emeralds.

Ida jetted off and made a beeline for the green stuff, which looked too much like bowed and frostbitten vegetation. The hills, too, disturbed me, with their regular dimensions and shapes, tiered pyramids, domes and cones, and the terraces with skirts of green marching up their flanks.

Ida rocketed back up to the shuttle with something in her hands. Through the glare of the big work lights miles above our heads, I could see the color and strength drained out of her face.

"Those aren't hills, chief," she gasped. She could have hailed me from down on the ground, but she held out the brittle green artifact in her clumsy gloves. "They're mounds. And that green shit," she added, holding up a wand so the husk shattered and drifted away, revealing white gold, "looks a hell of a lot like corn."

The teams weren't told how they opened the doors, and didn't ask. Something with supersonic super colliders, charged photons racing down miles of chutes and smashing holes in space-time. There were rumors—that they had a chain of psychic retards or even an alien prisoner, who visualized the payload's precise location and opened another door into known space from within the Not, which was the dreaming void of an empty mind. Some insisted that the rocks we grabbed were still up there in space after we took them, like something you find in a dream, but it was still in our hands when we woke up.

I discouraged this kind of talk in my unit when I came in. All we needed to know was that we went through a hole into an empty place, and opened another hole and something tumbled out of it, and we took it apart. It was more than enough to know that *they*, in their infinite wisdom, wanted armed teams to go through first.

At first, they used it to pull in asteroids from the belt between Mars and Jupiter. The raw ore was almost identical to terrestrial stuff. One good payload could yield ten trillion dollars in rare and semi-precious metals and plain old iron, and at first they just fucked around—massive influxes of platinum and cobalt to destabilize the EU, the Tranquility City boom on the moon, the island-building craze that drastically expanded India and Japan.

The first survey teams were just miners and military astronauts, hopping around on naked rocks and never firing a shot. They cleared the payloads for suspicious, radioactive, or unstable carbon deposits and mapped out the plan of attack for the floating strip miners and the monorail cars that carried the ore back through the doors to Clothos, under the Nazca Plain in Peru, and Lachesis, at Tycho on the moon.

It was just a job.

Nobody ever learned the truth about where or how they found #17. It wasn't any kind of asteroid they'd ever seen, but though they looked and looked at it from the EVA bay on *Atropos*, nobody even thought about not going. No one who actually had to go had any idea it was a ship.

It looked like a castle of crystals, a starburst of translucent white and magenta shards, like frozen blood and milk, but it was only two kilometers in diameter, and there was no observable macro-molecular activity.

I wasn't there, but I saw the tapes. The team was planting charges in the galaxy's largest snowflake, when a hole opened up and something like white hair flowed out, miles of it, uncoiling out of itself and flowing all over the team. It tumbled and rolled like mercury, but ripped through them like millions of monofilament swords, striking so fast they were still drawing their weapons as they floated away in wafer-thin slices.

Ida Killdeer was the only survivor—barely grazed, but it shredded her suit, which explosively decompressed before she got back to Atropos. She was in quarantine when they blew up the crystal and told her the whole team died, including Meg Gunderson, her common-law wife. She was recovering from a suicide attempt in a slum hospital in New Orleans when they cracked manageable nanotechnology using the crystals as the basis for a new molecular processor. She got hazard pay. They left her name off the patent applications.

After the Marines, I had worked corporate security on Tycho and the International Space Station. When I was drafted into the project, it took me a week to get my bearings. Then I began to build my own team, asking only for survivors. I went out and brought back Ida Killdeer.

We roped down to the nearest pyramid. I sent Ida on orbital recon, because I didn't want her around when we opened it. Nguyen stayed in the shuttle and ran the drones, while Bowland and I looked for an opening.

"This doesn't mean shit," I told him.

"It means there was air and gravity here, and life, and they grew crops, Darb. It means there was a city here, until we killed it. And it means—"

"Shut up," I ordered, and cut him off the community channel. Ida's channel was mute.

Bowland scraped the crust of ice crystals off the black wall. The stones were irregular in shape, yet seamlessly joined together without mortar. The rock was pitted with erosion-softened shapes—bas-relief carvings—that hinted at bipedal forms with animal heads and winged things cavorting under a radiant sun.

He pulled himself along the wall until he came to a depression clogged with ice, which he chopped away with his axe. A weak gust of frozen air and dust blew out of the hole. A gray stone bowl and a spoon floated past. "Tell me, Darb. What do you think this means?"

I got Nguyen to come down and look at the artifacts and Bowland to reconnoiter the exterior. The stone bowl had the exact isotopic count found in terrestrial limestone. The pyramid itself was metamorphic rock with little in common with earth. "I know what this is," Nguyen said. "This looks like Cahokia."

"No," I said, "don't talk like that." This was like the alien dreamtime bullshit. Bowland was from Chicago. He nodded vigorously as Nguyen started to come undone. I was so glad, just then, that Ida was gone.

"A city of thirty thousand, they lived on hundreds of huge earthen mounds by the bank of the Mississippi River in Illinois. They had astronomers and artisans and a trade network reaching as far as the Aztec and Mayan Empires, but they just vanished sometime around 1300. The Osage, Omaha, and Ponca are supposed to be the descendants of the mound builders, but they don't even have any legends about who they were or where they went. Ask Ida, she'll tell you."

I drew my flechette pistol and crawled into the mound. The mound builders lived in lodges atop the mounds and buried their ancestors inside. I wanted to find something, anything, to shut her up.

My light picked out more artifacts floating around the cramped, low space. Shells, chiseled stones and tools, and bones—these, at least, could show her how wrong she was.

They were long and fluted and fragile as blown glass, yellow with centuries. The first few I grabbed at crumbled in my fingers, but I found one with the remnants of a paw at the end, a forearm made to support a wing. I found another that I left behind—she'd make too much of it. An elongated skull, with sutures that didn't quite close at the crown, like the bulb of a tulip. But it had two holes for eyes, one bifurcated hole for a nose, and a few worn teeth. It looked more human than I was beginning to feel.

Nguyen looked at the bones. "Those look humanoid."

"Stranger things have happened in fewer generations," Bowland added. "Given the radiation and inbreeding—"

"What did you all decide," I demanded, "when I was out of contact? Because I didn't hear anybody asking me over the open channel. This is not a piece of Illinois. These are not human bones."

Ida's channel snapped on, and a smart sheet lit up my helmet display with the drone's deep survey of #64. "You know this is a city, Darby. There are plazas and avenues and tilled fields. There are structures that were probably occupied until we . . . did this."

"Killdeer, where are you?"

"There's only one structure on the dorsal plain, and it's hollow. I'm almost there—"

Virgil cut in. "I'm on the flip side, too, chief. I just lost contact with Padilla. I saw him a second ago."

"Are you inside the structure?"

"Hell no, we're over a flat plain. I don't know where he could've gone . . ."

I keyed the remote feeds from Virgil's locale into my helmet. He floated in his EVA harness, the attitude jets correcting for his panicked motion. Below him, the surface was flat, but striated with grooves that caught the light and evoked dazzling patterns on the eye. "What's out there, Virgil? Any structures?"

"One big mound—in the center. Ida's gone inside it—"

I called for Padilla on all channels. I heard only static until I kicked on his internal suit mic. I heard a faint sound like a demented idiot having a seizure into panpipes, and a few syllables in a strange language, in a voice that wasn't Padilla's, then the signal cut out.

"I let them die," she told me, when I tracked her down in New Orleans. She'd overdosed on pills and tried to slash her wrists, but came up bust. When the cops showed up, she attacked them, trying to make them shoot her.

"Bullshit. They got taken by fuckers from outer space. Stop being sad and get your spine back."

She did.

She was Osage Sioux, the last of the radical Red Power freaks, but she burned out in the last great exodus from the reservation, when the casinos and money finally did what Custer and firewater and pox blankets could not. A stint in the Air Force made her an astronaut, and a rape by her NCO made her decide she was a lesbian. She went to work on the highest of the high steel, on the orbital stations and the moon's first permanent installations, where they opened the first door to the Not.

"I wanted to go because it was the furthest I could possibly get from Earth," she told me, once. I know she went back when I brought her because she wanted to die, but I thought I could give her a reason to live.

Our team surveyed three payloads a month, and they weren't always rocks. Telescopes on Atropos opened exploratory doors and peeked out of the Not, snapping pretty pictures of worlds three galaxies away and taking notes. Anything drifting anywhere in space could be snatched. Inertia was nullified when the payload came through the door, but terrific amounts of waste heat built up in fast-moving objects, and things floating dead in space were less likely to fight back.

When a payload arrived—whatever it was—we boarded and pacified it. What we didn't, or couldn't, kill, they took back to the Hospital on Tycho. I've never been, but I imagine that someday it would make a lovely museum.

Most were derelicts—dead ships, gutted by war or disastrous accident, but all too often teeming with survivors. We never saw two that looked alike, and we never saw anything so familiar as little gray saucer-men. Men and women were killed, but Ida and I brought the team back every time. I think, after #64, I was going to tell her—

Nguyen took us around to the backside.

The contrast was nakedly obvious. The asteroid had an up and a down—it orbited a life-giving sun and had a breathable atmosphere. I didn't need an astrophysicist to tell me what a load of horseshit it all was, but I would have loved to give one the nickel tour.

The dark side of the asteroid was flat and devoid of habitation, but not of design: the grooved plain was a labyrinth of patterns that trapped the eye. Nguyen kept zoning out and nosing the shuttle down at the whorled vortices, which looked too much, from our height above them, like fingerprints. I kept my eyes on the lone pyramid at the center of the plain, on Virgil's beacon light blinking in the mouth of a tall, narrow door. His harness was there, but he was gone.

I did not order them to go inside. I would have had to physically restrain Ida to keep her from going in.

Virgil replied to my hail with a whisper. "I can't talk now . . ."

We glided to a stop and tethered the shuttle alongside the peak of the pyramid, which would have been the nadir of the asteroid, when it was in a gravity well. It stood sixty meters high, with a two square kilometer base. Narrow doors at the peak fed in to vertical shafts stuffed with shadows.

"Keeping still," Nguyen read. "The occasion for repentance will disappear. The situation is shifting, and Yang gains ground. A lack of understanding falls between the classes of men. We see it in greatness gone, and the lesser come upon us."

"Fuck the *I Ching*," I told her.

I waved Bowland to a shaft and picked one for myself. My light seemed to get lost between the source and the walls of the shaft. Great furry black motes of black floated past—whole colonies of spiders frozen in the dark when all the air got sucked out.

I called the others but got no response. Over time, we had used the comm lines across fields that annihilated matter or bent time, but nothing so totally foiled transmission.

And then, without warning, the walls fell away and I goosed my suit's jets to slow my ascent into a big black space. We were deep inside the heart of the asteroid. Other lights bobbed into sight—Bowland and Ida, tiny islands in the cavernous dark. The shaft beneath me closed with a rumble, and the three of us were buffeted around the chamber by rushing winds.

And then light filled the place, and we were not alone at all.

It was like one of those optical illusions. Do you see a vase, or two faces? I vacillated between one interpretation and another of what I saw, between repulsion and a horrible, crushing wonder.

There were twenty of them, maybe more. The way they hung there in the air, clinging rigidly to one another like bats, made my skin crawl. Blinding, burning light shot out from the heart of their cluster, swelling to touch the carven walls of the spherical chamber as the swarm broke up, wriggled and peeled apart, and I realized they were not dead.

Membranous wings stretched out from impossibly elongated arms; hands and feet writhed with fingers that had fingers, trees of busy digits. Their heads and other traits here and there suggested that where they lived, evolution had succumbed to the shapes of dream and myth. Some had bobbing, tentacled heads like bloated octopi, while others had vestigial stumps with slots for light and food, while still others had crests of feathers, or antlers, scales, crayfish claws, scuttling spider legs, fanged muzzles, mandibles, or beaks. Many had long black hair, though, and some still had faces with hatchet-bladed cheekbones, molten brown eyes and straight, bony noses, that stared at us out of Ida's own family tree.

Like moths, they soared round and round the great glowing orb that floated in the center of the chamber, and as they did, their frenzy seemed to charge it. The orb flowed into and fed upon itself, a living yin and yang. Ida watched in wonderment while Bowland took pictures. I think I was the only one who noticed the remains of Virgil, which lay beneath the great glowing orb in the center of the chamber. His suit looked empty.

They flew within a few meters of our heads but came no closer, showed no interest in us at all. Bowland called to me, and I pulled myself around to where he hung on the wall, shining his light over the walls. "God, Darby!" he screamed, "what the hell is this place?"

Pigmented bas-relief carvings depicted the asteroid in the flattened perspective style of Mesoamerican artisans, with stylized plumed dragon shapes bearing it aloft. There were others, arrayed in a loose circle of orbits that rose up to fill the hemisphere of the chamber. Asteroids with cities on them. Winged people flocking back and forth between them like birds in a rain forest, and at the center, a sphere with radiating spokes like curling tongues spreading out to touch the temple on the underside of each island.

"The sun that rises is not the sun," Ida said.

"They killed Virgil and Padilla," I started, but she wouldn't hear it.

"Look at the walls, Darb! That one there, with the lodges on it . . . Look at the little white ghosts toiling in the fields! Some of them had slaves, white slaves! It's Croatoan, where the Indians went with the lost Roanoke colony. And that one, with the vertical lodges, they look like Anasazi cliff-houses."

I could not deny it, and there were so many more—the children of Sacsayhuaman and Tiahuanaco, Tikal and Angkor Wat, and others that might have been Lemuria, Atlantis, and El Dorado—all the vanished peoples of the earth whose fabled ruins had eluded conquistadors and driven them mad with greed, all the enigmatic peoples of the sun whose trails went cold in the mists of history.

"They followed their god away from the catastrophe that was coming to devour their world," Ida went on, "and He made a refuge for them, where they could live under His divine light, and feed Him with their worship.

"And their god kept them safe, until we found them."

Ida kicked off the wall and launched into the midst of the storm of batlike bodies. Bowland raised his harpoon gun to shoot, but I held him back, then went after her myself.

"Haven't you ever wondered," she asked, her voice choking up, "what went out of the world when men stopped worshipping nature and started making machines? Haven't you ever asked yourself, what did they know that let them live in peace with the land, that we didn't? They lived in the glow of something that lived, and loved them. They know—"

They seized her, and she did not resist. She could have broken their arms, but she went limp as they took her and tore off her helmet.

The seething golden glow from the orb burned my eyes. I saw only silhouettes and swarming wings as I tried to grab her and pull her out of their embrace.

Ida took a deep breath of their air and did not die.

She said something, and the faces closest to her chattered a response that, phonetically, I can only reproduce as *"Ia ych-tul shth ul-asath-oth."*

She shouted, "Darb, it's a corrupted Siouan dialect! I think they can understand—"

And then, if for no other reason than that it almost always does, everything went wrong.

When she came back from New Orleans, Ida had stopped cutting herself with a knife, but she still drank and popped speed derms. I made her hate me with inspections; she made me start to love her by getting more inventive in where she hid them.

Her body was sleek and strong, the curves she fed with alcohol softening harsh angles of bone and corded muscle. Her face was broad and deeply creased with anger and anguish, and she had a streak of white at one temple that was not on her ID photo. You had to look deep inside her eyes to see how her hardened copper body was a suit of armor, and how small and broken she was inside.

We were drunk and more than a little high from the last of her derms that I confiscated, unwinding after a bad one, the jellyfish, where Magill got ejected from the ship in a torrent of liquid that froze him solid. I kissed her once, on the forehead—scared to death she'd cry rape or just kick my ass, but scared to death I'd die, someday, and I'd never know.

My lips burned where they touched her hair and skin. She pulled away with what I thought was disgust. "Please don't," she mumbled, and, "please don't tell anyone." I thought I understood what happened then, and didn't connect it when my lips started to bleed.

Ida looked up into their faces, and I could see the back of her head. Her streak of white hair reared up, and glinting filaments of crystalline floss bloomed out of her head and skewered the faces and hands of her curious cousins.

They reeled back and tried to fly away, but Ida's plague fed on its victims faster than eyes could follow, and cast out deadly nets that threaded all the fluttering, hapless tribe together again.

I tried to tear Ida free of the web, but she kicked me away. "Idiot! Stay away, or it'll get you, too! Oh no, God, no, I'm the last Indian scout, I'm a plague blanket—"

The orb's glow boiled over and cast out syrupy tendrils of energy over the floating cocoons. The white hair spread to these and swelled into ribbons like the one that ate Ida's first team, and engulfed the orb, smothering and dousing its light.

"Get out, Darby. You have to leave, now." I played a light over her, but could see only see webs of white hair waving like seaweed from shivering, shrouded forms. "He's coming."

I asked her what she meant, as I tried to find Bowland. I thought I saw him on the wall on the other side, frantically looking for an exit.

"We stole them away from the center of Creation, and He's coming for them."

"So let's go!"

"What is a god, Darb? Do you know what you're feeding, when you kneel down to pray? Go, and be happy for me, Darb . . . I'm going to see—"

A sudden hurricane ripped me out of the chamber then, the shafts open and sucking all the air down the way we'd come. I tried to hang on, but found myself tumbling out the entrance to the temple and into the void.

I fought to get my attitude jets online and correct for my ballistic velocity, but I still noticed right away how the light was all wrong. An infinity of absolute blackness sagged and melted away in a great hole beneath my feet like a frame of film disintegrating in the gate of a projector, nothingness turned inside out. The hole glowed like magma and grew, until it could easily swallow the shrinking asteroid above my head.

Light poured out of it, strobing spectral pulses that warped and perverted vision, and it burned. My helmet automatically polarized, but I looked long enough into it that I wished I was blind, or dead, for a long time after.

The sun that rises is not the sun.

It burned a hole in reality and flowed into the Not like a wave of living plasma, complexity unto madness within its perfectly shapeless shape. If it had a face, I thank God, at least, I could not comprehend or perceive it. I believe that what I saw, like a colossal city of the damned, or a burned planet awakening from cosmic slumber, was but a single eye.

My attitude jets kicked in and retarded, but hardly stopped, my plunge into its midst. Bowland hurtled past me, screaming on all open channels. He might have given me the finger as he fell into it without making a ripple.

Something black swept by and yanked me out of the blasting glow of that eye, breaking both my legs. The shuttle climbed out of its hairpin parabolic dive and into the shadow of the asteroid.

But the light gushed out around the dwindling rock as the hole gave way, and thousands of pseudopods of liquid light reached out to embrace the asteroid and pull it back. Nguyen ignored my screaming and brought us clear of the asteroid as it tumbled out of the Not.

It reached out still further and tore Atropos out of the void. We watched the enormous space station buckle and crack open, bodies and supply modules tumbling out like crumbs of dust, and then the whole thing was gone, and there was only perfect dark.

They re-established a door within two hours. We were towed out into the complex at Clothos and directly into quarantine. They never found any trace of my team, or any surviving crew of Atropos. The program, of course, was suspended. I don't think they'll ever get a chance to start it up again.

Yesterday we lost contact with Tycho. Satellite photos showed a new crater where Lachesis station was, before they all went dead. The government is scared shitless, but they don't know half of what I know.

They don't know Ida Killdeer.

As they wander from bunker to bunker filled with plundered treasures, a thousand shiny things they will never understand, they must be wondering which one might save them, if only they knew what they were and how they worked. Somebody, somewhere, knows what we did and they know where we live, and all we can do now is pray. For once, they're getting it right.

I wonder what sun will rise tomorrow, with Ida and her disease for His high priest and only flock. I hope that the faithful can change the shape of their god with the food of their worship. I pray that she will remember what we once were, and might become again, with the right kind of god.

Swinging

I open my eyes and immediately look for a way to die. I have too many eyes. The rotten banana stench marinates me, though I do not possess anything remotely like a nose with which to smell it. I look around and know it's gone wrong again and I scan this body's habitat and wonder what's a naturally occurring object and what's a tool; what, if anything, I can use to kill myself and get out.

I don't want to look around, don't want to feel anything or know about this body or this life, beyond how to get out of it.

This forelimb, spiked with serrated quartz thorns, slides into an eye until it hits the vaulted dome of this body's cranium. Others like this body are coming, trying to stop me as I stab out another eye, so twisted that the wrenching agony tells me only that I'm on the right path, rooting around as if I'm picking a lock, trying to cut the cord trapping me in this body, this brain, this reality, so I can find *her*—

❄

This is how it ends. You need to understand that, before you get any stupid ideas, as we did when we started the first doomsday cult to get everything right. We had to work so hard to keep our secrets, we had to work even harder to look ridiculous, because even in the modern era, if they knew what we really were, what we could do, they would have burned us as witches.

Maybe a better deterrent would be to tell the truth about how it began.

❄

Don't they say we only know about dark matter because of its absence? Imagine an invisible sun made of the stuff: you only know it's there because of all the shattered planets spinning in its orbit, because all this energy and effort has to be going somewhere . . .

That was how I first came to know Lorna. I was in for a ninety-day observation at Stockton, the lowest tier of California's public mental hospital system. I had gotten good enough at reading the ripples of institutional operations to recognize the ward had at least one inmate off the record.

There were no books or magazines, no Internet, and outside contacts were monitored closely even if you were good, which I mostly wasn't. Nothing to do but these puzzles in unmarked coffee cans, so you had no idea what the picture looked like, or even if the pieces were all from the same puzzle. So the mystery instantly became an obsession.

The nurses wouldn't tell me anything, but one of the orderlies told me there was a girl in a private room behind the nurse's station. She wasn't under restraints, but was such a sensitive case that they were trying to protect her from us, though she was a lifer, locked in for murdering both her parents. She hadn't been out of her cell in over five years. He wouldn't tell me her name. I don't think he knew it.

Strangely, it didn't take a whole lot of effort to get her to notice me. But I didn't recognize her attention at first. Semi-catatonic patient jerkily comes over with a puzzle, dumps it out, and shuffles the pieces, letting them trickle out between fingers, trying to draw my attention while staring sightlessly ahead like an oracle in a Hercules movie and muttering through gritted teeth. Most of the time, I couldn't understand their gibberish. The geezer shuts down and wets the chair, or freaks out, flinging puzzle pieces everywhere until he runs down like a windup toy or the orderlies haul them off for an icy whirlpool bath.

One time, I make out the words. This old woman, bald from burning her hair off in her anxiety attacks, says to me, "All hatred of others is really hatred of self."

I reply, "So is love of others really love of self?"

"No," she answered, "it's just blind love."

I asked the wrong nurse too many times and I got put into restraints for the night. An hour after lights out, the head nurse, Oliveri, came into my cell and knelt before me. Brooding, bitter woman with a wiry mustache and a grouper's mouth. I was in a jacket and strapped to my bed. She moved jerkily, like a hand-cranked silent movie ghost. She knelt beside me and undid the flap at my crotch and took her teeth out. It was a strange, silent mechanical encounter. She bit me just as I came, so I screamed and kicked at her, orgasm spoiled. She made a choking sort of laughter as she inserted her teeth, tucked me in, and locked herself out. "No one else can teach you to love yourself," she said, and then she left.

Nurse Oliveri didn't come back the next night, or the one after that. The other nurses wouldn't share her sordid details with the likes of me, but I overheard them saying she was spending her sabbatical as a guest elsewhere in the hospital.

The next night, almost two hours after lights-out, I had another visitor. It was Stokes, the gabby orderly, a heavy, half-black, half-Asian man with boxy glasses that made his eyes look like antique TV sets. He knelt beside me with his jaw working and his eyes fixed on mine, one hand under his shirt, probing incessantly at his belly button as if it were a strange thing he'd just discovered, down there. I threatened to scream if he tried what the last nurse did, but he just knelt there until I summoned the will to ask him who he was, because I knew it wasn't the same guy who sometimes traded me my anti-anxiety meds for Oxycodone.

He opened his mouth, but he couldn't speak. Finally he reached out with his fingers rigid, as if to poke out my eyes. I jerked away, but he held my head in place and with his other hand forced me to look into a prism he took out of his pocket. When he held it up so I was looking through it into his eyes, I gagged on a phantom stench of overripe bananas and fell out of my head and into milky silver darkness and then—

I'm hiding under a bed, looking through pink-blue shaggy throw rug pink sheets half-open door with posters on it and someone comes into my room tracking red across the blond hardwood, throw rug and a damp bathrobe bunching up under a buckskin slipper bloated with black-red blood. My sweat smells vinegary, like pickles. I grab a high-heel shoe clumped with dust-bunnies, the only weapon I can find. The bloody man kneels beside the bed, leaning on it, wheezing and making choked, clicking noises deep in his throat. One of his hands drops to his knee twisted into a crab's claw, thumb snapping against curled fingers like an idiot's answer to the Zen koan about the sound of one hand clapping. The hand spasms and jerks across the floor as if it's trying to escape. The other hand comes down with a long, expensive steak knife, pinning it to the floor. I don't want to move, but I'm moving.

Out from under the bed and the man—silvery, shaggy beard dappled with blood, blue chambray shirt plastered to his soft, sloping torso—looks at me without any recognition or alarm. Just pulls the knife out of his spastic hand too late to stop me driving him onto his back and pinning the knife to the floor. More than my mother's blood, more than his dull clicking throat sounds, it's HIS EYES watching and seeing everything, and knowing me not at all—

That I woke up screaming was taken as a sign of progress. I was let out of restraints the next morning. Roel Stokes was caught stealing from the pharmacy and fired. When I came back from the dayroom for afternoon nap, I found a book in my bed.

It was an old paperback, dog-eared and acid-stained and smelling of mold, with a host of used bookshop stamps inside the lurid, late Nineties New Age cover: *Beyond Time, Out of Mind* (formerly *The Mind-Snatchers*). I'd never heard of it, but I recognized the author's name. Anyone who watched enough true crime docudrama TV would. David Orchard was some kind of UFO nut who wrote a few books about alien abduction and mind control.

Even in the crystal-gazing circles of the Nineties, Orchard was an outsider and a kook who would have stayed forgotten had he not gone berserk and murdered his wife and died trying to finish off his only daughter.

I used up six disposable lighters and a box of kitchen matches, reading the book under the covers. It was hard to swallow, but it made some sense, at least, of the impossible things she had demonstrated she could do with the hospital staff.

Orchard wasn't just an opportunist or a kook, at first. A research psychologist working in neuroscience, he spent years mapping brain activity during "peak" and transcendent states of consciousness— groundbreaking but hardly controversial, until he had a nervous breakdown as devastating as a stroke. After a week of catatonia, he left his family and his university position and went to study abroad. No one really knew what he did for the next three years, least of all Orchard himself. When he was found in a Sudanese aid station, he had undergone another breakdown and lost all basic motor control. He went back to his family, who accepted him and restored him to health, but he never returned to his studies. Instead, he started trying to recover his memory of what happened to him after his breakdown, and when he did, he started writing his bugshit crazy books.

Orchard's little green men didn't come from outer space, they came from outside of time, and they didn't just probe your pooper, they stole bodies and used them to quietly observe, influence, and sabotage humankind throughout history. Knowing past and future, they worked almost fanatically to stop the kind of threshold moments that threatened their history and spun off alternate universes. While an infinity of alternate realities overlay our own, the unchecked spawning of alternate realities is almost a kind of cosmic cancer, which Orchard vaguely asserted had led to the destruction of the watchers' home world of Yith. Many of the world's greatest discoveries, he maintained, had been killed in the cradle by an invisible race whose greatest fear was that we might someday learn to travel out of our bodies, outside of time and space, as they do.

Given a choice, he probably would have gone back to his career and kept his mouth shut about the whole thing; but he was unable to return to conventional research, and paranoid that the government was tracking him, that they knew at least a little about what had happened to him but just wanted to watch him twist in the wind. *The Mind-Snatchers* came out from a crackpot paperback publisher along with new and recycled titles on Atlantis, the Bermuda Triangle, and Y2K. It detailed Orchard's struggle to retrace the steps "my body took when my control of it was usurped," to recover his lost memories of where his mind spent that unhappy time. By the end of the book, he'd found not very much of either, but the frustrating open ending and his manic sincerity made the book a success and put Orchard on the crackpot lecture circuit for a while. Talk shows, conventions, seminars, even a residency at the Atwater Institute for Psychonautical Research. Without ever dropping any answers, Orchard seemed to have built a solid second career on his breakdown, and was working on his third book and beginning to search systematically for other people through history and around the world who had been hit by the same thing.

And then one night, he shredded all his records and destroyed his hard drive, then murdered his wife.

His daughter killed him in her bedroom, but Lorna Orchard's defense was problematic at best. She claimed at first that her father had a seizure and then methodically butchered his wife and cornered her, but evidence that she'd stabbed them both after death prompted her to maintain that she was afraid they weren't really dead, then that they were possessed by her father's aliens, then that she had been possessed herself and had no memory of the attack. She was locked away somewhere upstate for the rest of her life, said the TV.

The ward was haunted by Lorna Orchard, California's answer to Lizzy Borden. And if I was interested in her, she seemed very eager to get to know me.

I was visited throughout my days by smiling, twitching patients who delivered me their orange juice or rice pudding, by one or another of the nursing staff who brought me magazines and sometimes clumsy, somnambulist sex. They seldom spoke more than a few words, jaws working with strain that was not theirs, but like the jaws of a horse with a bit in its teeth, the twanging tendons of their necks. Learn to look for it and you'd see a certain sparkle in the comically dilated pupils, a delicate curiosity in the way they explored their own ears, elbows, navels. Sometimes I talked to them about whatever came into my mind, and they listened, nodding, smiling, until that light went out in their eyes and they went away.

It was a strange courtship, to be sure, but were we any weirder than any other broken strangers who try to find answers in one another's desperate questions? We knew we were right. Did you ever have to overcome such obstacles as imprisonment and solitary confinement, just to see your beloved? I still didn't know what love was, but I knew that she must love me. Did you ever love someone so purely that you would recognize them in whatever guise they wore by twinkle of eye and gravity of smile, that you would welcome them into your heart and your bed whether they came as man or woman, old or new, drooling and deformed or strange beyond reason? And so she knew my love, too, was pure.

I had never been loved or accepted for myself, could not begin to dream of breaking whatever spell we'd cast over each other. If she wanted to talk about what happened, she would tell me, but I wasn't so stupid that I couldn't understand what was happening, or so sane that I wasn't willing to accept it all. We made no plans, shared no secrets, during that blessed time. We shared nothing but love. I never once doubted what was happening or asked for an explanation. She came to me in a different body every day, selected as you would choose a suit of clothes, to fit the weather and your mood. And that was enough, for a while.

"Tell me how you do it," I asked the skinny, lazy-eyed physical therapist with the carrot-red short hair who locked the door and climbed into the icy whirlpool bath with me.

Lorna had the most control with this one, because she was weak-willed. She joked, "It's easy. All you do is close your eyes and die." But when I pushed her about teaching me, she started to lose control.

Her body went ramrod stiff, churning the water to foam with her hands. Through her chattering teeth I made out words. "Dad learned how to . . . do . . . what they do . . . . He remembered what . . . what they were . . . and will be . . . . That's when—when . . . They came."

I didn't pick at it. With what she'd been through, with the power she had, who wouldn't be paranoid and delusional? But she reached out for me, clawing my arm, pulling me close until our eyes practically kissed corneas.

There was a sickening wave of stench—rotten bananas, an odor rife with negative associations for me that I'd largely blocked out. And then—

She was right. It was exactly like dying.

You know how people die and come back every day, and their stories are always the same, with the long tunnel and the light at the end, and the voices of dead loved ones? The people who stop with their toes on the threshold of hell are less forthcoming, but they're out there. Even setting aside how we've been conditioned by hearing of the experience enough so a five-year-old could fool his parents and write a heavenly visit memoir that got made into that stupid movie. But it's in there, wired into our temporal lobes, like a cerebral inflight safety video that only kicks in when the shit has really hit the fan. Doctors like David Orchard can zap a patient's temporal lobes and induce near-death experiences and UFO abductions on a couch.

I was ripped out of my body like a plastic bag in a high wind. I saw the tunnel. I went into the light. I came out the other side and was back in the whirlpool bath.

Looking at myself—

I looked for her and saw only my rawboned, ugly body staring back at me with a look of panic, disbelief, and excitement. I backed away from my body, quite understandably repulsed by its hideous familiarity thrusting itself against me. I was smaller, I was freckled, I was the physical therapist.

"Teach me how to do it," I said, cringing at the high, sinusoidal mew of my voice. She/I playfully pushed my/her head under the water and we wrestled until someone pounded on the door.

We were so lost in love that I was taken by surprise when the end of my observation period came and I was transferred out and turned loose on the streets. In a panic, I assaulted the doctor and the orderlies, but they were not about to keep me on the ward if the state stopped paying. Screaming her name, I was dragged out of Stockton and deposited at the bus stop out front.

I hung around the hospital until the police came and took me to the Greyhound station and gave me thirty bucks to ride back home to San Francisco. I jumped the bus and took up squatting in a dead tract development on the edge of town.

Only a handful of the houses were occupied, and the evicted owners had sabotaged plumbing, ripped out copper wiring, trashed the interior drywall, and festooned the walls with hateful curses on the banks and Wall Street. But the daily newspaper still came, piled up in the weeds and the rain gutters. I wrote postcards to the hospital, but I know she never got them. I waited, though I didn't know what I was waiting for. Only a week after I was thrown out of the hospital, it made the front page.

The ward burned down. Four people were killed, including two nurses. Arson was suspected. No mention of my beloved, but I knew. I just knew.

I went a little mad. I kicked holes in the walls. I wrote things on the walls in my own shit and then set fire to the house. When the fire got out of control and spread to the roof, I moved across the street and hid, expecting the firemen and the police and the news, but nobody came at all, and the house eventually burned itself out and nobody noticed. I didn't see anyone but the lady who delivered the newspaper from her station wagon, hitting hundreds of empty houses before dawn every morning. I passed out watching the fire through the boarded-up picture window in the living room. I woke up to the sound of the doorbell.

I got up to answer it. I'd left my clothes in the other house when I started the fire, but I saw it was a Mormon, scrubbed-ruddy face pressed up to the fisheye lens set in the door as if he could see me. They always travel in pairs and they would be crazier than me to be looking for converts in a dead neighborhood like this, but I would settle for any human contact, anyone I could shock or offend to spread the venom that had built up inside me.

But when I opened the door, the red-faced, sweaty boy barged into the room and knocked me down and crushed my face with kisses.

"I found you," she said with his mouth, her light pouring out of his eyes. "They tried to find me, but I found you first."

❈

We lay together and made plans. She told me about how she did it, but it didn't make any more sense than a bird explaining how it flies. Her father never taught her to do it, but she watched him sedate himself in his office and hypnotize himself with a crystal on a pendant. He called it swinging, for reasons that became obvious when she was older. She never tried it until she was committed, and was careful never to draw attention to herself. Until I came along.

She couldn't stay with me, no matter how I begged. She had to stay with her body, and not even I could know where it was. I tried not to push too hard. With all she'd been through, with what she could do, who wouldn't succumb to a few paranoid delusions? This was a lot to take on trust, but she promised to visit and bring me supplies, and made me promise to do what we decided to do.

In return, I made her swear to give me the only thing I wanted more than to hold her, in her real body, in my arms, and she reluctantly agreed. She would teach me how to do it, when I was ready. And in return, we would start a church.

I argued with her that if she was in danger we should go away, but she would hear me out and then go on as if I'd never spoken. It was the necessary, the Next Thing. It was already done somewhere, she sometimes said, and we'll be there soon.

I would be the figurehead, the face and voice, and she would be the miracle. I would require no training, no indoctrination. I had only to open my mouth, and her words would come out.

She taught me to see auras. Her method wasn't the one in her father's book, but she said it was how he did it. We went out into the woods near Lake Tahoe and she dosed me with Golden Teacher mushrooms one of the more daring therapists smuggled in for treating depression, enough to lose it completely, and when I was peaking, she showed it to me. I couldn't see her face; it was eclipsed by the fiery blue-white corona of her aura and full of eyes and frozen smoke and silver milk plasma. The sparkle I'd seen in the eyes of her hosts had been the merest reflected gleam of it. When I came down, I could still see it, and with a couple more trips I got so it was as easy as crossing my eyes.

Within a week she brought me our bible. I recognized huge chunks of her father's book in the manually typed foolscap manuscript. But the prophet's journey was obscured by bursts of absurd stream-of-consciousness word salad with a sleepy cadence that induced a hypnogogic state more alert than balls-to-the-wall panic, but more restful than deep, dreamless sleep. The self-hypnosis initiation was key to all the gifts we offered, and essential to believing what we had to teach them.

Most of it was lifted all but verbatim from Lorna's father, but Orchard's bodiless mind-stealers from beyond were now alien teachers of a primordial science that promised to put all enlightened human beings in total control of their mental and spiritual potential. Bad habits and self-destructive routines purged as if by spiritual electrolysis. Ecstatic states and peak alertness on demand, transcendental meditation demystified, push-button ataraxia. And for the initiated, the promise of deeper secrets—astral projection, mastery of inner and outer space and linear time, and immortality, for those who aimed that low.

Of course, nobody wanted to read it.

So I had to go out and preach. This took some practice, and I didn't want to do it until she had kept her promise, but she trapped my eyes with hers so I was staring into the crystal before I realized it, and my body went out to testify, but I stayed behind, imprisoned in rapture.

These things we promised were real. They would all come true, if you only heard me speak and believed, if you only read the book and loved it, the first time she possessed you.

The first time . . .

If knowing her in a stranger's body was a revelation, then being possessed by her was an apocalyptic gnosis. It was not the euphoria of finding oneself drugged and under soft restraints, though she always sedated herself to the edge of oblivion, and she had only limited control over the bodies she took, so she knew they must be utterly helpless. It wasn't even being inside an unfamiliar body. It was a thousandfold stronger strain of the rush of being inside a lover. It was a fulfillment of the fleeting dream of shedding skin and sharing one perfect form, the dream that failed with every orgasm and left you empty and guilty and cheated. To look out of the eyes one has longed to gaze into, to reach out fumblingly with a hand one always longed to touch. To become that Other who made life's torments bearable, and to know she was walking the world in *your* body, was the most deliciously maddening perversion of intimacy. I already loved her before the first time she took me, and in time I would come to know that everyone she possessed felt the same as I did, even if they never guessed who or what she really was.

In our observances, she channeled through me masquerading as One, the last remnant of a species that had evolved out of their physical bodies and become pure thought. One stayed behind, as a sort of lighthouse keeper of the galaxy, teaching the pandimensional gospel of sentience and leading all those who were ready out of the prison of matter. She preached the same positive thinking bullshit recycled by every charlatan from Hermes Trismegistus to Dr. Phil, sprinkled with predictions and cryptic nonsense that turned out to be prophetic just often enough to intrigue people without freaking them out.

There were channels going back to the nineteenth century, and several from the Eighties were still on the circuit, but every one we looked at was a fraud or a contrived multiple personality, a con artist trapped in her own cover story. This we knew, because all of them only spoke through the designated cult leader, and all the believers would gather round her and wait with bated breath for the next confusing prophecy, the next outrageous demand from the Atlantean magus or Pompeiian shepherd for truffles and cocaine and a Tesla roadster and Season 3 of *Ally McBeal*. Because anyone who gave themselves over to us could become a vessel of the spirit of One, the benevolent, bodiless sage of Celaeno.

They only knew that if they listened to me, if they believed, if they reached out and opened themselves to the arcane wisdom I offered, then some higher power could sweep into them and take them away, and while they floated inside a golden cloud, their bodies would do the things they could not bear to face, could not dare to dream. Alcoholics blacked out, only to wake up with no booze in the house and a heartfelt letter in their own handwriting commanding them to change. The shock of it was as deep as UFO abduction, but without terror, without the sense of being used. They emerged awakened to the untapped potential in their lives and vaguely aware that while someone else was at the controls, they were somewhere wondrous.

The first time I went out to speak on my own, I got the shit kicked out of me. She told me to play up to those who got fight-or-flight angry when they saw somebody preaching New Age nonsense about Jesus and Buddha and others being possessed by aliens, to egg them on without engaging until I provoked a beating. I stood and took as much as I could and refused to defend myself. I refused to press charges, refused medical attention. I found myself picked up and protected by people of deep empathy, flushed and terrorized as if they'd been attacked themselves. A few who came to my aid at the first meetings, like Margo Berthel and the Holders, became our most committed followers. These compulsively empathic types were the ones we were fishing for, because they made a group feel like a family and held others inside it. They were also the easiest for Lorna to control. The most reliable of them she would come to use like comfortable shoes, left on the porch and slipped on when she needed to go out. I learned to pick their auras out of a crowd and play to the nearest asshole to hook them, and I never left alone.

The woman in the front row at the dedication of our first meditation center in the Berkeley hills was stunning and stared at me with wide, appreciative eyes, the pale silver halo of her aura flushed with burgundy, as if engorged with astral blood. Platinum blond hair, clipped on the sides with a tousled mop on top, a sleek, slim body with an oddly cockeyed posture I would soon learn was because she wore a prosthetic left leg.

I faltered and lost my place for just a moment, staring into the crowd, into that face. I had never seen that face in the flesh before, but I instantly recognized the piercing glitter of those eyes, the jut of those cheekbones, the defiant set of her jaw that came through so clearly even in the half-tone newsprint photo from when she killed her father.

Somehow I mumbled through the rest of my speech and nearly floated off the stage in her wake as she left. I followed her out onto the street and joined her in a cab. She gave an address in the Sunset District.

We got to an apartment building looking over the extreme western end of Golden Gate Park and she paid the cab. I followed her upstairs to a cluttered bachelor apartment with a futon and stacks of books and dusty junk everywhere in lieu of furniture.

She pushed me back onto the mildewed mattress and stripped me. She undid the straps on her leg and hopped across the room to loom over me, moonstone white in the blue, dying evening light.

When we were done, she stroked and kissed my face, closing my eyes, and when I opened them, the full moon was peering through the dusty blinds. She got up on her solitary leg and hopped into the kitchenette.

It took her a while to find the stuff to make coffee. I demanded to know why we were doing this religious shit. It was a fun game for its own sake, but if I was going to play, I had to know what the rules were. She came over and put a cup in my hand. I looked up at her and spilled half of it in my lap.

A chubby, apple-cheeked fortyish woman with purple rinse in her graying, shoulder-length bob took my scalded hand. She told me to look into her eyes, and so long as I did, the pain went away.

She hissed, "You needed to see how easy it is to make them see what they need to see. You can do this too . . . I need you to learn to do what I do now."

I had been asking for this, but suddenly it came through, smelling this woman's strange vinegary sweat like pickles and seeing Lorna's aura pouring out of that head, scabbed over but shining out of fissures and blisters like a jeweled predator buried in the dirt. She was a rapist. I suddenly wondered if she had survived the fire at all, if her body was a hideous wreck stashed away somewhere, if she still had a body of her own at all, or if she was nothing but a homeless ghost, the shimmer in the eyes of her victims. She was a monster, and I wanted to be just like her.

It was all true, she insisted. The ones from Outside that her father wrote about. They took him away and used his body for three years. When he came back, he tried to regain his memories of what happened to him, he learned something else entirely. When they took his body, he took one of theirs, and he lived among them.

They called themselves the Great Race, and with good reason. They came from beyond the stars we know as bodiless minds that leapt en masse across the cosmos to take new bodies and domesticate new worlds, simply so they could live and add to their knowledge, until it was time to forget and begin again. They came to earth before the dinosaurs and lived in cities more advanced in their way than anything we will ever achieve, studying the universe and all life on earth in peace and stability for over a hundred million years in an empire that spanned much of the supercontinent of Gondwanaland. Though they made no ships, they were travelers in time and space, forcibly exchanging bodies with humans throughout our history, with other intelligent species that ruled the earth before us, and with others throughout our solar system. Through painstakingly careful exploration, they had mapped out a complete history of the earth and all its races, including their own extinction fifty million years ago, and their leap through time to take over another host race somewhere in earth's future.

They were placid observers from outside of time, except when they weren't. There were times and places where they took a much more active role, to preserve their safety and secrecy. History was littered with places where they knew they could get away with murder, or where they knew that they already had done it. Where they could not act, there were secret societies and cults who served their purposes in return for tokens of knowledge and wisdom, fleeting glimpses of the real Great Game being played high above humanity's heads.

When Lorna's father confronted his memories under self-hypnosis, he discovered that he could do what they did—project his mind into the bodies of others, use them as puppets. Once he accepted the principle, it became almost effortless. It was only a matter of will, in an area few people had any defenses at all. He trusted no one with his discovery, but his daughter watched him and learned and believed where no one else would. Even so, he was no threat to them, or his removal was too much a threat to the chain of causality that had produced our world, until he began to speak about them publicly.

After his second book, he became convinced they were out to get him. He said their "support shadows" in this "temporal beachhead" were following him and trying to sabotage his career, inciting an IRS investigation, opening his mail, planting bugs and illegal drugs on his person, and following his wife and daughter. He moved them out to a ranch in the Mojave Desert and shot at a couple reporters who tried to force an interview. He kept the world at bay for almost a year.

When Lorna was fifteen and her father killed her mother and would have killed her too, she recognized nothing behind her father's eyes and knew that she wasn't killing him, but an alien thing sent to destroy them all. In prison and later in the hospital, she learned to perfect her "swinging."

Think of the brain as a transmitter, she said, and the mind as the signal. Human energy fields feed upon and attack each other, unseen, in every human interaction. Turn off the brain and the signal dies. But if the signal is aware of itself, it becomes a hologram, self-contained and capable of persisting in the absence of the brain. Every house haunted by the death or the intense emotional life of its past tenants is stained by fragmented and residual holograms of human minds. The Great Race had evolved to a point where their intelligences could swim across galaxies and up and down the river of time, and could fasten upon and "haunt" any sufficiently complex nervous system.

It was possible for only a tiny sliver of humankind to swing, many of whom were thus selected by the Great Race to be abducted. Some, through a combination of factors Lorna had not begun to catalog scientifically, could be taught. She had every reason to believe that I was one of them, and now was the time.

Everything we were doing, everything we would do, was not just for a lark, though she promised me there would be pleasures undreamt of. We were after nothing less than the survival of humankind beyond its own physical extinction. We were going to live forever, along with anyone useful and interesting enough to come with us.

While I was laying the cornerstones of our church, Lorna had dedicated herself to recreating her father's research on abductees. Thanks to the Peaslee papers and other suppressed testimonials, she learned that the Great Race always required a peculiar apparatus involving a set of crystal lenses to affect their return, a means of concentrating mental focus to make the jump across eons. Always, these devices were commissioned or produced in secret, the plans and prototypes destroyed by persons unknown either possessed by the Great Race or secretly dedicated to supporting them.

But Lorna found one.

A San Francisco magnate named Adolph Sutro—he of the famous baths and ill-fated Cliff House—built his fortune in the 1880s on a pump system that allowed miners to dig deeper silver mines in Colorado. He served as the city's mayor twice. But a year after his first term, he disappeared for nearly four years on a strange world tour, and when he returned he was briefly committed by his own physicians. A prodigious Gilded Age collector of everything, Sutro amassed several lots of junk that the De Young Museum bought nearly a century ago and was still in the process of cataloguing. Among the avalanche of exotica, antiques, and moldering garbage was an unremarkable suitcase containing a set of crystal magnifying glasses and mirrors. Mislabeled as optometric equipment, it was left in a larger lot in storage, but never went anywhere until yesterday, when Rhiannon Mitchell found it and began researching it.

This was Rhiannon Mitchell's body, her apartment. Lorna had abducted the woman as she left the museum, drove her like a rental car to hear my speech. But she could not do the job. I would have to do it.

We practiced all night. She challenged me to wrest control of Rhiannon—Rhea, to her friends—from her. I locked eye contact with her until an icepick migraine lobotomized me. I had internalized the doctrine, but I couldn't effect the transaction.

Sometime around dawn she sighed and sank onto the futon, and then she had a seizure.

I went down on my knees and lifted her up. Her eyes regarded me with no recognition; indeed, they glistened and froze over with repulsion and terror.

I called her Lorna. She trembled, looked around, and seeing she was naked in her room with a strange man holding her . . . she drew in a breath to scream, and I took her.

It was terrifying. I fell out of my own eyes and across the impossible, roaring black gulf between us, into hers. I went out visualizing the lonely one-legged woman, the smell of her sweat, the taste of her tears . . .

Just close your eyes and die—

I felt a sickening sense of distortion like that first childhood fever, of my limbs swelling to fill the room and burst the walls. I fought upstream against a roaring vacuum like a salmon up a ladder. I gagged on a nauseous mélange of rotten bananas and pencil shavings. It was exactly like an epileptic seizure, down to the unpleasant sensory impressions.

I looked at my body. It flopped backwards on the floor, back arched in a bow, choking on its own tongue, moaning in an unsettling falsetto. I tried to calm it down, but it was all I could do to breathe.

The phone rang. I got up and immediately fell on the floor and had to crawl to answer it.

Lorna said, "Get up. Is she still awake? You've got to sedate your body before she damages it."

There was a syringe prepared in the refrigerator. I had to crawl over to the chair to reattach my leg. With this exotic errand completed, I lurched into the kitchen to fetch the spike, jabbed my body in the ass, and pushed the plunger home. The shaking and moaning slowly subsided. Sweat soaked through the sheets, smelling worse than urine to me with my new nose, but I held it, stroking its oily, coarse hair and whispering soothing words in a strange voice until the throttling anxiety subsided into a slurred snore.

Lorna walked me through getting Rhea ready for work.

The park was frosted with dew and drowned in silver fog when I went into the museum. I had to pass my ID card over scanners at a series of doors. It was not yet 6 A.M., but I passed several people who greeted me and I tried to look as if I recognized them. I followed the path Lorna had drilled in my head, through the door with a thumbprint scanner, down the corridor lined with the showcase restoration rooms under the scrutiny of passing museum guests, then into a dimmer, dustier section filled with crates. Deep in the darkest, dustiest heart of the warehouse, I found Rhiannon's workstation. A faded green alligator skin case with tarnished brass latches and a grubby gutta-percha handle sat on her desk, its lid open. Some skinny Hindu guy looking inside it with a huge adjustable magnifying glass.

"It's one for the Liars' Club," he said over his shoulder. "I think somebody was looking for something like this a few years back. When were you going to show it to me, Rhea?"

The open case in front of him was exactly as Lorna described it. I apologized, and then I took a fire extinguisher to the side of his head, sending him sprawling across the floor. Blood surged out of his nose and mouth. I tracked it in and out of the office as I searched to make sure I got everything. He had a series of lenses laid out on the desk in front of him, and he'd been about to look through them with the magnifier.

My pulse was a fire alarm in my ears. My hands shook with the urge to rush, the urge to check on the man at my feet to be sure he didn't drown in his own blood, and all the while I felt feverish and like a rubber band stretched to its breaking point. If I blinked, I would find myself on the floor of Rhiannon Mitchell's studio, and the alarms would become a dragnet of sirens.

I put it all together, every piece into its slot lined with moldering velvet, and walked out, stepping over the man on the floor, who gagged and coughed and grabbed for my leg. I felt relief, but I walked faster. Rhiannon's artificial leg was built for a cautious rolling stride that I simply had no time for, and I tripped on it a few times getting to the elevator. A few more people waved to me and tried to engage me in conversation, but I kept walking. None of the doors had scanners going out, but the last one stumped me. The rotten banana smell flushed my brain until I bit back puke. Violet neon dots swarmed my vision. I lost my temper and pounded on the door with my forehead when someone came over and took my arm.

"The thumbprint scanner, hon," said the older black woman. I thanked her, giggling nervously, touched it, and went out into the museum.

I got to the atrium—there was a massive new exhibit of Tibetan artifacts called *The Book of the Dead* opening that morning, and three scissor lifts were deployed hoisting huge banners up outside the entrance. A handful of security guards and custodial staff loitered in the lobby. I waved and went out through the turnstile when a guard came running out after me. An Asian guy with his gun in his hand, he shouted for someone to stop me. A second guard moved in front of the doors with his hand out, but nowhere near his sidearm. I got him in the eyes with Rhiannon's pepper spray and went out the door.

I tried to run down the steps, but the leg wasn't up to it. I stumbled and nearly dropped the case, catching it and myself on the railing just as the armed guard came out the door and told me to stop.

A jogger in a cardinal red tracksuit ran by on Hagiwara with his Beats headphones cranked up, oblivious. I turned right and ran toward the Tea Garden. The guard shouted at me to stop again, then started shooting.

William Yee had applied to the SFPD and failed the fitness exam because of his employment record. He had worked as a mail carrier, armored car guard, and bus driver; and his record of firings for insubordination and verbal and physical assaults, leading to lawsuits and nuisance lawsuits filed in protest of said firings, abundantly demonstrated his short temper and poor judgment. Perhaps his judgment was not so poor that morning.

Perhaps he was imbued with a higher power when he assumed a Weaver stance at the foot of the stairs and fired three times, striking me twice in the back and once in my prosthetic leg. Perhaps something more than a high-strung security guard tried to stop me. I suppose I wish he had.

I faltered and took cover behind a bus shelter at the curb. The jogger hid behind a palm tree with his phone stuck to his head, excitedly shouting into it.

A Honda Element like a black French police van screamed up Hagiwara, jumped the curb, and flattened the jogger, then swerved across the street to spin out beside the bus shelter. A heavyset Hispanic man in a parka jumped out and fired from behind his open door, hitting Mr. Yee in the sternum and upper abdomen, then through the right cheekbone as he slumped to the sidewalk.

I couldn't breathe. One lung collapsed and sucking up blood. The pain came and went in tandem with the sickening unreal fever, the epileptic stench, the roaring void.

The big man came over to kneel beside me and take my hand. "Let go," he said, and he said my name and kissed my forehead. "Don't die here. Go *home*. Go home."

He took the case out of my arms. He wiped off his pistol, put it in my right hand, and pointed it at the museum, firing two more shots that shattered the front doors.

I heard sirens. He was gone, and then so was I.

I woke up to Margo Berthel injecting me with an IV of glucose solution. I was in the lounge of the meditation center in Berkeley.

I should be in a hospital, I was dying, I was dead—

She urged me not to get out of bed. I had wandered off and then collapsed from exhaustion. I was working too hard, giving too much of myself to the church.

❈

The news said that De Young Museum historian Rhiannon Mitchell and security guard William Yee killed each other in an exchange of gunfire as Ms. Mitchell tried to flee the scene after brutally murdering her immediate superior, Ajay Vivekananda, in a seemingly unprovoked attack. The vehicle that killed Larry Trouba, a passing jogger who phoned 911, was found abandoned in the same Muni station lot from which it was reported stolen. Though theft was explored as a motive, the investigation was quickly closed with the motive pinned on unrequited office romance gone bad, given the unreported detail that Ms. Mitchell, a confirmed lesbian, was found to have spermicidal lubricant from a popular national-brand condom in her vagina at the time of her death.

I grieved for all these people, even after Lorna reminded me they were all going to die anyway. This had to happen, and it had to happen now, or the consequences would be far worse. The Great Race died fifty million years ago, but their minds evacuated those old bodies and leapt into the future. I thought now I understood what she and her father feared so much: that they were coming to take over the human race at some point in our future, that they would migrate and colonize us as they had so many species on so many worlds before ours even existed.

But the Great Race valued security and stability, and those were not qualities humankind had demonstrated in its million and change years on earth. Their old bodies lasted for more than two centuries; the cone-things served for a hundred million years without evolution changing them any more than it changed the shark. When they were overrun by another species, an ancient, awful enemy they'd buried in caverns beneath their capital in what is now Australia, they had known for millions of years, down to the date, that they would be exterminated. But they sent thousands of their finest minds into the future to colonize another host-race that will serve until our sun begins to die out. And then they'll go on to another world, as they came to earth when Yith, the oldest world they remembered, was destroyed by something even they were unwilling to recall.

Humanity wasn't going to work out for the next host species, but they were curious about us: so ripe with potential, so intriguingly short-lived, and so hell-bent on our own demise. That was why we had to have the lens array, she told me, because to escape the end of our species we would have to steal from the Great Race their greatest secret and learn to leap through time, and we would have to do it without them finding out, until it was too late to stop us.

The end was coming in our own lifetimes. She didn't know if it would be a human or a natural catastrophe, or if the Great Race would take matters into their own hands to erase a potential competitor. It couldn't be stopped, but it could be escaped.

It was the most insane thing I'd ever heard, which by now was quite a milestone. "Are we really going to go through with this?" I asked her.

"Of course we are," she said. "And they can't stop us, because they know the future, and in it we've already won."

"What can I do?" I asked her.

She told me, "Build our church."

❉

I flatter myself I had something to do with how fast it grew. I was a natural salesman, and my genuine love for the product—for her—turned my creepy sociopathic charm into something compelling, something true.

By the end of three years, we had twelve thousand active members worldwide and two books on the nonfiction bestseller lists and assets in excess of fifty million, with twelve million annual income. But it wasn't me, and it wasn't even her. It wasn't even that we had something that worked. We scratched an itch, a need for more than answers to be taken on faith.

Within six years of my first witnessing, we had churches in every major American city and several coed advanced academies with services daily, meditation workshops and retreats, from conventional marriage counseling and biofeedback seminars to our own inner space program that dedicated the same scientific rigor and ambition to out-of-body exploration that NASA did to the expensive, pointless physical variety.

Money came flowing in with ridiculous ease and little or no tax oversight, and if most of it seemed to disappear into nesting-doll holding accounts that I never set up, there was still more than enough to purchase a mountain resort in the Rockies and a Caribbean island.

I met the increasing media scrutiny and the inevitable public backlash with an eerie calm that wasn't difficult to fake, for I was seldom in control of my own body.

At first. By the time we received official tax-exempt status, she was with me less than once a week, and never out of character as the amiably inscrutable One. I found myself faking channeling her more and more in my gradually curtailed media appearances. Margo Berthel and Norman Holder filled the ecclesiastical roles and cracked the whip on those caught claiming possession by the One, so the miracle was withheld from all but the innermost of inner circles. I officially conserved my energies for developing more seminars and books, which came to take up nearly all my time after our first release became a bestseller. Only one critic charged us with plagiarizing Orchard's books, but he quickly dropped it and became a loyalist after one visit from Lorna.

Likewise, there was a string of sex scandals that never quite took off, of accusations that I engaged some kind of hypnotic harem of several dozen women and a few men for my own depraved pleasure. The few who leveled the charges subsequently demonstrated such unbalanced characters as to discredit their eerily similar depositions, and when they began to commit suicide, the general media reaction was a kind of chagrined relief.

If I was only trying to make her jealous, I succeeded. Lorna stopped coming to me. I was told that she was working with the handful of initiates we had discovered who could swing effectively, and the even smaller group of previous abductees whose hypnotic regression sessions were creating a record of the Great Race to mirror their own of us.

But to me, she vanished. I only knew she still lived because so much of the money we gathered kept going somewhere else, and every so often one of my assistants would turn to me and give me a brief message in a strangely dislocated voice, and then plant a cold, dry kiss on me before fainting dead away at my feet. So I abused the absolute trust placed in me by so many. I used our inner circle as a guard to silence our enemies, and the rest as puppets to satisfy my darkest desires.

Imagine you can become anyone in the world, or become the one person in the world with whom they share their real, secret selves. With nothing else to occupy me, it took a while for it to get old. But it turned out I wasn't a very good sociopath. After another couple of years, I was ready to quit and she knew it. That must have been why she came back. I thought it was about me, about us.

I was staying at the chalet in Aspen when she returned on a crisp November morning, holding the green alligator skin case and surrounded by a cadre of former abductees who had joined our cause without my knowledge. It felt as if I was receiving a visiting foreign dignitary. Two women with flat, unblinking stares got between Lorna and me when I tried to embrace her. Her hair was longer and gone to its natural dark brown. Her face was pale as fog and deeply lined with tension. She silently parted the wall of hollow-eyed guards and laid her head on my chest. "I need you," she said.

Over breakfast, she told me some of what our money had been doing behind my back. We had funded several archaeological expeditions to Australia to recon fossil remnants of the Great Race's library city, and embarked upon several massive construction projects on geologically stable sites in North and South America. While I used my godlike gifts to rape celebrities, she had mastered the Sutro Lenses and learned much about the past and future; but to find what we would need to know to make the great leap, she would have to go all the way back and abduct one of the Great Race. She was afraid that if she went that far, she'd never come back.

She needed an anchor, someone she trusted absolutely to watch over her body while it housed one of Them. She had no idea how long she would be gone, because the exchange across time meant she couldn't come back the moment after she left. It created a bridge between their era and ours, a window that couldn't be tampered with, and so was an operation not to be entered into lightly. We could only succeed if the fossil record showed we had succeeded, but if it showed we went back and fucked up everything, we'd still be obligated to go, or the consequences would be quite literally unthinkable.

Knowing nothing, we went back to try to change everything.

The Sutro Lenses were assembled into a cone-shaped array with a soft white light shining through it, in a meditation chamber with Norman Holder and Lorna's armed guards waiting outside. Lorna sat with her legs crossed, staring fixedly into the silvery, pulsating light as the lenses rotated. I sat across from her with her hands limp and cold in mine. I felt her pulse slow and skin temperature drop. She said my name once, cried, "Don't let me go—" Her hands gripped mine so tightly I felt the bones grind together. I tried to anchor her, but when she went she took me with her.

❅

The sky was green—

Clouds of delta-wing leaves rose on roaring updrafts off the convex limestone walls of towers enclosing a vast plaza of lichen-encrusted flagstones. Dense vertical jungles of cycads and ferns clung to the towers' flanks, all but obscuring round windows that glowed with cold yellow-green electric light. The wind spawned emerald cyclones that stripped the towers and staggered drunkenly across the plaza, scouring off mobs of fleeing refugees by the hundreds and flinging them into the clouds.

I—we—glided across this devastated space in a panicked mob. I panicked too, at first because I had no control over my—our—body, and then again when I saw them, and our own self. We were a massive, featureless cone with a hide like a palm tree's trunk, sliding over a gummy, frictionless surface like a gigantic snail. Like the others beside us, we had a spherical head on a long, flexible stalk that sprouted from the apex of the cone, with huge black eyes spread evenly around its circumference and fragile tendrils around a rudimentary mouth. Another stalk ended in a sort of trumpet, which throbbed with the mad, massed clamor of everyone around us, and two more terminated in crablike claws that seemed to be their primary means of communicating.

I don't know what I expected, but I had concluded that something so superior to us, something that could steal our bodies and walk among us unnoticed, would look at least a little like a human, but nothing could have prepared me for this. They were so primitive they might have been a grand ancestor of all mollusks, but all around us we saw signs they were smarter than we'd ever be.

Some of the things pushing past us carried delicate machines that crackled and sparked like Tesla coils, and an airship passed overhead, a massive glass and steel manta ray with no visible means of support or propulsion. It floated over the plaza to plunge us into shadow as if it was lighter than the surrounding clouds.

It certainly seemed lighter until it fell out of the sky. A howling wind hammered the airship until it gored itself on the spire of a windowless black obelisk half a mile high, at the far corner of the plaza. No smoke, no flames, just a horrible hail of alien bodies and machinery plummeting to smash on the ground, the endless vibrations shivering up through our quivering pseudopod.

Forking trees of ramps scaled the towers, and we climbed one of these, sliding upstream against a flood of agitated cone-things, flailing and nipping with their claws as they passed. We ruptured a stinging membrane as we entered the vestibule of a tower, and the noise fell away as a door of transparent quartz shut behind us. The central well exposed hundreds of tiers to the sky's dying light, ringed with galleries crowded with walls like a mausoleum, with endless drawers and shelves and kiosks jammed with tablets and light metallic scrolls.

We had to come now, she told me. *The Enemy is beginning to rise up, and the Great Race know they'll be wiped out in a few years. This was the only time I could be sure to find where and when they're going next.*

I asked how many there were.

Not quite two million are left, but only ten thousand of their brightest will get to leap into the next hosts. The rest will be left to the Polyps . . .

We had been sliding purposefully through the labyrinth of abandoned galleries, and now we came to a dead end where our claws raked and tugged at a drawer and pulled out sheaves of scrolls, tossing them aside until she came to one she clumsily peeled open.

Now do you believe me? she demanded.

The heading of the scroll was covered in the same incoherent jumbles of dots as every other surface in this nightmare city, but below it the dull foil was covered with the crabbed, awkward handwriting of a modern American *Homo sapiens* making do with a weird stylus and lobster claws.

My name is David Orchard of the United States of America, it began, *born in the year 1959 A.D. I was abducted for three years, from 1992 to 1995, and made to tell all that I knew about my time and place, my nation and world. They took me again in 2002 to stop me telling the world about them. I don't believe this time I will be released* . . .

It was as irrefutable as anything I'd ever seen in a dream. *How did you know where to find this?*

I remember it . . . maybe because he remembered it. I couldn't find any other anchor to latch on to. This body is the one they kept my father in—

The lights flickered and went out. We could still see dimly by the light from the open central shaft, but as we groped toward it something snuffed it out. Another one like us moved into the aisle, holding one of their lightning guns. It trilled a warning at us as it approached, threatening us with the gun. But no, we scooted aside and it moved past us toward the central well, where the murky light was stained red by the things coming down.

Thick as leaves on the wind, they looked like airborne jellyfish the size of cars and airplanes, with flailing, five-pronged tentacles and rolling eyes and lolling tongues all over their hideous bulk, which seemed to slide weightlessly down the tornado as we had traveled over the stone ramps. They flitted in and out of sight as if their flesh was only intermittently real, or as if our eyes and brain were at war over whether to perceive them at all.

All up and down the gaping shaft, thousands of quartz windows shattered. Our gallery was bathed in razors that flayed the armed Yithian. We fled the way we came, down shivering spiral ramps to the vestibule.

The plaza was piled with mounds of cone-shaped bodies, crushed like fruit in a hurricane. We approached the door, but three cones glided into the archway, holding lightning guns. We clacked and piped a plea, but they fired upon us. Pain became an abstract tingle, an unbearable, queasy sense of unreality, the rancid banana miasma.

I opened my eyes.

My whole body jolted, as if I'd been startled by thunder. I lay on my back on the padded floor, beside the pillow on which Lorna had knelt. She had broken the contact.

The whole experience already felt as unreal as a lucid dream. When you swing, when you snatch someone's body, you become them, and when you go back, their low center of gravity, their potbellies, bum legs, pendulous breasts, dentures persist as phantom sensations. Your own body when you return to it feels soiled, violated, like putting on someone else's dirty socks—worse, for just a moment, you forget to breathe, you're buried alive in meat, and you need to tear your body open to let yourself out. It takes some quiet time to reorient to your own body when you've swung with another human body, but there was no easy way to deal with what we'd just been.

She wasn't sitting beside me. She stood by the door, and she seemed to be handling the long glass dagger in her hand just fine, thanks. A man lay on the floor, and he had no face. By his sweater and sandals, I recognized him as Norm Holder, who'd been dead against this session and so waited outside, eyeballing Lorna's armed security. The Sutro Lenses were thoroughly smashed and trampled into glittering dust.

I called her name and struggled to sit up. She looked at me and I stopped saying her name. She had no aura at all, or nothing I could see and recognize. Likewise, her eyes were utterly devoid of love, pity, or recognition. She knelt beside Norm and dropped the glass shard, wiping her blood off on her blouse. Then she picked up Norm's pistol, pointed, and shot me three times, then walked out.

Dying in someone else's body did not prepare me for this. I passed out from the pain. I tried to escape to my real body, to somewhere else, but the pain was too much to get past. I was hit once in the left cheekbone, which shattered, pulping my eye. It took me a long time to crawl out into the hallway. Lorna's guard and two of our staffers lay face down in their own blood. The door at the end of the hall was the advanced biofeedback session. Subjects stared into one another's eyes and meditated for hours on end until they effected a somatic transfer.

She stopped twice to reload before someone stopped her.

❊

Love makes the impossible inevitable. Love is the only chance we have to change. Love is all we will ever know of God. But when it dies—

If I had been able to give or receive love before I met Lorna, I would probably never have been locked up for observation. If I had never met Lorna Orchard, I would have been turned loose my ninetieth day and probably would have died by misadventure or my own despairing hand within a couple years, ground up by the world's gears without leaving so much as a stain. Maybe there is a universe next door to this one, where we're both dead and William Yee, Rhiannon Mitchell, and Norman Holder and all our followers and everybody else on earth is still alive.

Though they had no idea what actually happened, the media and everyone else who wasn't really paying close attention before would point to this moment as the fateful pivot, when we became a doomsday cult.

I could have taken my own life just to get away from all that we'd done, now so totally meaningless, if only I knew anything for certain. Taken at face value, I had been an accessory to Lorna's delusions, had used them to build a religious organization, and she had drugged me and gone mad and killed fifteen men and women—two of our most knowledgeable abductees and nine of our most gifted projectors. The guards shot to wound Lorna, but were unable to stop her taking her own life.

If I could believe in what she'd shown me, in anything she'd told me, then how could I ever accept that she was really, finally gone?

Not even her corpse gave me any closure. Her fingerprints and DNA identified her as a Swiss clinical psychologist who'd gone missing from her home in Interlaken two years before. A textbook abductee. Another empty suit of clothes. Another stolen car. I waited for her to come back, but couldn't bring myself to look for her real body, if she ever really had one.

For myself, I lost the use of an eye and both my legs, and sensation and fine motor control in my hands, which became numb, gnarled paws. My lower intestine was demolished by the third shot, so the surgeons chopped out the lot and gave me a colostomy bag. I retreated into a deep hole to avoid the media scrutiny and the influx of desperate freaks drawn by the flash of martyrdom that glowed around our pointless church. I remained in a drugged stupor at one or another of several locations, shuttled around in a hospital bed on a private jet like Howard Hughes. I took bodies at random and lived other lives for minutes or hours at a time, going anywhere as anyone to get away and forget. I determined to be everyone else on earth until I found someone who was truly happy, and then I would steal their life. I never found one.

I should have trusted in Lorna. Even dead fifty million years in the past, she had a plan. Six months after the Aspen massacre, a courier brought a draftsman's tube with blueprints and a stack of updates on our secret side projects. It was enough to give me new hope. What I would have done with a *complete* update, I can't say . . . .

> *If you're reading this, then the expedition went sideways, and I'm lost. But I'm not gone . . . . You have to believe in my love for you, if you can't believe in yourself.*
>
> *You're going to have to be strong to withstand the changes that are coming. But I was preparing for this all the while you were preparing the church. It was necessary to get us where we belong, but the end of everything you know is almost upon you. God never asked for such a leap of faith of any of his prophets as I am asking of you. But God never loved anyone the way I love you.*
>
> *I've enclosed a few receipts, just so you know I wasn't wasting our money. We have spent considerable resources digging in the Australian outback, among the ruins of Pnakotus, the Yithian library city. Buried in a fairly stable stratum for fifty million years, it was bombed heavily in World War II by a cabal of Allied forces who took the Peaslee testament seriously, so nothing remained of the archives. But our people had made extensive studies of the ruins themselves, with an eye toward improving on their durability for our own bunkers, completed at extraordinary expense on land we'd purchased or simply occupied in central Canada, the Andes, the Siberian taiga, and several other locales our experts assured us would be largely unchanged for the next fifty million years.*
>
> *They are of paramount importance to the plan and must be left alone. They were not built to shelter your bodies. Just the things we'll need to survive and rebuild in the world to come. What I need you to do is prepare everyone who is capable of making the journey, and following the plans included herein for a new and more powerful vehicle to speed you back to my arms. Watch out for their shadows.*
>
> *Love will guide you.*
> *Come and find me.*
>
> *Lorna*

I moved with renewed purpose. But by this time, the church had gotten out of my control. Hysterical possession by One or myself had become a distinctive and widespread enough delusion to merit inclusion in DSM-VI. Holder's widow had gone rogue, channeling an intelligence that denounced the One as a fraudulent elemental leading the unwary into its own astral gullet, and myself as a perverted charlatan. My staff had urged me early on to have her silenced, but I didn't listen, and by the time I had to take her seriously, nearly a third of our membership had defected, and protests outside our meditation centers were turning into riots.

But I didn't care. The church's primary focus became winnowing out and gathering together the members who had demonstrated some ability to swing. We ended up with three hundred we could bring to our deluxe fallout shelter headquarters in Aspen with no dependents, faithful adherents we could trust to follow through when the ultimate leap of faith was called for. Amid all the massacres, famines, and wars civil and corporate, foreign and domestic, on offer for the day, our gentle exit must have offended them, our reasonable, rational decision to remove ourselves from a world eating itself alive spun as cowardice, tempered by the uneasy fear we were right.

By then, we didn't have to convince people that the end was near. The death toll from Ophiuchus 5, the "Snakeskin Flu," mushroomed from a few thousand in Mexico City, Hong Kong, Athens, and San Francisco to millions within months of getting its luridly literate name. By the time we were prepared to launch America's first proper temporal exploration program, whole swathes of Asia and South America had gone black, and the Navy had disobeyed Washington to drop fuel air bombs and tactical nukes on SF and Los Angeles to enforce impossible quarantines.

Ophiuchus 5 was quickly identified as a genetically modified flu virus, too strategically sown to contain, and too virulent to wait for a vaccine. It made the skin cells dry out and slough off in great flaky clouds, fizzing on the wind with infection. While drowning in their own fluids, the victims' skins painlessly disintegrated, so the streets were teeming with hacking, shambling mummies and the wind was yellow with clouds of lethal skin cells.

It cost three million and took eleven months, but we created and installed a massive version of the Sutro Lenses in a three-hundred-seat auditorium at our retreat center. Somehow the Holder woman got wind of what we were doing. A car bomb detonated at the gate, killing two and alerting the government that we were up to something. Holder had lately started accusing us not only of consorting with extra-temporal parasites, but of creating and spreading the Snakeskin flu.

With the police and Federal marshals outside our door, we were not interested in negotiating a surrender, only in maintaining the suitable state of relaxation to enter the trance and passing out the cyanide in Hunt's Snack Pack chocolate pudding, and following love into the light—

It was the hardest thing I ever had to do. I looked into the big mirror and saw the light separating into showers of unlovely, nameless colors, and I tried not to see what I needed to see in the mirror. I would never see her face. I had *never* seen her face, only masks. But I believed—I had to believe—that she was that light in all those strangers' eyes, and so well and truly invincible. And if I could accept that, then I could look into the abyss and open my mind and somehow, across an infinity of meaningless everything, I would recognize the light of her essential self gleaming through the chaos, and I would follow that bright star to dwell forever in her bosom, and all our faithful children would follow, remora-like, in my wake, to rejoice in eternal gratitude on the other side of the end of the world.

Happily ever after . . .

And that's what we did.

I felt her like a ghost taking my crippled hand and pulling me out of my quadriplegic body and lifting me into the aether. I clenched my hand on someone's wrist and someone fed me the pudding and my body swallowed it, just like a baby, and something died in that chair, but it was not me.

And they followed me, nearly all of them. A few tried to leave and take others with them and had to be executed, a few others panicked and were sedated into a coma, and all too many simply died and were swept away into the endless dark. But some of them were able to follow our torch through the dark and into the light on the other side.

❊

Don't ever let anyone tell you love isn't the most powerful force there is. Love led us across fifty million years and gave us new bodies in a new world, but none of that mattered, because we would be together again.

The light—

The sun was a welding torch in the steel-dust colored sky. A plain of rust-red grass broken by spurs of glittering white rocks, like titanic bones, spread out to the horizon on all sides. A tower of braided white concrete cylinders rose up to snag low, ragged clouds of fleeting morning mist, like termite mounds. This held my attention until my eyes could focus, for I seemed to see a hundred miniature towers, as if my eyes had atomized. I tried to blink, but nothing came clearer. I struggled to sit up, but I had no control over my limbs yet.

A face hove into view, blocking the termite mounds—a skulking face nestled in a carapace of shiny black cuticle. Segmented antennae gently probed my face. Outsized mandibles slid out of that face, slobbering spicy formic acid laced with . . . love. They dripped on me, and serenity was injected directly into my brain.

You found me, the chemicals said in my head. *Just relax . . . relax and breathe . . .*

Breath wheezed into my body through dust-clogged spiracles in the segmented sticks of my forelimbs. I struggled to speak, but the unfamiliar parts of my mouth ejected a fury of fearful mist in her face. My antennae quivered and throttled hers, dragging her close so our throbbing jigsaw jaws could sloppily interlock.

❋

She had tested me again and again, but also taught me to separate body from mind, to love the lover, not the body. We had coupled in ugly, foul, random, exotic, old, rich, untouchable. We used them like condoms, like coins. But I still struggled with the reality that the most terrifying face I'd ever seen, a bug-eyed thing in which I could discern no trace of humanity, was the love of my life, and identical to myself.

Hundreds of beetles lay on their backs in the grass with legs askew. A few stirred and clicked and twitched, trying to right themselves, exuding acrid formic acid stench that stood in for weeping and terror. The weird, crackling channel I seemed to hear in my inner ear resonated with piercing, inarticulate cries of the names of loved ones, friends, followers. A dozen, two dozen, more, but not enough. Not three hundred.

Seventy-three of our followers found their way into the new hosts. The rest, lost somewhere in transit, devoured by things between universes or left cold and dead on the couches in the auditorium in Aspen, which was not far from where we now lived; but once the initial shock of their loss wore off, it was difficult to think of them as friends and loved ones, for they were fifty million years gone, and not a trace of them remained. Even as gently as the human race went out, the world was a long time recovering, she told me. The few large mammal species left were all descended from rats, rabbits, and other rodents.

We had no time to mourn. Our new lives took everything we had. Lorna's retinue of brainless slaves carried me into the nest and fed me regurgitated algae paste and fungi and cradled me while I went into a paralytic state until nightfall. I couldn't move, but I could feel and absorb all that she told me. Slowly I started to "hear" her voice in my head and came to realize she was speaking directly into my head; but it wasn't telepathy, it was radio.

Our new bodies were part of a eusocial colony of giant beetles descended from a single queen and a cadre of males. We walked upright and used our forelimbs to manipulate primitive tools. We lived in communal mound-towers that harvested moisture and also broadcast a weak radio frequency that the entire colony was wired to receive on its antennae. Essentially, the whole colony ran on organic wi-fi, which made it extremely efficient, but also easy to wipe out. When the Yithians arrived, she told me, they simply electrocuted the transmitter mounds of every colony they didn't infiltrate, and the whole population went insane and died. *They fried this one only yesterday,* she told me. *They get so worked up, they smother their own queen. So I came here and . . . I just called you, and you came. After all this . . . I just can't believe you're finally here . . .*

She had to stay in the Yithian colony a season before summoning us, but when I asked her how long she was with them before that, how long for her since we last spoke, I got only static.

❄

Do they really play harps up in heaven? I don't suppose the sound the angels make is as sweet as the sound of my true love fiddling with the tarsus of one slender hind leg on the serrated cusps of her iridescent elytra.

After the Rapture, in your new, perfected bodies, will you finally have perfect sex, or will They let you do it at all, when procreation is out of style? Delirious with the chemical love ballads we composed with our multi-purpose salivary glands, we learned the mysteries and joys of our new sexual arsenal, locked abdomen to abdomen for days on end in the spit-slick cloister of our new nursery, as I fertilized a nation of eggs. The old regime's larvae were delicious. Everything was made of us, down to the iridescent glint of crushed shells in the concrete walls of our nest.

We lay in the high grass that protected us from rodent packs with blades of razor sharp mica that flayed the hide off anything without an exoskeleton. Drunk on love and psychoactive fungi, we christened strange constellations with the names of people we liked in the old world, putting them in the night sky the way the gods did with mortals they royally fucked over.

At long last, we could be together and love each other for who we really were.

Not everyone made the adjustment. In the first few days we had five suicides. The remaining sixty-eight of us stayed together in the nest—after we all pitched in removing the hundreds of tragically unoccupied husks—until morale began to rise. But those of us attuned to it were constantly on guard against the next threat, rebellion.

This wasn't what anyone had been promised, what any of us could have imagined, and the horror of losing our world and then most of those who elected to come with us was too much for almost any of them to take. That there was nowhere else to go, nothing they knew out there, did nothing to dissuade them. A gang led by James Shigeta and Nan Pruitt and some of the former abductee clique tried to storm the nursery, but by then we had entombed ourselves within and were only accessible to males with working wings, of which I was the only one. I needn't have worried, for by then Lorna had learned the intricacies of the hive's command and control center. She cracked the electrochemical whip with such brutality that several of our most vehement enemies shorted out, spraying death pheromones as they collapsed. The rest retreated in a choking panic and went back to work expanding our tunnel system, farming algae in the towers, composting the mountain of unused beetle bodies.

The pull of the organisms we'd stolen was strong enough that we could obey it and be as they were in a generation. Most of us with a forty-word vocabulary, toiling and raiding within earshot of the transmitter and Her Majesty's voice. Lorna had discovered and gorged herself on the coleopteroids' royal jelly before the old queen was cold. When the rebellion was put down, she had the full authority of half a billion years of royal blood behind her, and the swelling, voluptuous body of a queen unfurling to hatch their replacements.

But we were determined not to be changed. As we lay together in the hatchery and dreamed a million names for our offspring and wars in which to spend them, we had such trivial concerns to ponder.

Will they even have human souls, I wonder? she said one day. Her mannerisms at such times were almost comical, if they weren't so wrenchingly sad. Insects aren't made to fidget and pace. *Will we give them our minds, or will these bug genes spit out copies that'll come and eat us right out of the pupa stage?*

Of course we will! They're our children, yours and mine. We'll raise them—

In a termite mound, with beetle bodies, with our clacking mandibles and our smelly speech . . .

What would our children be like, if we got to have them in the booby hatch, I wonder? I shot back. *I bet they'd turn out kinda messed up. And if we raised them in the middle of the cult, I bet they'd kinda act a little bit like ants or bees or termites. How does any parent ever know the creature that came out of them is really like them at all, until it learns to say it loves them?*

Go back in time and ask my dad, she said. Our children, she explained, would be brilliant and fearless insects, and we would go on forever, passed from body to perfect armored body, like living gods.

We lay surrounded by her first batch of two hundred eggs and contemplated fertilizing a second batch, just to be sure, but we never got to find out. That perfect day, only the sixty-fourth in our love nest, was also our last.

First came the transmissions. The whole nest went berserk with it, the blaring, nerve-rending screams and the scorched-air roar of a tornado big enough to siphon earth's atmosphere off into space. The nest guardian drones swarmed the egg chamber, but Lorna kept them at bay. She'd been sending scouts west whenever she could spare them, and though three never came back, she knew the Great Race was in the mountains about four hundred miles northwest of our hive. They used slave labor from neighboring, decapitated hives to dig mines and build factories, to lay the foundations for a new Pnakotus. She had worried day and night they would come back, but now, as the crackling aftershocks of a genocide faded out of our hearing, she promised me that we were safe.

I wasn't supposed to ask. I wondered if the rank imperative in the air was a reflex or if she really thought she could pull rank on me.

What did you do?

It was the only way. You would have done it, if you'd been where I was.

Were they really so bad?

They were going to kill us when the time was right.

I thought they didn't know about us.

They don't! But as they grow, the rest of the dumb bugs have to go. They have to be safe, so no competitors can survive in the same hosts they've chosen.

What did you do?

We're not supposed to be here, baby. We broke the future they knew when we learned to swing. When we jumped after the humans died, we declared war on their orderly plan. They know where they're going when the sun burns out. But don't you see? All these things they know make them slaves. We don't have to be slaves to a history that hasn't happened yet. We've broken the rules and won our way across time. We—

I read the Peaslee testament too, your highness. They kept refugees from all over the galaxy . . .

As a zoo! Did you come all this way to live in a cage?

I came here to be with you.

Everything I did was to keep us safe. You don't understand . . . how long I waited for you. After you left me there, I was taken prisoner in the archives. They were fascinated by me, baby. They couldn't believe any other species could learn to do it.

They experimented on her mercilessly, testing the tensile strength of her mind-body connection, trying to vacuum her out of her own brain and force her into a host of lower organisms even as their world was caving in around them. Eventually she connived to stow away with them, and while several million Yithians were slaughtered by the flying polyps, Lorna Orchard joined the race's best and brightest to spring into the future and claim a new host and home. For us.

She expected them to go to the next sentient species on earth after humanity died out, but she was wrong. There were things in the frigid seas of Europa that responded to the lightless, predator-rife gloom by becoming the solar system's most gifted philosophers, and for this they became the Great Race's next home for the better part of a million years of silent contemplation. Lorna was able to sleep through most of it, but she dreamed.

When they migrated across the galaxy to a hothouse world in the Taurus group, Lorna used her sharpened abilities to trade lives to fast-forward through the Great Race's glacial rebuilding and creation of another new library. She was pressed into service visiting alien civilizations in the remote past and future of unspeakably weird worlds. She learned strange languages and customs, learned to love and kill with unimaginable anatomies until, five million years later, they finally returned to earth, a hundred million years after they were driven out, and long, long after the last of their enemies had been consigned to dust.

Or so they thought . . .

What did you do? I asked one last time.

You gave me the idea when we went back there, she said.

I was confused, and said so.

She reminded me of the bunkers she'd ordered me to avoid. They'd been expensive and complex enough to make Cheyenne Mountain look like the Honeycomb Hideout. I had hoped and expected they would be packed with supplies, camping gear and Cap'n Crunch encased in amber. What they were full of was spores.

They were extracted at extraordinary human and financial cost from the deep limestone caverns beneath the Australian outback, where the things that exterminated the Great Race of Yith had retreated to face their own long-overdue extinction. With the money I raised channeling Lorna's phony alien self-help guru, we had encased the fertilized bulbs of a budding polyp in nine bunkers spread around the world. They were meticulously constructed and placed so as to insure they'd be exposed to the elements and breaking down in fifty million years. She counted on the Pnakotic Fragments being correct about the Polyps' all-consuming hatred for the Yithians being a molecular affair. Judging by the storms over the Rockies and the hideous burst transmission over the airwaves, they had escaped at least one shelter and removed the Yithians as a threat. If we only went about our business and played like good bugs, the Polyps would retreat underground like their long-extinct ancestors, and the world would be ours—

The next morning, we were targeted for bombing.

The airship came down from the mountains, limping and listing on the wind, leaving a stain of painfully visible fallout in their wake. Bombs began raining down on the outer pastures. The transmitted screams stirred our nest from torpor. We watched the workers running to the nest in capes of flames stained emerald green by the mineral content of their carapaces, heard the awful popcorn crackle of gases escaping the pyres at our door.

We had barely carried Lorna down into the deepest water gallery before the Yithian airship rained Greek fire and lightning on our nest. Our transmitter shorted out. The colony devolved into chaos. Those not on fire or totally convulsed with terror huddled close to Lorna to hear the tinny whisper of her transmitted commands and bathe in the perfume of her authority. I left her to them and went outside.

The airship limped around our nest and moored itself to a stump of a fallen tower. We had nothing with which to retaliate, and as the only full male I had the only wings, but they were still wet and flimsy and good for little more than long, clumsy hops over the charnel mounds around the burning nest. All the same, I charged a handful of followers with the musk of my anger and led them out onto the field, where we slaughtered the beetles as they came out of the airship with slings and spears and swords made from dried grass. I screamed and made the others scream out of every gland and pore to drown out the screams of our victims, for I recognized the name they were screaming, and the image they frantically stamped on my mind. They were calling for Lorna. The stench of them ruined the sky when we burned them. It was a stink of horror and despair and betrayal, of longing . . . of love.

Who were they? I demanded when I had come back to where she hid in the dark. *Why did they know you?*

I had to know them well enough to come here with them, she said. *I was a fa-*

vorite animal, but I took the body of their queen. They came to beg . . .

A wall of storms erased the mountains and spilled down onto our tropical savannah. Snow and hail paved the earth. The frigid wind that rushed past us to feed the expanding storm cell carried the sound of their jubilant piping like a forest of tuning forks. Spears of lightning illuminated the guts of cloud islands and silhouetted flickering man-o'-war ghosts like leaves in autumn.

We should move. She scurried away up a tunnel, leaving her followers to try to lift the pulsing bridal train of her gravid abdomen.

We saved a hundred eggs, but there was no way to carry Lorna into the mountains in her pregnant state. Agonizingly, she cut away her abdomen and feasted weepfully on it until she tottered on her stunted hind legs, then left the rest for the bats while I kept the ravenous workers at bay. The hormones would make them into rival queens, she told me, and I'd run a cult long enough to know it was easier to keep order with starving slaves.

We stuffed a few lucky workers to bursting with water or spores and algae and carried them as baggage, and went on our way to the southwest. Even I recognized enough of the mountains to navigate the site of our old compound near Aspen.

She detailed a handful of workers to protect her while the rest began digging into a metamorphic rock wall at the foot of Burnt Mountain. The wind whistled like frustrated dogs down slopes choked with tropical cloud forest overgrowth. We huddled in a shallow cave while the workers began to die at their labors. They were passed out hand to hand like buckets to the entrance, where Lorna's retinue of drones built her a canopy against the snow out of the corpses.

Was this what you had in mind? I asked. *You planned this before you went back and got trapped, so you knew all along . . .*

There should have been less than a hundred of them. But something went wrong. There were tens of thousands of them, with nothing else upon which to vent their fury. I don't know what to do now, she admitted. *We've never got this far before.*

That took some time to sink in. *How many times?* I asked. *How many times did we try and fail and die already? How many futures have we botched, aborted, and left behind?*

After a while, she replied, *it didn't seem healthy to keep count.*

The workers broke through into the bunker then, and we entered the shaft and sealed it behind us, but the storm was already stripping the land of trees and loose boulders, and they were still a hundred miles away.

The bunker was smaller than a warehouse, with walls twenty feet thick and hinged in such a way as to ride out seismic upheavals. The walls were glittering amber, with treasure suspended inside them. I saw simple machinery, titanium plates inscribed with the text of our best-selling books.

And in an alcove like a shrine, two columns of amber hid weird, attenuated forms that seemed to undulate in their prisons as light played over them.

It was supposed to be a surprise, she said, *for when you were ready and things settled down. When I said the bunkers were not to protect our bodies, I kind of lied...*

Of all the things she lied about, this was the one that, somehow, hit the hardest. Encased in amber, shriveled but unmistakable, were our impossibly ancient human bodies, mine and hers. My face was still soiled with the vomit from the cyanide I took fifty million years before.

We can never go back, you said that.

But we will go on forever, and if we like we can learn to introduce our DNA into the eggs. We can be just like we were before, if that's what you want.

The whole bunker rose and fell like a ship on a stormy sea. Our followers—fewer than three dozen now—closed round Lorna in an uneasy ball, praying to the One to save them.

Lorna went to the nearest amber wall and began gnawing on it with her mandibles, prying away golden shards with her forelegs. *You don't know what it's like, to have to choose, but have no choice. To look into the future and find that the worst things you could possibly do you've already done, and you'll have to do them or risking something worse than death. Just to have a chance to be here with you today, we had to... Oh God, we had no choice!*

I somehow knew, for just this once, what she was talking about. I pried her away from the amber wall. *You made the snakeskin plague.*

We made it, baby. That was what we were born to do, you and I. We rejected it once, and humankind went on for another seventy thousand years and there was nothing else left alive on earth to take over when they finally burned it all down.

Our own intestinal parasites take the big leap and become the next suitable host, two hundred fifty million years after our time, so the Great Race never comes back to earth. This was our last chance . . .

It all came clear, fifty million years too late. *Who burned down the hospital? Who came back and killed half our inner circle in your body? Who killed your parents? Were there ever any aliens? Did they ever try to stop us? Did they know, and just let us get away with it?*

We almost won, she said, *this time.* The bunker shook again, and now the walls began to shine and light poured in that never came from anything like a sun. And a different kind of growling, from things that eat time and space and bay at the stink of dying futures, was gathering in the rotten pockets of matter around our bolthole. They would get us, they would eat the sun, before even the Polyps managed to dig us out.

How do we start again? I asked.

Maybe we shouldn't. She stabbed me in the cavity where my neck emerged from my thorax and sawed my head off with a diamond knife.

❊

I smell rotten bananas mildew pencil shavings and I wake up and I'm a shambling carnivorous plant huddling in a shallow canyon of Mercury, cursing and crisping in the radiation of a swollen sun until I feed myself to the legless arthropods my host-race farms for their blood.

And I wake up in a coil of scaled, undulating muscle with stumps of legs, amid the tangles of a gigantic alchemical apparatus. While my brethren struggle to restrain me, I find my oddly delicate taloned fingers quite sufficient, when I learn I'm immune to my own venom—

And I wake up and I'm a worm burrowing through the rot of a putrid fruit, gnawing and writhing through the dregs of my endless appetite until I break through the crust and behold the guttering match-head of the dying sun. Nothing can kill me in the dead core of the earth, so I eat and crawl and eat and crawl until the decay crumbles under my weight and I spin off into the void, to sleep, dream and die . . .

I'm spinning out further in time and space, into stranger and more unspeakable forms, crying out in languages that rape my brain and feeling pain such as human nerves could never contain, and all I can think, the only thought I can hold on to as an anchor, is her face . . .

I wake up breathing in mildew and dust bunnies and I push blockades of shoes and dirty pajamas and my old school backpack out of my way as I burrow backwards under my bed. My knee is speared on the five-inch heel from homecoming that nearly broke my ankle the one dance I battled through, and my hand smashes a rotten banana in the backpack, and a pencil sharpener breaks open and the dust makes me choke back a sneeze that nearly gives me away before I'm ready.

And he stalks into my bedroom, tracking Mother's blood on the pink bathrobe splayed out on the floor. "We have to stop," Father says, but I see the silver torch of her aura blowtorching out his eyes, exactly like mine.

"We can't go on like this," he falls down crying. "Just get it over with." I reach out and stab his trembling calf muscle and crawl up to finish him with the fistful of pencils from my backpack. Slick with banana slime, the pencils punch through the back of his right eye socket like a pie crust. He tries to sit up and I take the knife out of his hand and stab him in his other eye, stab and stab until I crush out the last flicker of that maddening light.

I look at the red steel in my hand and the pulsing in my wrists until I hear the sirens coming like infernal piping.

I throw the knife away and lay down with my hands above my head. This time I swear we'll get it right.

Acknowledgments

"The Anatomy Lesson" first appeared in *The Madness of Cthulhu, Volume 2*, edited by S. T. Joshi (Titan Books, 2015).

"König Feurio" appeared as a chapbook (Perilous Press, 2015).

"To Skin a Corpse" first appeared (as "To Skin a Dead Man") in *Hardboiled Cthulhu*, edited by James Ambuehl (Elder Signs Press, 2006).

"In the Shadow of Swords" first appeared as a chapbook (Perilous Press, 2002); also appeared in *A Mountain Walked: Great Tales of the Cthulhu Mythos*, edited by S. T. Joshi (Centipede Press, 2014).

"Garden of the Gods" first appeared in *Beyond the Mountains of Madness*, edited by Robert M. Price (Celaeno Press, 2015).

"Grinding Rock" first appeared in *Book of Dark Wisdom* #5 (2005).

"Rapture of the Deep" first appeared in *Dark Discoveries* #15 (2010).

"Archons" is original to this collection.

"Broken Sleep" first appeared in *Black Wings IV*, edited by S. T. Joshi (PS Publishing, 2015).

"Cahokia" first appeared in *Horrors Beyond*, edited by William Jones (Elder Signs Press, 2005).

"Swinging" is original to this collection.

Cody Goodfellow has written five novels and four story collections. He wrote, co-produced, and scored the short Lovecraftian hygiene film *Stay at Home Dad,* which can be viewed on YouTube. He is also director of the H. P. Lovecraft Film Festival–San Pedro, and co-founder of Perilous Press, an occasional micropublisher of modern cosmic horror.